Who Is Knocking at the Door

The Life Story of a Chinese Farmer and His Descendants Across Generations

Luo Weizhang

 **AMERICAN ACADEMIC PRESS**

Translator: Jimmy Billy Mkandawire

Project Editor: Tao Jia, Tang Junxuan

AMERICAN ACADEMIC PRESS

By AMERICAN ACADEMIC PRESS

201 Main Street

Salt Lake City

UT 84111 USA

Email manu@AcademicPress.us

Visit us at http://www.AcademicPress.us

ISBN: 979-8-3370-8932-4

Distributed to the trade by National Book Network Suite 200, 4501 Forbes Boulevard, Lanham, MD 20706

10 9 8 7 6 5 4 3 2 1

Contents

Part One..1

Part Two 93

Part Three...151

Part Four 222

Part Five 287

Part Six 358

Part Seven..427

Afterword 476

Part One

Chapter 1

My emotions and thoughts are rushing when someone is knocking at the door. The knocking sounds the same as the one who talks in his sleep. When that sound comes, it will go through one's chest along with anger, arrogance and reluctant acceptance under a cover of willingness, and then through the fingers and through the door before it is heard indoors.

The knocking made Chunhong, my eldest sister, realize that Chunshang, my younger brother, was waiting outside.

She tried to smile generously and walked to the door but she did not open it.

"How many of you?" she asked loudly, opening the shoe cabinet.

"I send our dad here, you know," Chunshang answered impatiently.

She put two pairs of slippers on the floor neatly and opened the door.

Chunshang bent down and undid the elderly man's shoelaces. After he removed his left shoe, he put one slipper on his left foot, and then moved the foot into the door; and he repeated the same process on the elderly man's right foot. Only then, the elderly man could be allowed indoors.

Chunhong put her father's poplar walking stick beside the door and helped him into the living room. Her brother followed them, looking angry and grave. As soon as he sat down on a plastic stool, it screeched and slid backwards, dissatisfied with the man above. He would have to change shoes whenever he came to his eldest sister's house, and he felt humiliated. He would have refused to do the task if I had not asked him to do so.

Our father had been living with Chunshang, but Chunshang built a house for his mother-in law and lived next to her. It was Guaizaoping located halfway up the mountain but it was over 200 metres lower than my hometown Yanerpo. I did not want to go to Guaizaoping to celebrate our father's birthday, but I had to come back for the important day tomorrow.

Neither Chunhong nor I intended to go there. Chunshang had had to find shelter under his mother-in-law's roof, and that was not an honour to our family. He, however, was eager to invite us to his house tomorrow so that he could hold a birthday banquet for our father and show off in his neighbourhood that he was the master in his family. Just let him do what he wanted to do. My sisters had discouraged him from building a house in Guaizaoping before he did so. After Chunhong's earnest persuasion turned out to be futile, she had to console herself: "If I had known he could not be persuaded, I would not have wasted my words. I should have saved my breath to make me feel better."

She had been a victim of toothache for several years and had gone through useless medical treatment. The toothache is not a serious disease but it is unbearable when it strikes. When she was attacked by the nuisance on the road, she would desperately need cold water for comfort; it was, however, unavailable; so she had to use her hands to scoop up the muddy water on the ground mixed with ox hooves, but soon the pain assaulted her teeth again. Later she got a folk prescription: use pieces of gauze to cover some highly toxic pesticide, and bite the gauze with the teeth to kill the pain. She did so and felt relieved, but she nearly lost her life after she swallowed her saliva blended with the pesticide. One early morning she would go to the vegetable market. As soon as she walked downstairs, she was hit by the toothache again. It was incessant and would start to annoy her just after she started a day's work, and it would make her burn with agony. She would use the pesticide again. But just before she turned around, she saw her maternal grandmother walking towards her from afar and gesticulated to let her open her mouth. She stood there and did so. Her grandma was nearby her now and put two pills into her mouth. The brown pills brought her a cool mouthfeel, invigorated her and made her wake up. It was dark around. A moment later she realized that she was lying on the bed. Just now she dreamed about her grandma who passed away many years ago. She had vivid memories of her grandma. Clean and dry air were the marks of the past windy autumn. Grandma's face was too blurred to be seen, but her bent body, her greenish-blue gown down to her ankles, and her hands full of age spots were shining in the darkness. Meanwhile, her words could still be clearly heard: "Save your breath for your good teeth."

Her toothache was cured by the two special pills. Since she saw her maternal grandmother in her dream, she had taken her advice – watch her mouth. But she had made futile attempts to discourage her brother from building a house in Guaizaoping, and she was too unhappy to go to that village.

After I entered Chunhong's house this afternoon, I put down my luggage, washed up, and called Chunshang. It was not a good talk. I just told him that I had come back and asked him to take our father to our eldest sister's house in the town. And I hung up the phone before he could speak.

He appeared on his motorbike after two hours. He would have come here within half an hour if he had acted quickly when we finished talking on the phone. The rest of the time must have been spent on quarrels: he shut his mouth and yielded to his wife's complaints about having a spineless, incompetent, poor husband belittled by his sisters. Today she would grumble much more: "We are living with our dad but we have to send him to your sister's house to celebrate his birthday."

That was what I had guessed, and I did not want to ask about the details. After several months in a cheap motel in Baima city he slept with a woman whom he had not met for so many years and who used to be one of his classmates in a junior high school. He told her what I had not asked him about. My guess was right: he had been scolded by his wife, which was nothing new. He told his sad story to that woman emotionally with teary eyes. She held him in her arms and let him weep over his sadness. He cried on and on and nearly called her mother. That was told to me by her.

"Hi, Chunming," she said. "Chunshang was on the verge of calling me mother. I would have said yes if he had said so, but he did not say it." She looked at me coquettishly while moved her large breasts which were sagging down her belly. She knew that both Chunshang and I were kids when our mother died.

Chapter 2

Chunshang could find an excuse if he did not want to send our father to the town. What's more, our father preferred the rustic lifestyle and he would get ill whenever he came to his eldest daughter's house.

Chunhong bought a house in Huilong Town perhaps nine or ten years ago. Her husband, a village party secretary, often travelled from the village to the town by bus for his work, but he did not live in the village. The villagers usually visited the secretary in the town with gifts, such as cigarettes, liquor, chickens and ducks for their business. Chunhong did not go back to the village unless she had to do something for weddings and funerals; as soon as those things were over, she would leave and have a forty-minute trip by motorboat and go ashore at the South Gate Pier and then set foot on the town. She had never been homesick. Hometown was nothing to a woman, and even a man could say goodbye to it and never returned. Where there was comfort, there was her home; so she chose to live in the town. Now her father had to go to the town to see her.

The pit-like fireplace was not provided in the town. Our father spent most of his time sitting beside the fireplace except during the dog days of summer. He disliked the air conditioner and the electric furnace, and he could not feel warm unless he was surrounded by the smell of the burning firewood. His birthday fell on the second day of the fourth lunar month. The calendar showed that date was summer already, but he could feel neither summer nor spring in his eldest daughter's house which was located by the riverside road along with chilly wind in the morning and at night.

Guaizaoping was an unwelcoming place to the father's children, including his third son who had come back from the provincial capital, so he had to go.

I, Xu Chunming, am the third son of our father. You may remember this name if it does not bother you, and it is okay if you forget it. You'd better let it slip your mind. You and I don't have to remember someone's name unless it is related to his or her good character. My name is not worthy of remembrance. Why? Because I say that you don't have to remember it, but I take it to heart, which shows that I am a hypocrite. You may remember my father's name: Xu Chengxiang, a name with good prospects. But he was getting old although the prospects had not come true. Those prospects turned out to be unattainable illusions through the end of one's life and would never be accomplished. The rest of his life resembled a ripe fruit off the branch, and you don't have to see it or learn Newton's principles of mechanics because you have known the result. Each birthday would be like the cold autumn wind blown towards the fruit. As a result, he was unwilling and worried to go to the town.

Chunshang could have used this as an excuse, but he did not mention it because he knew that it would be useless; what's more, I stopped him from saying it. After he hung up the phone and was scolded by his wife, he held our father by the hand and went out. He helped him stand and moved his motorbike along the muddy slope and parked it on the road. And then he scooped up our father in his arms, like holding a sack of potatoes, and put him down on the back seat of the motorbike. He mounted it and put the walking stick into his back collar. He started his vehicle after the elderly man put his fingers above his son's navel. He sat straight and drove in the wind down the zigzag mountain paths and across the flat ground until he reached the riverside road next to the South Gate Pier in the town. There was a row of buildings and Chunhong lived in the fourth floor of Unit Two.

We could hear the engine of his motorbike and Chunhong said that she would soon open the door. The sound of knocking seemed to come into our mind before the motorbike was stopped. She and I were wondering how he would act. When he was knocking at the door, however, things remained unchanged.

She and our father did what we had expected: she held him by the hand and walked towards the sofa in the living room; he stooped, grasped the sofa and then sat down, like a silently falling leaf. He curled up as comfortably as he could and leaned on the sofa wide enough for two people sleeping in. He huddled like a kid although he was an old man. He sat on one side of the sofa, his buns sideways, and looked at the cold place.

"I feel chilly and I worry that I may get ill," he sighed.

Those remarks irritated Chunhong. Our father would feel uncomfortable whenever he came to her house; he, however, became bouncy as soon as he returned to Chunshang's. Therefore, she concluded that our father pretended to be sick because he disliked being sent to his daughter's dwelling place.

"Stop being peevish, dad," she said. "You might hold the sun in your arms for your warmth, but the sun is not your own property." Our father laughed. He had nearly lost all his teeth, and his tongue could be clearly seen when he was smiling.

"You will get ill whenever you come here," she added. "Is my house a hellish place?"

She became annoyed. Our father stopped laughing and sat in the sofa quietly, his chest against his knees.

Chapter 3

Li Guangwen, the husband of Chunhong, did not come back until supper. He was calling Yang Jin on the phone to invite him to have supper together when he entered the door.

Yang Jin was a minibus driver. He used to be a truck driver for freight service in the steep Qin-Ba mountain areas. His wife was so worried about him that she made him change a new job to send passengers to districts and towns lest he should have a traffic accident or have secret moments with street girls. She treated Chunhong warmly and often shared sunflower seeds with her in her grocery store – the two women got along. Yang Jin was such a good driver that Guangwen often sat in his car to go to the village with the fare over 100 yuan each time. People could reach the town through water routes. The private business through land routes was bleak because regular buses were running and few passengers would go to the downtown. Now Yang Jin was happy with the perfect business deal brought by Guangwen, and gradually he became the chauffeur of Chunhong, her husband, her daughter, and even me. Today he picked me up in the railway station of Baima city and drove me to the town.

Yang Jin said that he had had supper and would not come here, so we started to have dinner.

Chunshang wanted to leave as soon as the supper was over. I tried to let him stay.

"If you return now," I said, "you will have to come here again tomorrow. Don't waste your time on the road."

I took a set of Chinese chess from the drawer in the TV bench. It had been put there for many years because Chunhong and her family members did not play chess.

After Chunshang sent our father to Chunhong's house, I bought the chess as a pastime for Chunshang lest he should go and leave our father alone. He was interested in playing chess at that time, but now he lost his interest in it.

"I'll go," he said hesitatingly, "and I'll come here tomorrow as early as possible."

Our father, looking at the doorway, softly told him to drive slowly. Chunshang had got drunk. He often drove his motorbike when he was drunken, and he had frequently fallen into the ditch nearby the road. In spite of that, he was so lucky that he had never fallen into a river or rolled down a mountain. After he left the town and went 1.5 miles downwards along the Qingxi River, he would have to go through a rugged mountainous terrain. Guaizaoping and Yanerpo were located in the Laojun Mountain. Winding and dangerous mountain roads with horrible screeching but without guard railings could kill drivers each year, including the father-in-law of Chunhong.

Chunhong's parents-in-law had lived nearby the bridgehead downstream, about one kilometre towards the town. Her father-in-law, who used to be good at making pilings and also a mason, left his hometown and built his own house nearby the bridgehead for better business both in the town and in the village. One day in May, he finished his farm work and mounted his motorbike, but disappeared after he drove past Guaizaoping. His family members knew that he might still be busy with his increasing workload if he did not come home at night. The next day he did not return, so they called him but got no answer, and then they called their boss and were told that he left yesterday. They searched for him at once and found his body in a pit under an abyss. He was dead, riding on his motorbike which had been thrust into the gap between rocks, grasping the handlebars, his eyes wide open. Rumours said that he did not fall to death: he died of fright before his body fell to the ground. Before his last breath was gone, he put his hands and legs firmly on the motorbike so that he could survive; that was what he had expected, but unluckily he died.

Our father was still worried about Chunshang, and he was eager to go home with him now. He desperately called the name of his youngest son, like a child who was left behind in the guest's house calling his daddy.

Our father had seven children. When our mother died, I was five years old, Chunshang two, Chunying less than three months. Later she was raised by another family, and Chunshang became the youngest child. As we grew up, our father grew old and got emotionally dependent on his youngest son. He wanted to go home with Chunshang now, but he was too afraid to say it lest Chunhong and I should get angry. When the sound of the motorbike was getting too far to be heard, our father lowered his head and cleared his throat, tilting his neck.

Chunhong was washing the dishes, so she did not see that. If she saw our father's expression, she would say: "You regard your youngest son as your only child!" Her husband did not see it either. He and Chunshang went out at the same time, and the former went to a tea house to play mahjong. Our father and I were sitting in the living room. I gave him a cigarette, he received it but returned it to me at once. He softly said that he preferred tobacco leaves to cigarettes, and then he was plunged into fear and sorrow. After a moment he realized that I was still sitting beside him, so he asked how things were going on in my small family. Chunhong came to us from the kitchen. She winked at me and, stifling her laugh, let me see our father's grotesque hair. He was in his eighties now, and he often combed his hair like a superstar's Mohawk hairstyle after he washed it every day. But his thin hair and wrinkled face made his head look like a bloodless cockscomb.

"Look at our dad's cool hairstyle!" she said jokingly, and then she sighed, "Things would be different if our mother were alive."

She often wished that our mother would be still with us. Whenever our father displeased us, she would retort in his presence: "God is unwilling to let us have good parents. Our mother rather than you should have survived!"

"If so, you would get a thrashing," our father smiled.

That was true. When our mother was alive, she was nicknamed "Hammersmith" because she wanted to have a good name for being a strict mother and would hammer us whenever we misbehaved.

On the contrary, our father was gentle. When we were beaten by our mother, he was worried about us but dared not persuade her to stop because he had to yield to her. After she died, however, his children suffered much more. The younger ones, including the eight-year-old second sister, were the victims of coldness and starvation; but the twelve-year-old sister, the seventeen-year-old brother, and the nineteen-year-old brother had realized how the world worked. The family members had been despised and been derided since the family master died. When you passed by someone's house, their kid would let their dog bite you but his or her parents just ignored that. Or, the animal waste provided by your family to be used as fertiliser in the village would be miscalculated deliberately so that some of it could be had by some household before it was given to the Production Team. What's worse, the plants in your farm land would be destroyed and your soil would be stolen. Those bad things were too many to be told. But we would not have been bullied if our mother had been alive.

Chapter 4

The wind ran past the window but did not enter the room at all, like a highly disciplined army that does not violate even an undemanding arrangement. Chunhong closed the doors and windows, turned on the air conditioner, and put a blanket on our father's body. The elderly man was taken good care of and started the same speech about our mother: her quarrels with one of her neighbours, Mrs. Hou, her hard work in the rice fields less than half a month after she gave birth to our youngest sister, her struggling in her sickbed, her curses when she was too weak to get up, and her death when she was sitting beside the fireplace.

The memories of our mother were related to her illness and her death, and we seemed to have a tacit agreement with our father that we tried to avoid recollecting those days when she was wielding enormous power in her family. Our father was just like a shadow when she was alive, and he became a pathetic man after her death. When a man with an enduring disposition does not fight back against dirt or arrows thrown on him, that is weakness, not kindness. We disliked our father who could bear insults but had never counterattacked. Chunshu, my second elder brother, even criticized that our father had put on a mask of kindness.

"It's a mask; otherwise his kindness would be useless," he said. Cowardice was worse than violence, which was the extended meaning of his words. "Love and hatred should go together," he added. "The deeper love is, the stronger hatred will be. Enmity is the root of affection. Devotion without hate is similar to early snowfalls melting before touching the ground." Bully the weak and fear the strong, and that's the way of the world. He was knowledgeable and gave many examples. The one impressed me was Lu Zhishen, one of the brave men in the Chinese novel *Outlaws of the Marsh*, who could save the girl named Cuilian and her father and could beat up a local tyrant Zhen Guanxi as punishment. He regarded Lu Zhishen as a kind man.

Guangwen came back when the talk about our mother was going on.

"You did not play mahjong?" our father asked.

"Both you and Chunming are here now," Guangwen said. "I'd rather stay with you."

"That's just your excuse!" Chunhong retorted sharply. "There were not enough players for the mahjong, right?"

"That's just your guess," her husband smiled, blushing. His lie had been exposed.

He had buddies to play mahjong and he could have big bets; if he had small bets, he would rather go home and sleep.

The small bets were called "chicken shit" in Huilong Town; if one lost, it would be a worthless game, not embarrassing. But Guangwen detested the small bets and the life in this way: life without the big bets would be useless, and the useless life would be death. He would not while away his precious time on the small bets with those men who would lose control as soon as they lost 20 or 30 yuan in a game.

Guangwen would close his eyes and snore after he sat down less than one minute if he had no alcohol, no mahjong, and no disturbance from villagers. But tomorrow would be our father's birthday, so he had to do something: he did not choose his special couch for his naps or sofa as his resting place, but sat down on the stool which had been used by Chunshang, and then he arranged the schedule for tomorrow just like he did to the villagers.

A birthday banquet should be held for such an elderly man as our father. Feasts, however, should not be organized at will in the villages, which was a rule stipulated by the government sectors in the town last year. The villages had been engulfed in feasts and liquor in these years: birthdays, weddings, newborns, the first month and the first year of babies, the crawling, walking, speaking and schooling of kids, building and moving house, hospital discharge, retirement, funerals, etc. Birthdays in the solar calendar and in the lunar month came one after another; family members would hold a birthday party for a dying patient, followed by a funeral just after several days. Mr. Wu, who used to be a teacher in the Huilong Town, enjoyed writing ancient Chinese poems. He would write verse whenever he took part in a banquet, and he left a thick volume of poetry after he died. For example, *Congratulations to Mr. Lin Dongquan on His Second Wedding*, *Congratulations to Mr. Lin Dongquan on His Third Wedding*, and *Congratulations to Mr. Lin Dongquan on His Fourth Wedding*. Mr. Lin Dongquan had married four times and had held four ceremonies. Mr. Wu had been invited four times and had written wonderful lines:

"Sitting in front of a mirror, you stand behind her, and silently watch her. Whispers can be heard, you are next to her."

"Your third marriage will be perfect."

There were notes following those words:

"The banquet cost me half-a-month pay."

That was behind *Congratulations to Mr. Lin Dongquan on His Second Wedding*.

"I should be thrifty from now on and I will have no egg for breakfast."

That was behind *Congratulations to Mr. Lin Dongquan on His Fourth Wedding*.

You must attend such a banquet with your gifts, otherwise you would be regarded as a ruthless person. And you should not pretend that you did not know it after you received it in your text message or in your WeChat. The host would call a VIP and would hang a sign in a street with drums and gongs. A guest with good connections would have to attend five, six or more than ten parties within one day, leaving him or her with a stuffed stomach, bills, and tears. The sufferers of these occasions would consider jumping from a building. That was true. A man did so and had his bones shattered.

No death, no ban. The town government officers tried to discourage villagers from attending banquets after they got the command, but they failed. Later they hung banners in the streets: "Shame on the organisers of the tasteless banquets! Shame on those guests!" So what? The villagers did not care two hoots about those curses. Give and take. No free lunch. Shame on the freeloader.

The persuasion did not work, so the officers made hard and fast rules: the host must apply for a banquet allowing guests to sit around three large tables, and he or she must give a reason and should not hold a banquet unless it could be approved with a written document; otherwise severe punishment would be carried out. Afterwards villagers often went to the town government holding good cigarettes covered with newspaper or good bottles of wine in a bag. The road to the administration building during the days before the Chinese New Year came would be teeming with those villagers. In addition, migrant labourers returned home with a lot of money and would spend it on the banquets during the Festival. As a result, anybody who went into the building could come out happily holding the written document.

It would be an easy job for us to get the written approval for holding a birthday banquet for our father because Guangwen was the village party secretary, but such a party should not be held at will. One of our villagers held a banquet for his 60th birthday when he was 59. Later he was diagnosed with gastric cancer and died in two months. He looked like a healthy man before the diagnosis, and he became a dying patient after it. So soon. Another man went to Shanghai to visit his son after his birthday, but he had a car accident, which left him partly paralysed. Such a thing had happened to our father, too. Chunshang organized a party for our father's 75th birthday and invited guests sitting around more than 30 large tables. Memories came to his mind. Since his wife died, he and his seven children had been ridiculed and been despised by the gossiping villagers. They cursed that Xu Chengxiang would be unable to bring up his children even if he could have reincarnation because he would be a good-for-nothing if without his competent wife. His children grew up and got married. His third son had been admitted to a prestigious university and had been a civil servant since graduation. Now his youngest son was holding a banquet full of guests inside and firecrackers outside. The past sadness and the happiness now made our father feel like crying. He came back from a hillside on the ninth day after his birthday. It started to rain as soon as he entered the room. A pair of shoes of Chunshang were in the rain beside a stairway. He wanted to take the shoes into the room, but he slipped and fell to the courtyard from the fourth step of a ladder. Both the courtyard and the ladder were made of stones. He fell to the ground and his hipbones broke.

Since then our father had had to limp with a walking stick and we had been too worried to hold a birthday banquet again. A family gathering would be needed although it would be difficult to have all our family members together: troublesome and tiring round trips from hometown to different and remote cities, and possible job losses because of absences. Few members would go home now. This year Ye Fengjuan (the wife of my eldest brother Chunshan) and her daughter lived in Zhejiang province, Chunhua and her husband in Hubei, and Chunying and her husband in Guangdong. The younger generation worked in various cities across China. Some of them had become regular employees, but the wanderer Xu Sixi, the son of Chunshan, would say on the phone that he was in Beijing, after five minutes in Hainan province.

The arrangement for the birthday banquet tomorrow would need a lot of discussions. Guangwen said that the family members of my brothers might come to the town and have lunch together in a restaurant.

"Chunshu is in the town now," Chunhong said. "I saw him in an oil-pressing mill before Chunming came here."

"Oh, I thought that he had returned to Yanerpo," her husband said.

"Why did he go there?" she asked with a mysterious smile. "Someone has not returned."

I did not understand that, but my question was stopped by Guangwen. "Mind your own business," he said.

"Aren't you meddlesome?" his wife retorted, scowling at him.

He became annoyed and silent.

"I don't want to pay for the special meal," she continued. "Others just eat in the restaurant. Either we or Chunming will have to pay the bill."

"Any other choice?" her husband asked.

"I'll cook at home," she replied.

"Well, you will have to buy raw materials."

"They won't cost me too much."

"You may cook if you think it okay."

Chapter 5

It was settled. Then our mother became the subject again. Guangwen had never met her. He had lived in the areas around Mount Lordhou opposite the river. Laojun Mountain and Mount Lordhou are the unimportant ranges of the Daba Mountains, just like outcasts. Each word needs to be explained with the other words. A unit of the world can be created by words, and even the whole world can be made by them. Ba Mountain is short for the Daba Mountains which connect Shennongjia Nature Reserve (located in Hubei province) in the east and Motian Ridge in the west, divide Jialing River and Han River, and also play the role of the geographical boundary between Sichuan Basin and Hanzhong Basin. What is unimportance? It is involved with politics, economy, and profound humanity. All in all, it is too complicated to be explained. The Laojun Mountain and the Mount Lordhou had extended nearly 3,000 metres before they became eye-catching.

Guangwen used to live in the Lijiayan Village, opposite Yanerpo. If you stood in your own courtyard, you could see the houses in Lijiayan, hear the moos, and even catch sight of the flickering will-o'-the-wisp on a starless and moonless night. Those things seemed quite near, but it would take a long journey if you walked there. The villagers seldom came and went to the two places unless their relatives paid a visit. Our mother was just like a mound of dirt in Yanerpo to Guangwen. He got bored with our conversation and felt drowsy; he lay in the couch and started to snore as soon as his head leaned on the pillow.

"Lie in your bed if you feel sick! Don't annoy us!" his wife shouted.

She wanted him to have a good talk with us so that she could let us be her good listeners. Her husband's companionship had been as short as droplets of water on a searing iron since they had been married for half a year. Many years ago he was poorer than Chunhong and he could not afford to hold a wedding. They agreed that they would go to Xinjiang province to seek for financial opportunities through one of his relatives. The departure date became their wedding. The rumoured good prospects in and out of Xinjiang were tantalising and enviable. She, however, came back alone after six months. She did not say anything about her life in Xinjiang or about why her husband did not return. She just spent one night in her mother's house and the next day she went to live in her mother-in-law's. I did not know her sufferings in her husband's family until many years had passed. What I knew at that time was that she had had a new home since she got married, and a person should not have two homes, otherwise it would not be a good thing. That worried me, and nothing more.

He did not return until his wife had been back for more than two years.

On the day when he appeared, he had a quarrel with his mother and elder brother, and he thought that he could make peace with his wife through the quarrel. Afterwards he worked as a village party secretary and frequently travelled between the town and the village, and seldom went home. After the couple moved to live in the town, he treated his own house like an inn and often brought three or eight people home when it was time for dinner.

After he entered the room, he would call his wife as if calling a maid:

"Cook chicken, Chunhong."

"Cook some beef, Chunhong."

She was burning with anger inside, but she had to keep calm and keep smiling, made tea and placed stools around a table, and rushed to the market. After the table was left with messy animal bones, her husband and his so-called guests went out at once.

Chapter 6

Guangwen did not stop his snoring until his wife yelled at him. He opened his eyes lazily, looked around in confusion, and realized that he was at home. He sat up and was surprised to see me.

"When did you come back, Chunming?" he asked.

His wife shouted at him while he was in a daze. And then he laughed, sat down on a stool, and gave cigarettes to me and to our father. The elderly man received it but soon gave it back to Guangwen. He said that he preferred tobacco leaves to cigarettes. It was unavailable here, so he had to swallow saliva. He worried that he might annoy his daughter if he had the strong tobacco leaf permeating the room.

"You can enjoy the tobacco leaf if you want," she said, glancing at him. "But don't pretend that you don't want it."

She turned off the air conditioner and opened the glass door between the balcony and the living room. Wind rushed in with the dampness of a river which became a raging torrent in the fourth lunar month.

"The air is fresh," Guangwen exclaimed, taking a deep breath.

At this moment he disliked stuffiness. But when he was sitting in a small room with other buddies and playing mahjong with big bets, he usually put large piles of paper money on the table regardless of a win or a failure. He was worried about the gossip rather than the police, so he closed the doors and windows. He was smoking on and on during the game and had no stuffy feeling in his chest, but he had it when he was at home.

Our father withdrew the blanket from his body, took a plastic pouch out of his bag and opened it to put some tobacco leaf powder into his pipe. Just before the pipe was ready, he began to drool. He was surprised to see his saliva, which looked like a jumping rabbit, dropping from his mouth. After he clearly saw it was his saliva, he tried to get a tissue from the table to wipe his mouth. When he lived in his hometown and in Guaizaoping with Chunshang, he would never spit in the way that a chicken or a duck would shit anytime in the room or in the cooking range or on the pot cover. Instead, he would spit in the ashes of the fireplace; and he would behave himself when he was staying at his daughter's house in which the floor was as clean as a mirror. She always mopped the floor as cleanly as possible and had to cook every day and would have to entertain the guests brought by her husband without an appointment. Her father did not want to soil the floor with his saliva, but it was flowing at will.

Our father could not grasp a tissue because his right thumb tilted backwards badly since it had been injured by a rock. The more the floor was scrubbed, the dirtier it got. His daughter looked away because she did not want to see that. But soon she came to help him because she was so obsessed about the cleanliness of the floor that she must clean it up whenever it became dirty. He was embarrassed when his daughter was sweeping the floor with two rolls of toilet paper. She threw the smudged paper into a trash can in the bathroom, and then she saw him drooling again.

"Oh, fuck…" he cursed.

Before he finished his words, his saliva gushed out. All of us including him got astounded by such a scene.

"Will you go to sleep now, dad?" Guangwen whispered, blushing.

The elderly man did not speak lest he should drivel again.

Chapter 7

I supported our father onto the bed. Chunhong had a very large house. Her husband bought the houses on the fourth floor both in the Unit Two and Unit Three in the residential quarter along the riverside road. Later he installed a door in the partition between the two Units, so the two houses became one. If you stood at one end of the house and called someone, he or she could not hear you; and you must shout. As the days went by, Guangwen started to worry that neighbours might gossip about his houses, so he blocked off the door in the partition and sold the one in the Unit Three. In spite of that, his house was still spacious. He used to have two houses in the Unit Two, but now just had one after the partition was connected.

Chunhong had made up the bed before supper. Now I led our father into his bedroom, fumbling for the switch on the wall. I did not know why she had had a large pile of new quilts occupy half of the bed, and our father had to sleep in the other half of it. I helped him to remove his shoes, socks and coat, to lift his damaged left leg, to lie down on the bed, and to tuck him in. He was a short man and had become shorter since he got lame. I had to fold the quilt to cover his feet.

"Are you feeling cold, dad?" I asked.

"Yes," he said.

I stood up on the bed, got another quilt from the pile as high as the ceiling, and put it on his body. Under the light he seemed to lie in a truck and I worried that he would be buried in the pile of quilts if they collapsed. He gazed at the pile which leaned on the window and would shield him from wind, and then he looked relieved. In fact, the wind could not enter the closed windows. He felt at ease in a small space and terrified in a large one.

"Are you feeling unwell, dad?" I asked.

"I'm feeling dizzy," he said.

"You may sleep now."

"OK."

But he did not sleep. He looked around.

An elderly man had eyes as curious as those of a baby, but they were no long clear and could not reflect the grass or the sky anymore. There was a smell like a withered leaf from our father's body, like time fading away. I took a towel from the box in the corner full of sundries, and put it on my father's head.

"I'm feeling warm," he said.

"You may sleep now," I said.

"OK. By the way, has Chunshang got home?" he asked.

"Several hours have passed and he must have got home," I answered. But I took out my phone and called him at once.

He was drinking when he was answering the phone. He had had supper at our sister's house. After he returned home, he saw two pieces of preserved pork ribs cooked by his wife. He worried that the ribs would go bad tomorrow, so he had them with some liquor. The couple must have prepared a lot of food for our father's birthday tomorrow. Nobody would come, so he ate the food without delay. Our father rested assured when he knew that Chunshang was drinking at home.

"Am I dying, Chunming?" he whispered.

Chapter 8

If a living person talks about death, it sounds unreal to anyone, even if that person is coming close to dying. Death is truth. What I had remembered was our mother's death.

On a night full of cold wind and rain in autumn, our mother, who had been lying on her sickbed for several months, suddenly became spirited.

"Chengxiang! Chengxiang!" she shouted in her bedroom.

Our father, who was having a bowl of corn paste with crumbs on his beard, put his bowl down on the table as soon as he heard his wife crying, and ran to the bedroom holding a kitchen knife. He thought that she had a twinge in her breasts again.

When our mother got seriously ill, she often shouted that she was having breast pain but she was still breastfeeding her youngest daughter, and Chunshang often sucked her nipples. She had been a quiet sufferer of afflictions, but now she could not help yelling that her blood was being sucked if her milk could not. In fact, at that time Chunying was sleeping and Chunshang was having fun outside. But our mother insisted that her breasts were being sucked and she tried to push the sucker away. Her forehead was teeming with sweat. Meanwhile, our father was so anxious that he got a kitchen knife and wielded it in front of his wife's breasts, trying to kill the monster who was tormenting her. But that did not work. Our mother did not feel less painful until she woke up from a coma, and blood drops could be seen in her nipples.

She had been unable to sit up for several months. Today our father, holding a knife, saw his wife sit up without yelling. "King of Hell kept me alive although I nearly died, my dear," she exclaimed happily. "He let me survive to bring up our children in the coming years of continued hardships, and he will take me away after they grow up."

All of us entered her bedroom which was located nearby a gable wall and which was dark and damp because of gutters underneath the wall. The dusty room was often hit by wind and rain at night and was dull in daytime even with a trace of light from the transparent-tile roof. Our father put the knife on the bedside table supported by a thin stand, and made the oil lamp lighter. Our emaciated mother was sitting in the middle of the bed with a linen mosquito net and two copper-plated iron hooks at both ends. She together with the bed seemed to be rippling in a river under the flickering light.

"Support me to the fireplace and I'll sit there," she said to our father smilingly.

When he was about to do so, someone shouted: "You should not do that! Your wife is having the momentary recovery of consciousness just before her death, just like the last radiance of the setting sun! She will survive if the radiance is kept and die if it is lost!"

Mrs. Hou, our neighbour, was screaming. We did not know when she came here.

Mrs. Hou, the worst enemy of our mother, visited the latter every day during her days of serious illness. My siblings and our father disliked her and said that she came here to see if our mother was living or dead. As a result, Mrs. Hou resembled an ominous shadow in each season no matter how gaudily she dressed, and what she said and did would be mantic. She did not sleep at night but sat with dishevelled hair in darkness and cast a curse on our mother through a thin wall. That was what I had thought until I grew up and realized that it might be another story.

Mrs. Hou was an illiterate but had an inner world totally different from Yanerpo villagers', so she must do something to turn it into the world she liked. She kept bickering with them including the mute except babies and dying people. When a dumb person made a sound like "Ah", she could guess the meaning through her imagination and would retort: "Fuck!" But that turned out to be ridiculous because both of them were women. What's more, Mrs. Hou often had rows with animals such as dogs, pigs, and birds, and even cursed their forefathers. The animals would not have become animals if they could have had a good previous life, but they would try to avoid her at the sight of her, which made her get bored.

She indulged in troublemaking and even pried into her neighbours' private affairs: whose grandpa had been a thief or an opium addict or had had syphilis; and then she would gossip about it. If those anecdotes failed to arouse the villagers' curiosity, she would make irresponsible remarks that some daughter-in-law moaned in a pinewood one night. The listener would ask why she moaned and if she had had a stomachache. Mrs. Hou would say something intriguing so that the listener could understand at once. Was it true or not? It was not important. When someday the daughter-in-law confronted her, she would deny that she had said about those things and then deny that the daughter-in-law had understood. So a fierce quarrel was started between the two women, which triggered days and nights of wrangles to satisfy Mrs. Hou.

But such a method became useless as more and more people and animals avoided Mrs. Hou at the sight of her. She got bored but soon found new fun in our mother who was her neighbour. A trifle could result in a quarrel, such as a chicken shitting across the boundary, a cat stealing a piece of meat, firewood falling onto the steps of the other's house, and mud falling from shoes on the doorway on a rainy day. Our mother had a bad temper and would never back off from any row, and Mrs. Hou had increased her bellicosity since she and our mother became enemies.

She needed our mother and hoped that the latter could survive, but our mother did not understand her and must fight back. That night when she heard Mrs. Hou speak, she struggled out of bed by herself and then moved her legs like swimming. Our father supported her with his hands and walked into the kitchen. She died after she sat beside the fireplace for less than twenty minutes.

During that period of time, Chunshu had been reading a dog-eared *Romance of the Three Kingdoms*, and he was still preoccupied with it when the funeral of our mother was prepared. When he was reading Chapter 63 *Zhuge Liang Cried for Pang Tong* on the eve of the funeral, he exclaimed: "Mrs. Hou was Zhuge Liang and our mother was Pang Tong. Pang died because he was egged on by Zhuge, and our mother died after Mrs. Hou did the same thing to her. Mrs. Hou was much smarter."

Chunshan, who was in mourning and was sealing the coffin with sticky rice paste, stopped after he heard his brother's talk. Chunshu, who was in mourning, too, was not as pious as Chunshan and did not help him for the funeral. Chunshan disliked him and got angry with him now.

"How dare you say that Mrs. Hou was smarter than our mother?" he snapped.

Chunshu went on with his reading. He used to be a top student in the district but he dropped out of junior high school. At that time a student must give a gift to the principal for further education. If you gave him a chicken and I gave him a sheep, I would be admitted into the senior high school; if you gave him bean curd and I gave him Chinese cabbage, you would be chosen. Chunshu did not want to do that, so our father brought a basket of Chinese cabbage bitten by worms to the principal who did not know the gift would be the food for our family for two days. The result would not be changed even if he knew that. Since Chunshu stopped schooling, he had been a regular customer in the tea houses and a good listener of good stories there, and also been an avid reader of romances in the musty books.

Chapter 9

Among my relatives, I have only witnessed my mother's death. Within the ten years after her death, my grandmother died, and then my mother's eldest sister, and then her son, and then my uncle, and then his wife – no, she suddenly opened her eyes after she was thought to have been dead for two days, but she kicked the bucket after a day and a half. I was studying in a university far away from my hometown when they snuffed it and when their funerals were held. Since then death had been like the wind and rain in autumn.

Now it was just the beginning of the fourth lunar month and was far away from autumn and death, but our father said that he was going to die.

"Am I dying, Chunming?" he whispered sadly.

What I was feeling at that time was the fragility of life rather than his talk about death.

"You should stop thinking about that, dad!" I retorted in an annoyed tone of voice.

Our father always worried that he might irritate his children. He was afraid of displeasing our mother when she was alive, and of riling us after he brought us up. Now he became silent after he saw my anger.

"I should not have increased the workload of your eldest sister," he said after a moment of silence. He meant that she must have mopped the floor since we left the living room, and that was what I had thought.

"She had done quite a lot for the crashers at home and she should do something for you." That was what I wanted to say, but I did not say it because I had been too shy to say caring words to him.

I worried if our father would slobber again when I saw him compressing his lips, but he didn't. He looked at the ceiling and then at me, and I could understand that he wanted me to stay with him – he was emotionally dependent upon me when Chunshang was not with him. I wished that Chunshang could be here now. At his bedside I sat down on a plastic low stool which was printed with a delicate red rose with fresh dewdrops on the petals. I frowned when I had to put my bottom on the flower lest I should dirty it or make my buttocks uncomfortable.

"Are you feeling cold?" he asked.

"No," I answered, fanning myself with my coat.

I felt uneasy and even impatient when I had to be alone with him.

"Has the football match begun?" he asked after a moment of silence.

At supper I told him that a football match would be shown on TV at 9:30 tonight, he knew that I loved it, but it was not even nine o'clock.

"Just let it be," I said.

"You may go to watch it," he suggested.

"Are you sleepy now?"

"I'm fine."

I thought that he was going to sleep although he did not say it definitely. I stood up and tucked him in, checked if the glass windows and the balcony door were shut, and closed the bathroom door beside the balcony.

"Turn off the light?" I asked.

"Yes," he answered. "Do not waste electricity."

I turned off the light, closed the door, and left him in darkness.

Chapter 10

When I saw Chunhong sitting alone on a sofa, putting her crossed hands on her belly and looking tired, I asked: "Is Guangwen sleeping?"

She suddenly opened her eyes. Her action reminded me of the inexplicable astonishment in Guangwen. The shock resembled a captive animal which would jump out of the cage in an unguarded moment. Perhaps I was too sensitive. I find that I am a hypocrite and also too suspicious of others; what's more, I have gradually lost trust in many things. I know that trust is the origination of everything – a seed will not sprout if it does not believe in the soil. If a tall, luxuriant tree is thought to have mistrusted the soil, that is either betrayal or affectation. That was me although I was not like such a tree.

Chunhong rubbed her face to remove her sleepiness, and said:

"Early to bed? That's impossible for him!"

"The deputy town chief Mr. Han had dinner with the leaders from the county," she added. "They left after the dinner was over."

That meant Guangwen had played mahjong with Mr. Han and the leaders.

She laughed unexpectedly at our father's dribbling as soon as I sat down.

"Did our dad slobber again when he was lying on the bed?" she asked.

"No," I answered.

"An old man may act like a baby," she added, feeling relieved.

I did not know why I was deeply sorry for our father's drooling, which was intensified by her laughter. So I changed the subject and asked her about her two children.

She had a daughter named Lily who had been a contract worker in

Zhoucheng Television Station since she graduated from university. Her son Li Zhi had been learning cooking skills in a restaurant since he went to Fuzhou two months ago. The restaurant owner was Jiang Hua who came from Huilong Town and used to live in the same village with Guangwen. Twenty years ago Jiang Hua went to Fuzhou and worked in construction sites, and later he had his own restaurant and gradually prospered.

When Lily was mentioned, her mother said:

"You should use your head and turn your niece into a regular employee in the Television Station as early as possible."

I realized that I should not have mentioned it because it was I who found the job for Lily. When she was in the fourth year of the university, her father called me and asked me to find a job for her in the city. He could settle the problems in the village and thought that he could do the same in the city through me. A man should establish his turf and become a big shot, which was his point of view. He could do it, but I could not. I was too shy to say no, and at last I pulled myself into a quagmire. I had to do what Guangwen had asked me, but the good jobs in the city had been specially made for the younger generation of the powerful and of the rich. I told this to Guangwen.

"You are useless indeed!" he snapped.

I had been unable to accomplish his tasks. Many years ago when the town government intended to promote village cadres, the local leaders would choose Guangwen, but such a thing should be decided by the county government, which was beyond his power. He asked me to use my connections in the city for his promotion. I was just a small potato in the provincial capital, but he frequently called me at midnight and importuned me.

I told him that I did not know any leader in the county government, but he got angry:

"You will be invited to all kinds of banquets in the county whenever you come back. Those leaders may be familiar to your friends though not to you. A friend in need is a friend indeed."

I had to use my connections, but I failed to facilitate the promotion of Guangwen. So I was looked down upon by him.

Fortunately, I got a job for Lily. At that time she had had her graduation certificate. Most of the students had left the university, but she and her boyfriend, who was one of her classmates, chose to stay for a few days longer. The campus was teeming with sadness. Few people would agree that the period of sadness would be of happiness in disguise. After you have gone through ups and downs in the society, you will become a hedonist, or be riddled with distress or depression, or persevere. All in all, you will be too preoccupied to be sad. Sorrow is confusion mixed with mild worry, which is needed by people in love.

But Guangwen thought that Lily would become an idler and waste her time if she did not go home after graduation, and I should be blamed for that. He did not know that I had been anxious to find a job for my niece through all my connections regardless of refusals since she had started her fourth year in the university. I had deeply understood the meaning of ineptitude in those days: you are an incompetent if you always need to be helped by others. But why do they have to help you? If they don't, you will complain and may belittle your old friends, and you will be reduced to being shameless, not useless. That nearly happened to me.

There would be a way. When Lily and her boyfriend enjoyed their longer stay in the university, I met one of the alumni named Xiang and had a chat with him about my niece.

"You should have told me much earlier, Chunming," he said with a glint in his eyes. "I know the director of the Zhoucheng Television Station, and I can introduce her to him."

"But Lily does not major in television," I said.

"The employment now has little to do with the major which is made for admissions rather than social needs," he retorted. "Most of the students go to college just for diplomas and don't care about if their jobs are related to what they have learned in the universities. Only the aspiring ones choose the specialty they love."

That made sense. Zhoucheng, an emerging city with a population of more than 4 million and with areas three-quarters more than downtown Baima, was next to Chongqing. I fawned on Xiang.

"I'm flattered," he said with a mysterious smile. "I would stand by if I did not know that you would need my efforts. But money will be needed."

Guangwen had stressed that I should tell him if I needed money for the special arrangements for his daughter's job. I told him that I would, and soon he transferred 50,000 yuan to my bank card which I'd carried with me. 50,000 yuan was too much. I withdrew a portion of the cash and put the banknotes into an envelope. And then I went to meet the man led by Xiang. I had to stay in Zhoucheng four days longer.

I could still member the scene, which was one of the bad experiences in my life: the man took the envelope and threw it on the sofa like a falling leaf, and then he started his idle talk; before he left, he put the envelope into his briefcase naturally just like he had owned the money. Later I was told that Xiang had been a wily old bird. The first man whom he had let me meet was not the key figure; after he took the money, he would give some to Xiang.

I dared not tell this to Chunhong and her husband. They would be satisfied with the good result, and Guangwen had never blamed me for spending too much money. He knew the advantages and disadvantages of money, and he often said that the thing would be done if the money was spent, just like the fire, but it would not be done if the fire went out. I felt uneasy at the thought of that.

Chapter 11

When Chonghong asked me to make Lily a regular employee, I took a sip of water, but remained silent. She did not elaborate further on her daughter's job because she was much more worried about her son Li Zhi. Whenever they talked about Li Zhi, people would say it's hard to buy the prosperity of one's descendants with money. Li Zhi had got married and had a daughter. At the beginning his parents funded his business, but he messed up each deal less than a quarter and had got more than ten bungles within three years. In addition, he went to work in the factory operated by his father and partners, but he turned out to be useless. At last his parents just let him be.

Since then he had been an idler and been unwilling to be a farmer. He indulged in playing snooker and he would go to a restaurant with his cronies when he got hungry. He always sprang for the meals and never ordered dishes. As soon as he entered the restaurant, he shouted:

"Serve food worth 300 yuan!"

The restaurant owner got busy in the kitchen at once; later he brought on the table a plate of shredded pork with green peppers, a big bowl of spinach and tofu soup, and three plates of vegetable dishes, no more. After he made a pig of himself, he did not calculate the bill but put three banknotes worth 300 yuan under the bowl, and then he went on to play snooker. If he was told that there was good fish in a reservoir or a pond, he would call his cronies and go there by motorbike with fishing gear. After he got the fish, he would go to a restaurant, have the fish cooked and eat them. Both he and his father seldom had meals at home. Most of the time he did not sleep at home; sometimes he returned with four or five buddies for sleep. The rooms often stank of socks which had not been washed for many days.

His wife Qingmei turned a blind eye to his loafing. She spent the mornings in her mother's house located at the bridge with her daughter and came back for lunch; she and her daughter shopped and went to the newly-established North Gate Pier and Banese Plaza in the afternoons; or, she chatted with other women like her and ate sunflower seeds in a store, and went home just before supper. Later her daughter had preschool education. She went to the other places after she sent her daughter to the kindergarten. The little girl had lunch in the kindergarten. She picked up her in the afternoon and did not return home until supper. After her father died, she often had supper with her daughter in her mother's house and spent the night there (like tonight). She did not speak to her husband even if she met him in the street.

He did the same to her. If his daughter was with her mom, he would kiss her in the cheeks, hug her and lift her up, and then put her down.

"Be a good girl," he said. And then he went on with his idling. If his daughter was not with his wife, he would ignore her. They were not on bad terms although they were not a sweet couple.

At noon two months ago, a man at 24 or 25 wearing women's clothes and earrings, was walking with his bottom wiggling, his hands on the trousers seam but his little fingers upwards coquettishly. He would not have been recognized as a man if without his flat chest and his Adam's apple. He was like a two-legged, eye-catching monster. Among the crowd, Li Zhi took an instant dislike to that guy, so he punched him and that man fainted at once. Guangwen rushed to the site and kicked Li Zhi as soon as he got the news.

"Fuck!" he cursed in a low voice. "Run now! Go to Fuzhou and find Uncle Jiang." He put a wad of banknotes into his son's pocket.

After Li Zhi fled, his father called for an ambulance to send the injured man, who was bleeding in the mouth and nose, and having convulsions at the corners of the mouth and in his legs, to the hospital in the county directly because he could not be treated in the health centre in the town. The president of The Third People's Hospital in the county used to be one of the classmates of Guangwen in the senior high school. The doctor said that the patient was not at risk, and Guangwen felt relieved. He called Jiang Hua in Fuzhou, and said he wanted his son to learn cooking from him. Jiang was glad to hear that. Soon he called his son and knew that he was on the journey to Fuzhou.

"Tell Uncle Jiang that you want to become a cook," he warned. "Do not tell him that you have been a troublemaker."

The patient was discharged from hospital after twenty days. Guangwen paid the medical bill and gave him the nutrition fee of 20,000 yuan, cost of lost labour, and mental damage compensation. That man tenderly expressed his gratitude to Guangwen and left the town. He was a visitor to Huilong Town. That day he sat in a yacht and went ashore in the Town; later he enjoyed sightseeing in the street along the river, but was punched unluckily.

The buddies of Li Zhi sent messages to him that the patient had left hospital, and he started to pack his bags for his return trip. Jiang Hua could not understand why Li Zhi was eager to go home before he could become a good cook. Li Zhi had been learning the skills in the kitchen and he was talented – a glutton might be a born cook. He refused to stay longer, so Jiang Hua called his father. Guangwen wanted his son to continue his apprenticeship so that he could run a restaurant in the town and could have more opportunities to make money for the whole family if his father had few.

"Let him stay in your restaurant until he becomes a leading chef," the father said. "It's your duty!"

Guangwen could speak to Jiang Hua in this way because he had done a good deed for the latter. When a rural highway was being built many years ago, a route would pass through the ancestral graves of the Jiangs according to the design drawing. Jiang Hua returned from Fuzhou and implored Guangwen to find another way. At last the highway neither passed through nor behind the ancestral graves of the Jiangs. Geomantic omens would become disastrous if a road was made behind ancestral tombs. The Jiangs had so many auspicious omens that four sons of the five had left the countryside, and that two of them had established their career in Chongqing and had become deputy directors in government sectors. Jiang Hua was still a villager but he had made his business prosper in Fuzhou.

Jiang Hua told what Guangwen had said to Li Zhi. He put away Li Zhi's luggage, kept closer watch on him, provided him with meals, liquor, and cigarettes, but gave him no money. Since then the apprentice had stopped learning cooking skills.

Chapter 12

"Li Zhi may return soon," Chunhong told me.

He used a boning knife to cut on his arms in Jiang Hua's presence. The latter was so frightened that he called Guangwen lest his son should cut off his own arms.

"Blood! Mr. Li!" he screamed. "Your son is self-harming and I can't control him!"

Chunhong cursed her husband and her son, and then she thought of her daughter-in-law.

"Qingmei is an incapable wife," she sighed, shaking her head. "A husband should be educated by his wife, even a good-for-nothing can become promising if he can be well instructed by his tough wife. But my daughter-in-law is too weak-minded."

"But she is faithful to our family," the mother-in-law continued. "A daughter-in-law would have forsaken us if we had been poor! A wife nowadays will have a new relationship if she can't endure poverty. The daughter-in-law of Lame Liu in the middle section of the new street has married four times with men living in the villages around the river: Huilong Town, Qingping Town, and Golden Town. She does not feel ashamed of herself; instead, she often comes to Huilong Town and shows off, wearing gaudy clothes and a large necklace like a dog leash, and walking like a whore. She saw me and greeted me this morning, but I ignored her!"

The sound of water flowing could be heard, and then Chunhong checked the kitchen and the bathroom.

"Did our dad relieve himself before he went to bed?" she asked.

"No," I said.

"Let him do it now. Our dad is like a baby."

I had never seen an old man act like a baby. Our mother died when I was a boy, and I did not live with my parents-in-law after I got married. The days that I had been able to stay with our father since I went to university were less than a week within one year.

In fact, Chunhong infrequently stayed with our father, but she anxiously cared for him – she must have been influenced by her mother-in-law. Our mother died early and Chunhong's mother-in-law became a widow at 30. When she was engaged to her fiancé, she felt that her husband's mother was sullen. She did not realize that she had a cruel mother-in-law until she came back from Xinjiang and lived with her. The mother-in-law despised her because the latter had not been toughened before the marriage.

"When will Erwazi (the nickname of Guangwen, the second son in his family of three sons) come back?" the mother-in-law asked one day.

"He will return after one or two years," Chunhong answered.

"But why so long?"

"Don't ask me. He will come back at the right time."

Immediately the mother-in-law slapped Chunhong hard across the face, pushed her away, pulled her hair, and beat her with a club. The first son of the old woman was there, too, and was ready to punish her.

At that time Chunhong was pregnant. Her mother-in-law did not hit her in the belly, but grasped her by the collar and thrashed her in the shin bones.

"Physical pain is nothing compared with mental pain," the daughter-in-law said, holding back her tears.

"You have been an ill-bred girl since your mother died," her mother-in-law snapped.

Chunhong would wail for her dead mother whenever she was cursed. Since then she had started to hate her mother-in-law, and she would yell at the latter:

"I hate you! And I'll hate you as long as I live if you can't kill me!"

Fight back and have a sharp tongue, these were the characters shared by Chunhong and our mother; the latter taught the former the decency of being a person, so the former did not grapple with her mother-in-law for the sake of her baby in her belly and of good manners. Chunhong, however, said that she should have had a fight with her mother-in-law. The old woman would be helped by her first son, and Chunhong would be at a disadvantage and might be beaten to death. Human beings and animals will die sooner or later whatever kind of life they live.

Her mother-in-law died in her seventies without illness. When she went to the toilet one night, she fell into a cesspool and drowned. The outhouse, which had been surrounded with yellow mud for decades, had a leaky roof and repairs did not work. The old woman had a mason pave slates around the squatting pit. The slates, which had been dug out of ownerless graveyards in the back mountains, triggered a disaster: the ghosts in the tombs got so angry that one night they were lurking in the bamboo forest beside the outhouse and were waiting for her. She came, squatted, and was soon pushed down by them. She slipped as soon as she felt an evil wind around her. Shit and urine together with the spectres enshrouded her quickly before she could make a sound. She moved up and down, and then became as quiet as the night.

Chunhong never talked about the death of her mother-in-law. Whenever she was asked, she would say: "Everybody dies in his or her own way. There is nothing strange."

Someone died downstream before her mother-in-law did. That person was a woman, too. Whenever she saw a human being scratch himself or herself, even though the being was a hundred meters to her, she would feel like being tickled and would be on the verge of laughing. Later she would do the same at the sight of a cat or a dog scratching itself and even of a backscratcher resembling a bent thumb. She kept guffawing for several months until she choked one day and died at the age of 34. People talked about the death of the ridiculous woman and that of Chunhong's mother-in-law. In fact, death is not a topic. All the gossip is about a person's life before death. The death is the outcome, and all kinds of deaths are the same. The monotonous thing is not worth talking.

People's topics are and will be the same; in this way they can protect the embarrassing details related to themselves from being revealed. Meanwhile, they are eager to know the details of others although the two groups have similar secrets. The secrets are like shadows which will not hurt their owners under attack. Therefore, Chunhong had to give the same answer to the repeated question.

"I hate you!"

"Everybody dies in his or her own way."

Rumours said that Chunhong had hated her mother-in-law and cursed her to die; and at last the old woman died in a cesspit, which satisfied her daughter-in-law.

To be frank, at the beginning I thought so. But one day Lily told me that her grandma had been living alone. After her mother went to the market and bought cakes, she would give them to her children without being noticed.

"Do not let your grandma see these cakes," she whispered.

The children did what their mother had said, but they would save some cakes for their grandma.

"Enjoy your desserts, my dear," the old woman said. "Your mom gave me many pastries after she came back from the market." And then she opened the cupboard and the pastries were more than her grandchildren had eaten.

I did not know why Chunhong had hated her mother-in-law but bought cakes for her, and why she would not treat the latter well overtly. What was more, I wondered when the old woman started to act like a baby, and how Chunhong would get along with her. And I also wanted to know what Chunhong's husband had done during his two-year stay in Xinjiang. I was too shy to ask them about it, and the couple had never talked about their days in that place.

Chapter 13

Chunhong was still angry with her daughter-in-law. She did not mention the latter but shouted: "My husband gives several thousand yuan to Qingmei each month. He is such a fool that he should not have financially supported her to raise her daughter! She is just a freeloader!"

I had never heard of that before.

"Human beings will become extinct if a woman wants money to bring up her own children!" she continued in a huff.

But soon she realized that she had said the wrong thing and she blushed.

"We have our own problem," she added. "Li Zhi is a leech living off us. He is a pathetic, embarrassing loser, and he cadges money off his parents!"

I knew that Chunhong had blamed her husband for having given money to their son, and for the sake of that, she had smashed cups and bowls. Whenever Li Zhi needed money, he would go to the mahjong parlour much frequented by his father and waited for him. After his father appeared, he would stretch one of his arms forward and get a wad of banknotes at once. Li Zhi could get money from his father, but could not from his wife.

"Qingmei can have a windfall each month but she is unwilling to buy food for her family," Chunhong complained.

I had looked at my phone several times because the football match had begun. I wanted to turn on the TV but I had to continue to be the good listener.

"Don't overthink," I tried to console her. "Qingmei is faithful to her family and is a good wife and a good mother. Li Zhi is a glutton, not a gambler or a drug addict, not a swindler like Sixi."

She smiled because what I had said was truth. Huilong Town, a wharf in the Qingxi River, was a mixed bag, including gambling and drugs. The gambling in this place referred to illegal private banks rather than playing mahjong or cards in tea houses. Li Zhi had never been a gambler or a drug addict.

People could take drugs easily in Huilong Town. Guangwen had been operating excavators and sand excavation vessels with Ho Laosan since he came to the town. Ho Laosan took charge of business operation and Guangwen of accounts. Ho Laosan, the greater contributor, got more revenues, but his money had been squandered by his son, a drug user. His son and Li Zhi used to be childhood playmates, but one day the former took drugs. Since then his family wealth had dwindled. Ho Laosan had sent his son to a drug rehabilitation centre several times, but that turned out to be useless. At last the father came up with a solution: he had a blacksmith named Zhang in the old street make iron chains weighing more than 30 pounds; he chained up his son and locked him in a dark room.

This afternoon I sat in Yang Jin's car to return home. When the car entered the town, I heard snarls from a brick wall at a fork and I shuddered. Yang Jin told me that the crazy yeller was the son of Ho Laosan. The young man had become skinny and hoary-haired and would die soon. He often shook the chains hard whenever he wanted to shout. His father had built two more walls outside to avoid disturbing his neighbours, but his son frequently screamed.

There were many young junkies in Huilong Town. Rumours said that Li Zhi refused to have a taste of drugs when he was egged on in a bar. Sixi was a fraud. The comparisons made Chunhong feel relieved and even feel that she had a good son. She sighed and went to sleep, and she would be busy tomorrow.

Chapter 14

Dawn had not come when someone was knocking at the door. Acquaintances often knocked at the door in the acquaintance society of a village or a town. When I lived in Yanerpo or stayed at Chunhong's house, especially the latter, I often heard someone knocking at the door in the early morning or at midnight. On the market days, a lot of villagers from Yanerpo and Lijiayan came to visit her before they sold their products. The business hours had not started, so they chatted and smoked after they entered the house, and she would have to entertain them just like our mother did. After the guests left, she would have to mop the floor and would yell when she became exhausted: "Damn it!"

But someone was knocking at the door again, she would have to throw the mop, open the door, and entertain the new guest.

The villagers would often store their things which they had bought or failed to sell in Chunhong's house, and they would take them away after they played mahjong or finished their unimportant tasks. Baskets and bags were often stacked in the living room. The baskets were stained with mud or dung, and there were piglets in the bags tied up with ropes. The piglets who had left their mothers and who were now in a strange place could not run, but they looked around, squealed, and shat on the floor. The whole house stank.

"Throw these fucking piglets into a river!" Chunhong shouted.

If their owner had not come, however, she would make a meal with soup and cold rice, and put the food into a basin for them; if no cold rice, she would give some vegetable leaves to them. When the piglets were too scared to eat, she would say nice words to them. When they started to enjoy their meal, she would smile and stay with them.

"Oh, don't be afraid, my dear piglets. How pathetic you are!"

Nowadays few villagers would put their things in her house for temporary storage. Most of them had bought their own houses in the town. Guangwen's younger brother had bought his house in Golden Town rather than Huilong Town. He had operated a tofu shop in the Golden Town rich with good soybeans. Chunshang had not purchased his house yet. Chunshan could have bought one, but he had nearly become the poorest man in Yanerpo because of his son Sixi. Guangwen's eldest brother had a patient at home: his wife was a leper. He told others that she had been cured; in fact, she would be taken to another place after she relapsed, and she would come back after a few months. The medical treatment could be partially reimbursed, but a family with a patient would be teeming with worry about shortage of money.

Someone was still knocking at the door although the comer might not use Chunhong's house as a free left-luggage office. Today was not the market day, but a guest was waiting outside. I woke up and found myself sleeping in the sofa. Last night I watched two football matches on TV. Sleepiness came to me after the first one was over because of my tiredness after a whole day's sitting in the car. But the second one should not be missed, so I brought the quilt and pillow prepared by Chunhong in the bedroom to the sofa in the living room. When I passed by our father's bedroom, I stopped and tried to hear something, but it was quiet. I did not open the door because I would have to have a good talk with him if he was awake. After I watched the second match, I fell asleep, leaving the TV on. But it was off now. It might be turned off either by Chunhong's husband when he returned to his bedroom or by her when she used the toilet at midnight.

There was sound in the living room. I thought it was made by Chunhong, but by our father. The button was fumbled for but it could not be turned on. The person must be our father. Last night I forgot to bring the walking stick to his bedside. He could walk if without it, but he had to push himself forward by putting his left hand on his knee. I got up and the door was opened. The voice-activated light in the corridor was off and it was dark.

"Chunshang," our father said.

Someone was stamping outside and the light was on. The comer was not Chunshang. Last night he said that he would come here tomorrow, but not so early.

The man at the door knew our father although the latter did not know the former.

"It's nice to see you, Mr. Xu," the man greeted loudly, smiling in a friendly way. "When did you come here?"

Our father answered him and hesitated if he would let him come in. The man entered the room and did not change his shoes. And then he saw me in the dark living room and said:

"Oh, you are here, too, Chunming."

It was light at the doorway but dark inside, and he could see me. I did not know him, so I called Chunhong. She had got up and was putting on her clothes when she was trotting towards the door.

"Oh, it's you, Laosan," she said.

Now I knew that comer was Ho Laosan.

"Come in and sit on the sofa, Laosan," Guangwen said drowsily. "I'll get up soon."

"You should turn on the light, Chunhong," Laosan said, stepping into the room. "Are you saving electrical energy?"

He turned on the light deftly, and the living room glared at once. He said loudly to Guangwen, "The ships in the early morning have returned to the town, but you haven't got up yet."

And then he smiled at me, showing his white teeth beneath his moustache. He was a spirited man with a resonant voice. I would have been unable to imagine that he had a son addicted to drugs and chained up at home if I had not known about the fact. He soon drank up a bottle of mineral water given to him by Chunhong.

Guangwen came to the living room, stripped to the waist, and fumbled for a cigarette in his pocket. Ho Laosan gave me a cigarette from a case in his trouser pocket. The cigarettes were neatly placed in the case, unlike the bent, wrinkled ones in Guangwen's pocket. He was a careful man. Rumours said that his grandpa was Mr. Pao well known in the wharf area of Huilong Town. He had inherited the imposing manners from his forefather, but he had put more than 30 pounds of iron chains on his son's body and locked him up. That bewildered me. I saw him carrying a Chinese style briefcase under his armpit. The briefcase was gleaming under the light. After Guangwen walked out of his bedroom, Ho Laosan opened the briefcase full of bundles of banknotes (each was 100 yuan) tied up by rubber bands.

"Take it easy," Guangwen said. He lighted a cigarette and then led Ho Laosan into a passageway on the right side of which were the bathroom and the kitchen, and on the left side of which were two rooms: the bedroom for the couple and an empty room. The two men entered the empty room, and after a moment Ho Laosan came out holding an empty briefcase. Ho Laosan settled accounts with Guangwen each month. The latter said that the business of operating excavators and sand excavation vessels turned out to be so profitable. Ho Laosan gave more cigarettes to us and left smilingly. He declined to have breakfast and lunch with us invited by Chunhong.

"He will be busy the whole day," Guangwen said.

Both our father and I had seen the bundles of banknotes, and Guangwen had often explicitly done in this way. That was the good cooperation between him and Ho Laosan. But Chunhong would prefer that our father should not have witnessed such a large amount of money. Her husband said "Take it easy," which was done after his wife winked at him. She would not worry that I had seen the briefcase full of money, because she thought that I was able to earn more money than her husband. But she would worry about our father because he would consider that his eldest daughter should use 90% of her money to financially support her poor siblings in the village. If his eldest daughter was rich but his youngest son was poor, she had done the wrong thing, and that was what our father had thought.

Chapter 15

After Ho Laosan left, our father went to wash up, and Guangwen returned to his bedroom for more sleep. Chunhong sat beside me and, pointing at the bedroom, whispered, "Guangwen enjoys showing off and he has been influenced by Ho Laosan, but he had not given us the money during the second half of last year."

Guangwen had told me that Ho Laosan was a man of his word and of integrity in doing business, but Chunhong did not know that. She was wary of me. She said so now, and I pretended that I did not know it.

"When will you call Chunshan?" she asked.

"In the morning," I answered.

I finished the cigarette given to me by Ho Laosan. Just before I started to dial, Guangwen came out.

"My sleepiness has been gone," he said. "I'll call your brother, Chunming. If you do, that'll be an expensive long-distance call."

He started to smoke after he made a phone call. His wife cooked in the kitchen. When she saw the smoke, she fully opened the balcony door. And then she took a warm coat of her husband's out of the wardrobe and threw it on the sofa.

"Let our dad put it on after he washes up," she said.

Our father was walking towards us without his walking stick; instead, he pushed himself forward by putting his left hand on his knee.

"You are walking in a cool manner!" she laughed.

"What kind of water did you use to wash your hair?" she asked anxiously when she saw our father's newly washed hair.

"Tap water," our father answered.

"You should have asked me to turn on the hot water valve!" she shouted at once.

The master valve on the gas cylinder should be turned on to supply hot water for Chunhong's house.

"You often say that you are feeling cold," she yelled. "But you use cold water to wash your hair!"

"I did not want to bother you," our father said.

That annoyed Chunhong because she thought that she had been treated like an outsider by our father.

"You try to make yourself get ill so that you can return to your youngest son's home," she yelled. "His home is like a paradise to you. But others will say that I'm not a filial daughter! No wonder my brothers have nursed grievances!"

Our father became quiet and sat beside one edge of the sofa, just like he did last night.

"Use a hairdryer," Guangwen said to lighten the atmosphere.

"Do not use it," his wife retorted. "Let it be."

Her husband brought a hairdryer, but it was snatched by her at once.

"The hairdryer is too much for his thin hair," she shouted.

Our father's wet hair was like the farmland with its crops taken away. She put away the hairdryer and took a dry towel from the bathroom. She rubbed our father's head disorderly. After his hair dried, it looked like a Mohican hairstyle. Both she and our father laughed.

"I'm not jesting!" she said.

Our father stopping laughing.

The breakfast included poached eggs with cubes of brown sugar, and braised beef with potatoes left last night. Guangwen asked me which wine I would prefer. Richly packaged wine bottles made by pottery or glass were nearly placed in an eye-catching shelf. I was a teetotaller. People living in the areas around the Qingxi River would have alcohol in the morning. When I left the River, I had not learned to drink yet, so I did not have the habit. He brought a half bottle of tartary buckwheat wine and poured it into two cups: one for himself, and the other for our father. The elderly man enjoyed his breakfast while frequently glancing at the door as he used chopsticks to pick up food.

"I called my brothers-in-law and asked them to come here as early as possible," Guangwen said.

Our father realized that his eagerness had been discovered, so he stopped looking at the doorway.

"You treat my house as a prison," Chunhong said.

"No!" our father retorted at once.

"You know it."

But soon she laughed and then asked, "Did you remember last night, dad?"

Our father lowered his head, blushing.

"I woke up at midnight and wanted to see if you were well," his eldest daughter said. "But I did not turn on the light lest you should drool again."

"I'm getting old," he said imploringly.

She wanted to joke but she didn't; instead, she used the spoon to put pieces of braised beef into his bowl.

"No! You are still young!" she continued. "Our mother died early, and her unfinished years of life must be accomplished by you."

"I'll try to make it," he said. "I'd told Chunshang that I would live until I was 100 years old.

"Why not 200 years old?" his daughter asked.

"I would become an old demon," her father chuckled, opening his mouth without teeth.

"That might not need 200 years," his daughter said. "Mrs. Hou lives like a demon now."

Chapter 16

Mrs. Hou was nine years older than our mother and one year younger than our father. Chunhong said that she lived like a demon now because the latter had become bouncy since she reached 80 years old: she could cut firewood, carry buckets of faeces on a shoulder pole, and walk fast. Since our mother died, she had got bored with her life. Everybody was too busy to quarrel with her, so she plucked fruits and vegetables without permission: she did that just for fun.

Mrs. Hou had had three children: two boys and one girl. One boy and the girl died of tetanus, but the eldest son Xu Limin survived. After he grew up, he married a girl named Zheng Saner. Since then Mrs. Hou had killed time by bullying her daughter-in-law: she slapped her hard across the mouth and made her cry much more by punishing her if the latter dared retort. As a result, the daughter-in-law often had a swollen mouth and eyes. People could become so tough that they would not be tormented to death easily. Chunhong would get furious at the thought of her sufferings in her mother-in-law's house, and she sympathized with Zheng Saner. As a result, the two women got along.

Zheng Saner did not kill herself although she had been maltreated by her mother-in-law. As time went by, the former had a son and since then she had been able to have her own status in the family. The mother-in-law found it difficult to continue to punish her daughter-in-law. Later, the old woman's son and his wife had their own nest. Although the couple lived next to Mrs. Hou's house, Zheng Saner would no longer be afflicted by her mother-in-law's torture.

Mrs. Hou got bored again, so she began to treat her husband as a new punchbag. Her husband was Xu Chenggui who had been a production team leader and a good carpenter. We usually called him Uncle Chenggui. Several years ago he spent 15 days making a pigsty for a villager who provided three meals a day for him and paid him daily wages. It was indeed a very good pigsty and its owner was satisfied with it. However, he had bad luck later. One night he woke up, groped for a water vat and used a gourd ladle to have some water, and then he went on with his sleep. When it was time to get up, he moved extremely slowly. Since then he had started to do everything at a snail's pace and had often been cursed by his wife and even been tardy in responding. After his wife finished her farm work (such as splashing manure into the crops) and came back holding a half basket of grass for cattle's food from the farm land through a long journey, he, who was two years younger than his wife, had not got to the kitchen from the bedroom. His wife threw away the manure bucket and shouted: "Be quick! Don't pretend to be ill!"

Chapter 17

The good health of Mrs. Hou was the envy of our father.

"I don't think she could be as hardworking as in her youth," our father said.

"Sour grapes," Chunhong jeered. "She can walk fast carrying a shoulder pole with two manure buckets each weighing nearly 70 pounds. Can you do it?"

"I could have done it if I had not slipped," our father retorted, glowering at her.

"Get real."

Our father became quiet and tried to put the wine cup closer to his mouth. The wine was wobbling in the cup. His hands started to tremble as soon as he held the cup, and they quivered hard when the cup was reaching closer to his mouth. He gulped the wine just before the cup fell from his hands.

"Do you know why the cup dislikes your lips?" his daughter asked, watching him sadly. "Your blood detests liquor, so you should not drink it."

"The alcohol I've had in my life can flood hectares of farm land," our father said. "And my bones will itch if they can't be nourished by liquor."

"Don't you remember the father-in-law of Chunshang?" she asked.

That man used to be a drunkard and he died of liver cancer. With a growing belly and a thin body, he had been huddling and been waiting for death at home for several months, and been ignoring all his family members. He was a dying man, so he treated their longer life as a sin, and everybody should beg for being forgiven by him. As a result, his family members dared not walk fast, not fart, not laugh; instead, they must look sad. If he saw someone smiling, he would think that you must have pretended to be sorrowful and you must curse him to die soon and then you would get rid of the burden. His hatred made him become a cold fish. When Chunshang called him father, the man would greet him; if the former asked how the latter was feeling, his father-in-law would shake his head with a meaning of having let it go, and would have a chat with his son-in-law. Chunshang was so grateful to his father-in-law for being so good to him that he built a house nearby his mother-in-law's after his father-in-law died, and he would take care of his father and his mother-in-law. But he was stupid. He should have taken his mother-in-law to Yanerpo to look after her. She had a daughter and a son. After Chunshang lived in Guaizaoping, his mother-in-law's son would gradually make things hard for him, and even his mother-in-law would grow dissatisfied with him.

"He was unpromising," our father sighed at the mention of that man.

"You may get ill no matter if you are promising or not," Chunhong retorted.

"I would not be good enough if I died before 100 years old," he said.

"You have outlived many people, and you are much better than them," his eldest daughter remarked.

Our father laughed.

"This is a blessing!" she exclaimed.

"It won't be a blessing unless I can reach 100 years old," her father said.

"Don't be upset if you leave us when you are 99," she continued. "The funeral for a man who dies in his eighties is a good one. I would not cry if you went to heaven."

"I must reach 100 years old," our father added. "And then I'll die."

"You are such a fool!" cried Guangwen, hitting Chunhong in the hand with the chopsticks. "Anybody who can reach 100 years old will be rewarded with a TV set by the county government leaders. And the TV set will be given to Chunshang."

Our father's true intention was exposed, and he looked embarrassed.

"Oh, my God!" Chunhong shouted. "All your children should have a share in the TV set. Why do you favour your youngest son?"

"He is short of money," the old man said in a low voice.

"Who is rich?" his eldest daughter yelled. "Chunshang has a TV set in his house. Will he get rich if he can have the TV set which will be the gift for your 100 years of life?"

And she started to blame Chunshang and Sixi; the two men had become our constant topic and fun. Sixi was seldom met, so Chunshang was often targeted. His wife frequently cursed him that he could not earn much money. That was true. Our father looked at Guangwen when he was listening to our talk.

Chapter 18

Guangwen could make a fortune through operating excavators and sand excavation vessels and through his position in the government sectors of the village. He was a big shot in Huilong Town, and he had to solve problems in the town although he had not been chosen to be a leader in the town government. Three small villages were made into a large one named Lijiayan, and he became the village party secretary. Many years ago natural gas was discovered in Mount Lordhou, and a number of households should be relocated before the gas was exploited. A new town secretary named Feng Quan let Guangwen be the coordinator to deal with the matter. All the villagers would do what Guangwen said.

Guangwen had won his good reputation among villagers through his own efforts. He had been busy raising money before roads were built in the village. After the roads were accessible to the villagers in Lijiayan, he did not charge them fees; what's more, he brought more benefits to them: 0.5 hectare of farm land had been occupied, but he suggested a section of the road should be turned into the farm land, at last the occupied farm land reached 0.6 hectare. Beyond that, only ten trees could grow tall and big in the villagers' forests which had been occupied. They timidly reported eleven, but Guangwen said thirteen, including the two small alders. The foundations of villagers' houses would have to be measured before relocation, the front and the left areas should be calculated, but the back and the right areas not. Guangwen measured all the areas in the four directions for each household. He snored as soon as he got home and lay down on the recliner, but he could work day and night to solve villagers' problems. When a fire happened in Mount Lordhou because of a lightning strike, he spared no effort in firefighting. His lower legs and back had been burnt, but he without any rest or medical treatment was busy finding shelters and food for the victims. All the villagers were grateful to him.

"But I don't believe that I can't deal with such a local despot as him!" Feng Quan, the new town secretary, snapped.

He went to Lijiayan and held five successive elections. The result showed that only Guangwen got the most votes while the rest of the candidates got less than five votes. The county government leaders pressured Feng Quan on projects and taxation in the village, so he had to implore Guangwen to help him. Guangwen was broad-minded to the leaders and cooperative.

An accident, however, happened after six months. I had mentioned it many times, but I had hidden its relation with Guangwen. Concealment was manipulation. When it was mentioned again on the warm winter afternoon, the truth must be told now.

It was not complicated. On a rainy day a ship capsized. There were more than twenty people aboard, and five of them died. The county government stipulated that the death toll of an accident such as a mine disaster or a shipwreck should be less than three, otherwise the head of the local government sector would be relieved of his post. The head referred to the leader in a town and above; those in the village, although called the lowest ranking officials, were actually not officials. Feng Quan, who had been the secretary in Huilong Town for less than eight months, would lose his job soon, but his position was secured by Guangwen. The river section in which the accident happened did not belong to Lijiayan geographically, but the three villagers among the five dead people came from Lijiayan. The county government leaders had divers search for the bodies in the river while the TV station and public security bureau had their men record the process. Only two bodies were found and the third one could not be discovered. After several days, the conclusion was reached on the case: two people dead and three missing. The three missing people were the villagers of Lijiayan.

Guangwen did something after the accident. He had a long talk with Feng Quan.

One day he visited the family members of the three missing people and told them: "Your beloved one may rest in the river, just like in the earth. The river is so deep that the body can't be found. You'll need to tell this to the high-level officials, and it will be solved."

And then he gave a lot of money to them, which was the compensation fee and the hush money. The villagers could understand the meaning even without an agreement. The village leaders gave 15,000 yuan to the divers, and let them remember the gender, the age, the appearance, and the clothes of the three missing men, and asked them to report the information to the TV station and the public security bureau. It was planned that the two missing villagers would be reported, but Guangwen worried that the funeral of one of the victims (if his body could be found) and the sorrow would trigger a troublesome petition. Therefore, he decided to announce that three villagers had been missing. Since then Guangwen had become the close ally of Feng Quan and also of the town government leaders. That was because he would be extremely helpful at the critical moment and had successfully persuaded the villagers not to appeal to the higher authorities for help. The burdens were removed and the local leaders felt relieved. In return, they often brought business opportunities to him.

Chapter 19

When our father looked at Guangwen, the latter had seen it and could understand it. He had a mouthful of wine and, watching me, started his speech: "I can be a contractor and I have many business deals, but I won't subcontract the projects to my relatives on both sides, and I won't let anyone of them work in my construction site because they are lazy, careless, and greedy. So I'd rather hire professionals to finish my tasks. They are serious with their work, respect me, and are grateful to me. For example, if I give a packet of cigarettes to a professional, he will say nice words to me. If I do the same thing to one of my relatives, he will grumble that I should have given him a carton of cigarettes, and will think that I'm a stingy man."

When he was speaking that, he did not look at our father. He would let our father know that he would not help those lazy, careless, and greedy relatives. Meanwhile, the elderly man was chewing his food silently. What Guangwen had said was truth. He used to subcontract projects to his relatives, including his own brother and my brothers and my brothers-in-law, but they bungled the projects. Since then Guangwen had stopped working with his relatives: they would sponge off you and mess things up, and would turn your power into a knife, use you and sharpen the tool, and at last you would be hurt by its point.

But his words made me feel uneasy. He would give me a carton of cigarettes whenever I came back. His cigarettes were much better than mine. His buddies and the local leaders would have dinner with me after I returned, and Guangwen would be embarrassed if I smoked cheap cigarettes. I thought that he should have given me two cartons of cigarettes. But why did he give me just one carton? I saw him looking normal, but I still felt uneasy.

Yesterday afternoon I washed up and was led by him into his bedroom. He opened the cabinet full of branded cigarettes, such as Double Ninth, Nanjing Cigarettes, Guizhou Cigarettes, and Yellow Crane Tower. But he just gave me a carton of soft Chunghwa cigarettes and then closed the cabinet. He should have given me another carton. Later I often thought about it. I visited him in a special place after many years. When he took a cigarette from my hand, that thing came to my mind again.

Chapter 20

Chunhong often scolded him when her husband was speaking, but today she did not do that. She tried to stop his speech because she had more relatives on her mother's side than those of on her mother-in-law's side.

"I'll refill your bowl with hot soup, dad," she said, holding her father's bowl.

"No more," he said, snatching the bowl.

She asked if her husband would need the soup.

"Not soup," he said. "More wine. I'll have another half cup."

"Chunming has finished his breakfast," Chunhong said. "You may have more wine at lunch."

"I'll have it," he added after a moment of thought.

He drank up the wine at once, ate a piece of potato, and then stood up.

When our father wanted to have more liquor, his eldest daughter snatched his cup. "Stop drinking!" she cried. "Your hands are still trembling!"

She splashed the liquor on the table, and then she cleared the table with a cloth, soon the table turned shiny. It was a cinerous marble dining table patterned with clouds and waves. Chunying and her husband had had it made in a stone mill in Guangdong province and had it transported at a high price. Chunying had been raised by another family since she was a baby, and she spent each Chinese New Year with us. We were still like a family.

Guangwen walked towards the door when his wife was cleaning the table.

"Are you going out again?" she asked.

"Qian Wen will be here soon," her husband answered.

"When did you contact him?"

He became quiet. He would not answer most of his wife's questions; but if he had answered, he would have become the sole secretary of his wife.

He heard the footfalls before he opened the door fully. The comer must be Qian Wen. He was at 34 or 35, not very tall, his left cheek looking like frosted glass, perhaps it had been burnt or scalded. He entered the room, greeted nobody, changed his shoes, and walked into the living room. He followed Guangwen into the empty room although the two men did not speak to each other. They started their talk inside but the content could not be heard. Guangwen yelled angrily but their conversation was still inaudible.

"Give me a pen, Chunhong!" he shouted.

She found a pen in the TV bench and gave it together a memo pad to her husband in the special room. She came out, sat down on a stool, and went on to clean the table. It was shiny but she was moving her hands mechanically and thinking about the conversation in the room. Later the two men came out. The left cheek of Qian Wen had become darker. He greeted nobody and walked towards the door. Guangwen saw the visitor out. After Qian Wen changed his shoes, he said, "Don't worry, Mr. Li."

"I don't worry," said Guangwen. There was anxiety in his tone of voice, but he could get rid of all his misgivings and make things well done.

Qian Wen closed the door with the sound like a gunshot. The footfalls could not be heard until five minutes passed. It seemed that the man outside had been shocked by the sound.

Guangwen walked into the living room.

"What did he say?" his wife whispered, with her back towards our father and me.

Her husband stuck out one finger and soon withdrew it. I guessed that Qian Wen must have borrowed money from Guangwen for secret use, otherwise he would not have acted mysteriously.

Guangwen started to smoke and his wife washed the dishes. After she finished, she saw her husband was about to sit in the recliner, and she moved it away at once.

"A lot of visitors will come to our house today," she said. "The recliner will take up too much of the space."

And then she quickly moved the recliner into the empty room.

"Look at your eldest sister, Chunming," Guangwen said calmly. "She is much more bad-tempered than Yukun."

Zhang Yukun, the Secretary of the County Committee, was transferred here from a county in the western Sichuan province half a year ago. Rumours said that he was so aggressive that he had even yelled at the deputy secretary; what's more, if someone was called by him in the roster, he must stand up and would have to endure Yukun's abuse.

Chapter 21

When the conversation was going on inside the house, someone was knocking at the door hard. Guangwen immediately knew that his granddaughter was waiting outside, and he rushed to the door.

"Who is there?" he asked jokingly.

"Li Dou and Yang Qingmei," a little girl answered.

"Oh, Yang Qingmei is your mother," Guangwen laughed.

"You're being naughty," he added. "And I won't open the door."

"You are being naughty," the little girl said loudly.

He opened the door, beaming. The little girl, screaming, ran inwards.

"Change your shoes, Dou!" her mother yelled.

The girl did what her mother said. Her grandpa lifted her up and kissed her in the cheeks happily.

The little girl called her grandma cordially but was surprised to see me and her great-grandfather sitting on a sofa. She, tilting her neck and blushing, was a strong girl.

"They are your family members," her mother said. Her daughter silently held her mother's leg.

"Today is my grandpa's birthday," Qingmei said, smiling at us. "I knew that my third uncle must be here, too, and my grandpa would go downstairs. I take Dou here to say hello to you, and then I'll take her to school. I'd told her that she should greet her elders. But now she is too shy."

"Good," Chunhong said, winking at me and our father. "You still remember the birthday of your grandpa. Have you had your breakfast?"

"Yes," Qingmei answered.

Qingmei asked Dou to greet the elders, but the little girl just put her head between her mother's legs. Her mother persuaded her to show respect for the elders, so the girl at last greeted her great-grandfather, but not me.

Obviously, she was the centre of our family. Before she appeared, the centre was our father or me; after she came here, she was in the limelight. One generation came after another, and the previous generation was made pale by comparison. How time flew! The third generation was growing up. Chunshan's grandson, the son of Sixi, was an elementary school student now. Our father was aging and so were we. I became estranged from the younger generation in my hometown, and I felt that we were living in two different worlds externally and emotionally.

Dou was nestling in the arms of her paternal grandmother. Chunhong asked Dou about her meals in her maternal grandmother's house, the animations she had watched, the health condition of her maternal grandmother, and if she was liked by her maternal grandmother.

Qingmei washed peaches that she had brought from her mother's house, placed them in a plate, put it down on the table, and let me have one.

"You may have a taste of the peaches, grandpa," she said, smiling at the elderly man.

"The peaches are too much for his toothless mouth!" her mother-in-law retorted.

"I've never seen him eat a peach, so I want to see it now," Qingmei smiled. And then she went to another room.

After a moment she came back, wearing makeup, new clothes, and a pair of golden earrings. She looked much more attractive if without makeup. She married the nineteen-year-old Li Zhi when she was seventeen. At that time they were too young to register a marriage certificate; they post-registered it last year. She had become a wife and a mother at such a young age that she had missed her girlhood. When her daughter was three years old, she looked immature and was quiet, but she had some smartness and warmth, both of which were hidden by the makeup now, leaving loneliness. After Dou had one peach, Qingmei took her into the bathroom to wash up, and then took her to school.

Chunhong wanted to mop the floor, but soon she dropped the idea because of too many visitors and a large workload today. She went to the market and bought fresh fish, spiced goose, rabbit meat, spiced dried bean curd, rattan pepper duck tongue, spicy haggis, and bought herbs and spices in a supermarket. After she got home, she heated up a pot of water on a stove and then she went out with a kitchen knife to kill some chickens. She kept them in a stairwell in the ground floor. Stores were operated in the front of the buildings nearby the river and the chickens were kept behind the buildings. There were stairs in the front and back of the buildings, and outfalls were installed in the basement of the buildings at the back for drainage in case of a rainstorm. Chunhong placed these animals in the stairwell when no water flowed. The chickens had to stay in a dark place after she shut the stairwell with an iron grating. They had been given to her by the villagers and the children who used to be looked after by her.

Chapter 22

A lot of children regarded Chunhong as their mother, and a man named Guangli, who was older than her and her husband, did so. She told me that she drove Guangli away when he came to her house to make a ceremony to worship her as his mother, but he did not give up even if he had been turned out of doors eight times. At that time he was a farmer living in my hometown and often helped Chunhong do farm work. Since her husband had been the village party secretary, the couple had seldom done farm work; instead, they often hired workers to plough fields, rake soil, sow seeds, and harvest crops.

In one spring rich with rain, Guangwen hired a man to plough his fields the next day. The next morning the worker, carrying farm implements and leading an ox, came to the fields and was surprised to see that the fields had been well done. The couple knew who was the contributor. Guangli started to plough the fields at midnight and came back before dawn. Chunhong sighed but still refused to treat Guangli like her son. But he kept working silently in her farm land every day; she did not speak to him, not invite him to her house, and not make meals for him. He just worked on and on until he finished a day's farm work and went home with mud or salt all over his body. He did this for a week and Chunhong started to falter.

"What should we do?" she asked.

"You'll decide," her husband said.

She sighed.

"One day I called his name in a friendly manner," she told me. "Later he ran to the fields, knelt down beside me, and called me mother. Oh, my God!"

She closed her eyes, gritting her teeth and shaking her head, like enduring agony.

"As I watched him kneeling with grey hair covering half his scalp and heard him calling me mother, it felt as though a knife slicing through my body.

I did not get used to that until he kept calling me mother for six months."

"You are a capable man, Guangli. You may call my husband your father now," she said, pointing to her husband beside her.

Guangli did so at once.

"He calls you mother, and calls me father. This is good news indeed!" Guangwen said cheerfully.

Since then Chunhong had stopped doing heavy work. Guangli had been cultivating crops in her farm land since her family moved to the town. After he harvested sorghum, maize, sweet potatoes, and white potatoes, he would keep some for himself and give some to Chunhong. After unhusked rice and oilseed rape dried off, he would carry them on his back and visit her. What's more, he would send vegetables to her house whenever he sold his farm products on the market day. Those vegetables were the best ones for the farmers. It was said that farmers did not use pesticides on the vegetables and fruits which would be served on their own tables, but used pesticides for those to be sold to customers. That was bullshit. Insects grew with crops. No pesticides, no harvests. If the fruits and vegetables were to be consumed by the farmers themselves, they would pluck them after the withdrawal time. If the fruits and vegetables were to be sold to customers, they would use pesticides today and sell them tomorrow, or use pesticides in the morning and sell them in the afternoon. The buyers in the town were unaware of the smell of the agricultural chemicals lingering on the fruits and vegetables. The farmers would provide grass, cereals, and soil blocks for the chickens to be eaten by themselves. If the chickens were to be sold to customers, they would put ripener and antibiotics against fowl plague into the fodder. As a result, the eggs and the chickens bought by the town dwellers contained chemicals.

Guangli always gave the best farm products to Chunhong. She did not buy vegetables today because she received a large basket of them from him yesterday. They had been put into a refrigerator and were still fresh now.

Chunhong had always asked her husband to treat Guangli well since he called her mother. Her husband said that Guangli could hold his head high now.

Li Zhengshe, a neighbour of Guangli's, had been making things hard for the latter for so many years. The path into the courtyard had to pass in front of Zhengshe's house, but he blocked the path so that Guangli and his family members could not enter. Guangli had to build a flight of stairs connecting the protective wall which nearly reached seven meters high outside the courtyard. It was dangerous when one walked on the steep stairs. Guangwen criticized Zhengshe, and the latter swore not to do that again. Zhengshe did what he had said, but Guangli was too scared to believe him.

Now Guangli could stand up with his head high and even deliberately made faecal sewage spray on the ground in front of Zhengshe's house. Guangli raised one or two pigs each year for Chunhong. He would kill one and cut the meat and send to her house before the Chinese New Year. In fact, the benefits he had received from Guangwen would be far more than three or four pigs. After Guangli's sons had had three children more than the family planning policy stipulated, their family was not punished. Guangli called Guangwen father, the results turned out to be rather advantageous to himself.

Many left-behind children called Chunhong mother. Their grandpas or grandmas were either too busy with farm work or got too tardy or too ill to cook for their grandchildren. When it was time for breakfast, lunch, or supper, Chunhong would bring such a child to her house for a meal. Later more than ten children went to her house for meals.

"You must behave yourselves and study hard," she shouted when she was cooking, "and you should not waste the meals I've made for you!"

The children got so frightened by her yelling that they cried. She tried to placate them, but that did not work: their blubbering made the birds outside feel sad or overwhelmed, so they flew away.

"Stop crying!" she snapped. "But tell me why you cry."

"I miss my mom."

"I miss my dad."

The children wept on and on. Chunhong, with tears in her eyes, put more meat into their bowls. Their parents had not known about that. After they knew it, they made phone calls to Chunhong from different cities across China. They said that they would let their children repay her and her husband for their kindness after they grew up.

"If he (or she) fails to do his (or her) filial duties to you, I'll break his (or her) legs before he (or she) is punished by God!" the parents swore.

"You don't have to say that," Chunhong replied calmly.

The children used to call her sister, aunt, or grandma. Later all of them regarded her and her husband as their mother and father. They grew up now. Six of them were studying in the university, and one in the military academy. Whenever they came home for holiday, they would carry their luggage with themselves and visit Chunhong and her husband before they returned to their own home.

Chapter 23

The chicken given to Chunhong by the villagers and by those children had been killed and been plucked and could be put into a pot after they were washed. Later the senders found that she often gave the chicken to others, such as Yang Jin. She covered the chicken with a lotus leaf and went to the store operated by Yang Jin's wife.

Yang Jin's wife was Huang Ermei. She used to live in the same village with Zheng Saner, the daughter-in-law of Mrs. Hou. That village was famous for two things: height and easy naming. Huang Ermei was 1.75 metres in height and Zheng Saner about 1.70 metres. It was an easy job for the villagers to make straw into sandals and make bamboo into mats, so they chose to name their children easily: Laoda (the first child), Laoer (the second child), and Laosan (the third child). Sometimes they would make their names better: Zhangda (the first child), Xizhangda (the second child). Later the parents could polish their children's names: Dawa (the first son), Erwa (the second son), Damei (the first daughter), and Ermei (the second daughter). The parents of Huang Ermei gave their daughter a polished name.

Huang Ermei, 28 or 29 years old, was tall, fit, and charming. She was neither affected nor seductive, and would look at everybody sincerely no matter he or she was a farmer, a gelder, a butcher, a whore, or a leader. Chunhong got along with her and often gave her the chicken which was too much for her own family.

Chunhong had given more chicken to Xiaolan who was the daughter of Chunshu. After Chunhong and her family members moved to the town, soon Xiaolan and hers did in the same way. After the latter had rented a house for less than one year, they bought a large one and later a truck to transport raw materials from the city. Zhu Guibing, the husband of Xiaolan, was a plasterer. His toilsome but profitable job was calculated by square meter although not by square foot in painting. After more people moved to the town from Lijiayan, they would set up interior walls; and Guangwen would bring the business opportunities to Zhu Guibing rather than the other plasterers. After several years, Chunshu and his wife moved to the town and bought a new house. They did not live there all year round because they would have to return to Yanerpo to plant crops. Living in a new house was like driving a new car; if the car or the house was not used, it would be too tantalizing to be resisted. In addition, their new house was the special symbol of ownership in the town. Chunhong gave chicken to Chunshu and his wife, and to Chunshan and younger one. She would not bring excessive chicken to them at a time because they only came to the street on the market day and had no refrigerator at home. After Li Zhi got married and Qingmei's parents moved to live in a house at the bridge, Chunhong would pluck one more lotus leaf to cover more chicken with it.

Chunhong did not avoid her husband when she was wrapping chicken. The couple sometimes shunned each other and sometimes not.

"When Mr. Pao, the grandpa of Ho Laosan, was the big shot in Huilong Town," Guangwen said, "the food sent to us by his men, such as fresh pork, mutton ribs, sirloins, and venison, had to be hung both inside and outside our house, and even broke the stair railings when they had to be hung there. But even a leg of pork was not given to others lest the senders should become disappointed if they knew it. When the excessive food could not be consumed by us anymore, they were tied up, were carried to a river by rack truck, and at last were thrown into the river at midnight."

"That was a sad thing, too!" his wife retorted.

"The river won't speak after the food is thrown into it," he explained. "But if you send some food to someone, he or she will tell everybody that you have given food to him or her. Just show off, not show that you are kind."

"You are one of them!" his wife exclaimed. "You often show off!"

"You are ignorant!" her husband yelled, blushing.

"You should cherish the things given to you by someone," he continued. "But you waste them if you give them to another one. In a TV drama, the sender often says: 'The gift is for you, my lord. And you may award it to anybody you like.' In fact, nobody wants you to award the gift he has given to you to another one."

She got confused and could not understand who was the waster: the one who threw the excessive food into a river, or the one who awarded the gift he had received from someone to another one.

In addition, she could not understand many things done by her husband. He used to treat well a man named Huigoer in Lijiayan. Whenever Huigoer appeared, Guangwen would invite him to a restaurant rather than his home; he would not drink but pay the bill. Huigoer was a rascal and often fell to the ground deliberately after he had a short quarrel with someone. And then he groaned that he had been beaten or knocked over by a man, and he would need money for his medical treatment and nutrition. He often fell down in front of a car, and even crept under it, lying between the two tyres. whenever car owners attempted to resolve this issue at the local police station in the town, they were met with scolding and were often requested to pay 10 or 20 yuan to Huigoer. The car owners cursed that they would run him over if he dared do that again. But that did not happen. Huigoer had been living in this way since he was 18 or 19 years old. Now he was in his fifties and was fine. Guangwen often invited him to restaurants and gave him cigarettes. His wife disliked that and often expressed her dissatisfaction.

"You are ignorant!" he retorted.

She realized that her husband had found a pretext on Mr. Pao. He had been such a victim of poverty and starvation that he would not throw the good food into a river. He was displeased with the fact that his wife had given the chicken to Chunshu.

Guangwen detested Chunshu and thought the latter put on airs. Chunshu, who used to be an avid reader although he read no book now, remained a cold fish; dropped out of junior high school and was a farmer in Yanerpo nearby Laojun Mountain; bought a house with the borrowed money; his daughter Xiaolan and her husband made good business deals, but his son Hongquan was a braggart and an incompetent. Hongquan and Lily used to be classmates in the senior high school. Later he went to a third-rate college in southern Sichuan and his major was unknown. After graduation he was jobless and started to sell mature vinegar with the swindler Sixi. He took away the advance wages of 4,000 yuan from the factory, loafed around, and did not sell any bottle of vinegar. He had done that several times in the other factories; later he left Sixi and went to Suzhou. Lily played matchmaker and had one of her female classmates in the junior high school marry him.

Chunhong disliked my second elder brother, too, and thought that his family members were ungrateful. She had often invited them to dinner since they came to live in the town, but she had never been invited in return. Xiaolan, just like her parents, had never entertained Chunhong. The latter had complained to me that both Xiaolan and her parents were ingrates, and they were jealous of her wealth. That was true. Jiang Zhuqing, the wife of Chunshu, did not compare herself with Chunhong whose husband was a village party secretary, but with Chunshan and his wife. She would remain quiet as long as possible if she heard that Sixi had fallen on hard times; if she was told that Sixi had prospered, she would shout at her husband: "Chunshu!"

She was startled by her own yelling and was in a trance. A moment later she continued to shout: "The sun is setting, and you should do your farm work now!" Sometimes she would add: "She is cunning. But you?"

Ye Fengjuan, the wife Chunshan, had never retorted. She was a good, broad-minded, agreeable, and humorous woman, and she was respected by our family members except by Chunshu and his wife. The couple were displeased with our respect for Fengjuan, claiming that we favoured her and they often scowled at me and Chunhong. Zhuqing might be less peevish, but her husband could sulk at will, that was because he cared for nobody except himself.

Although Chunhong was dissatisfied with the ingratitude of Chunshu and his wife, she continued to give chicken to them, just like she did so to her friends. She realized that her husband's words made sense. When she was considering if she would give more chicken to more people, her senders changed their way: they gave her living chickens rather than chicken. Since then she had been keeping chickens in the outfalls. They would die if there were too many of them, so she had to check them every few days and would throw away the dead ones. It was a pity, but she treated them like the ones who had had fowl plague and she discarded them. She would not eat the chicken infected with the disease, and she should not give it to anybody.

Chapter 24

The pot was boiling and was screeching like fighting animals. I turned it off and Chunhong came back. It would not take one hour to kill a chicken, so she must have had long chats with her idle acquaintances if she met them, and she must have forgotten her maternal grandmother's advice because her toothache had been gone for many years.

Guangwen was out.

"Where is Guangwen?" she asked.

"Someone called him and wanted to see him," I said.

In a sulk she went to the bathroom holding the pot of hot water, and came out a moment later with an empty pot, and then she went out again.

Our father was sitting on a sofa sleepily. I asked him if he was going to have a nap, he shook his head and looked at the door. I called Chunshang but I got no answer. I said that he must be on the way, and the elderly man looked much better.

"Is Yuling coming here?" he asked.

"She may come here for your birthday," I replied.

I was not sure whether my father asked the way because he wanted her to come or didn't want her to come. My siblings said that Yuling had treated our father badly. When they lived in Yanerpo, she made rice crust for our father who had lost all his teeth. Even Mrs. Hou was angry about that. She told Yuling a story. Barber Sun had been keeping a dog for ten years. Every day the owner cooked thick gruel mixed with chopped vegetable leaves and minced meat for his toothless dog. Its aroma could be smelt even in the distance. Yuling might understand or pretend not to understand that.

"He treated his dog well!" she jeered.

The rice crust had to be soaked in soup if soup was available, and in water if soup unavailable. The crust did not become soft until the soup or water cooled off. That was each meal for our father. Chunhong saw that when she visited him one day. Later she sent him to Chunshan's house; and she went to see him after he had been living there for a period of time.

"How are you doing, dad?" she asked.

"I'm fine," our father replied.

"Which one is better, living here or living in your youngest son's house?"

"Here."

"You look bouncy now after you have been living here for a month," she smiled. "That's your good choice."

Our father gave a forced smile.

"Listen to me, Chunhong," he said after a moment of silence. "I want to live with Chunshang."

"But why?"

"I don't want to be a burden on Chunshan."

Chunhong soon sent our father to Chunshu's house.

"You will live in your sons' houses and they will take turns to look after you," she said.

Our father, however, went to his youngest son's house with his walking stick after he stayed at his second son's for ten days.

"Leave our dad alone!" Chunhong yelled. "That's his life! Things would have been different if our mother were alive!"

Yuling was glad to see our father whenever he went to stay at her house. After two or three days she started to treat him badly again.

When Chunshang worked in Wanyuan city located in the border between Sichuan province and Shaanxi province, his wife treated our father worse. One day she had sauted meat at home when our father was having a chat in his neighbour's courtyard. He went home before she finished her meal, and saw her throw the unfinished food into a pigwash bucket. After one week Fang Yun brought fish to him. He lived in Huanglingtan nearby a river. After he caught some fish, he would walk three miles against the river direction and walk two miles in the mountain road so as to give fresh fish to our father. The elderly man told the matter about the pigwash bucket to Fang Yun, and the latter told this to his wife. She at once called me and asked me to come home. Our father said that he would rather live in a cave. When an old man who had children was determined to live in a cave, that meant that he had been hurt by his unfilial children; what's more, that also shamed them.

"That'll shame both you and Chunhong although I don't give a hoot about the gossip!" Chunhua exclaimed.

If someone has done something bad, it will embarrass the whole family, the whole clan, and even the whole country. Chunhua worried that the rotten apple would disgrace the whole family's name.

The problem must be solved no matter whether it would be a disgrace nor not. I returned home and asked Chunshang to come back. Living in a cave was just an angry remark, and our father did not mention it again. But he would prefer living alone to living with my eldest and second brothers. Before he fell and hurt himself, he had been living with me in Chengdu, and he insisted on returning to his hometown after one week. It would be dangerous if he lived alone because he had to limp now and he could not cook by himself. What was more, there was no available house for him to live in. I looked at Chunshu at the mention of the house. He had a spare one but he looked away.

It was impossible to have our father live in the spare house of Chunshu.

"You should live with my eldest and second brothers, dad," I said. "I'll give you 3,000 yuan each year, and you can give the money to the people you choose to live with."

"I'll use the money," our father said.

The money should be controlled by himself.

"You have difficulty in walking now," I explained, "and you don't go to the market. So you don't have to keep the money."

"What if I have someone go to the street and buy something for me?" he retorted.

"We know your plan, dad!" Chunshu snapped, glowering at him. "You don't want to waste your money on us because you want to give it to Chunshang!"

"No!" he cried.

"Chunming gave the money to Chunshang when you were living with him," Chunshu said.

Our father did not argue with him because he could not find an excuse. Meanwhile, Chunshang looked at nobody, hand on chin, blushing.

After he got home, he asked his wife what had happened.

"I swear that I did not have the sauted meat," she shouted, "and I did not throw the unfinished food into a pigwash bucket. If you could be rich, I would toss the meat to a pig. I'd rather burn down the shabby house and live in a new one!"

Her husband became speechless.

"I'll live alone!" our father said loudly and firmly.

But there must be a solution. It was disliked by our father, by Chunshan, and by Chunshang, so its details were not shown here. Our father finally had a new nest. The next morning he changed his mind before I was about to leave.

"I'll live with Chunshang," he said with teary eyes, holding me by the hand.

That happened frequently from then on. Since then he had been a doormat in Chunshang's house. Nobody believed him after he had said his angry words again and again: "I won't live with Chunshang any longer!"

Chunshang's wife called the shot. Since he moved to live in his wife's village, she had become bossier and bossier. Our father, however, tried to please her and worried that she might divorce his youngest son. Chunhong had said that a wife nowadays would divorce her husband if she had to live in a poor family. Yuling might do so because she had said so. The word "divorce" was like a machete which did not scare her husband but had been worrying her current father-in-law.

Chunshang was not good enough for Yuling indeed. She was an attractive woman but her buck-toothed husband, who had scalds and scars in his arms in childhood, was too weak to support a family. Our father chose to live with Chunshang so that he could give more money to his youngest son, just like Chunshu had said, and could keep an eye on Yuling. But that annoyed Chunhong.

"Let Yuling go if she wants, dad!" she yelled. "Let Chunshang leave that woman if she wants to divorce him! I don't believe that she can have a new, better husband! She will bully you if you are afraid of her!"

Our father was quiet and sad, and he was anxious about the word "divorce". At that time Yuling wore a pair of golden, large earrings, and it seemed that she would divorce her husband soon. The elderly man hoped that Yuling could come here with her husband, and he worried about her being alone at home. No wonder Chunshang went home by motorbike as soon as he finished supper last night, and he was not stopped by our father although he had got drunk.

Chapter 25

The sun cast its rays over everything and the glass door in the balcony gleamed. The wind blew against the river current and brought chilly air into the house. I put the blanket, which was used last night, on our father's body. He forgot that after he had got up and he said that he was not feeling cold. The temperature in the morning was much lower than that of at night, but he had washed his hair with cold water. He did not want to bother me. I covered his whole body with the blanket.

"How about going out for a walk, dad?" I asked.

"No," he replied. "Are you going out?"

"Yes. And I'll be back soon."

I stopped walking when I was standing at the door.

"The door is ajar," I said. "When Chunshang and his wife come here, they can push the door and enter."

I saw a lonely figure when I closed the door. I walked down the back stairs and wanted to see how busy Chunhong was, but she was not there. I walked through the front buildings and across a lotus pond I saw her squatting along the wide embankment in the riverside road. The Qingxi River often flooded during the autumn rains in west China and even had inundated half of a street. Since embankments and railings were set up, town dwellers had learned to feast their eyes on the ferocious floods safely at home although they used to be frightened by them.

The lotus pond in front of me used to be a huge construction site. The real estate developer from a city said that he would set up top-end buildings in Huilong Town and the prices would be more than twice as expensive as the others. The locals realized that the Huilong Town was teeming with rich people when they saw the crazy buyers standing in a long queue and giving 50% of advance payments to the developer. He, however, disappeared after a pit was dug. Eight years had passed. The developer was wanted every year but he had not been caught. Later bad news came: he was not an ordinary citizen, he was the younger brother of the wife of a municipal government leader. The buyers were not rich; in fact, they had become broke since they borrowed a lot of money for the down payments. Dongxuan County had propagandized whole-area tourism. Huilong Town, with the relics of the remote Banese culture (the reason for the establishment of the Banese Plaza), would become a famous tourist town. A good house bought by a town dweller would become a golden egg.

But that turned out to be a pie in the sky. The town government leaders introduced the developer to the buyers, so the latter petitioned for their payments in the government office. When I returned to the town several years ago, I often saw long and short banners made by paper or cloth, with words written with ink or paint, hang in front of the government building. The appeals were not stopped until recent years. The petitions, however, were going on. As a result, the town government leaders were frequently asked to go to Chengdu (the provincial capital) or Beijing to pick up those angry buyers. The government leaders wanted to backfill the pit after the developer had been gone for three years, but the buyers stopped them from doing so because they argued that the pit was shame on the government and also the evidence of the victims. As the days went by, water accumulated in the pit and a pond was formed, later lotuses bloomed in it. Now the pond was teeming with lotus seeds. Drops of water rolled on the leaves in the rain or under the sunshine. The beauty now concealed the past shame and evidence. In summer croaks of frogs might make people sleepless at night.

Chapter 26

Chunhong waved her hand to let me go there when she saw me. She was holding a chicken and was removing fine hairs from its body after it had been plucked. Chicken's neck looked long in its naked body, or it had been lengthened because of its excessive weight. The air stank of a dead chicken soaked in boiled water. Its eyes remained wide open, which was the first time for me to see such a thing.

"It had been locked in the dark place for so long that it went blind as soon as it saw light," she explained.

Light could be sharper than a needle.

"But it's dead now anyway," she added.

If a human being dies with eyes open, he or she has unfinished business. What if a dead chicken?

"It killed itself," she said. "It pounced on my kitchen knife before the iron grating was lifted by me. Its feathers were flying. It might not see the knife at the beginning, but it rushed at the knife after it saw the tool."

"You said that it lost its sight at once when it saw light," I remarked.

She laughed and told me the details of catching and killing of the chicken. And then she continued to talk about the process of killing a rabbit the other day. She slayed it on the back of its ears, which were the Achilles' heel. The animal had convulsions and died; but it suddenly sat up and cried after it was skinned by 50 percent.

I knew she told me those things on purpose. I was afraid of watching the process of killing small animals, and I dared not speak it out lest I should be laughed at. Once I was too emotional to hold it back, and I was derided.

"Don't be such a hypocrite!" Li Zhi, my nephew, criticized me. "You still eat meat although you are scared of watching their death."

That was true because I would feel uneasy if I had no meat each day, but I did not want to retort. Later I could not bear to see the slaying of all living creatures.

"You are such a hypocrite!" Li Zhi sneered. "You will swat a buzzing mosquito to death with your hand before it bites you."

Chunhong worried that I would be so soft-hearted that I might become a monk someday.

Zou Deng, one of the villagers in Yanerpo, had been afraid of killing animals and later of seeing the process of killing them. One day he went into the mountains to chop wood, but he did not return at dusk. His family members found the machete used by him rather than its owner in the mountains; they walked along ridges and saw a brood of boars, two foxes and several hedgehogs. But his whereabouts remained unknown. After seven years, Wang Qingguang, one of our neighbours, went deep into the mountains for mondo grass. At the foot of an escarpment, a naked wild man came out of a cave which had been excavated by bandits during the Republic of China era. He had super long hair and had moss all over his penis. There were rock dowels on the walls of the escarpment. With his feet stamping on the dowels, hands grasping the dowels, and teeth biting them, he moved across the walls; then he plucked Lagotis leaves, tied them with couch grass, put them around his neck, and returned to the cave. Wang Qingguang flopped on the ground, paralysed with dread. But he was afraid of the wild man no more when he saw the back of the latter, because he recognised that the man was Zou Deng who had a tumour as large as a bowl on his back at the age of nine and it looked like his face. Now the tumour was covered with moss, yet its shape unmistakably bore the hallmark of Zou Deng. Wang Qingguang told this to all the villagers after he returned, and they became excited. At night the family members of Zou Deng, holding torches and carrying long ladders, marched towards the cave with the help of Wang Qingguang and more than ten young and strong villagers. What could be seen in the dripping cave covering more than 30 square meters, however, were the visitors holding torches and their shadows. The fresh, leftover Lagotis leaves proved that Wang Qingguang's words turned out to be right. The family members of Zou Deng had been searching and waiting for him for months, but they could not find him. In the twelfth lunar month next year, someone came across him in the temple which had been built in the True Buddha Mountain during the Hongwu era of Ming Dynasty and which was two hundred kilometres to the Huilong Town. The man was no longer Zou Deng in Yanerpo, but the monk with Haideng as his Buddhist name. The visitors told him that his mother had gone blind for him and his younger brother broke his legs when he searched for him. Zou Deng, however, remained calm and said "May the Buddha preserve us" putting his palms together devoutly, and then entered his meditation abode. It was said that monks were filial but Zou Deng, who had ignored his family members, had a heart of stone. The villagers considered that the monk Zou Deng was ruthless.

One could not survive if without his or her family members in the villages. I was regarded as the backbone of our family and things would become terrible if I followed Zou Deng. Chunhong wanted to toughen me, and I tried to build up my courage when I saw her killing a chicken. I loved meat and I should not be afraid of watching the process of killing an animal. But I had been influenced by Li Zhi. Was he a competent, reliable man? I doubted that.

I told Chunhong that I would take a stroll in the street. I walked east along the river embankment before I saw the street. There was luxuriant grass under the embankment but the nearshore areas were engulfed with rubbish. Chunhong threw into the river the chicken feathers and the boiled water which had been used to wash the chicken. Plastic bags full of used toilet paper of each household were tossed down the embankment, and the paper might fly in the wind if the bags were loosened. Dirty water flew out of drain outlets and went into the river. In summer the whole place stank. A thin egret was walking along the river, like an old farmer watching his ruined crops.

South Gate Pier was nearby. I would go to the street after I walked upwards a rough-textured slope. There were two streets in Huilong Town: the old street and the new one. The old street was nearby the river. It used to be more than 200 meters long. Since half of the street was submerged by floodwater, the rest of it had been the hustle and bustle of Huilong Town: business deals, fights, gatherings and partings. Now the street was like a desolate place. Three or four old men were sitting in front of their houses which used to be their stores, and were wasting their time in decay.

Today was not the market day. The old street was made pale by comparison when the new street was thronged with people on the market day. The new street, which was divided into the upper section, the middle section, and the lower section, was busy and full of activity. In the old street, however, some vendors squatting in the corner were selling sun-cured tobacco leaves, and some fortune tellers were waiting for customers. The houses in the old street had been built with wooden partitions and wattled walls, and they were not allowed to be renovated or be demolished. It was said that these houses had been the relics of the Qing Dynasty and also been the settlements of the ancient Banese. Under the wall nearby a river someone found a rusty bronze sword carved with a dragon. Experts said that it was a snake rather than a dragon, and it represented the emblem of one of the ancient branches of Banese: Snake-Banese more than 3000 years ago. The archaeological teams from cities and the provincial capital found nothing except the sword. But the sword would mean much more, and everything in the old street should be protected as cultural relics.

I walked in the old street and saw Blacksmith Zhang sitting in a bamboo chair in the centre of his room and having tea. The doors of the other houses were open but they looked like empty rooms. I could not be attracted by them, so I walked into an alley. It was the middle section of the new street outside the alley.

Chapter 27

Gongs and firecrackers could be heard from the alley. A swarthy young man, wearing red underpants and a white bra and holding a gong, was walking in the crowd towards the lower section of the new street. It was a wedding. The bridegroom had to walk with wiggles of the hips; if no wiggle, a firecracker would be tossed at his feet. The gongs must go on and on; if paused, a firecracker would be thrown at the gong beater's feet, too. Huilong Town did not have such practices in the past; the locals learned them from the other places. The bridegroom was parading and his father carrying the bride on his back was doing the same thing.

"Burn! Burn!" the father-in-law yelled.

No burning, no ash. After setting a fire, one tends to clean up the ashes. What he was shouting was a metaphor in China - a sexual relationship between a daughter-in-law and her father-in-law. So, the father-in-law today had to yell and slobber. That was just a joke. But if he did not do that, a firecracker would be tossed at his feet, too.

I heard Guangwen call my name as soon as I stood in the middle section of the new street, but I could not find him. He came out of the Congee Restaurant and waved at me. He must have had breakfast and he usually had it with his friends or other people. Perhaps he was watching the wedding. I did not want to join him but I saw a man standing behind him. That man greeted me cordially. I could not remember who he was although I had met him before.

"Do you still remember him, Chunming?" Guangwen asked, pointing at the man.

I gave a forced smile but I did not know who he was.

"He is Dachao," Guangwen said.

Oh, he was Zhang Dachao. He had been released from prison. When natural gas was extracted in Lijiayan many years ago, a drilling machine was stored in a brick-wall room of Liu's house in the upper section of the new street. It was empty, so a natural gas company rented it as a temporary warehouse. One night, Zhang Dachao and his accomplice from the upstream Golden Town pried the bricks open with steel bars, snuck into the room and stole the drilling machine which looked small but weighed over 100 kilograms and was worth more than 200,000 yuan. One gram would be worth more than 1,000 yuan. It was used to drill for natural gas, so it could glare in a dark room. Zhang Dachao took off his coat and covered the machine with the coat. He managed to carry it onto a ship and took it to Golden Town that very night. After he had noodles in his accomplice's house, he would go to Chongqing by boat to sell the machine. But he got caught when he was at the tail end of the Jialing River.

Zhang Dachao, the prime culprit, was sentenced to 13 years. The whole thing had been the hot topic around the Qingxi River for one year. Such a severe sentence had never been heard of in this place. People had often carried baskets and stolen vegetables and corn during years of famine. Those things were privately owned, but the natural gas and the drilling machine were nationally owned. So, the locals concluded that the belongings of households and the Production Team could be taken away, but the state-owned resources could not. Zhang Dachao, however, had been a rich man. The Congee Restaurant used to be a two-storey inn many years ago. He had had a lot of houses and operated profitable businesses such as steel bars, rapeseed oil, tobacco and wine, incense and candles, and hell money in the middle and lower sections of the new street. It was hard to understand why such a millionaire as him should steal a drilling machine worth 200,000 yuan. Perhaps he should be sent to prison.

He had an early release yesterday after he had been in prison for nine years. His houses had been sold and only one was left; and his businesses were ruined. His wife moved from the lower section to the middle section, and she had to subsist on the unpromising Congee Restaurant which had only three tables inside. At breakfast there was no customer. We entered and sat at a table, even tea was not served. The locals often gossiped about the uses of the money she had earned: to repay debts, to be carved up by her brothers, or to be transferred to the bank accounts of her secret lover in the town who had had her money but refused to divorce his first wife to marry her.

I knew that Zhang Dachao had been one of the four faithful friends of Guangwen in the town, at that time Ho Laosan was not one of them. His friends were here today, including Wan Ping and Chen Ya. Wan Ping was nicknamed "wax gourd" because he looked like the plant. He was responsive to wax gourd rather than his true name. Chen Ya was a short man. His lips resembled a piglet's and he said that he was good at telling jokes.

This was his joke now. A migrant worker returned home early to surprise his wife. When he entered the bedroom, he saw her sleeping like a log with another man in bed. They must have had a crazy night so they were too tired to notice him. He found the adulterer was his younger brother although the windows and curtains were closed. He punched his brother on the mouth and one of his front teeth fell into the woman's mouth immediately. She woke up and her husband beat the other man on the bridge of the nose. She spat out the tooth and jumped out of the bed, naked.

"How dare you batter your brother, you prisoner?" she yelled. "Would you beat Mr. Wang, our neighbour, to death?"

Wan Ping guffawed, but Guangwen stifled his laugh. The joke was too stale to make me laugh. Chen Ya realized at once that the joke was inopportune and it contained the word "prisoner". Zhang Dachao sat down opposite me. I glanced at him and saw his smile like a withered leaf.

Chen Ya asked me when I returned home. Wan Ping gave cigarettes to us, and Chen Ya lit them. They had a lively talk with Guangwen, but Zhang Dachao kept smiling silently – he could not keep up with the life now. They started to feel bored, and Guangwen stood up.

"I'll have to go home," he said. "I'll hold a party for Dachao and Chunming soon. All of you will join it."

Zhang Dachao, smiling, showed us out.

Chapter 28

They departed. Guangwen and I walked towards the lower section of the new street. The bridegroom, the bride and her father-in-law could not be seen now. It was quiet and windy and the sun cast its rays on the newly renovated road. The new street was flanked by stores. A thoroughfare, also a national highway, was connected with southern Shaanxi province upwards, and with districts, counties, and cities downwards.

"I'll have to leave tomorrow," I said. "When will you hold a party for Dachao?"

Wan Ping and Chen Ya had left. Guangwen looked at the Congee Restaurant which had no customers now.

"No party!" he snapped. "He was a prisoner."

He greeted the people in the street.

"I've been estranged from wax gourd and Chen Ya," he added. "Both of them are good-for-nothings. Wax gourd often drinks, brawls, swears, and smashes windows and bottles in restaurants. Chen Ya is useless. He can't support his family and is often beaten by his wife. I don't want to waste my time on crap."

Guangwen started to blame himself because he could not understand why he had befriended them. The wind was blowing hard because it could not understand it either. The apple of discord had been planted since Zhang Dachao was arrested, and that was what I had known. The locals did not believe the gossip at the beginning, but later they did. Rumours said that Guangwen, Wan Ping, and Chen Ya were his accomplices because the four men were good friends, but they were not. The locals worried that they might do something illegal someday and be sent to prison, and also considered that their friendship was not reliable: Zhang Dachao chose a man from Golden Town rather than his buddies. Guangwen had been so disappointed that he kept himself far away from Wan Ping and Chen Ya. But today someone called him to see Zhang Dachao.

Chapter 29

Chunshan, Chunshang and his wife Yuling came here. They sat at the marble dining table and greeted me and Guangwen as soon as they saw us enter the room. I found Yuling getting old. She looked attractive one year ago but now unattractive although she wore a pair of plastic yellow earrings prone to dirt.

"You don't like to visit us, Chunming," Yuling said. "My husband can take you there by motorbike. But Guangwen may have Yang Jin drive you there. Well, it isn't expensive."

"I have to pay the gasoline bills," Guangwen retorted.

"I would reimburse the driver for the bills if I were the village party secretary," she argued.

"Oh, it's a big surprise that you should be so generous," he sneered.

"Humph," she complained, and became speechless. That was how she mitigated her relations with her parents-in-law because she was a stupid arguer. My relatives disliked talking with her, only Guangwen spoke to her. She would roll her eyes and mumble if she could not retort. So, my siblings and the younger children often laughed at her.

"Yuling treats our dad too badly!" Chunhong often grumbled. "If she had looked after him well, we would have brought wine and meat to him. In fact, he can't enjoy the food even though I send it to Yuling's house."

But Chunhong often brought food to Chunshang and his wife especially on the market day. If chicken was unavailable, she had villagers in Guaizaoping send delicious beef shanks to our father if cattle were slaughtered in Lijiayan. She cooked the meat, covered it with lotus leaves, and fastened it in a bag to avoid gossip.

"You are a big shot in Lijiayan," Yuling said.

"You are just flattering me," Guangwen sneered.

Chunhong walked out of the kitchen and heard the bickering. She glowered at her husband and took a packet of iodized salt she bought yesterday into the kitchen.

"You should help your sister-in-law in the kitchen," said Guangwen.

"She does not need my help," said Yuling. "And that's why I'm sitting here."

"Chunhong tries to make her less tired," our father remarked.

"She does no farm work, so she is not tired," Guangwen added.

"You often sweat from hard farm work," Yuling continued. She took a peach and started to eat it and walked towards the kitchen.

Chapter 30

After Guangwen stepped into the room, he gave Chunshan and Chunshang a pack of cigarettes respectively. It was not the well-known brand, but it was the locally ordinary Bafine.

After the bronze sword was discovered, rumours said that Huilong Town used to be the dwelling place of the Banese. Historians came here from Chengdu for researches and later published a number of papers and monographs in which recorded the Banese had brewed a kind of liquor named Bafine, they usually had the liquor before they went to the battlefield with King Wu of Zhou, and they even drank and danced in the battlefield to frighten away their enemies. The county government leaders considered that they had found a cultural relic and would produce liquor named Bafine. But a local cigarette plant had registered the brand with the name, and those leaders approved of it because they could get more taxes from cigarettes. Folklorists and historians did not draw a sharp line between cigarettes and alcohol.

Bafine was also graded: the best one with a red case priced at 15 yuan, the second one with a green case priced at 10 yuan, and the third one with a white case priced at 5 yuan. The villagers in Lijiayan often gave Bafine cigarettes in red cases to the village party secretary to express their gratitude if they could not provide good meat for him. The secretary accepted the cigarettes because he knew that both the villagers and himself were neither rich nor powerful.

He never smoked Bafine. When his son was at home, however, he would give it to the latter and require that he should not smoke branded cigarettes: do not indulge in the things that were beyond his capabilities to obtain; otherwise he would get himself into trouble. Li Zhi was not a promising man, but he was neither a gambler or a drug addict, which made his father feel proud of him. In addition, he would let Huigoer, his brothers, and his brothers-in-law have Bafine.

My brothers, who usually had the Bafine cigarettes in white cases, were attracted by the cigarettes in red cases at the sight of them.

"Give me more," said Chunshang.

"You've had enough," said Guangwen.

What Guangwen had said this morning about the differences between giving cigarettes to family members and to outsiders turned out to be true. The red marks left by excessive drinking could be clearly seen in Chunshang's face when he laughed. Chunshan and our father guffawed. The elderly man looked spirited.

Chunshan put the cigarettes into his pocket and asked Guangwen about Li Zhi. "Jiang Hua called me last night," said Guangwen. "He gave my son 15,000 yuan as his homeward-bound allowance. Li Zhi went sightseeing in the Three Lanes and Seven Alleys, the heritage buildings; and then he went to the Altar of Islands in Pingtan and spent one night there. Yesterday he returned to Fuzhou and had dinner with Jiang. He said that he would go to Gulangyu Island and would go home from Xiamen. The two guys ordered too much seafood. Li Zhi got drunk and Jiang paid the bill."

"Your son is a freeloader," said Chunshang, puffing on a cigarette. "But I had to do sweated labour." He used to toil in Wanyuan.

Chapter 31

Wanyuan, a rugged and dangerous place located in Daba Mountains, is a county-level city and is under the administrative jurisdiction of Baima city. The Red Army had a tough fight there in the 1930s. General Xu Shiyou depicted the fight in his memoirs that it was at the expense of countless sharp weapons and blood.

Chunshang used to carry large bags of cement and sand for a project on the mountaintop along steep slopes in August. When local farmers whipped their horses to death, Chunshang felt like being one of the horses, and he was whipped, too. After three months, he got 6,500 yuan, excluding house rent and fees of meals and cigarettes.

Our father felt pity for him. When he worked in Wanyuan, his wife often cooked meat at home and would rather give leftovers to pigs than allow her father-in-law to have a bite of it. He often exaggerated his difficulties and he had been pampered by our father since childhood. The elderly man did all the farm work after my brothers and sisters got married and I went to university and before our father broke his leg.

One day, when Xu Limin saw our father cleaving oriental white oaks, he said to the latter, "You should have Chunshang do this."

"He is not good at this," our father replied, wiping away his sweat and panting.

Later the villagers said that Xu Chengxiang would look after his youngest son as long as he lived. Chunshang got embarrassed after he heard that, but he was too lazy to change himself. After he got married, he was often scolded by his wife. As a result, he tended to make a mountain out of a molehill to build an image of being a hardworking man.

Chunshang showed us his hands full of calluses, a symbol of self-improvement. But Chunshan retorted, "My wife's hands were badly damaged by brine when she was making roasted meat. Swallow once said that nobody would have dared to buy the meat if her mother had not worn gloves."

"Oh, your wife is a good woman indeed," said Guangwen. He talked on and on about Fengjuan before the other family members came.

Fengjuan treated all the members sincerely and carefully. When we returned to Yanerpo, she would cook if her sisters-in-law were unwilling. If she was not at home, we did not go back to that village. She was the key figure in our family.

Chapter 32

I have only one son, Chunhua has two sons, the other siblings have one son and one daughter. Swallow, the daughter of Chunshan and the younger sister of Sixi, was beautiful and kind-hearted, but she was headstrong. At the age of 16, she went to Suzhou and Hangzhou with other young female fellow-villagers to find a job. Later she was employed in a rock mill located in the border between Shanghai and Zhejiang. She, holding a baby less than 40 days, like a sick kitten, in her arms, returned home with a man named Sheng Jun for the Spring Festival. He was nine years older than her and had a fierce look on his face. He was an unwelcome guest but he did not give a hoot about it. He soon went to the courtyard to smoke.

The whole village was covered with heavy snow. Sheng Jun went to see a neighbour and introduced himself, "I am Swallow's husband."

Before the family meal in Chunshan's house was over, Sheng Jun said to

Chunshang hastily, "You'd better be quick and we can play mahjong." Everybody soon understood how he had tricked Swallow.

After the meal, Zhuqing said, "Fengjuan does not like her son-in-law, but she gives a thick coat of her husband's to him lest he should feel cold."

"She wants him to win in the games of mahjong," said her husband.

"She is not short of money. Sixi went to Singapore with a new boss. Mrs. Hou said that Sheng Jun's home was nearby."

"Does she know him?"

"No. He visited our neighbours just now and Mrs. Hou asked him about the details."

"But he may be a poor man."

"He is richer than you anyway! He has one brother who is more than ten years older than him and has left the village. The three large rooms left by his parents belong to him."

"Oh, you are so lovely," Fengjuan said to her grandson, holding him in her arms. "Look at the snow outside."

"The baby is wall-eyed," said Zhuqing. "He won't be a promising man after he grows up."

"Let's visit our family members," Fengjuan said to the baby again.

Zhuqing carried the baby in her arms and tried to make him smile, but soon he cried like a sick kitten.

You will be gradually accustomed to the things and people you dislike at the beginning. For example, after Guangwen and I visited Zhang Dachao, I found that Yuling and Chunshan were getting old. But the more I stayed with them, the less I felt that they were aging. When I saw Sheng Jun for the very first time, I considered that he was far beneath Swallow; but as time went by, I thought that their relationship might be acceptable although they had no marriage certificate. Their son was named Huchuan and he was looked after by his grandparents when he was less than six months old. Swallow and her husband worked in different factories in different provinces; later they started to do pyramid selling in Wangping, Jiangxi province. After one year, Swallow left Sheng Jun and resumed her job in the stone mill in Zhejiang. Their relationship broke up.

Swallow told others that Sheng Jun often took away sacrificial food from graveyards after visitors left, so she did not want to be with him anymore. That was a ridiculous excuse. Zhu Zhanhui, one of the villagers in Yanerpo, said that her younger male cousin (on the paternal side), who worked in a restaurant, was asked to take away sacks of food from cemeteries on each Tomb-Sweeping Day (a traditional holiday to honour ancestors in China).

Zhu Zhanhui also said that Swallow and Sheng Jun had been engaged in pyramid selling. Those people bragged that they would buy half of the properties in Huilong Town, but they were poor and miserable. Many villagers guessed that Swallow broke up with her husband because they failed to earn money. In fact, Sheng Jun had had an affair with a married woman from Hebei province and made her pregnant.

Chapter 33

After Swallow went to Zhejiang, she had a new boyfriend named Ren Dayou. Nobody had seen him except Fengjuan. Swallow used to send a picture of his to Xiaolan on the phone. His physiognomy showed that he could not be trustworthy. Ren Dayou's home was located in the mountains behind Yanerpo. That area was Cotton Infertility. Geographically Yanerpo covered a village, Yangshutai in the west, and Cotton Infertility in the mountains. When I was in the second grade at an elementary school, the government leaders required that villagers should replace wheat with cotton so as to build a cotton planting region in Huilong Town. The attractive cotton bolls failed to bloom and the bolls were as tough as stones. Kids plucked the bolls and put them into baskets. Their mothers threaded the bolls on a string, and their children wore the "necklaces" and went to school. Nobody dared to bully them. The cotton plantation turned out to be economically futile, but the place Cotton Infertility was left.

A fast walker could reach Cotton Infertility from Yanerpo within twenty minutes. The two places did not belong to the same production team. The villagers seldom visited each other after the elementary school was relocated in the town. The Rens did not have a good reputation in Cotton Infertility. Mrs. Hou was a nosy gossiper but she could be straightforward if she was no longer hostile to you. She used to be on bad terms with our mother, but she washed the corpse of the latter. Few people were willing to do such a job. Ren Dayou's ex-wife had been raising their son who was six months older than Huchuan. Swallow would become a stepmother and would not listen to reason.

"It's Sixi's fault!" Guangwen snapped.

Swallow and Sheng Jun would not have engaged in pyramid selling if Sixi had not coaxed them into doing that. If Sheng Jun had not gone there, he would not have had an affair. What's more, Sixi had swindled Chunshang, Chunhua, Chunying and Xiaolan out of more than 200,000 yuan. Chunshan felt embarrassed by his son's deeds. Shortcomings were constant topics.

Chunshan changed the topic. "Chunshang was better-off during his days in Jiangxi."

Chunshang became spirited at once. He had been to two places only: Wanyuan in Sichuan and Wangping in Jiangxi. When he was a new comer in the pyramid scheme, Sixi was a director in the organization. Everybody respected Chunshang; later more of his family members joined him, and the leader praised them as a great family success in meetings.

Now they guffawed, including our toothless father.

Chunshang had mentioned it so frequently that it became stale. The pyramid sellers had showed off to local villagers; but as there were increasing sellers, they would rather glance at each other than greet. They were chance acquaintances.

"Enjoy your dinner," Chunshang said, tapping the table with his index finger three times in a row.

"You have finished your meal and you should go now!" Chunhong ordered. "Call Qingmei and ask her to buy half a kilo of ginger. I forget to buy it this morning."

"Come home and help your mother-in-law," Guangwen said to his daughter-in-law on the phone. "Buy half a kilo of ginger and I'll reimburse you for the expenses."

Qingmei's words made her father-in-law laugh.

"Do not pamper her!" Chunhong said angrily. "She may become greedy and find a new, rich husband!"

"She does not dare to do that!" her husband retorted crossly.

Chapter 34

Guangwen opened the door and saw Qingmei, Chunshu and his wife.

"I changed my clothes this morning and I left the key in the pocket," said Qingmei. "I came across my second uncle and aunt in the market." She went to the kitchen with a pouch of ginger.

"How much?" asked Guangwen.

"10,000 yuan," Qingmei replied jokingly.

"Will you let your father-in-law reimburse it?" asked Chunhong.

"Yes," answered Qingmei. "I saw Yaqiong and we had a long talk."

"Both of you get along."

It was busy in the kitchen. Chunshu and his wife changed shoes.

"We'll hold a birthday banquet for our father," Guangwen said to Chunshu.

Chunshu should have called Chunshang.

"When did you come back?" Zhuqing asked me.

"Last night."

I stayed in Chunhong's house when I returned to the town. When I was asked by Chunshu and his wife, I would not say that I came back early lest they should grumble that the rich ignored the poor. They and many villagers claimed that I was a rich man; if I denied that, they would retort that I pretended to be poor. Later they boasted that I was a billionaire, but I did not want to argue with them anymore. The local people were braggers and kept up appearances at a high cost; what's more, they often cursed a corrupt official who brought shame on his ancestors. I had been admitted to a good university before higher education was popularized. After graduation I worked in a provincial government organ. I was respected by others although I was neither powerful nor wealthy. One day, however, things changed, and I was not treated with regard. As a result, I had to keep a low profile so that I could still be respected.

If you pretend to be rich, you will have to give money to your family members in festivals, but they won't be grateful to you; instead, they will become greedy. If they want to borrow money from you and you refuse, they will hate you. If you lend money to them and ask them to return, their hostility to you will be increased. Respect is like a veil which may be ripped. This is a warning, but the same mistake will be repeated.

If I told Chunshu that I had returned home, his wife would have to prepare meals for me and would talk about it everywhere. So I would rather visit them at the right moment and leave soon. "Why are you in such a hurry?" Zhuqing asked unctuously. "You don't have to do farm work and you may think about your business in a room. When the dinner is ready, I'll call you."

I should not take it seriously.

Guangwen gave a Bafine with a red case to Chunshan, and the latter put it into his pocket. Chunshang put the cigarette case on the table. Chunshu glanced at the two cases, and Guangwen soon gave him a packet of cigarettes.

"Our dad is thin," said Zhuqing. She felt that she should not have said that. She looked at Chunshang and asked, "Where is Yuling?"

"She is in the kitchen."

Zhuqing went to the kitchen, too. "Oh, my dear sisters-in-law," she said, opening the kitchen door and hearing the sharp sound of frying.

"What does Xiaolan do?" Guangwen asked Chunshu.

"She plays cards every day."

Xiaolan and Guibing worked as plasterers when they came to the town. She stopped working after she had four daughters and one son. She looked after two daughters and had two families adopt the other two little girls: one in Shapingba and the other in Jiulongpo. That was a farewell. Several years ago she went to Chongqing and had to watch her two daughters in the distance, but she ran away with teary eyes. Later she was scolded by her husband, and then he went into a bathroom and washed his face full of tears. Afterwards she did not go to Chongqing again.

Xiaolan and her husband doted on their son. The boy was in kindergarten now and the two girls were in elementary school. Xiaolan sent her son to kindergarten in the morning and picked him up in the afternoon. The two girls had lunch in the school. Guibing usually had a large bowl of spicy noodles as fast as he could at noon, smoked a pipe, and went on with his work. Xiaolan idled away an entire day by playing cards in a tea house which provided lunch. There were many women like her. Their husbands went to different cities to make a living.

Guangwen helped Xiaolan and Guibing when they were just new comers in the town.

"Xiaolan should quit playing cards," said Guangwen. "And she should help her husband."

"Guibing would rather prefer to have her take good care of their son," said Chunshu.

The couple cherished their son but neglected their daughter.

Chapter 35

Their daughter was Clever at the age of 12. Her father often slapped her hard across the face, leaving blood in her nose and mouth. But she refused to yield to him.

Last year I came home for the Spring Festival and spent one night in Chunhong's house. When I came across Clever on the street, I invited her to have tea in a tea house in a stilted building located in Suwan behind the middle section of the new street.

When I was standing in the stilted building, I could have a panoramic view of Huilong Town and the old street looked like a slum. The river outside the town was thinning and the ripples were too eerie to be told to Guangwen. Mount Lordhou was opposite the river, near Lijiayan, Guangwen's hometown. The mountain might be renowned for Lord Hou in history, but it was declining. A political commissar, a director general of bureau of finance, and an editor-in-chief of a newspaper group came from Laojun Mountain, but few personages from Mount Lordhou. Guangwen said that he would become the acquaintances of those influential people if he had come from the Laojun Mountain, and he could not believe that I did not know them although I worked in the provincial government organ.

Guangwen often said to me, "You are like Chunshu. Those big shots graduated from famous universities. The director general of bureau of finance has built two cement roads for his hometown located in a place higher than Yanerpo geographically. But Yanerpo needs good roads, too. You are an official working in the provincial capital, but you haven't done anything for your hometown. Rumours say so. Others' higher education turns out to be useful, but yours useless."

Chapter 36

There were few customers in the tea house during the Spring Festival. Two cups of herbal tea were served. When Clever was sitting opposite me, I wondered why I invited such a little girl like her to have tea. I may feel at ease in the presence of a child. I'm an editor of an illustrated magazine in Chengdu and I write poems in my spare time.

The villagers in my hometown had had to be farmers throughout the generations and they had been eager for comfortable spaces. Now they have to make a living in different cities across China, but they are still longing for the spaces. Urban and rural areas serve as the standard for classifying spaces. I should have done something good for my hometown, but I haven't. As a result, I often feel embarrassed when I'm with my fellow-villagers. But Clever did not make me have such a feeling.

Meanwhile, I felt pity for her. "You are Clever and you should know what to do when you are scolded by your parents," I said to her. "Just turn a deaf ear to those harsh words."

"Since my younger brother was born," she said, sipping the tea, "my younger sister and I have become punchbags. Before he came into the world, we and my mom were often scolded by my dad. I am headstrong, but I'll be beaten by him anyway."

"But they love you," I argued. "Because you are their daughter." Clever gave a forced smile and continued to have tea. She seemed to laugh at my ignorance of the reality: many children had been forsaken by their parents, which made physical punishment pale by comparison.

I was thinking about what to say when I was having tea. I wanted to ask her about her schoolwork, but I knew that she was not an academically good student and she would retort sharply and even fight back if she was provoked by her classmates. I should not preach at her.

I asked her if there were interesting things in school. She happily talked about the math teacher's nose and the dress of the representative of Chinese lesson.

"Oh, I've changed my world outlook!" she added.

"Can it be changed so easily?" I asked.

"Yes," she replied. "When I went to the town with my mom, we spent a long time waiting for the traffic lights to turn green. That afternoon my dad drove to pick us up, and we repeated the thing in the morning."

I smiled. And then I asked whom she and her classmates adored. She mentioned the names of a lot of superstars, and she continued shyly, "I like my dad the best because he is the most handsome man. He has been working hard for our family. When I went to see him and gave him the paint, I saw him standing on the stairs and painting the ceiling. He was covered with the white paint from head to foot. I was so shocked that I thought that he became an old man so soon."

I refilled her cup.

"Do you smoke?" she asked me.

"Yes."

"You are sitting here but you don't smoke."

"I should not do that in front of a child."

"My dad smokes when he holds my younger brother in his arms. And I can suck on a cigarette if now you do it, too."

Chapter 37

I did not tell the details of our conversation to anybody.

One day when Guibing was holding his son in his arms, I said to him, "Your daughter understands you."

He smiled, but his wife retorted, "She wants to have swimwear and a trolley school bag when she sees others have them. If she knows that her dad is toilsome every day, she should not be greedy."

I said no more because I had never helped them, but Guangwen had. Chunshu and his wife complained that I had given assistance to Chunhong and Chunshang, but never to them. I had Lily employed by a television station through her father's money and my connections. I gave 3,000 yuan to Chunshang each year because he lived with our father. Chunshu and his wife considered that I only helped the rich.

When Guangwen said that Xiaolan should quit playing cards, Chunshu looked unhappy.

"You are the initiator," Chunshan said to Guangwen jokingly.

Our father smiled meaningfully.

Chunhong's husband had indulged in playing cards since he returned from Xinjiang. His wife could not stop him from doing that while she was maltreated by her mother-in-law. As a result, she had to take Lily to her hometown and told all her miseries to her father. She blamed her father for the marriage. Her fiance was impoverished but her father said that he was a promising man. Later she eloped with him without a wedding. After two years, he came back and spent too much time playing cards and mahjong. His wife was determined to change him.

"To compare me with others?" Guangwen asked proudly. He said this to his father-in-law deliberately to prove that he was a successful man now.

"Xiaolan should help her husband," he continued. "She should cook and bring food to him so that he can work harder and earn more money."

"She can manage it," said Chunshu.

"An addiction to playing cards can be disastrous," said Chunshan. "Yaqiong had been a victim. Luckily, Xiaolan does not do that when she looks after her children."

"She should do her duty," said Guangwen.

"What do your son and daughter-in-law do?" Chunhong asked her husband, putting liquor bottles and cups on the table.

"I don't have a promising son," said Guangwen.

"His wife is an idler."

"She is cooking. And she picks up our grandchild every day. That's very good."

"Has salt been put into the fish soup?" Qingmei asked loudly, standing at the kitchen door.

Yaqiong, who lived in the Yellow Flowers Lane of the lower section of the new street, became the topic at once.

Yaqiong looked after her son at home when her husband was working in an architectural decoration company in Hanzhong city, Shaanxi province. One morning she put a heating tube into a baby bathtub and put her son into it after the water became warm. Before she removed the tube from the bathtub, her partners asked her to play cards, so she locked the door and went outside at once. Several hours passed. When she saw the lunch provided by the manager of the chess and cards room, she suddenly realized something, screamed and ran towards her house. The baby had been reduced to bones. His hair and the remnants of flesh were sandwiched between his legs. One of his ghastly feet was sticking out of the bathtub. Her husband came home and buried their five-month-old son and left, never to return. Afterwards she often spoke and acted like a mad woman, either shutting herself at home or wandering the streets day and night.

Ordered by Guangwen, Chunshang took a bottle of Kweichow Moutai, one of China's top liquor brands, from a rack, and cups from a TV bench. Guangwen called Xiaolan and asked her and her husband to come here for lunch.

Chapter 38

Calls to Chunshang came one after another. He gave the phone to our father, but the latter could not hold it close to his ear.

"I can't hear you clearly," said our father.

Chunshang put the elderly man's hand closer to his ear, But his hand holding his mobile phone like holding a firewood axe, keeping it half a foot away from his ear.

We smiled but Chunshu did not. He thought that our father did it on purpose and he did not like clumsy people. He had said that the world had two kinds of men: the smart and the goofy.

"I'll hold the phone for you," Chunshang said to our father.

"OK," said the elderly man. "Are you recovering from your hand injuries?" he asked Fengjuan on the phone. "Keep yourself warm if you feel cold, and you may return home if you don't want to stay in Zhejiang anymore."

"Just like you!" Chunhong exclaimed.

"Take good care of your mom, Swallow," our father continued. "You may start a new relationship if you meet a good man."

"Gossip is terrible," said Guangwen. He had bought two houses, but he sold one lest he should become a topic.

"Sheng Jun has left you, Swallow," our father continued. "But it's not your fault. I suggest that you should be less self-opinionated from now on."

And then Chunhua's call came.

"I wonder if you are brave now," said our father. She used to be too chicken-hearted to go outside. When she heard rats squealing in fights, she realized that the rats in cities and in her hometown were alike. Afterwards she could communicate with non-locals.

"Does Ziguo have a new girlfriend now?" our father added.

Chunhua had two sons. The first son Fang Ziqiang had got married and had two daughters. The second son Fang Ziguo was now in his early twenties.

Early last year, Ziguo came home with a girl named Shanrui from Suining, Sichuan. Her parents had been doing business and had bought two houses for her and her elder sister in Chengdu, each covering more than 100 square meters. Ziguo met Shanrui when he worked in Chengdu. Their relationship was strongly opposed by her parents and she was locked in a room by them. Later she escaped and left a note: she would be with Ziguo even though she could forsake her house and money. I had never seen her but I was told that she, a beautiful girl dressed in summer wear before summer came, had served Ziguo like a maid but returned to Chengdu after six months.

Ziguo was still single. "Let Shanrui be with Ziguo again," said our father.

"She has jilted him," Chunshang whispered.

"Nonsense!" our father retorted.

Chunhua thought that she was being talked about. She said something more and our father smiled.

"You should treat your sons equally," he added.

She hung up the phone.

Chapter 39

Chunhua disliked such a remark as our father's. She had been favouring Ziguo although Ziqiang was much more hardworking and reliable. Ziguo was usually a slacker in bed when Ziqiang was busy in a farm.

Chunhua also disliked Ziqiang's wife named Fu Anping, much taller than her husband.

"You treat your daughter-in-law well, aunt," Anping complained to Chunhong, "but your younger sister can't. She often scolds me in front of everybody."

Chunhong had never done such a thing to her daughter-in-law.

"Just turn a deaf ear to your mother-in-law's nagging," Chunhong consoled Anping.

"I would have swallowed rat poison if I had taken her words seriously," said Anping.

If Anping put more oil into a pan, her mother-in-law cried, "Don't waste oil when you are cooking!"

When Shanrui lived with Chunhua, the former often plucked reeds and saxifrage and then put them into a broken bowl. What's more, she often put excessive oil into a pan when she was cooking; but she was praised by Chunhua for having good cooking skills. Chunhua bought a house for Ziqiang in Huilong Town, covering 125 square meters; and bought one for Ziguo in Qingping closer to the county, covering 128 square meters and much more expensive.

"Parents can't treat their children equally," Anping said to Chunhong and others. "I'm not a fool. Even my father-in-law obeys my mother-in-law. My husband is clumsy in speech."

By contrast, Ziguo was a glib talker. "I'm so lucky to be your son, mom," he often said to his mother, gripping her sleeve. But Ziqiang would never speak to his mother like that.

Because Ziqiang was honest, we sometimes asked his mother to advocate for fairness on his behalf, but his mother retorted, "I've bought a house for Ziqiang and I've been treating him and his wife well." And then she talked about her expenses on furniture in Ziqiang's house, on Anping's daily necessities, and on their daughter's food and medical bills. What's more, Anping had been keeping the couple's money.

"Gossip and complaints incur catastrophic consequences," Chunhong complained. "Chunhua lives with Ziqiang and his wife now. If they live in different places someday, the sad daughter-in-law will be unwilling to treat her mother-in-law well."

Things became complicated after Ziqiang's second daughter was born.

Chunhua had looked after the baby for several months, but later she let the baby's grandparents do the job after she went to work in another city. The grandparents had been raising eight grandchildren with difficulty and they could not afford to bring up one more. Chunhua was unwilling to continue to be the babysitter so as to avoid trouble, which had been her character since childhood. Chunhong said that Chunhua would rather do farm work than cook at home. But Chunhua considered that it would be a much better thing to work in a big city.

So Anping had to take care of her own children. Qingmei could get 4,000 yuan each month for looking after Dou from her parents-in-law who could provide meals for her. Anping wanted to have the benefit, too, and would need 6,000 yuan each month although she did not need 10,000 yuan.

Chunhua got shocked and called Chunhong at once. Chunhong blamed her husband for that but she told Chunhua that she should give money to her daughter-in-law.

"It's miserable to be the sister of a rich family!" Chunhua retorted bitterly.

Anping frequently grumbled that her own children had to be looked after by her own parents. As a result, we often persuaded Chunhua to treat her sons and daughters-in-law with equality. But Chunhua got fed up with our preaching, so she hung up the phone now.

Chapter 40

But soon Chunhua called our father again.

"Chunhua," said the elderly man.

"It's a bad signal," she explained. "So I changed a place. My husband will speak to you."

Her husband was Fang Yun, as good-tempered as Fengjuan. He had been loving his wife heart and soul.

When I was a middle school student, Fang Yun visited us on the first day of the Chinese New Year. The next morning I came across a piece of paper when I was looking for a shuttlecock in Chunhua's bedroom. It was a love letter to her sent by Fang Yun. He wrote in it that he had felt pain over her irritation at the sight of him. He must have sneaked into her room, put the letter on the bed when he came here yesterday. But he did not know that his letter turned out to be futile because Chunhua could not understand the letter: she stopped schooling when she was a second-grader with the worst academic record.

She would have taken Fang Yun as a bad egg if she had been able to read it. I threw it into a fireplace. When others were out for fun, I asked our father about her friends. For companionship, girls in Yanerpo usually persuaded the other girls to marry the men in the village where their new home after marriage was located no matter if they were single or not. Chunhua was one of the candidates. Later I often praised in the presence of her that Fang Yun would be a very good husband. She got angry at the beginning, but her anger gradually turned into anticipation. In October the same year, when Chunshan came to see me in the school to give me food and money, he told me that she and Fang Yun would soon get married.

Our father and Chunshan often said that Chunhua would have become an unlucky woman if she had not married Fang Yun.

"Her bad temper is trouble," Chunhong said.

In Yanerpo, Chunhua once was annoyed by something unimportant. She was in such a sulk that she pinched her husband's arm as hard as she could. He endured the pain lest others should talk.

"I don't know why Fang Yun loves Chunhua," Chunhong added.

Li Zhi came home, covered with mud after fishing. "If love is toxic, someone will be the antidote," he explained, stripped to the waist after a bath.

"That may be true," his mother said reluctantly.

Chunhua was the most beautiful one among the three sisters. If love is driven by good looks, it can't last long. Fang Yun was good at fishing, repairing watches, stamp carving, and street vending. He would buy snacks for his wife after a day's work, and buy her favourite cloth after several days. She was a stunning dressmaker and embroiderer. But the younger generation like Anping, disliked the old fashion and would rather buy ready-to-wear clothes. Fang Yun was a thrifty man and bought moderate cloth so that his wife could show her wonderful skills.

However, Fang Yun's business declined. Fishes were often electrocuted, and nearly 4,000 kilograms were poisoned to death. Fang Yun had to find new jobs in big cities, just like his son and daughter-in-law did. Labourers would become exhausted in a busy season and idlers in a slack one. Fang Yun would rather keep himself busy even when a seasonal labourer was needed.

Fang Yun worked as a stevedore: walk along steep stone stairs and carry a large bag of goods weighing 90 kilograms into a warehouse above the stairs. All the goods of a ship must be finished; if one bag was left, the labourer would have no money. Each labourer wrapped a piece of cloth around his head and the two ends were gripped with his teeth to prevent sweat falling into his eyes. Meanwhile, he had a thin bamboo stick in his mouth and should spit it out into a basket for counting. He would get no payment if he fainted or left halfway. Fang Yun fell into a river as soon as he stepped out of the planks between the ship and the shore. He felt extremely thirsty but the water did not flow into his mouth, and he was too exhausted to tilt his head forwards for some water.

Fang Yun had to work hard for his two sons at the cost of his own health. Our father hoped that he could come home if he could not endure it anymore, and he could have a rest when he was not busy with farm work.

"We'll have to make a living in other places if we can't in our hometown," said Chunshan.

"Our dad may give money to his children if they come back," said Chunshu.

The elderly man laughed with tears. "If I were rich, I would give each of you 10,000 yuan each month and I would rather have you stay in our hometown." He cried at the thought of his miserable children.

Chapter 41

Chunying called our father. Her current name is Lian Ying because her adopted father's family name is Lian. But we usually call her Chunying.

"Do you still have heart pain?" our father asked her.

She had had heart pain since she started to do pyramid selling. She disliked noodles but she had had noodles for one year. What's more, she had suffered from distress.

She and her husband had worked in Hunan province, but the couple was deceived by a call from Sixi. The couple had to pay 3,980 yuan as soon as they reached the place; they were unwilling to leave with shame while they could not earn any money although they had to spend money every day. Sixi, Fang Yun, Chunshang and Swallow had been there for several months and also had played a part in persuading Chunying. Sixi told Chunying on the phone that she could earn at least 5,000 yuan each month in the factory in Jiangxi. She and her husband went there by train so as to be reunited with her family members and to make a fortune.

But Chunshu considered that Chunying had suffered from her own actions.

Chunying and Sixi conned Xiaolan into doing the pyramid selling, and even tried to get Guangwen and me involved. Sixi had been scolded by us so frequently that he dared not call us. So he chose to call Chunshang and then the latter called Guangwen. With a glib tongue Chunshang told him to join him, but Guangwen did not believe him. Later Chunshang called me. After I heard his speech, I retorted, "That's the pyramid scheme."

"That's the multi-level marketing," Chunshang argued.

"I often watch law programs on TV. It's the pyramid scheme and it's illegal."

"The regulation is overt but a participant will soon be released from custody if he is arrested."

I could not understand that. And then more of my family members tried to sway me. Chunying, who was suffering from heart pain, talked with me more than 30 minutes about the pyramid scheme.

Our father was full of remorse at the thought of Chunying. She often complained, "You could raise my siblings except me."

When she was less than three months old, our father could not get any breast milk for her. Even neighbours had insufficient milk. He finally found a couple who was willing to adopt her. The foster parents had no children but could afford to cook rice gruel for the baby. In spite of that, she never stopped her complaints.

"I called your dad just now," she sometimes said to me on the phone. "Your dad" was our father in fact. After she knew that she had been raised by her foster parents, she often looked sad by a casual glance from them.

Our father spoke to her slowly and caringly on the phone. He asked her about her husband Yao Xianhe and their children. Qiuyue was the elder daughter and Huatian the younger son; both of them studied in Qingping Town: Huatian in elementary school and Qiuyue in middle school. Qiuyue was attractive with a lachrymal mole. Clever could be educated by her parents but Qiuyue was too rebellious to be educated. When Xianhe called me in summer vacation, I asked him about his daughter's academic record, he said, "Her mom and I dare not mention that!"

Lily, Li Zhi, and my wife called our father successively, but Hongquan and Sixi did not. Hongquan could not remember his parents' and his grandpa's birthdays. We disliked Sixi, but sometimes he could become so emotional that he cried in front of everybody.

"Too many calls!" Chunshu exclaimed impatiently. He got annoyed because his son did not call our father.

My son did not either. He could only remember his own birthday; what's more, he must study hard for the forthcoming National College Entrance Examination.

"Sixi may be busy now," Chunshan said mysteriously.

We became much more curious about him: what was he doing?

Part Two

Chapter 1

Xiaolan greeted her relatives. Her father was Chunshu, and she had called him Uncle Chunshu. A term frequently employed by the village children. She thought that Uncle Chunshu was another name of her dad. Whenever he gave her physical punishment, she did not cry or admit her own mistake, but she shouted: "Beat me to death if you can!" Now she complained that her own daughter was too stubborn. If children have good appearance and good character, their parents will say that they inherit theirs; if they don't have good qualities, their parents will get angry. If the mother and the father are on bad terms, they will curse: like mother (father) like daughter (son)!

Everybody in the room laughed. Xiaolan was rather delighted; what's more, she had had good luck in playing mahjong today. Several hours ago she received a call from one of her family members to celebrate her grandpa's birthday and then she could leave the chess and cards room with a good reason. She talked with her partners and paid for their lunch. When she was walking on the street, she bought 2.5 kilograms of loquats for one of her partners who had been coughing so much so that she could not hold a mahjong tile.

"You don't treat me as generously as you treat your mahjong partners, Xiaolan," Chunhong complained.

"I have such a good aunt as you," Xiaolan said, blushing. "And I enjoy the meals cooked by you, not by others."

"You may have a taste of the meals made by your other relatives."

The door was opened again.

"One more guest," Chunhong added.

Guibing smiled and tried to find slippers.

"You don't have to change your shoes," said Chunhong. "Because there won't be any difference."

Guibing was covered with white paint all over. The dried paint fell off after he sat down.

"Everybody is here," said Chunshang. "Let me pour you liquor."

He peeled off the red cover from the bottle cap with difficulty, but he could not unscrew the cap. Guangwen winked at me,signaling for him to continue.

"I'll have to use a hammer," said Chunshang. He found a walnut opener made of iron under the table and used it.

Guangwen snatched the bottle from Chunshang's hands, shook it, and poured the liquor into a cup.

"Just like this," Guangwen said gloatingly.

"He could have opened it if he had ever seen it," said Chunhong, holding the last course.

It was the famous Kweichow Moutai.

"You have been keeping it for a long time," Chunhong added, looking at the bottle.

"Moutai is for our dad's birthday," said her husband.

Chunshu glowered at Chunhong and thought that she was unwilling to share the good liquor with others. Chunshu had said that Chunhong was as stingy as our youngest maternal aunt who had been living in Qingping Town. Her husband had worked in the supply and marketing cooperative. They had been better-off but they did not help us at all after our mother passed away. When Chunhua and Chunying went to Qingping and saw the aunt take the medicine or sunbathe in a cane chair in front of her house, they just ignored her. Chunshu had said that Chunhong was miserly in the presence of Chunshan, Chunhua, Chunying and me. Chunhua and Chunying gave a forced smiled while Chunshan and I kept silent. Whenever my two sisters came home from other provinces, they would stay at Chunhong's house for one week. Ziguo had been a freeloader in Chunhong's home and been idling away his time with Li Zhi. Chunhong was a bighearted woman.

Chapter 2

Chunhong saw Chunshu scowl at her and realized that she had said something wrong. She fetched a plate from the kitchen for the discarded bones.

"It's Moutai," Chunshang said sourly. "But we can't distinguish if it is genuine."

"You haven't seen much of the world," Guangwen retorted sharply. "It was given to me by Chengzhong. Moutai is usually for a military leader."

Chengzhong was one of the adopted sons of Guangwen. He was studying in a military academy.

"Let Chunming judge it!" Guangwen added.

I sipped the Moutai liquor and said, "It's genuine." In fact, I could not tell whether it was fake or not.

Others tasted the liquor and their eyes and mouths stung.

"Why not taste it?" Guangwen asked our father.

"How much?"

"More than 1,000 yuan."

"Too expensive!" our father exclaimed, sipping it.

"We are not rich enough for such good liquor," said Chunshang.

Others laughed.

"What are you laughing at?" asked Guangwen.

"Nothing."

"You'd better let us enjoy some ordinary liquor, Guangwen," said Chunshan. "We are not good enough for the superior Moutai."

"It is extravagant," said Guibing. "Cheap liquor is much better for us the toilers."

"You are unappreciative," said Guangwen.

"Slap-up tobacco and liquor will make us have more and more," said Chunshan. "Chunshang can come to your home easily and enjoy your wonderful meals because he does not live far away from you. But I can't."

Others laughed.

"I may take a bottle home to avoid trips," Chunshang said jokingly.

"You have a good plan," his wife said.

Chunshang put two chicken drumsticks into our father's bowl.

"The drumsticks are for you, dad," said Zhuqing.

Chunhong put a piece of fish into our father's bowl, too.

"There are fishbones," said Chunshang. His wife removed the fishbones and put the fish into the elderly man's plate.

"Enjoy yourselves," our father said.

Zhuqing put another bigger piece of fish without bones into the elderly man's plate.

"Our dad loves fish," she said. "I used to cook sweet and sour fish for him, and he had a lot of it. The fish was brought by Fang Yun."

The elderly man smiled.

"Your children provide endlessly delicious food for you, grandpa," Xiaolan giggled.

"Are you one of them?" asked Chunhong.

"His children are excessive providers and I'm one of his grandchildren."

In Yanerpo, whenever Fengjuan cooked dinner, she would always let our father have a share of it. Zhuqing seldom cooked; but whenever she did, she would tout it and she might not let our father have it if she cooked for her own friends. When he lived in Guaizaoping, Chunshan and Chunshu brought no food or liquor to him.

"Chunming gives our dad 3,000 yuan each year," said Chunshu.

"Chunming is considerate," said Chunhong.

"We are considerate, too," Chunshu added sourly. "But we have no chance to show consideration for our dad."

"Let's continue to have some liquor," said Guangwen, stopping his wife from saying more.

Chunshan gulped the liquor in his cup. "Bring us cheap spirits."

There were 2.5 kilograms of liquor jars and 5 kilograms. When Qingmei was holding a jar of 2.5 kilograms, it had such a smooth glaze that it fell from her hands. She quickly used her belly and feet to stop the jar from breaking into pieces. We were waiting for her to open it.

"The jar has been buried under the bamboo roots for 40 years," said Guangwen. "And it was nearly destroyed by you."

"Oh, I'm sorry," Qingmei said, blushing. "Just now I performed acrobatics for my grandpa's birthday."

Everybody laughed.

Qingmei put the jar on the table and removed the rope and yellowed plastic sheets from the seal. The fragrance spread quickly through the air as soon as the cap was opened. She poured some emerald liquor into Chunshan's cup. As soon as Chunshu, Chunshang, and Guibing gulped Moutai, they put their cups for the thing in the jar.

"You are eager to taste the ordinary liquor," said Guangwen. He did just like his brothers-in-law did.

I used to have him join a banquet in Chengdu and we had Moutai, too.

After it was over, he said, "I did not drink to my heart's content today."

"Why?" I asked. "I thought that you had drunk too much."

"Too much is as bad as too little."

Chapter 3

"Not everybody enjoys the liquor stored in a jar," Chunhong said to her husband.

"Chunming and our father like it."

"They won't have much."

"Store the rest of the liquor if it can't be consumed wholly."

"I'll have much more," said our father. "It's very good."

"Oh, you can judge its good quality," said Chunhong. "But you should not have too much."

"OK." Our father's hands were shaking when he was holding the cup.

"Your hands dislike alcohol," said his daughter.

He tried hard to grasp the cup and he was being watched by his children and grandchildren. He gulped the liquor and smiled awkwardly at them. They kept calm.

Chunhong laughed.

"Are you crazy?" her husband asked.

Both our father and I knew why.

Xiaolan stood behind Chunhong and gave her a back massage.

"My mom wears a new blouse," said Qingmei.

"Do you know what happened last night?" asked Chunhong.

Our father worried that she might tell everybody that he had slobbered, but she did it. Chunshang watched our father and recollected that the latter looked like a forsaken child when he called his name last night.

"Excessive drinking had killed my dad," said Yuling. "Don't repeat it."

Yuling was disliked by her sisters-in-law, so she was a little afraid of us.

"Did your dad's hands shake?" our father asked Yuling.

"No."

He held the cup again for another gulp.

"Let our dad enjoy it," said Chunshan.

"Qinglian would not let him drink if she were here," said Yuling. Qinglian was her daughter. After Yuling's father died, Qinglian stopped her grandpa from drinking too much: he could have no more than one small cup of liquor during each meal.

"Qinglian has done the right thing," Yuling added.

"I'll keep drinking until I meet your mother in heaven ten years later," said our father.

"Don't boast," said Chunshu. "Mrs. Guier, much stronger than Mrs. Hou, had passed away much earlier."

Mrs. Guier was Wang Qingguang's mother. Before Qingguang was born, his father was stabbed to death when he was selling sugarcane on the street. He was holding a peeling knife, but the murderer grabbed him by the wrist and thrust the weapon into his belly. Mrs. Guier had lived independently since Qingguang got married. In March the year before last, she had a meal soaked in cold water after she finished farm work. But soon she started to belch. The hiccups did not stop until she died five days later. Mrs. Hou cleaned Mrs. Guier's corpse.

"I've neatened 29 bodies," said Mrs. Hou. "But I've never seen such a stiff, pop-eyed, open-mouthed body as Mrs. Guier's."

"Say something auspicious for our dad's birthday!" exclaimed Chunhong.

"You started the topic," said Chunshu.

"I asked our dad to drink less."

"You said that he had slobbered."

The elderly man glowered at Chunshu.

"Our dad will live up to one hundred years," said Guangwen.

"He should cut down on his drinking," said Yuling.

"He will live as long as possible for all of us," said Guangwen.

The elderly man would be rewarded with a TV set by the township government if he could reach 100 years old, and the TV set would be a gift for Chunshang. Chunshu and his wife stifled their sighs.

"Our dad knows if he is treated well by us," said Yuling.

"Very well," our father said hastily.

"If you say so," said Chunshu, "we'll have no objection."

Chunshang looked embarrassed because their conversation reminded him of the fact that he had been asked to return home from Wanyuan.

"The villagers in Yanerpo say that our dad should reach 130 years old before Chunshang reaches 80 years old," Chunshu added.

Chapter 4

Chunshang was in a sulk. Chunshan changed the topic: "Let's drink!"

"What's the alcohol content?" asked Chunshan, watching the thick liquor.

"60%," replied Guangwen.

"It'll be expensive," said our father.

"It may be sold at 100 yuan per gram," said Guangwen.

"Guangwen's house is full of valuable objects," cried Zhuqing.

Chunshan put a potato chunk from the chicken soup into his bowl but did not eat it.

"To have a cigarette?" he asked our father.

"No."

And then he gave cigarettes to Chunshu, Chunshang, and Guibing. He asked if Guangwen and I would need some, I had one but Guangwen did not. Zhuqing watched Guangwen and Guibing, meaning that Guangwen should provide good cigarettes for Guibing.

"I gave a carton of cigarettes to Guibing the other day," said Guangwen.

"The day before yesterday," Guibing smiled.

"We all know that you treat him well," Zhuqing said to Guangwen.

"But I don't think so," Guangwen retorted.

"We will always be grateful to you," Xiaolan said to Guangwen ingratiatingly. And then she gave him a back massage.

"You have had too many famous cigarettes and liquor," Chunshan said, smoking. "And you have a lot of guests. They don't care about the liquor jars, but they do notice the precious liquor bottles in your room. Fengjuan asked me to tell this to you."

"He refused to listen to me," said Chunhong. "The liquor racks are too showy."

"You are the village party secretary," Chunshan added. "You have done many good things for the villages. People in our village said that a few kilometers of road would be built if we could have Li Guangwen work as the village secretary for a few months. But you should keep a low profile."

He glanced at me and continued, "But others are jealous of your wealth. Jealousy incurs trouble and snares."

"The liquor has been sent to me by my adopted children," Guangwen explained, smoking. "The senders also include Mr. Wang, the general manager of a natural gas company, and successful fortune seekers in other provinces. There is no covert deal."

"But others don't think so," said Chunhong. "They say that you can get those things easily because of your leadership in the village."

"You would not have had so many adopted children if you had not been a leader," Chunshu remarked.

"I raised them," Chunhong retorted.

"Did you bring up Guangli?" asked Chunshu. "Your husband's leadership has been giving you money and reputation."

Chunhong looked downcast because her efforts of raising her adopted children were taken as fishing for compliments.

Guibing refilled the cups and said, "The liquor is soft. Sixi told me that the liquor in Shandong made his throat burn."

"When did you drink with Sixi?" asked Zhuqing.

"When he came back in March the year before last," replied Guibing.

Sixi had not returned since he left two years ago, which meant that he had sufficient money that he did not need his parents'.

Zhuqing glowered at Chunshan. The latter said that Sixi was too busy to call his grandpa. All of us wanted to know what he was doing. Meanwhile, another one was knocking at the door.

Chapter 5

Chunhong opened the door, got surprised, and whispered to the comer.

"Will you join us?" Chunhong said loudly.

"Thank you," the female comer replied. "But I'll have to go."

Chunhong closed the door and held a heavy bag.

After she put the bag into the room, she said, "It's Huang Ermei."

"I guessed right," said her husband. "Yesterday Yang Jin asked me why Chunming returned home. I told him that we would hold a birthday party for our dad."

"So she brings us gifts."

"I did not invite her."

"She and Yang Jin would be sitting with us if you did it," she continued in a low voice. "She gives us 8,000 yuan and says that it's sent by the township government leaders."

"How did they know?" her husband cried impatiently.

"Yang Jin must have spread the news. Ermei says that Li Qiantao has let Yang Jin provide the money in advance."

Li Qiantao was a clerical assistant in Lijiayan and was trusted by Guangwen. I'd seen that man: he was tall and walked like a snake.

"Keep the money," said Guangwen.

"You should return it," said his wife.

"I can't today."

"I'll give it back to Ermei."

"You should have given some food to her," said Guangwen, smoking.

"I wanted to give her two chickens, but she refused."

After Guangwen told the story of Ho Laosan's ancestors, villagers and his adopted children often gave chickens to him. Sometimes Chunhong let Qingmei take one chicken to her mother's house, but the former stopped giving chicken to Chunshu, Xiaolan, Chunshan or Chunshang. Chunshu and his wife delivered sour looks when Chunhong took 8,000 yuan from the bag, which could be used as available evidence that money comes after power. Even Huang Ermei would not accept the money if it was returned; instead, others would give her the money in return. Chunshu considered what Chunhong was doing was hypocrisy. Later when he told this to Chunhua and Chunying who did not go to Chunhong's house on that day, he said that Chunhong would profiteer from each dinner party in her house.

Chunhong did not know what Chunshu was thinking about, but she realized that she had said something wrong. She put chicken and potatoes into bowls. Qingmei held the pot and Chunhong sat down and talked about Huang Ermei. Chunhong seemed to make three mistakes in a row but she might not take them seriously.

"Ermei is attractive and often helps me whenever she sees me carrying heavy things," said Chunhong. "What's more, she often sells high quality products at affordable prices to me."

"You have brought business to Yang Jin," said Chunshan, "and she should do something good for you in return."

"But Huigoer is different from them," said Chunhong. "He never lends others a helpful hand unless he is paid. When he was walking with me along the riverside road before he visited Guangwen, he was just an onlooker when I was carrying a crate of milk."

"Huigoer would have become a good man if he had been broad-minded," Guangwen explained. "He would not have become a troublemaker if he had been respected, and the village would have remained peaceful if he had not made trouble."

"Early this month he stopped Mr. Gao's car on purpose!" his wife retorted.

Chapter 6

Mr. Gao replaced the former Mr. Wang in the natural gas company. The natural gas company was located 20 kilometres north of the town nearby Ba Valley, which belonged to Huilong Town. Ba River was an important tributary of Qingxi River. Fertile soil brought good harvests and profits while animals could enjoy delicious food. The company complex, however, was built at the expense of farmland and crops. Employees of a desulphurization factory, established in the Valley, too, also lived in the dormitory area of the natural gas company.

The senior leaders often checked wellheads. Early this month the blackmailer Huigoer lay on the ground deliberately when Mr. Gao's driver jammed on the brakes. The driver sounded the car horn frantically, but he was ignored by Huigoer. He opened the door and it pressed against a pine tree. He cursed Huigoer, but it did not work.

Mr. Gao and an office director were in the car. The latter got off and hurled abuse at Huigoer, but it was still useless. Mr. Gao walked out of the car and swore, too. Huigoer spat on his hands and rubbed his ears. The office director kicked him in the legs, but the latter rolled his eyes and spread his arms on the ground.

"Run him over!" Mr. Gao snapped.

Mr. Gao got stuck: Huigoer did not move at all; and he could not back the car in such a steep place. He had to call the township government leader and the latter called Guangwen. Yang Jin soon drove him to the site, and Guigouer opened his eyes and sat up, but he did not stand up because he pretended to have broken his legs.

"He is a wretched guy," Guangwen to Mr. Gao. "You may have a good talk with him and pay medical bills for him."

"Bad eggs come from bad places!" Mr. Gao roared.

Guangwen sneered and left. He asked Yang Jin to stay in the car lest the latter should beat Mr. Gao. Yang Jin used to solve problems with his fists, but it would be troublesome if he did that again. Guangwen knew that some employees in state-owned enterprises had lorded over poor villagers. In the lower reaches of the river there were wellheads in Mafu Ridge where those men had battered villagers. If Mr. Gao and his men started the fight, Guangwen would make their life have ill luck. Yang Jin backed the car expertly as soon as Guangwen sat inside. The former had frequently driven in the much more dangerous roads located in the Qinling-Daba Mountains.

After Guangwen left, Huigoer lay on the ground again. Mr. Gao looked at the office director with a nod, and the latter ran towards Yang Jin's car.

"Let's have a good talk, Mr. Li!" the office director cried.

Yang Jin stopped the car and Guangwen asked on purpose, "Are you Mr. Gao?"

In fact he knew who was Mr. Gao.

"No," replied the office director. "I'm not."

"I'll need to speak to Mr. Gao," said Guangwen.

The office director had to let Mr. Gao go to meet Mr. Li. Mr. Gao made a sour face at the beginning but he fawned on Mr. Li when he was getting near the latter. The former lit a cigarette for Mr. Li and then the latter made a long speech.

Yang Jin told me about the speech in details yesterday. It made him worship Guangwen.

"This had been a poor place since Pan Gu created heaven and earth," said Guangwen. "The natural resources, which belong to our country, have been raising countless generations, but poverty is still here. The natural gas will be transmitted to Shanghai. West-East Gas Transmission is a national strategy, and this region is also a part of the strategy, and we feel proud of it. But the local people haven't benefited from the taxes you have paid. Gas storage holders and firewood are still used here. Underdeveloped areas give way to developed ones. We know why some villagers have been angry although you don't. If they are cornered, they will throw a burning match or a lighter into gas wells. Now we are in the birthplace of the Banese. They were hunters and warriors and had made a nation surrender through their singing and dancing. If the foolish ruler of the State of Ju and the greedy one of the State of Shu had not brought the army of the State of Qin here, history might have been changed and the Banese might have unified China. According to your words, the natural gas is nationally owned, but the locals are not. The indigenous resources and human beings are interdependent. You could not have driven a car here if we had not built roads. We should treat each other well and gratefully. Whenever Mr. Wang, your predecessor, came across a villager, he would drive him home."

Mr. Gao looked pale when Guangwen was talking.

"You will have good results if you get along with the locals," Guangwen continued. "Whenever you have a problem, you would rather call your leaders than think about why it happens. Both your leaders and mine will not have a 24-hour watch here, and it is impossible to have military vehicles guard this place. What's more, the problem will be ceaseless if it can't be solved radically. I work for the town and you for your company. If we fail to do our job well, what will our bosses think about us?"

The burnt-out cigarette in Guangwen's fingers was left with a stinking filter tip after he ended his speech. He took out another cigarette which was much more expensive than Mr. Gao's.

"When he passed the cigarette to Mr. Gao," said Yang Jin, "the latter could not hold it firmly. It is unbelievable that Mr. Li, who had no higher education, should have forceful arguments. He is an extraordinary man."

I kept silent although I felt the same way. I was not as eloquent as him. Later Mr. Gao was on good terms with Guangwen and often invited him to dinner. Mr. Gao provided him with a lot of scrap iron, and the latter could make a fortune by selling it in the town, much more than the earnings of several households.

"Mr. Li is good at turning hostile leaders into his friends," Yang Jin added. "He would have had more power and money if a coal mine had been discovered in Lijiayan. The village party secretary of Randeng in Guihua Town is also a coal mine manager. He is not as smart as Mr. Li, but he is so rich that he can sway the township government leaders."

"What happened to Huigoer that day?" I asked.

"Mr. Li said that 1,000 yuan could solve the problem," replied Yang Jin. "But the office director would pay only 200 yuan. Mr. Li retorted that he would no longer be a troubleshooter if the 1,000 yuan could not be paid. Mr. Li suggested that Huigoer should be sent to a county hospital lest a township one should be insufficiently equipped or lest the one in the charge of the natural gas company should favour Mr. Gao. The office director knew that medical examinations in a township hospital would cost much more and it might have connections with the local township government. The office director said that he would pay 300 yuan, but Mr. Li insisted that he must give 1,000 yuan to Huigoer and apologise to him if they did not choose to go to a hospital. After a moment of silence, Mr. Gao did according to Mr. Li's requirement."

"Huigoer stood up as soon as the office director gave him 1,000 yuan," Yang Jin laughed. "Before the apology was made, he quickly waved his hand at Mr. Li; but soon he realized that he must pretend to walk with a limp."

I could imagine Huigoer's gait: like carrying his buttocks on his back.

Chapter 8

The mention of Guiouer reminded Chunhong of Chunshu. She could not understand why Chunshu said that she had raised her adopted children for the sake of a good reputation. Did she want a reputation when she sent food to him? No wonder he was unwilling to help her. She thought of Lily's wedding.

Lily got married with one of her classmates, Yu Peiliang, after she was employed in a television station. His hometown was nearby the Qingxi River and was much remoter and poorer than the areas in Laojun Mountain and Mount Lordhou. But Peiliang, the only son of his family, was lucky. He was born when his mother was nearly 40 years old. He was taken to town with his parents when he was just a kid. They rented a house and sold vegetables. After Lily worked in Zhoucheng, Peiliang found a job in the same city. Their wedding was held in the town. For a thrifty ceremony Chunhong did not reserve tables in a restaurant. She borrowed kitchenware and more than twenty tables from Mr. Gui, a retired teacher; and she must return the whole set intact; if not, she must pay for any damage.

Chunhong and her female friends cooked delicious dishes along the riverside road to entertain guests two days before the wedding. Food, laughter and firecrackers permeated the air. At night a man would be needed to guard the place, so Guangwen asked Chunshu to do the job.

"I can't sleep well if I'm not in my own bed," said Chunshu. That was a refusal.

At that time, many relatives and even Chen Ya and Wan Ping helped Guangwen and his wife. Guangwen got rather angry with Chunshu.

Each household needed a room in the ground floor to keep a corpse before it was sent to a crematorium. The room should neither be located in the second or third floor nor be under the eaves of another one's house. One man had died in the house sold by Guangwen. Chunshu was not afraid of a dead body because he had been engaged in funeral business for so many years and had earned a lot of money. What's more, he did not want to be disturbed by the rats raging in those rooms.

"I had intended to sleep in one of those rooms," Chunshu explained. "But I disliked such a bossy man as Guangwen."

Chapter 9

Guibing realized that there were insinuations in the talks about Huang

Ermei and Huigoer. He quickly finished his meal and left. The rest of the relatives would rather say something auspicious for our father's birthday. We tried to remember happiness in hard times when Chunshang mentioned our childhood. After our mother passed away, we were still able to wear new clothes made of good cloth. Whenever a tailor ripped a piece of cloth, that was the most wonderful sound in the world; and we were waiting for the Spring Festival when sewing machines were working. In addition, we could have some pork after a lot of it was given to the Production Team. We applied salt, chilli powder and rice wine to the pork, and then had it smoked or dried in the cold wind. After it was cooked, it was too delicious to tell.

However, now we were not as excited as Chunshang.

"Did you feel cold just like our dad did?" his wife asked.

We gave a forced smile. We had said goodbye to the past and we should let our memories sleep to avoid nightmares. All of us have carried burdens as we grew up. We were isolated and we could not clearly remember our father's age although we had cared about so many things. The villagers gossiped that our father was about the same age as Mrs. Hou. When Chunshang held the seventy-fifth birthday party for our father, the age was just an estimate. His birthday was the second day of the fourth lunar month, and it might not be true. The birthday should be decided by one's parents, while parents had become my father's remorse.

Our father was sure of his birthday and we had no objection. Time went on and on, and every day was a new day. But his days were getting increasingly closer to the end. His birthday was a chance to enable him to stay with his children and grandchildren, counting his minutes before he said goodbye to the world.

We had to continue our talks with the topics from other people.

"What did Yaqiong say?" Chunhong asked Qingmei.

"Lunatic ravings," said Guangwen.

"She will go to Hanzhong soon," said Qingmei.

"Has her husband buried the hatchet?" asked Zhuqing. "They can have another child."

"She says that her son goes to Hanzhong with his dad for a new job," Qingmei added. "And her son has a girlfriend. They will hold a wedding in

Hanzhong and she will attend it. She has bought blankets and will buy new clothes for her daughter-in-law."

"The other day I saw her walk into her house, smiling and each hand holding a blanket," said Xiaolan.

"Rumours say that she had bought 30 quilts," Qingmei continued.

They became silent. The large pile of quilts was terrible.

"Where does she get the money?" Zhuqing asked on purpose.

In fact everybody in the town knew how she earned money. If she did not shut herself in her house, she would go to the Ba Valley and the town. She was a beautiful woman and was good at dressing herself up. After she had the money, she would return to the town, in her arms holding the baby bathtub in which her son had lost his life. In the past she madly said that her son was too big to be held, but now she said that her son would get married soon.

"Sinful!" Chunhong cried.

"That's true," said Chunshan and Yuling.

"Her son would have become as tall as Dou if he were alive," said Yuling.

"He was born eight months earlier than Dou," Qingmei explained.

"Change the topic!" Guangwen ordered.

"What's the matter?" our father asked in perplexity.

"It's over," said Chunhong.

Guangwen asked everybody to have the liquor. "Is it good?"

"Guibing says that it's very good," said Zhuqing. "And Sixi …" She tried to start the topic about Sixi which all of us wanted to know.

Chapter 10

Sixi had been a troublemaker in the whole family. He had been scolded by his relatives so much so that he yelled at his father, "I'm a good man but you take delight in speaking ill of me! And then you can show that you are much better than me!"

Chunshan did not fly into a rage; instead, he said softly to his son, "I do hope that you can become a good man."

Others consoled Sixi but Chunshu glowered at Chunshan. During Lily's wedding, Guangwen asked Chunshu to be a night watchman, but Chunshu refused that. Yang Jin did the job. When it was not even 2:30 a.m., Chunshan got up and made a fire. Chunshu felt that he was humiliated by Chunshan: the latter was an early bird but the former was a picky rejecter.

But his words were not convincing. After our mother passed away, Chunshan had to help our father to support our family. Chunshu spent most of his time reading and did not have to toil. Family members usually talked about Chunshan's merit.

But his son Sixi was the topic. Before the Spring Festival several years ago, he went to Singapore with a boss and came back after several months. He was still in Toa Payoh on his grandpa's birthday. He said that he was so busy that he could have only four hours of sleep each day. This year he might become busier: perhaps he had a much more powerful boss. Being busy was connected with wealth and status. The villagers thought that bosses were drinkers, gamblers, playboys and sunbathers based on what they watched in the television programs. After they went to work in big cities, they came to know that bosses should be extremely busy. Sixi had a hectic work schedule, and his boss must have a tighter one.

Chunshan talked about his son's girlfriends. Sixi told his cousins that he had slept with actresses and airline stewardesses, and we did not know if that was true. But we knew the two women who had had a relationship with Sixi. The first one was his wife, Ran Qing. They got married and had a son named Tian, but they divorced when the baby was just six months old. Chunshan and his wife looked after Tian. The second woman was Kang Furong. They had a daughter named Rong although they did not marry. Sixi left Furong when she was sleeping one night. At that time they lived in the house owned by Furong's parents. After he went away, Rong had to be raised by her mother. And now, the third woman was Shen Xiaofei who came from Harbin and who had a bachelor's degree. We could not believe that she should fall in love with Sixi who had not finished junior middle school education.

Our father smiled but Chunhong cried unhappily, "Sixi is a swindler!"

"He is a good-for-nothing and a fraud!" her husband snapped. He would protect his daughter, who had a bachelor's degree, too, from being deceived by such as man as Sixi.

Chapter 11

It was true that Sixi, who had parents, women and children, had achieved nothing. The boss whom Sixi had followed and the company that he had joined turned out to be the things that he had borrowed but returned. Old, poor things were still with him. Nobody knew if he had really been to Singapore, how he got there, and with whom. After he "returned" for two months, Chunshan received a call from a company in Shanghai. His son had bought a mobile phone priced at 6,000 yuan in instalments. The call was made because of overdue payments and of Sixi's changed phone number. He had left his father's number as the guarantor, and he replied on the phone that he was Sixi's father. At the beginning he thought that his son had become a boss and let one of his men call him to have fun in a big city, but he got furious after he knew what had happened.

His father got shocked by such a figure. Sixi should not have bought such an expensive phone because he was not a rich man. He had never given money to his parents, and he would ask for more from them before he went to another city for his so-called business. During one Spring Festival, he gave some money to his son.

"You should study hard," he said softly to Tian. "A man with a fake graduation certificate of middle school may earn more money than an undergraduate. But that's the hard-earned money from a labourer. You should make a fortune with your wisdom, and that's the reason why you should be a hardworking student now. I had little schooling but I've been learning knowledge and skills since I started to work. And I won't sleep until I finish reading every night."

Nobody could prove if what he had said was true. But he had a superficial understanding of economics, laws, military affairs, history and music, and he could play the accordion. In one August several years ago, he returned to the town and came across a beautiful young girl when he was relaxing in a cool place in front of an acquaintance's store. She, carrying a Bayan accordion on her back, a new graduate from a normal college in Chengdu, was surprised that a man in a rural area should ask her about chords, and she had a nice chat with Sixi. He wanted to have a try, so she let him play the accordion. He performed *Valurile Dunării*. It did not matter whether he was good at it; it mattered that he could play it and he would let everybody know that.

In one early autumn morning the year before last, I received a poem *Banks of Xiang River* on my phone from an unknown number, perhaps a lover of poetry. I sent a message "Very good" to him. Soon I got this: "I feel honoured to be praised by you!" It was Sixi. I did not think that it was a good poem when I read it again, but I could understand loneliness, helplessness and perplexity in it.

Sixi should educate his son. "This is the lucky money for you for the Spring Festival," he said, giving a banknote of 5 yuan to Tian. This banknote was the only thing which he had left for Tian and which was the only nursing expense he had given to his son.

After Chunshan received the call from Shanghai, he recollected another thing.

When Sixi got drunk one day, he told it to Li Zhi. After the former went away, the latter told it to his family members excitedly: "Sixi met a sexy female cyber friend in Kunming. She was a wine seller in fact and she conned him of 7,000 yuan within two hours."

Chunshan angrily called Sixi about the matter.

"Leave it alone, dad," Sixi said lightly. "They are troublemakers. I'll handle it."

Chunshan got so annoyed by the incessant calls that he said that he was not Sixi's father.

"Are you Sixi's father?" the caller asked.

"No," said Chunshan.

"But you said that you were the other day."

"It rained but it's sunny now."

"If it kept raining, would you say that you were Sixi's father?"

"It depends."

He turned off the mobile phone. When he turned it on after seven days, he received no call. He did not worry about Sixi because the caller could not find him in such a remote place. What was more, Sixi was a cunning hider.

After several days the village party secretary received a court summons in which the company in Shanghai sued Sixi. The summons was sent to the township government and it was given to the involved party. When Chunshan was holding the piece of paper, his hands were shaking much more severely than our father's when he was holding a liquor cup. He was too wrathful to curse.

"You should be sent to prison," he said to his son. "Because you have brought shame on me."

We did not know how Sixi dealt with it, but he was not jailed. It embarrassed all of us. Shame comes to everybody sooner or later. If so, they would prefer to lose it outside their hometown rather than within it, because losing face in one's hometown is truly shameful The same thing happened again and again, and Chunhong had a terrible quarrel with others because of him.

When Sixi was a wanderer in Zhengzhou with a man named Lianwazi who came from Cotton Infertility, each of them paid 5 yuan and bought a lottery, and later Sixi hogged the lottery prize of 4,900 yuan. He did not give any to Lianwazi after several years had passed. Lianwazi could not find Sixi, so he told this to his mother. On a market day she met Chunhong in the area between the middle section and the lower section of the new street. She talked about it politely at the beginning, but as she went on, she said that Sixi was a swindler.

Chunhong had been aware of that. Sixi had defrauded his parents with an excuse of needing investments, but he squandered the money which they had got with difficulty on dating and sleeping with women. Later he deceived his relatives with the pyramid scheme and other tricks. He once told me feebly on the phone that he had had no food or water for two days. I hastily asked my wife to transfer money to him.

"Where is he now?" she asked.

"In Dongguan," I replied.

"Swallow is there. She may give some food to him. He is too weak to go to the bank."

I soon called Swallow.

"Sixi is nearly starved to death," I said worriedly.

"He had a wonderful meal in my house just now," she said. "And he will go to Sanya for fun."

Sixi had frequently cheated his parents and relatives out of money, but each time they thought that he might tell the truth. He would not change himself. I considered that he had pretended to be lonely, helpless and perplexed. The former victims did not want to suffer anymore, so Sixi had to find new ones. Chunhong was clear about that.

Chapter 12

Sixi had been often scolded by his relatives, but he should not be cursed by an outsider. There were a lot of onlookers at the scene of the quarrel between Chunhong and Lianwazi's mother. Two villagers of Lijiayan helped Chunhong, but Lianwazi's mother hurled insults at her: "Li Guangwen has been leeching upon the villagers and has raped your mothers and daughters. And you are eating his shit!"

Whenever it was mentioned, Chunhong and her husband would burn with rage. If Guangwen was criticized for something else, he would not take it seriously; but he was cursed as a leech, he was teeming with anger and sadness.

But Sixi had been the culprit. At that time, Guangwen called him and the latter was in the town. If others called him, he would say that he was in a remote place. Sixi thought that Guangwen and his wife supported him most although they had been two victims of his blandishments.

"Come back to the town at once," Guangwen ordered.

As soon as Sixi entered the room, Guangwen asked him about the lottery prize.

"I haven't seen Lianwazi for ages," Sixi exclaimed in surprise. "And I'd given him the money much earlier."

Chunhong told Sixi about her quarrel with Lianwazi's mother in details. With various expressions on his face, Sixi took out a cigarette and gave it to Guangwen. It was the well-known Chunghwa. Guangwen did not receive it. Sixi wanted to smoke but dared not, so he sat down on a plastic stool.

When Chunhong mentioned the dirty words from Lianwazi's mother, Sixi yelled, rising to his feet: "I'll stab that guy to death!"

Guangwen flung him a scornful look, and then Sixi sat down. After Chunhong finished, Sixi explained, "I'd given the money to Lianwazi. When he lived like a beggar in Zhengzhou, I bought him shoes and clothes, and provided him with meals for several days."

Chunhong and her husband kept silent while Sixi went on and on and at last said that it was ungrateful of Lianwazi.

Suddenly Sixi stopped. The whole room became quiet.

"Too many kind-hearted people have been deceived by your low tricks," Guangwen said after a moment of silence. He took a puff on the cigarette and then raised his voice, "I don't believe that Lianwazi should take away your money!"

Sixi gave up the idea of further argument.

On the next market day, Chunshan sold a pig and met Lianwazi's father in a tea house in the middle section of the new street, and he gave the money to the latter. That whiskered man returned 300 yuan to Chunshan awkwardly and told the truth to him. Lianwazi had lost all his money when he went to Zhengzhou, and Sixi provided meals and shoes for him. Later Sixi led him into a construction site with meals and accommodation included. Sixi stayed in Zhengzhou for several months and he was invited to dinner by Lianwazi after the latter got paid. They had some liquor, wandered on the street, and then came across a lottery shop. Each of them paid 5 yuan and bought one lottery ticket. They had very good luck.

Chunshan and his family members could not have known about it if Lianwazi's father had not told him. That man thanked Chunshan gratefully and apologised to him for his wife's harsh words. Later he insisted on apologising to Chunhong and Guangwen, led by Chunshan. Chunhong was still angry but her husband was mild: "Quarrels do not deserve praise. Otherwise, the township government offices would be boiling with rage and shouts."

At that time they gave a forced smile but Chunhong was in a sulk. Her husband would get irritated at the mention of it. He had never been cursed in that way; and he would have felt much better if he had vented his anger. But he chose to let it go although it was like a bullet shot into his heart; and the bullet would not have worked if Sixi had not been troublesome. Now there was one more victim of Sixi's tricks.

Chapter 13

Chunshan felt embarrassed and regretted that he had mentioned Shen Xiaofei. Guangwen usually treated Chunshan well, and the latter always did his best. When he was still in the hometown, he would need bamboo to make baskets and mats. The bamboo could not grow tall in the lush Mount Lordhou, so Chunshan chose the best one in his own bamboo forest, bundled it up, and carried it towards Guangwen's house. The walker in the mountain carrying the heavy bamboo must protect himself from falling off a precipice, and he would have to wait half a day for a ferryboat if the owner was not at home.

After Guangwen lived in the town, one day he invited Mr. Wang, the general manager of the natural gas company. The manager said that he would have a black-bone chicken, and the best one came from Xiangjia Valley in Laojun Mountain. At noon Chunshan received a call from Guangwen, and the former ran towards the Xiangjia Valley without lunch in scorching heat. After he bought one, he brought it to the restaurant as required by Guangwen before supper.

Guangwen remembered all those things and considered that Chunshan was a much better man than Chunshu. Today, however, Guangwen was infuriated by Lianwazi's mother's curse that he criticized Sixi as an irredeemable man in the presence of Sixi's father. He did not stop until there was a phone call.

Chapter 14

The caller was Yang Jin. "When will you start?" he asked.

"What?" Guangwen asked in perplexity, but soon recovered it. "Oh, I'm too busy to go there. Send a message to him."

"Where would you go?" asked Chunhong.

"I made an appointment with old Zhang," her husband replied. "But today is our dad's birthday."

"Why did Zhang contact Yang Jin?" she asked doubtfully.

Guangwen smelled the thick liquor, gasping. His wife did not say more.

Guangwen seemed to have many complicated drawers in his mind. His wife had never opened them. Even if she had, she would not believe what she had seen; instead she would rather compromise with him. Many couples live like this. But she could not figure out the reasons, so the compromise might become torments.

"Who is old Zhang?" asked our father curiously.

"You don't know him," Chunhong answered hesitatingly.

"He works in the food bureau of the county," her husband explained. "I want to buy his house located nearby the environmental protection bureau in Narcissus Road."

The topic could not be stopped.

"The floor space and the price?" asked Chunshan.

"140 square meters to be sold at 600,000 yuan," answered Guangwen. "The decoration and furnishings will cost 200,000 yuan additionally. I want to buy it because its price is not expensive."

Guangwen talked about the price lightly, which brought me a sense of inferiority. A poor man is self-abased in front of wealth. I thought that I was an idealist. But the world is not set for idealism because it can't work if without money, and the same goes for human beings.

"For Dou's better schooling in the future," Chunhong explained hurriedly.

That might be plausible. Dou would go to school in the town; if she studied in a better one located in the county, Chunhong did not have to buy a new house there.

"The new house may be used for Li Zhi's business," Chunhong added. "He is a good-for-nothing now and he should have material guarantee."

Qingmei rolled her eyes and went into the kitchen to heat dishes.

"We don't know if we can have loans from banks," Chunhong sighed.

Everybody knew that was untrue. Chunshu glowered at her.

"I thought that you would have Li Zhi own your current house," said Chunshan.

"We would have no place to live in if that happened," said Guangwen. "I plan to live in Lijiayan when I'm getting old. I'll build recreational facilities, enjoy the scenery, and go fishing. And I hope that my wife can agree with me."

"You may talk about it many years later," said Chunshan. "You should buy a good house for Li Zhi now. Did Lily's house cost more than 900,000 yuan?"

"It may be more than 2 million if her education tuition is included," said Guangwen.

"Where did you get so much money?" Chunhong snapped.

"Her house in Zhoucheng cost 1.07 million," replied her husband.

"Did her education expenses reach 900,000 yuan?" Chunhong asked crossly.

"Your eldest sister always supports Lily," Guangwen said awkwardly, looking at me.

"She is a promising girl," Chunhong said in a low voice, looking at the kitchen.

"Unpromising people should die?" her husband retorted in a low voice, too. "Only Chunming is the brilliant man among us."

"Let's say something better for our dad's birthday," Chunhong said, tapping a bowl with chopsticks.

"Better and better," her husband said.

I got nervous at the mention of Lily. Chunshu and his wife had complained that I had found a job for Lily, but I had not for Hongquan.

"Does Lily become a regular employee?" asked Zhuqing.

"It's up to Chunming," said Guangwen, watching me.

"She will have many tests before she can be formally employed," I replied.

"It is your own sayings," Guangwen said angrily.

"But there are rules," I argued.

Chunhong got annoyed and thought that I would evade it.

"The rules may be changed," she said.

"Others know that, too," her husband said.

That reminded him of the personages who had come from poor areas in Laojun Mountain, and he also regarded himself as one of them. He knew more rules than I did, and that they could be altered as the situation demanded.

Chapter 15

Chunshan sensed the topic had gone too far. He swallowed some food and then asked Chunhong and her husband if they had visited Lily's parents-in-law in the county recently. Guangwen would pull a wry face whenever his son-in-law was mentioned.

I wondered if Guangwen had ever asked Lily to find a rich, powerful husband. She did not do that in fact. Her father considered that a good marriage should be established between two families of equal social rank. He was a farmer, so he hoped that his son-in-law and his parents were farmers, too. In addition, he was a village party secretary, so he hoped that they would be better-off farmers.

Yu Peiliang's parents were farmers who had rented a house and lived in the county. When Lily took Peiliang home to meet her parents for the first time, her father had one more cup of liquor than he usually did, and after lunch he rested in a recliner without snoring rather than play cards, which showed that he thought Peiliang was a good man. Meanwhile, his wife felt the same way: the polite and hardworking Peiliang used to study in the same university with her daughter and they had a good understanding of each other. Lily's parents would visit Peiliang's so that they could have a good talk. But Guangwen got shocked after he got there.

Guangwen had frequently gone to the county since he became the village party secretary and Yang Jin became his chauffeur. Just like Huilong Town, the county was surrounded by mountains and a river. It had been a place of animals and wilderness, but now it was full of tall buildings and commercial activities. Migrant workers boast about the prosperity of big cities. In fact, people and things in urban areas are ever-changing and totally different from those of in rural ones. They were perplexed, while they speak highly of a city to cover up their failures there.

Guangwen had had frustrations, too. Thirty years ago he and his wife went to Xinjiang to meet his distant relatives. He returned to his hometown after he went to Urumchi, Changji and Shihezi. The names of the places did not leave a deep impression on him, but the experiences there were too engraved to be mentioned. As time went by, those names faded away, along with his distress. During recent years, he had been to big cities such as Chengdu, Shanghai, Shenzhen, Beijing and Qingdao; and also to Mr. Wang's hometown, a medium-sized city in Shaanxi province. Later he went to

Thailand with Yang Jin, Ho Laosan, and Li Qiantao; they wore sunglasses and beach shorts and sightsaw in Bangkok and Chiengmai. After they took photos with shemales, he often told others that the ladyboys had bad breath. What was more, he took delight in talking about the tax-free dinner for ten thousand visitors in Bangkok. He said that he would spend his retirement in Lijiayan, but he loved cities. He was familiar with the roads and alleys in the county.

Peiliang said that his parents' house was located behind the city moat. The slope there, which immediately came into Guangwen's mind, was flanked by hair salons, hot pot restaurants, tobacco and liquor stores, and residential buildings in which occupants hung clothes racks full of underwear in the balcony. The ancient moat was left with dilapidated walls and ferns. These lifeless plants were like an old man, frowning, squinting, putting his hands into cuffs, and waiting for the sun.

Chunhong and her husband followed Lily and Peiliang through damp alleys. They had to walk on tumbledown, screeching stairs. Guangwen was gloomy about the location and wondered why pedestrians failed to hear the sound.

A door in the fourth floor was opened. A fat woman and a thin man greeted their guests. They were Peiliang's parents. The ground was paved with frosted stone and the interior looked dirty although it had been cleaned. A wall was plastered with certificates of merit of Peiliang from kindergarten to senior high school, and the certificates were flanked by a painting of *Chairman Mao in Anyuan* and a stage photo of *The Red Lantern*. When Chunhong sat down on a sofa, it screeched and sank.

Chunhong was speechless with shock and her husband, who had been familiar with the county but knew nothing about the internal situation, was teeming with worry.

Guangwen, standing, gave a cigarette to Peiliang's father. The latter kept silent with a sweaty forehead when he was smoking. Peiliang's mother's belly was moving up and down when she was talking. What she had said could not be remembered by Lily's parents.

The farmers living in a county would feel much more embarrassed than those living in the countryside. Guangwen knew that and would treat Peiliang like one of his adopted children. But Peiliang would become his son-in-law.

"I'll cook our lunch," said Peiliang's mother.

"Let's enjoy it in a restaurant," said Guangwen.

She had to agree with him. Guangwen ordered a large number of dishes and paid the bill. All in all, he did this for his daughter.

After lunch Chunhong and her husband went home. The next day Lily came back alone.

"Where is Peiliang?" asked her father.

"He is in temporary company with his parents," said Lily. "And we'll go back to Zhoucheng the day after tomorrow."

"Have you ever visited his parents?"

She did not answer. She kept calm in Peiliang's parents' house yesterday, which meant that she had been there.

"His parents are so poor," she sighed after a moment of silence.

"You have chosen him," said her father.

The daughter was considering what her parents would say. They would have strongly disagreed with her relationship if they had disliked Peiliang.

"Don't care about his family background if you want to be with him," said her mother. Chunhong had told this to her husband many times before Lily returned home, because Chunhong was in the same situation thirty years ago. Guangwen did not retort and his daughter felt relieved.

Chapter 16

Buying a house is extremely important for a couple in China.

"Lily and Peiliang can earn their money step by step," said Chunhong. "We, the parents, can make a down payment on their new house in Zhoucheng."

"The balance more than 100,000 yuan must be paid if the full payment can't be made," Guangwen argued.

"A small house can be bought with the total payment."

"Our daughter deserves a large one and we should protect her from becoming a laughing stock. The couple will have their children and need more space. What's more, I don't want to live in a hotel when I go to see her in Zhoucheng."

Guangwen asked Lily and Peiliang to go to real estate agencies at weekends to choose their favourite house.

Guangwen disliked the house types provided by Lily and her boyfriend, so he went to Zhoucheng in person and chose a simply-decorated one priced at 1.17 million yuan. Later he went to see Peiliang's parents and talked about the matter.

Peiliang's father kept silent while his wife said, "We can't afford a house, but you can buy one with your own money."

Guangwen was too shocked to smoke, leaving the cigarette between his fingers burning, just like when he made a long speech to Mr. Gao.

"How much will you pay?" Lily's father asked.

"At most 100,000 yuan," replied Peiliang's mother.

"You should think about my daughter."

"I know. But you should know our conditions."

Guangwen looked at the old and shabby place in which Peiliang's parents had been living, and then he said, "Transfer 100,000 yuan to Peiliang's bank account."

After five days Peiliang received 100,000 yuan in his account. Guangwen transferred 1.07 million yuan to Lily's account. The house could be bought at last.

Later Guangwen complained, "100,000 yuan to buy a house? A drop in the bucket!"

Guangwen was displeased that his son-in-law had a windfall. "A carrot and stick approach should be adopted," he said. "I told a white lie to the young couple that I'd paid 270,000 yuan and borrowed 800,000, and they should return to me little by little. Everybody believes that I can borrow as much as I want."

Guangwen wrote a certificate of indebtedness with his signature and mine. He showed it to his daughter and daughter-in-law, and he kept it. There was no copy. The family members knew the truth except Peiliang. One day the soft-hearted Lily told it to her husband; afterwards he worked harder and harder.

After he was promoted to director in the company, Lily was so excited that she told to her parents that her husband had known about the white lie.

"You did tell him," cried her father.

Lily's parents were satisfied with their son-in-law although they were dissatisfied with his parents. It is said that raising a son is money-consuming, and the same is true for raising a daughter.

"Child-rearing is expensive," said Chunshan.

Guangwen got angry with Sixi who had a girlfriend with a bachelor's degree. Now Chunshan tried to restart the topic on Sixi.

Chapter 17

Shen Xiaofei was born in Harbin and worked in the same city after she graduated from a local university. She was the apple in her parents' eyes and they would have her stay with them anyway because they considered the world outside Harbin would be full of perils. After they knew that their daughter had a boyfriend who came from another province, had graduated from Faculty of Arts of Fudan University, and was working in a top event planning company in Harbin, they worried that he would take her far away from them someday. In fact, Sixi's diploma and job were fake. One day Chunhong said, "Xiaofei's parents should have gone to the company which Sixi had mentioned and asked the staff if there was an employee named Sixi."

Xiaofei's parents would meet Sixi. They had mixed feelings when they saw him in a steak restaurant: he was a glib-tongued, obsequious hunk. They asked him about his future planning. Xiaofei had told him that her parents would not let her leave Harbin, so he retorted bluntly, "I'll seek for better opportunities in the south within three or six months."

Xiaofei got shocked because he had never told her about it, and he should not have mentioned in the presence of her parents. They looked grim but Sixi went on with his speech about the history of the three provinces in the northeast of China.

"Harbin has got stuck with history and been obscured," he argued sophistically. "It's indulgence and oblivion. A city, like a man, can't get real if without memories. If reminiscences are taken as a shelter rather than a lesson, he will gradually lose his sense of crisis and become lifeless. So, I'll go to the south for much more vitality."

Chunshan did not know the details about Sixi's sophistry. After twenty days, he took Xiaofei to his home far away from Harbin; he told the process to Li Zhi and Ziguo, and Li Zhi told it to others generally. Later Chunshan knew what happened after his son made his speech that day: Xiaofei's parents were too astounded to have coffee or steaks. After they went home, they required that their daughter should break up with Sixi as soon as possible; what's more, they helped to ask for sick leave for her and had her stay at home. As the lovelorn girl pined away, her parents met Sixi again in a coffee house and asked him either to leave their daughter or to settle down in Harbin.

"Xiaofei and I love each other, you know," said Sixi. "You do hope that your daughter can live a happy life. She is on the way to happiness, but you are trying to pull her back. You, rather than I, should let go of her. I'll make a fortune in the south so that I can afford a house in Harbin. If you are worried about your daughter, I can go there alone and I'll come back three or five years later."

Three or five years would aggravate the girl's lovesickness. Her parents talked with each other outside the coffee house for a moment and then returned.

"We can buy a house for Xiaofei and you in Harbin," said Xiaofei's father.

Chapter 18

"Chunshu!" Zhuqing suddenly snapped.

She took it out on her husband when she heard the good news of Sixi. That was because her son Hongquan did not have highly suggestible parents-in-law.

Hongquan's wife was Qiu Bihua whose hometown was located in the areas around Mount Lordhou. It belonged to Cypress Ridge, not Lijiayan. Deep forests divided Cypress Ridge and Lijiayan. Birds flying in the sky in Lijiayan might be regarded as eagles in Cypress Ridge, and smoke in Lijiayan as clouds in Cypress Ridge. Lily and Bihua used to be middle school classmates. They met in the town during winter vacation when Lily was a senior student in the university. They could recognise each other. Lily still looked like a middle school student and Bihua had always been a beauty during her schooldays. The charming Bihua just graduated from a vocational college in a city six months ago. Now she was an office clerk in a small company in Baima. While it was not a highly paid job, it was neither tiresome nor toilsome She declined Lily's invitation to her house but was glad to have tea with her in a tea house.

They went to the tea house located in the stilted building in which I had had tea with Clever. The two girls had a nice chat and then talked about their boyfriends. Bihua was one year older than Lily.

"You are still single," cried Lily in surprise. "You must be demanding."

"No man wants to date me," replied Bihua.

Lily realized that no man dared to date her. When Bihua was studying in the vocational college, many students had fallen in love. The college was located in Nancheng in the urban district. It was an area which was developed ten years ago. The streets nearby coach stations and bus stations were thronged with motels. Chunshang used to sleep with one of his middle school classmates in one of those motels.

Zhou River (its largest tributary is Qingxi River) passed outside the college. Young lovers rented apartments outside the campus, and few students lived in the dormitory. Bihua had four roommates and all of them had got married. Boys had to speak to her carefully so as not to annoy her.

Bihua worked in a small company in which there was a poor computer, a printer, and a copying machine. The streets were jammed with stores selling food, liquor and funeral products. Parents often went to the company in which Bihua was working. A girl's father nearly forty years old frequently visited her, but she declined his invitations.

After three years she met Lily again. Bihua looked sad.

"Hongquan is one of my relatives," said Lily. "We used to study in the same senior high school. He went to a third-tier college because of bad luck in the National College Entrance Examination."

"Had I met him before?" asked Bihua.

"No. You were studying in Qingping Town but we were in the senior high school in the county. Perhaps you had met him on the street in Huilong Town. He is a handsome, tall man and wears floral shirts in summer. He would have been admitted to a much better university if he had not loved those shirts."

"There were many gay couples when I was in the college."

"He loves girls although he is fond of those shirts. He had two girlfriends in the senior high school and one in the university. But all the romances failed."

"What does he do now?"

Lily did not know that Hongquan had gone to Suzhou alone. She called him.

The phone call was the beginning of a relationship. Lily sent a picture of Bihua's to Hongquan's phone, and he sent his to hers, and the phone numbers of the two people were exchanged. Later Bihua learned accounting by herself, passed the exam, and obtained an accounting certificate. She went to Suzhou and worked as an accountant in a small company.

Chapter 19

A large house must be bought before the wedding. Bihua's parents asked Hongquan to buy a house in the town; luckily, they did not ask to buy one in Suzhou.

"How much money do you have?" Chunshu asked Hongquan.

"I'll be a rich man."

The father scolded his son on the phone. Chunshu had frequently given physical punishment to Xiaolan, but he was reluctant to do so to his son who had been born in violation of family planning at the expense of a lot of money. After the father stopped lecturing his son, the former went to real estate agencies.

Chunshu should buy a large house for vanity in front of his relatives. What was more, Bihua was a beautiful girl with a bachelor's degree. Her bigoted father, a carpenter, considered that few men in the world could be chosen as the candidates of his son-in-law; and he had even driven away matchmakers. His daughter was getting old, so he had to become the relatives of Xu Chunshu by marriage.

Chunshu wanted to buy a house covering 135 square meters priced at 160,000 yuan. Its price was much lower than the houses located in the riverside road which had become lotus ponds. Chunshu had had a bit of private money of 42,000 yuan. He told it to Limin in a tavern on a market day; Limin got along with Chunshan, so he told it to him. Chunshu said that he had borrowed money from his relatives so that he could buy a house for his son.

After Chunshan found Chunshu's secret, he told us about it. Chunhong had known that because Limin's wife, Zheng Saner, got along with her. After Chunshu finished decorating the house, he and his wife returned to Yanerpo.

"You have had a new house," Zheng Saner said with derision.

"We've bought it with the borrowed money," Zhuqing replied.

On the next market day, Zheng Saner came across Chunhong and had a chat with her.

"Zhuqing said that she had borrowed money to buy the house," said Zheng Saner. "Chunshu and his wife have deposited more than 40,000 yuan for more interest, and they have borrowed money from others."

Chunhong got annoyed but she did not tell it to her husband.

"The borrowed money should be returned," said Guangwen. He knew it through Chunshan's talk.

The wedding would be held in the town. Six cars would be used to pick up Bihua from her hometown. One car was owned by Yang Jin, another one by Guibing who also had a minivan and a Hyundai; the rest of the four cars would be charged for use. Zhuqing was not helpful, so Chunhong had to borrow kitchenware again from Mr. Gui, just like she did for Lily's wedding.

At 11 p.m., Hongquan received a call from Bihua. She was weeping.

"What has happened?" asked Hongquan.

"My dad does not allow me to marry you," she answered.

"If he disagrees, I won't marry you, either!" he snapped.

Bihau was heartbroken. Hongquan was playing mahjong with his cousins in the new house. His father asked him about it, and he told him sharply.

Chunshu looked grim because the house and the wedding had taken away most of his money. Several days ago he had to borrow from Xiaolan, but she refused.

"I'm not a bank," she retorted. "You have borrowed too much money from me for Hongquan's education and house, but you have never returned!"

She had to ask her husband. Guibing knew that his father-in-law was unwilling to use his own secret wallet, so he smoked in a sulk. Xiaolan told her father that Guibing had no spare money. Chunshu felt helpless and humiliated. The wedding would be held tomorrow and everything was ready, but the bride said no.

Hongquan and Bihua had not got a marriage certificate. They decided to register after the ceremony. If the bride did not appear, all the preparations would turn out to be futile. Chunshu cursed her as a nun and her father as a break-promiser, but he had to come down to earth.

Chunshu urged his son to call Bihua.

"I'll play mahjong all night long," Hongquan said lightly. "And tomorrow I'll return to Suzhou."

"I've spent so much money on your house and wedding!" his father roared. "You must return the money to me before you go to Suzhou! And I'll sell the house!"

Hongquan silently rolled up his sleeves. He was wearing a white linen shirt. Since he had had a relationship with Bihua, he had stopped wearing floral shirts.

When Zhuqing and Xiaolan were preparing the things for the wedding the next day, they heard a quarrel and later they knew what had happened. Zhuqing swore frantically but she was stopped by Xiaolan.

"I'll call Bihua," Xiaolan said calmly. "And you should keep quiet."

She tried to reach Bihua, but the line was engaged. Someone was knocking at the door. Xiaolan opened the door and saw Chunhong calling someone, looking angry.

"It's from Bihua," Chunhong said after a moment of talking on the phone. "Listen to me. This is what she has said."

Chapter 20

Diamond ring, diamond earrings, and diamond necklace must be provided for the bride. Villagers had never seen diamonds, so they would favour gold ring, gold earrings, and gold necklace. Bihua's parents, especially her father, required that his son-in-law must provide the three gold jewels for his precious daughter. Several days ago Hongquan and Bihua returned from Suzhou. They went to the town and bought the gold earrings and gold necklace, but not the gold ring.

"We did not find the suitable one that day," cried Hongquan, grasping a mahjong tile. "And we'll buy it later."

"But you may forget that after the wedding," Chunhong retorted, glowering at him.

"I'll remember to buy it!"

"But I don't think so! The gold ring must be put into the case tomorrow. If not, the wedding will not be held."

"The ring is not available in the town, but in the county," Hongquan's mother yelled. "What's more, it's getting dark. Even we set off now, the shop will be closed after we get there."

"Bihua implores me to help her," said Chunhong. "Her dad says that the wedding will be cancelled if the ring is unavailable."

It would be a long journey to get to the bride's home, and take a long time to visit ancestral graves and the elders and to have breakfast. And it would be too late if Hongquan went to buy a gold ring the next morning.

"If that old guy gives up the wedding, we give it up, too!" Hongquan's mother snapped.

"A financial loss will prevent disasters," Hongquan's father said loudly.

"I'll continue to play mahjong!" cried Hongquan.

"You should take remedial action instead of shouting here," Chunhong exclaimed, glowering at everybody. "Bihua's parents need your sincerity before they let Hongquan marry her."

"We would not have bought a house nor have made preparations for the wedding if we had not been sincere," Zhuqing retorted.

"Only Hongquan's name is written on the property ownership certificate. Is that sincerity?"

"Your daughter Lily bought a house after they got married. Both her name and her husband's name are written on the house proprietary certificate. And we are not as rich as you."

"Does money have anything to do with sincerity? You should have Bihua's name written on the certificate so that her parents can feel assured. They'll need a gold ring and a new gold necklace and gold earrings for the good match. What's more, meat, fruits, cakes, clothes and hats for Bihua's parents and grandparents, and 20,000 yuan in cash will be put into the case."

Hongquan and his parents, Xiaolan and her husband became silent.

"Bihua is waiting for your answer," said Chunhong.

"I have no answer," said Chunshu.

"And you, Hongquan?"

"I'll go to Suzhou tomorrow morning."

"It shows that you don't love Bihua and you don't want to marry her."

"Her parents are troublemakers," Zhuqing argued.

"You can be the trouble-shooter," said Chunhong.

"To take her away by force?" Chunshu said snidely.

"Get real!" cried Chunhong. "Greedy parents want 150,000 yuan as the bride price, and they even soak the banknotes into water and then weigh them. A girl may insist that her husbands must own a house and a car and prefer that his parents have died, because she doesn't not want to look after them. Bihua's parents are not that greedy and she is a good, diligent girl with a bachelor's degree and an accounting certificate after graduation. And she helps me to do housework whenever she visits me, but you don't! She must have had a long quarrel with her parents before she calls me tonight. She is now in trouble, and you should support her because you are her husband. Don't be such an irresponsible man!"

Hongquan lowered his head silently and his father's sardonic expression was gone.

"But it's so late," said Zhuqing.

"Listen to my aunt!" Xiaolan ordered.

"Barber Sun lives in the upper section of the new street," said Chunhong. "His wife's younger brother operates a restaurant in the county, and that brother's brother-in-law has a clothing store, and that brother-in-law's wife's niece runs a jewellery store. Call Barber Sun now and tell him to call the jewellery store manager. Do your best to buy a gold ring before morning comes. Guibing has to drive you to the store to save time."

"I'll do it," said Guibing.

25,000 yuan would be needed. The people on the spot provided their available money, but it was not enough. The bank only worked in daytime. Chunhong knew that her husband could provide some because Ho Laosan had paid according to the contract after supper and he lent some to Qian Wen and kept the rest of the money. Chunhong called her husband hesitatingly.

Guangwen was playing cares and roared on the phone. It is said that a man will have bad luck if he has to receive a call during playing cares even though he is about to win, and he will lose much more if he does not win. His wife knew that, so she talked to him softly on the phone.

"Come to Chunshu's house now," she said.

"For what?" he yelled angrily. He hung up the phone.

After half an hour Guangwen appeared to everybody's surprise. Chunshu and his wife treated him submissively. Guangwen usually smoked famous cigarettes, but now he received the ordinary one given by Chunshu. Chunhong told her husband about the matter when he was smoking.

"I lost much in the chess and cards room just now," he said. "And I don't know if the rest of the money will be enough." Usually he dared not tell his wife that he had lost money on playing cards, but now he told it to her confidently.

"How much do you have?" asked Chunhong.

Her husband took banknotes of 29,000 yuan from his wallet, and then put 4,000 yuan back into the wallet.

"I'll lend you 25,000," he said. "After you receive red packet money tomorrow, you must repay me at once. You have borrowed 30,000 yuan from me, and you must pay me 55,000 totally tomorrow."

Chunshu looked grim. His wife argued, "We can't receive red packet money of 55,000!"

"Return to me as much as you can get," Guangwen said coldly. He recollected that Chunshu had refused to be a night watcher for Lily's wedding, and then he walked away.

Chunhong phoned Barber Sun while Guibing and Hongquan went to the town. Barber Sun was woken up by the call but soon reached his contacts. He was helpful and he had been asked to photograph Lily and her husband and record her wedding.

Barber Sun was a lover of photography and he was often asked by villagers to photograph them on important occasions at a cheap price. When he was engaged in recording, he felt that photography was much more interesting. I saw the professional photos he had taken for Lily's wedding. He did not know me, so I had Guangwen tell him if he could publish his works on the illustrated magazine in which I had been working. Later Guangwen told me that Barber Sun had declined my invitation: if his works were published, he would be upset by his own desire for fame and money.

"I know Chunming is working for an illustrated magazine," Barber Sun said to Guangwen. "I would have contacted him if I had wanted to make myself famous. But I just want to be carefree."

I pondered over his words: was he unwilling to deal with editors or was I regarded as a seeker of fame and fortune?

Perhaps he was a proud man. Sun Jun, his grandson, the first and the only man in Huilong Town who had ever studied abroad and returned from Britain with a doctor's degree; later he became a professor in a prestigious university in Shanghai.

At last, the wedding between Bihua and Hongquan turned out to be a very good one. At noon, Hongquan's parents got red packet money of 73,000 yuan, and on the spot Guangwen had his share of it: 55,000 yuan. Chunshu and his wife complained that Guangwen was greedy.

Chapter 21

Chunshu's son's wedding was full of twists and turns, but Chunshan's was easy and smooth. The former envied the latter.

Ran Qing, Sixi's ex, did not ask him to buy a house or to pay a high bride price although she was not a money tree. The two people got married inconspicuously and had a son.

Kang Furong did not marry Sixi, but had a daughter for him, but she was forsaken by him. His parents did not know that until she carrying the baby went to Yanerpo one day. At that time they had no mobile phone. They called their son with her phone, but he rang off. After Chunshan and his wife scolded Sixi, they apologised to her, and she forgave them and had dinner with them. Fengjuan wanted to give her some money, but she declined politely because she knew that they were not better-off. She, carrying her little girl in her arms, said good bye to them. After two years, Sixi visited her; she did not claim alimony. The other day she told Chunshan on the phone to take good care of himself.

Shen Xiaofei did not demand bride price; instead, her parents had bought a house for her relationship with Sixi.

Chapter 22

"Chunshu!" Zhuqing shouted. "We should go home now."

The lunch was over. It was 3 p.m., and it would be the last meal of the day after several hours. The children would have the leftovers with their grandpa and great-grandpa for supper.

"Let's go now!" Zhuqing roared.

"Don't waste your time if you want to go now!" Chunshu cried crossly.

"I won't wash the dishes for you," Zhuqing said to Chunhong.

"I'll do it by myself," said Chunhong.

She and our father tried to let Zhuqing stay a little longer. He was eager to return to Guaizaoping with Chunshang, but he wanted to be with his children and grandchildren. The family reunion was dwindling for him.

Uncle Chenggui often told us stories in Moon Dam when we were kids. He said that he and other men would have to trudge through dangerous paths; toil made them vomit blood and they were riddled with distress.

Our father felt the same way now. Even though he could live 100 years, he would have less and less family gatherings, and he felt that each party was so short.

"You may stay and have supper with us," he said to Zhuqing.

She did not sit down again and her husband stood up.

"We are full," he said lightly, ignoring the elderly man's imploring look.

After Xiaolan saw her parents leave, she helped Chunhong to clear the table.

"You may go if you don't want to clean up," she said to Xiaolan.

"You are considerate, auntie," Xiaolan whispered. "I've got a lot of text messages and I'll need to go to the chess and cards room. After I win, I'll pick up your grandchild." She left.

"I won't have to cook more dishes," Chunhong talked to herself.

Chapter 23

After the lunch was over and several relatives left, the rest of the people in the house looked tired. Guangwen lay in a recliner and snored. Later Chunshan had a nap, too. When his wife was not at home, Chunshan would skip his supper and sleep and get up at midnight to cook meals for pigs. And then he would go to the mountains under the moonlight and would still go there with a flashlight if there was no moon. He would see a frog, a snake, or a stone. When he was watching the stone, he wondered where it came from: having fallen from a mountain, or having been kicked here, or having rolled here. He concluded that either an animal or itself had brought it in this place. The number of villagers had been decreasing.

Less and less villagers would help to slaughter a pig or to find a graveyard. The relatives would have to seek assistance from the township government. Young officers would be sent to the village to support farmers to deal with funeral matters. By contrast, the situation in Yanerpo was much better. In the past, such an important contributor as Mrs. Hou would clean the corpse and wound be provided with meals in the family of the deceased person. Now those things would have to be finished although the contributor would be very busy.

Chunshan, who was not afraid of ghosts, often turned off the flashlight and stood in front of tombs, waiting for a spectre; but it did not show up. It was said that ghosts feared ironware. He, with a woven belt or a straw rope in his waist and even without his keys, could not see any apparition. The cloud of corpse light suddenly turned into lines and wandered around the mountain. It became smaller and smaller, and at last it disappeared. He walked out of the graveyards and could hear his footfalls, the wind, and frogs jumping into a river. The night was enlivened. But soon the animation was gone and the whole area fell into silence. What he could hear was his own footsteps. His lessening footfalls occurred in the mountain night after night. He went home in the wee hours and slept in his clothes. That was the best moment for him. He knew that morning came when he opened his eyes again.

Now Chunshan strained to keep himself awake. He would waste the whole afternoon if he had a nap. It was still in the daytime if he went home now; but he would see his grandson. The boy was a first grader. He, Chunhong and her husband were worried about Tian's schooling.

The elementary school did not offer accommodation and meals. The kids' parents, including Chunshan, who had to do farm work and whose wife was not at home, had to rent houses. Chunhong and her husband would let Tian stay in their big house and take good care of him.

That did not work.

Yumei rented a house and looked after Chunshang's and other relatives' children. Ziqiang's mother-in-law, who had to take care of eight children, was regarded as a principal because there were four kids in some rural school. She might be taken as a principal in charge of two elementary schools. However, there were insufficient space and food for those naughty kids. Qinglian was no more a top student, which worried his parents. They were not rich enough to rent a house and had no time to look after kids.

Chunhong would become exhausted if more kids stayed in her house. Chunying's children were studying in the schools located in Qingping and were looked after by Chunying's foster mother who had got bored with baby-sitting. Huatian was a good boy but the rebellious Qiuyue was disliked by the elderly woman. If Chunhong's house could be used as a temporary nursery, Chunying would send her children to Huilong Town. Chunshu had a house in the town. Hongquan and Bihua, just like Peiliang and Lily, were too busy to have children. Chunshu and his wife would complain if those kids could stay in Chunhong's house like in a child care centre.

Chunshan concluded that he should not let Tian live in Chunhong' house. But she and her husband helped Chunshan. Zhu Zhanhui in Yanerpo looked after one child, so Chunhong gave her money to take good care of Tian. Only I knew that. One day Chunhong said to me, "We help Chunshan, that means we help Sixi, the useless, trouble-making son. He is the biological father of Tian but he does not carry out his obligations at all."

With a complicated expression she thought of her own son and fell into silence.

Chapter 24

Chunshan's sleepiness made our father sleepy, too.

"What will you do, dad?" asked Chunshang.

"You will decide," the elderly man replied.

"I'll visit my elder sister," said Yuling.

"Bring Qinglian and her sister here," said our father.

"School is not over," Yuling said in a sulk.

"Can't you speak to our dad friendly?" Chunhong retorted, glowering at her.

"Well, I'll have to wait," Yuling said, blushing.

"Will I go with you?" asked Chunshang.

"You know it," his wife said coldly.

Chunshang stood up.

But I wanted Chunshang to stay. If he left, Chunshan would get impatient, Chunhong would clean the house, and I would have to be alone with our father.

"Let's play chess, Chunshang," I said.

I was not an avid chess player. I seldom played chess unless I returned hometown and met Chunshang or Hongquan.

When Yuling was walking down the stairs alone, Chunhong cried behind her, "Bring your children here to have supper together. They should have nutritious food."

Chunhong would rather keep busy than feel the loneliness after everybody left. When I was playing chess with Chunshang, Chunshan and our father were watching us. Nobody spoke to Chunhong. She could not clean the room occupied by us, so she went into her bedroom. Our father was smiling at us although he was a layman in chess. He could have had a talk with Chunhong, but she did not speak to him. Our siblings except Chunshang were not willing to stay with our father alone. He had raised us, but as he was getting old, he made us unable to be alone with him.

Chunshan wanted to leave. He could have waited for Tian and had supper with us; if it was too late, he could have spent the night in Chunhong's house. But it would torment him if he was asked to sleep in another place. We often visited relatives when we were kids. It would take a long journey to reach the one who lived nearest to us. What was more, our relative might feel unhappy if we returned on the same day. Chunshan usually led us home even though he could see our relative's house in the bamboo forest and hear the chirping, he would go back anyway. When he was employed in another province, he returned home before he could stay there longer; and he complained of having a sore throat and stomachache when he was working in another place. Now he was no longer young; and he would rather sleep in the old room in Yanerpo and would go to the mountain at midnight, which had become a part of his life.

Chunshan looked at Guangwen and then at Chunhong's bedroom.

"Will you go to the mountain with me?" he asked me.

"No," I replied. "I have a tight schedule."

"Tell Chunhong to let Tian have supper with you."

After Chunshan left and the door was closed, Chunshang said, "I dislike him."

He might think that Chunshan acted willfully. "He left just now so that he can save 20 yuan for motorbike fee," Chunshang added. "He will get home before it gets late. He would have asked me to take him to his home in the mountain if my wife had not been with me. She is here, so he was too embarrassed to let me send him home. He is stingy!"

Whenever my sisters and I went back to Yanerpo, Chunshan always entertained us with the best food in his house.

"Chunshan would give the best things made by his own bones and blood to his son Sixi," Chunshang continued. "But he is as closefisted as Chunshu to the others."

Our father did not talk about that. Chunhong once told me that there were reasons why our father was unwilling to live with Chunshan or Chunshu: he could not feel at east in their houses. Fengjuan treated him well, but he could not feel comfortable. He had to stifle his cough at night and it would be a difficult job for him to go to the toilet at night. When he lived in Chunshang's house, he would put a chamber pot in the room; if he lived in Chunshan's or Chunshu's house, he could not feel homelike. During his stay in Chunshu's house, after Chunshu and his wife went to the farm land, they locked the door; as a result, our father could neither use the toilet nor eat in the whole morning until they came back at noon. Later the elderly man went to live in Chunshang's house. He could cook for himself but he could not do the same when he was in Chunshan's and Chunshu's house because he worried quite a lot.

My family members except Chunshu had not spoken ill of Chunshan. But today it was a surprise that Chunshang should say those harsh words about Chunshan. I lived in the capital, so I did not know too many things. I did not let him send Chunshan home because he had got drunk, but I asked him to move his chess piece as quickly as possible.

Chunshang felt boring and had to play chess with me to kill time. He liked playing mahjong with money. His wife asked him to go home a moment ago, but he didn't; now he was worried.

"You can go now," I said in an annoyed tone of voice.

Chunshang did not stand up at once, but he could see what I was thinking about. I was often called to go to the hometown when I was working in the capital, and it seemed that I could have the company of everybody after I returned. In fact, I was left alone. Before departure, I felt that I was saying goodbye to my hometown. It was not because of decreasing villagers, collapsed houses, or barren land; I was losing my intimacy with my hometown. When I went back many years ago, I could have an intimate feeling even with the grass there, because that was the place where I had grown up. But now the feeling was gone. When I talked with my sisters about our mother, we fell into nostalgia. No more.

"I'll bring my children here after school is over," said Chunshang.

"You should go as quickly as possible," our father said anxiously. His tone was teeming with worry that Yuling would elope with another man if Chunshang was tardy.

Both our father and I are humble. When I'm working in the editorial office, No. 5, Baihua Road, Chengdu, I will envy anybody who has a prize or gets promoted. When I greet my boss in an elevator but I'm cold-shouldered by him, I'll keep agitated for a whole day and wonder if I have done anything wrong. Humbleness, under the cover of detachment and resistance, can also be seen in my poems. Our father did not have such a mask, and that's the difference between us.

Chapter 25

I had to be alone with our father.

"Are you going to have a nap, dad?" I asked.

"No," he replied. "And you?"

"I'll sit here for a while."

I was annoyed by Guangwen's snoring so much so that I woke him up. He looked around, belched, and took a cigarette out of his pocket. His wife woke up after his snoring was stopped.

"They've left?" she asked lightly.

"Chunshan left," I answered. "Chunshang, Yuling and Tian will come here for supper."

Chunshang called me and asked me if Chunhong had got up. I gave the phone to her. She talked on the phone and then the call was ended. She said that Yumei had got a cold and would ask Yuling and Chunshang to cook supper.

"So they won't come here tonight?" our father asked anxiously.

"No," replied Chunhong.

"That's just an excuse," said Guangwen.

"Yuling wants to stay with her elder sister," Chunhong added. "She is happy when she is with her mother's family members. But she is unhappy when she is with us."

"Now it is much better than in the past," said her husband.

"Half a month ago Yuling's mother cursed Chunshang," said our father, "that he was incapable of supporting a family."

"Didn't you get angry when you heard that?" asked Chunhong.

"Chunshang plays cards after he has breakfast," our father replied. "And he does not stop even at noon."

"You are pissed off when we criticize Chunshang," Chunhong argued. "But you are not when he is cursed by his mother-in-law."

"Come off it!" said our father. And then he explained why things about Yuling had got better: when her mother scolded Chunshang, she would take sides with her; but one day Yuling put in a good word for her husband.

"It'll be good for him," said Chunhong. "He should be educated. The farm work could not have been finished if without the diligent Yuling. They should work hard to earn more money for their children's schooling."

"You can't feel at ease during your stay in Chunshan's and Chunshu's house," Chunhong added, staring at our father. You are too dependent upon Chunshang. But you must be looked after when you are left alone at home. You are worried about Yuling if she goes outside. Chunming gives you 3,000 yuan each year. Our sisters can earn that money within half a month. Fengjuan can earn more than 3,000 yuan monthly by selling roasted meat, and my brothers can benefit from your stay in their houses. If you live in Yanerpo, you can often chat with your neighbours. Even Mrs. Hou is a good listener. When you are in Guaizaoping, you have nobody to talk with."

Our father looked unhappy.

"That'll be useless," said Guangwen, putting out a cigarette.

"I'll have Chunshang go to work after I return," said our father, lowering his head. "Yuling does not annoy me anymore."

"He will live with Chunshang anyway," said Guangwen. "And he will be rewarded with a TV set when he lives 100 years old, and it will be a big gift for Chunshang only."

"Yuling has improved her cooking skills," our father smiled. "And she often pours warm water into the foot bath basin for me."

"It's up to you," said Chunhong, combing her hair. "Don't take Chunshan's words seriously."

"What?" her husband asked.

"He treats you like an errand boy. Don't get yourself involved into any trouble!"

Chunhong's words were like a puzzle.

"Don't talk about irrelevant things," said her husband.

"Don't show off your famous liquor!"

"People will doubt me if I stop accepting their bottles of liquor."

"Be cautious!"

"The liquor are legal gifts. Chunming knows that I won't be questioned by lawyers if villagers don't sue me. I get along with everybody in the streets and in the village. Only greedy men will get caught. I've never heard of such a thing that someone should bring a suit against another one because of justice. Such a thing is done for his own interests, and justice is just an excuse."

Chunhong could not understand his words fully. She threw a lock of hair into a trash can.

Chapter 26

Chunshang's wife and children did not come to supper, and we forgot to have Tian brought here. Chunhong could not find Zhu Zhanhui's phone number. She would call Chunshan, but called Chunshu by mistake.

"Oh, it's you, Chunshu," she said. She talked for a while and ended it. She laughed and her phone nearly fell into the bowl.

"That's ridiculous," said her husband.

And then she called Chunshan. He could not use his phone well, so he did not know how to record phone numbers into it. But he could remember all the numbers, including Zhu Zhanhui's. She had been looking after his grandson Tian.

Chunhong called Zhu Zhanhui and knew that they had finished supper.

"Who will come here?" Dou asked curiously.

"Tian," answered her mother.

"I don't want to see him because he will snatch the remote control from my hand!"

Dou was watching the cartoon *Boonie Bears*. Chunhong dropped the idea of bringing Tian into her house. Soon Chunshang came and had got drunk. Yumei's husband had been working in another province and had no liquor, so Chunshang must have bought some.

"You may stay with Chunming for one more day, dad," he said anxiously. "Are you going to leave tomorrow?"

"Yes," I replied.

"Are you busy now?" our father asked.

"Yuling's elder sister has got a cold and some children have got it, too," said Chunshang. "Luckily Qinglian and Zhaohui are fine. Yuling helps her sister to run the store for several days. And I must go back to cook meals for pigs."

"Does your mother-in-law ask you to do it?" asked Chunhong. "She can do it if you are not at home."

Chunshang smiled awkwardly.

"You may call her now," said Guangwen.

Chunshang took out Bafine in a red cover and stared at the only two cigarettes exaggeratedly. "I can't smoke in the store."

"You just want more cigarettes!" cried Guangwen.

Chunshang smiled in embarrassment, which he often did whenever his request was refused.

Guangwen received a message, and then put the phone into his pocket and grasped his coat, ready to go.

"You let me stay, but you do something else," said Chunshang.

"You may go now if you want to," said Guangwen. "And you want to play cards in Guaizaoping because you'll lose if you play in the street."

He threw a carton of cigarettes to Chunshang, and then he changed his shoes without bending, and wore his shoes like a loafer did. His wife scolded him for that, but he turned a deaf ear to it.

"I'll come back before you sleep, dad," he said. "And you may have some fun."

Chunshang sat down after Guangwen left.

"Are you going to stay or leave?" Chunhong asked Chunshang.

"Leave."

"Take our dad to your home now. There is a storm tonight. Protect him from a cold."

She mentioned that our father slobbered last night. Chunshang looked at him, like a father looking at his son.

"I'll leave soon," he said.

"This is for your mother," Chunhong said to Qingmei in the kitchen, holding a large bag of food. "I did not call her because she might not be interested in talking with your uncles."

Qingmei put the bag down on the table.

"Hurry up," Chunhong urged. "It's going to rain."

"Dou prefers watching cartoons than doing homework," said Qingmei. "I don't want to bring her to see her grandma."

"I will go to see my grandma!" the little girl retorted. "And I'll do homework in her house!"

Dou ran to the door and she would spend the night with her mother in her grandma's house.

"Do you smoke bad cigarettes?" Chunshang asked me.

"Bad?" cried Chunhong, glowering at him. "My husband will give you cigarettes no more if you say that again!"

Chunshang and our father laughed. The elderly man was huddling in the sofa.

"Can you drive a motorbike?" Chunhong asked Chunshang, watching our father affectionately. "You've drunk quite a lot."

"Yes, I can," Chunshang replied confidently. "And I can drive through Laojun Mountain."

"Be careful."

Chunshang and our father stood up.

When our father was standing, one of his shoulders was higher than the other.

"You may stay in Guaizaoping for one night," he said to me.

"I'll return to Chengdu tomorrow morning."

Chunshang helped our father to put on his shoes, and then he squatted and carried the elderly man on his back.

"Look," Chunhong whispered to me. "This is why our dad treats Chunshang well."

Our father was thin on Chunshang's back. Chunhong and I went downstairs, and Chunshang started his motorbike. Our father sat on the motorbike and put his walking stick into Chunshang's back collar, clinging to him.

About thirty people were dancing beside a lotus pond.

"Are you going to return home, grandpa?" asked Xiaolan, dancing in the crowds.

Chunhong told me that Xiaolan was experiencing back pain due to her excessive card playing, so she would dance after supper as a form of exercise, and then she would continue to play.

Chunshang said yes.

"Xiaolan does not invite her grandpa or you or Chunshang into her house," Chunhong said to me.

"I'll go to the street," I said. I knew that she would clean the room.

"Come back early," she said, watching the cloudy sky. "It's going to rain."

Chapter 27

People were walking leisurely in the South Gate Pier to miss the old days and to dream of the future.

I walked into the old street in darkness. It was like beneath an ocean. Blacksmith Zhang's house was the only source of light. He was sitting in a bamboo chair and having tea. He was wearing a shirt full of holes, as a symbol of his toilsome job. All of his clothes were like that. He had stopped doing his business since he made iron chains for Ho Laosan's son.

There was a barren beach nearby a river to the east of the old street. A pit much bigger than that of in the riverside road appeared in the beach, which was left after soil was excavated for building roads organized by the township government. A lake was formed in summer and autumn, and green duckweed could be seen in the lake. When it became dried, it stank because neighbours had thrown everything into the lake, including dead pets. The bad smell forced the officers in the new government building to make a landfill, which was two meters lower than before. Later an area covering more than 300 meters was provided with hardening of cement, and a stall was set up selling beer. There were few customers but aroma of oil and chili could be smelt. I found nothing interesting, so I walked out of the old street from an alley connecting the new one.

There was no customer in Congee Restaurant. Local people had had congee excessively so that they would rather have it for breakfast rather than for lunch or supper. Zhang Dachao was sitting inside alone. He had been wearing grey clothes for nine years. I could not understand why he should steal a drilling machine nine years ago. He would do the same if there were time traveling. The soul beneath his body was too weak.

His accomplice was a bricklayer who had had an ordinary life before he committed a crime. His sin was triggered by Zhang Dachao. The accomplice ran to his home in Golden Town when Zhang Dachao got caught. More than twenty policemen encircled his house and searched for him. In the room, a police officer saw a wardrobe was not closed and saw shoes. The wardrobe door was opened at once. As soon as the man saw the comer was a woman, he punched her recklessly. But soon he was arrested and died in the prison after several years.

Would Zhang Dachao think of him?

Six middle-aged men from Chongqing were talking in front of a hardware store. They used to be sent to Huilong Town when they were young, and today they came here again. They were missing the past days quietly and they had bent to fate.

Yang Jin was sitting in the light nearby a grocery store. His fatness made his height pale by comparison. I walked in a shadowy area to avoid being seen by him. Later Guangwen walked out of a store. He took a bottle of water and gave money to Yang Jin. The latter shook his hand.

"Ermei," cried Guangwen.

Huang Ermei did not receive the money when she saw the bottle of water. Guangwen sat down with Yang Jin, opened the bottle cap and had some water. Guangwen did not play cards because he thought that I would leave tomorrow; so he loitered in the street, chatted with Yang Jin, and returned.

I did not greet him. Instead, I entered a deserted oil-pressing mill. I saw a dog and I wondered what it had been protecting. Whenever I came back, I found its dirtiness and gloom intensified, and its chains graver. It had been kept in captivity. It was sleeping and the distant light fell on its head. I tried to walk tenderly, but it sensed my footsteps. It suddenly woke up and glared at me, but it was too old to stand up. It would die without being noticed someday.

The riverside road was nearby. I knew Chunhong was busy cleaning rooms. I watched the dark river. Its darkness was impenetrable. I went upstairs after I felt cold.

Chapter 28

Chunhong's house looked clean. She was still wiping small things with dishwashing liquid. I entered the bedroom. It was a tidy room prepared by Chunhong, and there was a desk. I took a laptop from my travelling bag and put it down on the desk, but I did not know what to do. I could not write a poem now. It existed in its heart only. I seemed to see someone standing in the shadows, and then I heard: "You were born on the same day with that man. But you treat yourself as an on-looker."

I was puzzled.

"Illusory sadness lies between moonlight and snow," it continued. "Forget the fruits of youth and lift its sweetness above your head."

I was at a loss.

"A new miracle will come," it sighed. "It's not about space, but about metabolism."

I got angry and drove away the shadow and the sound.

Chunhong entered when I was choosing one film in my computer.

"What are you doing?" she asked, sitting on the edge of the bed.

I would rather be left alone now. She seemed to have a long talk with me, so I turned around and faced her.

"Our dad is getting old," she said.

When our father was with us, I felt my heart was full of emotions; when he was not, I felt devoid and empty. I wished that he could stay here; but I would feel sad if he did. I was silent.

"He does not flush the toilet after he uses it," she complained, looking much more disgusted than our father's drooling last night. "I've taught him, but he can't do it well. I flushed the toilet once yesterday, but I did it three times today."

I did it, too. Our father was not a slovenly man, but he did not know how to use the toilet. When he stayed in my house in Chengdu, he complained that he could not shit when he was sitting on a toilet. He had always used the latrine pit.

"People get old too fast!" she added. "Our dad was still young and bouncy when our mom died. Now he is grey-haired and has to walk with a stick. And he often gets ill and feels cold in hot summer. He hopes that he can live 100 years!"

She laughed. I thought that it would be about the TV set.

"I should have called Chunshan about Zhu Zhanhui's phone number, but I called Chunshu by mistake," she explained. "She has had an affair with Chunshu."

I was surprised. Zhu Zhanhui and her husband Xu Xing were taken as the younger generation. She and Guibing had the same family name.

Chapter 29

Guibing found it last year. When Chunshu and his wife were busy digging sweet potatoes in our hometown, she hurt her feet accidentally with the hoe. Guibing and Xiaolan went to visit her in Yanerpo. It was Sunday, and Zhanhui went to Yanerpo to hold a party for her one-month-old grandson.

Zhanhui was the same age as Chunhua, got married early, and had one son and one daughter. The son was good at singing dirges. They got married early, too, and had smart children. Like Xiaolan, the daughter finally had a son after she had several little girls. The grandson was born in Zhanhui's house. The mother-in-law looked after the baby, but Zhanhui was still worried about it. She was hardworking day and night. She would hold a party when her grandson reached one month old. Guests were not invited, but they could participate willingly. Chunshu visited her with gifts.

Such a party included a major one and a minor one. Friends and relatives took part in the major one and gave an old hen, a piece of pork tripe, four crucians, and 40 eggs to the host, and could give much more, like clothes or a longevity lock made by gold or silver. Neighbours took part in the minor one and gave 30 eggs, an old hen, and 50 yuan to the host. However, Chunshu gave 60 eggs, an old hen, and 100 yuan to Zhanhui. He did not belong to either of the two kinds.

Guibing visited Zhanhui, too. Zhanhui had two houses. The old one was located nearby a bank and the new one was nearby Chunshu's house. After Zhanhui moved into her new house for more than ten days, Guibing went to see her in the old one but could not find her. He asked Zheng Saner and knew that she had moved into her new house and the cattle would be moved there, too. Later Guibing went to Zhanhui's new house.

When Guibing heard his father-in-law's voice, he realized that there must be something wrong, so he hid himself in a bamboo forest. He would say that he would catch chicken if he was discovered.

"Does your wife know this?" asked Zhanhui.

"She knows that I give you a hen," said Chunshu. "But she knows nothing about the eggs and the 100 yuan. I've kept the eggs secretly."

Guibing was shocked and went to another path. He saw Xu Xing trimming a tree. He greeted him and threw a cigarette to him. Guibing received it but dared not smoke it. He threw it away on his way home.

Guibing had to keep it secret. After Zhuqing recovered, she went to the town with her husband. At dusk one day, Guibing saw two people in the Banese Plaza. He could recognise that one of them was his father-in-law and the other was Zhanhui. He went home as quickly as possible.

At home his mother-in-law was making a pillow. Guibing felt pity for her. After she left, he said to Xiaolan, "Your dad is having an affair with Zhu Zhanhui."

After Xiaolan scolded him, he told the details to his wife. Xiaolan called her father at once.

"You should not tell him that I've told you about it," said Guibing. He was so worried that he went outside.

His wife was angrily sitting on the sofa and waiting for her father.

Chapter 30

Guibing went to a store and chatted with the keeper. Soon he saw his father-in-law.

"Xiaolan calls me," he said. "But I don't know for what."

Guibing and his father-in-law went upstairs, but Guibing left halfway, so the other man went to the fifth floor. After he entered the room, the door was closed.

"You must repay the money right now, dad!" Xiaolan shouted angrily. "My husband has earned it with his hard work. You've borrowed my money for yourself, for my mom and for my younger brother. But it should not be used by the bitch Zhanhui!"

"Nonsense!" her father retorted nervously.

Xiaolan told the details to her father, but he tried to argue: "I came across Zhanhui tonight. She said that Tian was a good boy. That's what she had told me."

"You do care about Tian," Xiaolan cried. "But you don't care about your own grandchildren!"

Her father dropped the idea of finding an excuse. Meanwhile, she yelled on and on. Afterwards she tried to find evidence. On a market day she mentioned the subject to others.

"I've known it long before," said Chunshan.

In last September, Chunshan's mobile phone fell into a vat, so he found Chunshu and would borrow his phone. At that time Chunshu, holding a barrel of swill, gave his phone to Chunshan.

Chunshan wanted to tell Zhanhui to take good care of Tian. Before he spoke, Zhanhui said coquettishly, "Are you thinking about me, my dear?"

"This is Chunshan," he said after a moment of shock.

"Oh, it's you," she said unctuously. "I thought it came from my husband."

Xiaolan hated her father after she knew the truth. And she hated Zhanhui, too, and she would curse her whenever she saw her shadow.

Chapter 31

"Shame on her!" Chunhong said to me.

She told me similar thing about her husband many years ago.

"Zhanhui is a whore," Chunhong added. "She has slept with so many men."

Now I could understand why Guangwen asked if Chunshu had gone to Yanerpo, and Chunhong replied "that person has not returned."

"The wives of those men, including Baohan, Xueqin, and Zhenxun have quarrelled with the shameless Zhanhui," Chunhong continued. "Xu Xing has been cheated on again and again."

Those men had not come back to Yanerpo since they had worked in other provinces. Zhanhui found good soil in Xueqin's farm land, so she planted maize and sugarcane. The good harvests brought sweet food to her.

"Only Xueqin's farm land can produce such good sugarcane," she said proudly.

Chunhong had never quarrelled with her and she even treated her friendly, but she could not understand why Zhanhui should turn out to be so shameless.

"One should hang himself if he behaves so disgracefully," Chunhong added. That became a prophecy for her.

Chunhong went to her own bedroom at 11 p.m. I was sleepless and I could hear the river roaring outside. Today was our father's birthday. A new day would come after thirty minutes. The storm did not come, and Guangwen had not returned yet.

Part Three

Chapter 1

I could have stayed two days longer, but I left even without breakfast the next morning. Guangwen had not got up.

"I'll have Yang Jin send you to the railway station," he said loudly in his bedroom.

"I can get there by taxi," I said.

Chunhong gave me a large bag of pickled mustard roots, a jar of thick broad-bean sauce, and a box of allium chinensis, which were my wife's favourite food. I declined much more because of insufficient space. Chunhong insisted that she would send me to the station. I planned to go to the county to meet my old friends. I could go to Baima city by bus and then take a bullet train to reach Chengdu; or I could take a speed boat in the county, or take a bus in a fork. A shuttle bus came every few hours; or I could carpool and the car would go when there were four passengers.

"I'll go to the county and then to the city," I said. "There are more buses in the city."

"You should have let Yang Jin send you there," said Chunhong. "You may call him now."

But I had put my luggage into the trunk of a private car and I was helped by the car owner. I waved my hand at Chunhong. I could hear someone shouting and iron chains clunking. The passengers laughed and said that man had lived one more night. I saw Chunhong looking at the car in which I was sitting. When her figure faded away, I called my friends.

It was Thursday. My friends were wily old birds in their companies. Discipline and time had lost their effect on them. Less time resulted in less restrictions.

"You are a famous editor," one of my friends said. "But you should not sit in such a car."

The car entered the Ba Valley after the call was ended. Office buildings, a hospital, and living quarters in the charge of a natural gas company could be seen in the distance while smoke was floating from a desulphurization plant. The road was wide and smooth. It was Boar Ridge. Divided by the Ba River, two areas were like two strings with different fates. The azaleas in Danxia landform cast spectacular hues over the mountains. Buildings were obscured in the birch forests while few people could be seen. There used to be an industrial park, but it turned out to be a deserted place. Sunshine was reflected in the foliage and a wind had the light over the park and the road.

I received a call and I was told that a room in Pahsien Hotel had been booked for me and I could check in with my identity card. The Hotel was located nearby Central Garden: a sago cycas planted in a flower-stand in the centre of a street.

My room was in the eighteenth floor, also the top floor. Humans and cars were like living beings at the bottom of air. A crucifix could be seen. Sï-Shen-Tsï Methodist Church, the only church in Dongxuan County, a Gothic architecture, had been designed and built by Canadian missionaries. Tall buildings were set up nearby the Church. The river could be seen much more clearly. The bottom board and railings in a low steel cable bridge had been covered with red paint. It was the submersible bridge established by the previous local government. Citizens could sightsee and fish on good days. Dancing was forbidden, but dancers would choose the bridge if there was no suitable place. A prohibition might be a temptation.

Stone staircases led to a road towards Bijia Mountain which used to be forests and villages. Trees were felled and old houses would be demolished. Bijia Mountain would belong to a part of the county for mitigation of overpopulation and for tourism according to the planning. Mr. Zhang, the Secretary of the County Committee, was dispatched from another place six months ago. When he was working in a county in southern Sichuan province, things were often arranged vertically both in offices and in houses. I concluded that was the essence of space. Mr. Zhang missed it, so he made a blueprint for Dongxuan: he would build roads in mountains, discard the submersible bridge, build a barrage downstream, raise the water level, turn a river into a lake, and create lake landscape in a county.

Chapter 2

Two friends came to see me after I washed up. One of them was working in a cultural centre and the other in a television station. The man from the cultural centre had operated a book store named Single Braid, just like his hairstyle; but now he had a new one. The other man was Tan Ruisong. He wrote poems in middle school and novels in university; worked in a hydroelectric board in the county after graduation. After severe years he retained the job but suspended the salary, and went to the south and operated an advertising agency. One night he met a woman in a club and then they lived together. After six months, his wife visited him from hometown and found that her husband had cheated on her. She cried and persuaded him to go home with her, but he argued that he and that woman had been obsessed with each other. His wife had to go home alone. After one year he returned in gravely bad health. He was too embarrassed to be reunited with his wife, so he rented a poor house and waited for his death. However, he survived after two months, and he was determined to study traditional Chinese medicine to reinvigorate his life. He had lost his former job but he was employed in a television station as a copyreader. He had not divorced his wife. One day he, in a suit and holding a bunch of roses, met her in the road which she walked every day, went down on one knee. His wife brought him home. He frequently told me that his wife was his saviour whom he should have worshipped. In our talk one day, he suddenly slapped a telegraph pole many times and cried, "I was a sinner! I will finish two important tasks for the rest of my life: atone for what I had done to my wife, and make myself foolish. I used to write poems and novels in top publications, and made a fortune in the south although I was not hardworking. But cleverness had overreached itself."

Ruisong said that he would drive me to Fengming Mountain which was his hometown and which I'd never been to. The three of us went downstairs. His car, a white Excelle, did not show that he was a rich man. He was a seeker of literature rather than of money. A plaza could be seen past the Central Garden and a street. Ordered by Secretary Zhang, stores and occupants were relocated within 20 workdays so that the plaza could be established and it was named as Ballad Plaza by him. It was a scenic spot in Dongxuan although it had nothing to do with folk songs. The world has been governed by concepts since intellectual revolutions came into existence.

The city moat in which Peiliang's parents had been living could be seen, and then the No.1 Middle School in the county.

"My younger brother has bought a house in the tall building behind the No.1 Middle School," said Ruisong.

I was surprised. His younger brother was a village party secretary. Guangwen had the same job title, but there was natural gas in the village he had been serving. The one in Ruisong's brother's had local products such as tea and tobacco, but he could afford a house. The prices were exorbitant and the house was located nearby the best middle school. The property developer was Chen Shuliang. He used to work in the urban construction bureau, but later he did business: reselling bad overseas products, running coal pits, and managing real estate. Gradually he became the richest man in Dongxuan. After several years he started to sell the best and the most profitable buildings. Per square meter of a house in Dongxuan was priced at 3,000 yuan, but the house run by him at 5,000 yuan. Guangwen bought a second-hand one with less than 1 million yuan, which was not expensive by contrast.

"My brother had spent a lot of time in the county before he bought a house," Ruisong explained. "He had often gone to restaurants, tea houses, and clubs to fawn on high officials. What's more, he had given tons of good food to them."

"My mom should not have had the banyan felled behind our old house," he complained. That tree was a symbol of his literary fortune. However, not long before his graduation, her mother had cut it down and built a house for his brother. Since then it had become his brother's good fortune in his political career.

"She had intended to turn me into a fool," he added. "Fortune favours fools. I would not have gone through those bad things if I had been able to understand her much earlier."

Chapter 3

Fengming Mountain was another world. In history, local people had hidden themselves there to protect themselves from being killed. The walls in the cave were smooth. Visitors might think that ancient people had wings. Single Braid, I could call him with the name of the book store operated by him, took photos of the caves. He had been there many times to explore and preserve intangible cultural heritage. Most of the coffin hanging caves were located in the Three Gorges, but the Bright Gorge was different from them. Single Braid had declared the Bright Gorge as heritage five times, but it had not become successful. He respected the ancient people.

"Single Braid keeps working hard for it," said Ruisong. "He is practicing his arm power and will enter the cave with ropes for details."

I had seen how hardworking he had been. One day the three of us went to Wuhua Town and visited the Qianfeng Ridge in the deep forests in which hundreds of aborigines had been living. Single Braid met a wizard and stammered, "He may be the last one in the county."

The Wizard Dancing had been invented by a man. It used to be court dance, but it was taken as superstition as time went by. Now it was protected. Single Braid gave him 200 yuan for a performance, the wizard declined it at the beginning because there was no ghost for him to expel. After a moment he chose to strike a gong. He hanged a picture of a female deity, put on a mask and a headband, grasped a chair and moved forwards or backwards after he sang a line. He sang from one to twelve. When he sang two, I heard: "There is a charming lady."

Ruisong and I yawned, but Single Braid was so busy taking photos that he fell into chicken manure. Suddenly a golden pheasant flew from the grass nearby Single Braid towards a valley.

Ruisong and I felt relieved when we saw Single Braid was safe and sound.

"Fengming Mountain is rich with golden pheasants," Ruisong explained. "There were many of them when I was studying in university. But now there are few. Today we are lucky to see one of them. It shows its charm to us because it is the essence of local culture."

Chapter 4

Fengming Village was located behind the forest, and it was also Ruisong's hometown. Dangerous roads ran across tea mountains. It was like my hometown. A brown Lacrosse was parked in front of a courtyard.

"This is my younger brother's house," said Ruisong. He continued to drive.

"I did not tell him that we came here," he added. "He has driven to the county in his Buick. I would not have brought you here if he were at home. He does not like men of letters."

"That's true," said Single Braid. "He has treated us perfunctorily."

"Village cadres wore well-buttoned shirts even in hot summer," said Ruisong. "Town cadres carried briefcases under their arms. County cadres had the slicked back hair style. Now things are different. My brother goes to the Great Hall of the People in branded clothes. Official rank can be distinguished only in the power system."

Ruisong talked about my hometown and felt pity for Single Braid. The county leaders wanted to create Banese culture and would build Dongxuan into a cultural landmark. Single Braid had written a detailed investigation report of nearly 50,000 words, including historical argumentation.

"It's a very good report," said Ruisong. "Explore the world with culture. Understanding is for prediction. The county leaders would invite experts from Chengdu, but later they threw the report into a trash can."

The Ba Valley, the capital city of the ancient Banese, was chosen by a natural gas company which would bring a lot of profits. Bafine, the name of liquor originally, was used for lucrative tobacco.

"Money talks," said Ruisong. "Culture works like an embellishment and it will be neglected when it becomes useless. But culture can save people. Human beings should be liberated from the necessity of presenting their spiritual wealth. Officials prefer power to culture, so they don't respect men of letters."

A seminar on the Banese was held in Hong Kong last year. County leaders gave an invitation to Single Braid but would not fund his trip if he took part in it. He participated in it at his own expense, but later the costs were reimbursed by a businessman who was one of his friends.

Meanwhile, Single Braid was sitting in the back row silently.

"You work in Chengdu, Chunming," Ruisong added. "But you came from Dongxuan. You are a famous poet and you should be received by county leaders and your talent should be appreciated. A man from Beijing has been funded to write an article of 400 words on Dongxuan with the payment of 300,000 yuan. But you would not do such a thing."

"It was said that only 150,000 yuan had been accepted by him," said Single Braid. "But it was 300,000 yuan on the signature sheet."

"I heard that writer had got only 100,000 yuan," said Ruisong. "200,000 yuan had been shared with others. That may not be true. Outsiders can be regarded as professionals. Clifford Geertz, the author of *The Interpretation of Cultures*, says that he will feel uncomfortable if he has no direct experience of social life. That means the direct experience is the foundation of culture. Whether experience is needed or can be had is the essential difference between social science and natural science. How can a man who has no local experience write an evocative article? Secretary Zhang values culture."

His car was parked in front of an old house, two tea forests away from his brother's house. His parents had passed away and it was a deserted place.

"My brother often has it cleaned," said Ruisong. "He thinks that an old house is like glory for a successful man."

He let us see the tree stump. It was like a table around which four or five people could stand. It had been felled, and the rotten stump resembled damp soil. Death and life formed a circle. Before we left, Ruisong kicked the stump hard.

Chapter 5

At 2 p.m. we were so hungry, but we could not find any restaurant. There were few villagers. At last we met a couple.

"Any food?"

"Only noodles. You may go to the farm land and dig vegetables by yourselves."

We plucked chameleon plants. The woman cooked noodles for us.

"To have liquor made from maize?" her husband asked.

The delicious beverage excited us. We persuaded Ruisong not to drink because he would have to drive.

"It's sweet, very good," he exclaimed, gulping down a mouthful of the liquor. "Ancient people were happy when they could have a wonderful meal with a beautiful female boss!"

She smiled and then put bowls of noodles in front of us. After we enjoyed the food, we gave some cigarettes to her husband. My cigarettes had been given by Guangwen, and Ruisong's by his brother, the same brand; Single Braid's was more than 20 yuan.

"Put it away," said Ruisong.

"I bought a better one for Chunming," said Single Braid. "Usually I smoke cigarettes of 10 yuan." He took another a packet of cigarettes, which was 6 yuan. The woman's husband laughed.

"Privilege is a good thing," said Ruisong, giving cigarettes to everybody. "An official is much better than a scholar."

"So your younger brother dislikes men of letters," argued Single Braid.

"Well, let's change the topic. I enjoy the privilege brought by my brother."

The woman served preserved meat. We talked and drank on and on. Ruisong told us about his days in the south humorously, even the couple laughed. At dusk, we would pay the bill, but the couple declined. Single Braid received a call and he was invited to dinner by his friend who had funded his trip to Hong Kong. Soon we reached the hotel. Some young women in cheongsam were showing tea art. The tea came from the countryside in which we stayed just a moment ago. The dinner began. There were more than ten guests. The females treated me coquettishly.

Urban culture is ambiguous and indirect, which cannot be sensed in rural areas. City dwellers can understand that after they go to the countryside.

Suddenly I received a call from Guangwen.

"Where are you?" he cried.

"I'm still in the county," I replied. I should not tell a lie in the presence of my friends. "And I'll go to Chengdu tomorrow."

"You must come back now! Our dad gets ill!"

Chapter 6

Yesterday our dad slobbered, but that was not illness. Guangwen seemed to get angry with me because I was having fun with my friends. He was a bossy village party secretary. I continued to drink and talked with the host whom I'd never met. After thirty minutes I received another call from Guangwen.

"Where are you now?" he cried.

I got nervous and soon I got a message from Chunshang: "Our dad was drooling and could not speak clearly." I should go to the township health centre as quickly as possible.

Two female poets said, "Let's sing at a Karaoke bar after dinner."

"Let's have roasted beef later," said the host. "The owner has run a barbecue restaurant for ten years in South Korea. He came back last month. I had the beef yesterday. It was so delicious that I would have much more. There are so many customers that I can't book a table for us at 6 o'clock tonight, but I've booked at 9 o'clock."

They continued to drink. The dinner was set up for me, but I had to tell them that I should leave. I had to give a forced smile when I was worried about my father. At last I stood up and said, "I'm so sorry, but I must be going now."

"For what?"

I showed the text message to them. They could understand me and saw me out. Guangwen did not have Yang Jin pick me up because he knew that I could sit in my friend's car. But they had got drunk, so the host had a driver send me. I packed and checked out of the hotel.

Chapter 7

My relatives were standing in the room while our father was lying on the bed, crying and holding Clever's hand. She seldom visited him unless she had dinner in Chunhong's house. He released his grasp when he saw me.

"I'm a dying man," he said.

"What did the doctor say?" I consoled him.

"If you came back drunk tomorrow," Guangwen said angrily, "you would know what the doctor had said!"

What would they do if I returned to Chengdu?

The doctor said that our father had a cerebral haemorrhage, and he should have a CT scan. The CT scanner was provided only in the hospital in the charge of the natural gas company. He had not had the examination because of money. Who would pay? Guangwen would not because he was just a son-in-law. Such an important thing should be decided by his own son.

"Let Yang Jin drive our dad to the hospital," I said to Guangwen.

Xiaolan and her parents avoided the subject, which was perceived by Guangwen.

"Who has driven you here?" asked Guangwen. "Will he send our dad to the hospital?"

"He has left."

It was not a good thing to have a private car send a patient. Guangwen called Yang Jin after a moment of hesitation.

Yang Jin arrived soon. Chunshang carrying our father walked downstairs and got into Yang Jin's car. Chunshu was just an on-looker, so Guangwen, Chunshang and I accompanied the elderly man. The CT scanner was damaged, and the doctor said that the patient must be sent to a general hospital in the county by ambulance. Our father was shaking all over. The First People's Hospital was the best one, but we had no friend there. Mr. Gou, the President of The Third People's Hospital, used to be one of the classmates of Guangwen and they had kept in touch. At last we went to The Third People's Hospital. Dr. Kang, a young attending physician, said that our father had a cerebral haemorrhage and should have conservative treatment although it was not serious.

I did not have too much money, so I borrowed 5,000 yuan from Guangwen. Our father was hospitalized after I paid 4,000 yuan. All the wards had been occupied by patients, so he had a bed in the corridor in the third floor. After the medical equipment was provided, Guangwen and Yang Jin left, Chunshang and I stayed.

Chapter 8

00033428 was our father's admission number. I thought those figures could bring good luck to him. However, he fell into a coma and his whole body convulsed violently. Chunshang and I tried to press his body.

"Doctor!" Chunshang shouted.

A slim female nurse with an ID badge written Cheng Fangbing flapped our father on the back; after a while his trembling eased. She put a long grey hose into his throat for aspiration of sputum. After a moment he became quiet.

And then she pulled back the quilt, took off his pants quickly, put a medical hose into his private parts, and then hanged a urine drainage bag on a shelf.

"There is a button," she said to Chunshang and me. "Turn it on every few hours. He will have urinary incontinence if it is on all the time. After the bag is full of urine, open the bag and pour it into the bedpan and then into the toilet. And you'll need to buy adult diapers and towels."

I went downstairs to buy those things.

"I can buy them," said Chunshang.

I walked downstairs directly. It was the first time for me to see our father's private parts: loose skin and grey pubic hair.

Ms. Cheng was still waiting for us after I returned. She opened a diaper and put it under our father's buttocks. She looked at us, seeming to let us learn it. She went to another hospital bed. Caregivers had to sit on the ground because there was no bench in the corridor. Guangwen knew the President, so two stools were prepared for Chunshang and me. We were soaked with sweat all over.

Before I wiped myself with a tissue, Chunshang cried, "Our dad is shaking again!"

Those words and the procedure were repeated eight times.

Chapter 9

I felt exhausted after our father became quiet.

"You'll stay here," I said to Chunshang. "I'll have a cigarette."

When I was smoking in a corner between the second floor and the third floor, I saw a large display screen with various shocking names of surgery. I looked away and went downstairs.

In a hall a young man was swearing on his phone at his relatives: his grandpa needed a blood transfusion, but the hospital was in short supply of blood and asked the patient to transfer to another hospital. The young man's relatives did not sign the document lest they should pay more money. He wailed.

I looked at the street to make myself less sorrowful. There were many stores selling products to patients and their relatives. I had bought the diapers and towels from one of them. Overloaded trucks were still going at night, but I did not think they were noises. The sound faded away soon and the street became silent. Several hours ago I was drinking and talking with my friends, but now I had three cigarettes. After a long while I returned to the hospital.

The corridor was full of beds. An elderly woman sat up and lay down frequently.

"Are you hungry?" one of the patients asked her.

"Yes."

Her husband had died and her son had been working in another province. Her daughter-in-law would not send any meal to her unless she was paid. As a result, she often felt hungry. Sometimes the patients shared their food with her. Tonight she could not have sufficient food again.

"I just want to cough," she added.

She coughed as many patients did.

The sound of high heels could be heard. A woman with chestnut hair holding a large bunch of flowers came to the third floor and looked for the patient she would meet, but she could not find him or her. She made several phone calls but could not get a good answer. She sat in the car which she had rented in the downtown area and got here. It was waiting for her outside, and she left.

It was 3 a.m. Now someone yelled: "Don't move! You haven't worn your trousers!"

He was the young man whom I met a moment ago in the hall. His grandpa had gastric perforation, and blood poured from his mouth and anus. He was so hungry that he wanted to have some food, but the doctor asked him to keep an empty stomach.

"Keep still!" his grandson shouted again. The stench made him run away as soon as he pulled back the quilt.

Our father had convulsions again. Ms. Cheng repeated her measure. The elderly woman, who often felt hungry, with a limp walked towards Chunshang and me.

"Your father may die soon," she whispered.

He was breathing with difficulty, eyes closed and mouth opened.

"Dad!" cried Chunshang. He got no reply.

"The doctor says that he can be saved," said Chunshang, touching our father's face.

"That's what doctors always say," she added. "If he dies here and you have friends in this hospital, his body will not be cremated, and you can bring an intact corpse to his hometown. But his body should not be put in the central room anyway!"

After a man dies, his soul will return home and take a last look at it, and then he will be reincarnated. If he dies in a hospital or other place, his soul can't find its way back home; it will have to spend so much time searching for it that it will be late for its reincarnation, and at last it will become a ghost. Therefore, the body of the man who has died somewhere else should be placed in the open air rather than be put under the eaves so that its soul can find it. That's the way how people living around the Qingxi River understand death and believe in it. However, Chunshang and I disliked the elderly woman's words.

A thin, middle-aged man carrying a woman's bag watched our father. He shook his head and then went downstairs.

"That man is a patient, too," the elderly woman whispered, looking at his shadow. "He has got pancreatic cancer. When he feels better, he goes everywhere to pretend that he is still healthy. But he looks deathly pale and will die soon."

She returned to her bed and moaned.

Chapter 10

Chunshang watched the wall blankly and then bit his nails.

"Are you thirsty?" he asked me.

"Yes." I gave him some money and let him buy bottles of water.

It was muggy, but he was wearing a well-buttoned shirt to cover up scars in his arms. He was just a kid when our mother passed away in January more than forty years ago. He fell into a basin of boiling water, and we pulled him out of the basin at once. His arms were scalded and since then scars had been left. He had never worked in another province and had been unwilling to meet strangers. What's more, he would never unbutton his shirt even though he was soaked with sweat. He was always poor and had no money to buy some water. He must be thirsty, too.

He came back and gave me a bottle of water and the change. His bottle had been emptied.

"You could have bought more," I said to him.

"I've had enough," he said, looking at our father. "He is better now."

With his mouth opened and eyes closed, he was still in a coma although he could breathe calmly.

After a moment I had to go to the toilet. On the wall I saw some words:

"Sell guns. No bargaining."

"I love you, Leena!!!"

The words seemed to have been written by the same man. Love and guns might be regarded as the same thing. I guessed that Leena had stopped loving him. The three exclamation points were shocking.

Doctors and nurses were rushing into an ICU. The patient was having convulsions and his heart rate was 130. Our father's was 147 when his body was shaking. I saw the patient's grandson just now. He could not suffer anymore. His grandson was making a phone call. More people came. A man was walking with a limp towards the ICU. The patient died and his oxygen hose was removed. His daughter was crying. After a moment they carried the corpse wrapped in a purple blanket from head to foot.

The deceased man's children and grandchildren were living in the county. One of their relatives and some leader in the hospital were fellow-villagers, so the corpse would not be cremated. It would be buried in his hometown. What the elderly woman had said turned out to be true. But nobody knew whether his soul could return.

Chapter 11

Morning came.

"You may go to have breakfast, Chunshang," I said.

"Let's go together," he said.

I knew he would feel lonely. And me, too.

Ms. Cheng came and made aspiration of sputum for our father. He was breathing with difficulty with his eyes closed. She lifted the quilt and asked Chunshang to wet a towel. Later she used it to wipe our father's private parts and changed his diaper. She tucked him in and left. After a few minutes she walked out of the office wearing fashionable clothes and carrying a blue handbag.

She was a charming woman.

"Doctors will soon have a ward-round," she said. "Stay here."

"Have you had your meal?" a man in his sixties asked her.

She fudged the question.

Chunshang and I stayed in the ward. The man asked doctors the same question, but he was ignored. Later I knew that man had been hospitalized for a long time and his medical bills could be reimbursed by government agencies. He often walked around and greeted doctors and nurses. At 6 p.m. he would ask if they could get off work.

Nurses pushed our father's bed into an ICU in which a patient died several hours ago. It was clean and tidy with a smell of disinfectant.

I was asked to pay the bill every day. It was a long list. Last night 78 items were consumed, totally 3662.54 yuan. I told my wife on the phone that I would need more money for our father's medical treatment. And then I called my boss to extend leave.

Chapter 12

At 9 a.m. Chunshan and Chunshu came. Our father was still sleeping, looking pale. Chunshan asked me about the situation while Chunshu was watching the elderly man.

"He can't be saved," Chunshan sighed.

"I couldn't agree more," said Chunshu.

Dr. Yu, the chief physician, stood in front of our father's bed, followed by interns.

"Give me the CT scan picture," said Dr. Yu.

Chunshang gave it to him at once.

"He has a cerebral haemorrhage," said Dr. Yu. "Very serious."

But yesterday Dr. Kang said that our father could get better soon. This morning he told us that hypertension, arrhythmia, coma and trembling were normal reactions. Right now he kept silent when Dr. Yu was here. Dr. Yu led his interns to other beds.

"He can't survive," said Chunshan. He soon told this to our relatives on the phone. They had been waiting for the news since Guangwen told them yesterday.

Tears were falling down from our father's cheeks although his eyes were still closed. Chunshang wiped away the elderly man's tears with his left hand, and much more of his own with right hand. I talked to Chunshu so that he could not see the crying Chunshang. Chunshu had been engaged in funeral business for so many years that he knew death would come to everybody sooner or later. He might look down upon Chunshang.

Guangwen and Yang Jin came. They spent last night in a hotel.

"Zhang asked me to see the new house," said Guangwen, "so I could not come here earlier."

Guangwen knew that his father-in-law was in a dire situation through my two elder brothers.

"Mr. Gou wanted to examine our dad," said Guangwen. "But he was given notification of attending a meeting in the municipal health bureau. He told me that our dad would be well treated."

We could understand that our father's intact corpse could be carried to his hometown.

"Have you had breakfast?" asked Guangwen.

"No."

"Let's go together."

Chunshang would stay with our father.

"We may bring some food to Chunshang," I said.

The restaurants were full of customers, including patients: bandaged up, in plaster, walking alone or with a stick or being supported. It was like in a battlefield. Everybody will go to the battlefield sooner or later, and one's enemies are illness, old age, and the combination of the two. He may have a win against illness, but old age will make everybody a loser. Diseases and senility, which are beyond all human beings and won't treat the latter as their enemies, are more of dirtiness, a necessary condition before death.

Chapter 13

Yang Jin and I had congee and steamed stuffed buns, others had some wolfberry wine. We brought steamed stuffed buns and a box of milk to Chunshang. Yang Jin returned to his car, Guangwen and we went upstairs.

Our father, who seemed to have gone through a tough fight, was sleeping.

"He hasn't eaten anything since last night," said Chunshang.

"He can have nutrients in his body," said Guangwen, looking at the infusion bottles. "But what should we do next?"

"He can't survive," Chunshan and Chunshu said.

They wanted our father to be sent home right now, but he would die soon if that happened.

Chunshang and I were like in the battlefield with our father last night, but my two elder brothers were not the witnesses. I knew that they were worried about money.

"I'll pay the medical bills," I said. I would regret, but I did it.

Chunshan looked embarrassed but Chunshu was in a sulk.

"You should decide this," said Guangwen. "And you should prepare for the funeral. Has our dad's coffin been painted?"

"No," said Chunshan.

"A dead body should not be placed in the central room. We'd better send our dad home on his deathbed. What's more, the transportation expense of a corpse is much higher than that of a patient. We can't use Yang Jin's car to carry a corpse and we'll have to rent another car."

Guangwen glanced at Chunshu. When the elderly man was in a coma, Chunshu and his daughter did not say anything. Things would become complicated if our father died in Guibing's car.

"And we should find a suitable place for our dad's body," Guangwen added.

The elderly man should be buried in Yanerpo, the place of our ancestral graves. But Chunshang's house in Yanerpo was too dilapidated to be used as a mourning hall.

Chunshan cleared his throat and looked at Chunshu, but the latter avoided his eye contact.

"You have a spare house," said Chunshan.

"It has been used to store all kinds of things," Chunshu retorted.

Chunshan cleared his throat again and the brothers did not speak. Shadows, voices and smells were mixed outside.

"You force me to use my house," Chunshu said crossly after a moment of silence. "And I'll have to do it."

Our father used to threaten us that he would live in a cave, or live independently if not in a cave. At that time I suggested that Chunshu should let the elderly man live in his spare house, he did not agree with me until I gave him 2,000 yuan each year as the rent. But that made Chunshan, Chunshang and our father unhappy.

"Your mom had left an old house before she said goodbye to us," our father said to me one day. "Later two houses were built for your two elder brothers. Chunshu's house was built by himself after he got married. I am your father and I think it is absurd that I should pay the rent to live in one of my sons' house."

He changed his mind. That was not for Chunshang's sake, but he would feel sad if he lived in that house.

Would our father feel better if he overheard our talk? Chunshu would use his spare house as his mourning hall free of charge, was that an honour for our father?

Chunshan and Chunshu would return soon: the former would buy black paint and firecrackers, and the latter would prepare for the mourning hall.

Dr. Kang came and whispered, "Your dad can recover." And then he left.

"Who is he?" asked Chunshu.

"He is the attending doctor of our dad," replied Chunshang.

"He is a quack!" cried Chunshu.

"The chief physician's conclusion is believable," said Guangwen.

They would act as planned.

The coffin of our father was bought more than ten years ago. When cedarwood was sold, Chunshan called me that we could buy a cheap coffin lest we should be fleeced in case of an urgent need. In fact he wanted me to pay the money. Uncle Chenggui made a coffin out of the cedarwood, but since then it had not been painted. Other families usually painted caskets each year as a symbol of extending life. The coffin had been stored in a barn and had been protected from animals' excreta. It was often windy, but the coffin had been kept dry for eight years. It was placed in the bedroom in which our father had slept after he lived with Chunshang in Guaizaoping.

"Is your elder sister getting better?" Chunshang asked his wife on the phone.

"She can hold on," she replied. "You should go back to Yanerpo at once and ask Magpie to paint the coffin."

Magpie was a lacquerer in Yanerpo.

"Where is mom?" she suddenly shouted. "Why is dad so angry?"

Chunshan and Chunshu wanted to sit in Yang Jin's car, but Guangwen said that he would have to deal with other problems and then went downstairs. They talked about the transportation: a cheap but slow motorboat with long waiting hours, or a speedboat faster and costlier than a car. They decided to go by car.

Chapter 14

Chunhong came. She did not expect that our father should get seriously ill. Yesterday the physician in the health centre said that he might have a cerebral haemorrhage, but his family members thought that he could recover soon.

"Open your eyes if you love your children, dad," Chunhong said anxiously. But he did not.

"Are you going to do just like your wife did?" she asked.

Memories came into her mind. Our father had been living a hard life since our mother passed away. He frequently suffered from hunger so that he could leave more food for his children. He wailed after he sent his youngest daughter to another family. He implored others to lend him some money so that he could support my schooling, and he did everything he could to repay. He carried countless trees at midnight to earn more money so as to build houses for his two sons and to prepare dowries for his two daughters. Our father was the mainstay of our family.

"I'll belch after I sit a car in the morning," said Chunhong, trying to cover up her sadness.

"Have you had breakfast?" Chunshang asked her.

She did not reply. Instead, from a bag she took insulated barrels containing chicken soup and fish soup.

"Have a taste of fish soup, dad," she said, holding a spoon. "This is your favourite."

She asked Chunshang to lift our father's pillow and then she put a towel under his chin.

"Open your mouth, dad," she said.

The elderly man did not do what she said, so she put the spoon into his mouth. The towel became wet. We did not know how much soup could enter our father's stomach. She washed the towel and the spoon.

"You should live 100 years and keep your word," she added.

She put the spoon on the barrel and the towel on the chair, and then rubbed her eyes.

"I should not have held a birthday party for our dad in my house," she complained. "He will get ill whenever he goes there. Luckily he returned the day before yesterday, otherwise I did not know what to do."

"If our dad stayed with me and got ill," Chunshang argued, "would I be blamed?"

"I blame myself," said Chunhong. "Perhaps the geomantic omens (feng shui) of my house are not good."

"Where should our dad celebrate his birthday?" Chunshang retorted. "You won't go to my house anyway. If he had got ill because he had had his birthday party in my home, you would have pinned it on me!"

"You could have had a good life in Yanerpo," she continued, glowering at him, "but you've chosen to live with your mother-in-law in Guaizaoping. People will gossip that you've hogged her house and farm land, and she must think so. She won't be grateful to you! If you look after her, what will Yuling's elder brother think about you? You are her son-in-law, not her own son! He has borrowed your money but has not repaid. Don't you know why? He thinks that you have possessed his house!"

Chunhong mentioned the thing which occurred many years ago. At that time Chunshang had less than 10,000 yuan earned in Wanyuan and borrowed 30,000 yuan from Chunhong and me to buy a house. We would give him more if he chose one. However, he built a house in Guaizaoping. It was sold to him at a cheap price by a villager who would move to another place. He neither paid much nor repaid the money to me and Chunhong. To our surprise, he lent the money to Du Kun, the younger brother of Yumei and also the elder brother of Yuling. Du Kun had several children and worked in another province with his wife, but he refused to repay with various excuses.

Chunshang had urged him but got a refusal on the phone: "I could pay back if I were a rich boss!"

Even now Chunshang had not reclaimed the money from Du Kun.

Chapter 15

Chunshang stifled his words although we knew what he would say. When he was living in Yanerpo, he was often criticized by Chunshan and Chunshu; what was more, they said that Yuling would seduce other men. One day she quarrelled with Tang Qun, the wife of Wang Qingguang. Zhuqing used to be on bad terms with Tang Qun, but as soon as she saw the confrontation between the two women, she immediately prepared corn cakes and handed five of them to Tang Qun. In addition, they said that Yuling had treated our father badly. Yuling would rather pour the leftovers of sauted meat into a pigwash barrel than let our father have it. Zhuqing told that to Mrs. Hou, and the latter told that to others, and finally those words reached the elderly man's ears. He was highly suggestible that he believed that.

Chunshang had told that to Chunhong and me many times. We doubted that. Chunhong did not believe when Chunshang put in a good word for his wife.

"Parents do not expect that children become rich and powerful after they grow up," said Chunhong. "They need filial ones. But Yuling treats our dad badly."

In one Spring Festival after our father lived with Chunshang in Guaizaoping, my sisters were unwilling to visit them because they disliked Chunshang's mother-in-law who often complained that she had been a victim of poverty and derision. At that time everybody was living a hard life.

"She regards herself as a martyr," said Chunying. "But she is one of the elders. If we don't send her some food when we visit our dad, we will be talked about by others. In fact we don't want to buy any food for her. It's not worthwhile."

At last they decided to return to Yanerpo.

During our father's stay in Guaizaoping, my sisters felt that they did not take good care of our father when they visited our mother's graveyard.

"I don't believe that Chunshang's father-in-law could sway him before he breathed his last breath," said Chunshu. "Yuling must have persuaded him to look after his mother-in-law."

Chunhong considered that Yuling must have a secret lover so that she would divorce Chunshang. In Chunhong's opinion, a woman should love her husband heart and soul; if she mentioned divorce, she must have had an affair with another man.

Chunhong did not argue anymore when she saw Chunshang rubbing his face silently. She knew that Yuling still lived with her husband. The latter often scolded Chunshang and even quarrelled with our father, but she had never harbored resentment towards her husband for taking good care of her father-in-law.

"It's unbearable that our dad should get seriously ill suddenly," she said, tidying Chunshang's shirt.

I got nervous at once. Last night Dr. Kang asked me about our father's condition. I told him that he had slobbered.

"If a man drools when he is sleeping," Dr. Kang explained, "that means his spleen is not in a good state. If he drools when he is awake, that is the forewarning of a cerebral haemorrhage."

"His hand was shaking when he was holding a liquor cup," I added.

"Well, that's the forewarning indeed."

I did not tell that to Chunshang because he was in a pharmacy at that time. Now I did not tell that to Chunhong either.

Our father had seven children. Only I had been working in a state-owned institution, and I had an obligation to him. He was getting old and I should have arranged for him to undergo a medical check-up. The township health centre was not provided with advanced equipment, and I should have adhered to the doctor's advice and allowed him to take medication for high blood pressure. But I did not think that such a thin man as our father should have hypertension.

Chapter 16

After the lacquer and firecrackers were ready, the coffin was painted and then was moved into Chunshu's spare house. Our father woke up! Chunshang worried that the soup brought by Chunhong might go bad, so he rushed downstairs to buy fresh food for him.

Li Zhi visited his grandpa when I was staying with our father in the ward. He was fatter and happier. He was wearing a shirt and the scars could not be seen in his arms: his body and heart could recover as quickly as possible. After he talked with his grandpa delightedly, he left hastily because he was eager to see his buddies whom he had not met for a long time. Chunhong was worried about him, so she went back yesterday. What's more, our father was lying on the bed with the naked lower part of his body; when a urethral catheter was checked or a diaper needed to be changed, Chunhong, a daughter of his, should avoid those things.

"Dad," I whispered, squatting.

I did not know what to say. I had seldom met him since I went to university. But I was feeling that I had not seen him for ages. It seemed that I had been a fatherless child but I suddenly had a father now. I was sad but soon Chunshang came back. He bought dishes and congee with meat.

"I met Dr. Kang just now," he said. "He told me to feed our dad the food."

And then he did it with a spoon and the elderly man enjoyed the meal. Meanwhile, I called Chunshan.

"I don't think our dad can get better," said Chunshu.

I hung up the phone. The elderly man was getting worse and worse.

It was the first time for our father to be hospitalized. After he broke a leg, he was sent to the township health centre and had his legs x-rayed. The doctor suggested that he should avoid using biomedical titanium alloy lest it should block blood circulation in the bones, and that he should be hospitalized for conservative treatment. His children decided to send him home because they considered it was not a fatal disease. They had a barefoot doctor treat him, and gradually he got better although he had to walk with a limp.

Dr. Yu came for a ward-round and was surprised to see that our father was eating.

"His physical signs are good," he said, looking at the electrocardioscanner. "And he may make a miracle."

Dr. Kang glanced at me and tried to cover up his complacency in front of Dr. Yu. After they left, I called Chunshan and told what Dr. Yu had said to him.

However, everything was in a mess in our hometown now.

After Zhuqing returned to Yanerpo and heard that our father was getting better, she saw the house had been emptied and then hurled abuse at her husband. He could not endure it anymore, so he lifted a knife and would kill her. She ran crazily and was protected by Mrs. Hou.

"You have read a lot of books, Chunshu," cried Mrs. Hou, "and you know that it is a crime to kill a person. Your dad is still lying in a hospital bed!"

Chunshu went into the room crossly. Zhuqing wailed in Mrs. Hou's arms and she was consoled by the latter. Mrs. Hou wept, too, when she talked about our mother.

"I don't know why Mrs. Hou had missed our mother so much," said Chunshan.

She was bouncy when our mother was alive. After she passed away, Mrs. Hou desperately needed punchbags and pried into others' affairs much more. We always felt that she resembled a shadow of our mother's and we got along with her. She was getting old and was not as nosy as she used to be, otherwise she could have known the affair between Chunshu and Zhu Zhanhui, and the gossip would have reached Xu Xing's ears. The gossip perhaps had run amok even though Mrs. Hou was less inquisitive. In spite of that, Xu Xing had to accept the reality.

Zhuqing had no sense of security and had borrowed a lot of money. She would have committed suicide if she had known that her husband had been loving another woman and had given her eggs, money and beautiful clothes.

Chapter 17

Relatives rushed here for our father's funeral but they were told that he was getting better, so they had to refund their bus tickets at the cost of service charge. Guangwen often visited our father. He talked with him for a while, smoked with me, and then left.

My friends in the county called me, but I did not tell the details to them. One day when I was having breakfast nearby the hospital, Ruisong's wife saw me. I had met her once, but I did not greet her. Later she told this to her husband, and he could judge that my father was staying in The Third People's Hospital. He came to see me without a phone call.

When he was looking for the ward, he reminded me of the woman who could not find the patient she wanted to see that night. I wondered the relation between her and the patient. Had the patient died? What was she thinking about on her way back home? How would she dispose the flowers?

I tried to hide myself in a balcony with a curtain in the ICU lest other friends should know this. I would rather be left alone.

In fact I was lonely. I felt that I had been attacked internally. Was it our father's anguish? It was more of the feeling that had been forced upon me by agony. Illness and old age were the reason for distress while the source was life. Was life dirty? I could not tell, so I did not want to be disturbed. What's more, I stank all over.

"Is Chunming here?" Ruisong asked Chunshang.

"Yes."

So I had to meet the guest.

"Both of you look alike," said Ruisong.

The gene made him recognise me. It was the sadness which human beings could not escape. Ruisong could understand me and called more friends to see me. I was very glad when I was chatting with them, just like in a banquet.

Mrs. Hou was the loneliest person in Yanerpo and she had been with loneliness since girlhood. Her mother's home was located in Dahuozhai in Laojun Mountain, even more remote than Yanerpo. Mount Lordhou was independent but Laojun Mountain was overlapped and zigzag. Dahuozhai was a poor, bleak place in which maize was the only product. The local villagers could not afford a millstone, so they always stewed the maize. They would suffer from hunger if there was no harvest. Many people had lost their lives in the slippery, dangerous roads. In addition, their bodies were full of moss. Local people including girls smoked sun-cured tobacco leaves to remove dampness from their bodies. After Mrs. Hou quit smoking those leaves for one year, she got married with a man in Yanerpo, and her teeth gradually turned yellow from black. Remoteness and poverty had always been with them. Mrs. Hou could have rice but she was not satisfied. She had been feeling empty even when our mother was alive. She had much more loneliness than I did.

Chapter 18

Chunshan and Chunshu saw me and Guangwen when they came to hospital again at noon. Yang Jin drove Guangwen here and they visited our father.

"I'll have to deal with something urgent," said Guangwen.

Chunshan asked them to wait for him because he wanted to sit in their car.

"I must go now!" cried Guangwen.

"How is our dad?" asked Chunshan.

"You can see him now," Guangwen replied impatiently. He sat in the car and it started.

When Chunshan, Chunshu and I went upstairs, Chunshu said, "Guangwen is not busy. He stopped us from hitching a lift."

"Chunming!" Chunshang yelled, rushing towards me. "Our dad is delirious!"

"You should ask the doctor, not me!" I said.

"He is not shaking."

"I'll live 100 years old!" our father shouted.

"Yes, you can," I said calmly.

"Qinglian and Zhaohui would have poured me a glass of water if they were here." He used to be taken good care of by his two grandchildren.

"Are you thirsty?" I asked.

"The water system in Liangjingwan is broken! Repair it now!"

We did not know that at all.

He was looking in the distance. The light in his eyes was fragile.

Chunshang soon brought Ms. Cheng here.

"Mr. Xu!" she exclaimed, looking at the monitor. Her voice was like magic which could make our father come to his senses. The light in his eyes was gathering.

"Speak to him as much as you can when he is awake," she said, and then she left.

"Who I am, dad?" Chunshan asked.

"You are Chunshan," our father answered in an annoyed tone of voice. "You had your 19th birthday yesterday."

"Do you know how old my siblings are?"

"Chunshu is 17, Chunhong is 12, Chunhua is 8, Chunming is 5, Chunshang is 2, and Chunying is less than 3 months."

He replied quickly and correctly. That was the age of us when our mother passed away. His memories stopped when his wife said goodbye to the world. He wished that we would always be kids and have a mother. But her death made him too distressful to move on. Chunhong often told him that our mother rather than he should survive. Even villagers talked that such a good-for-nothing as Xu Chengxiang should die, and he felt the same way.

Chunshan did not know what to say, and we fell into silence. Chunshang could see Chunshu in a sulk, so the former opened the two insulated barrels: one was empty and the other was left with congee. He would let Chunshu know that I did not lie to them on the phone. He became silent. Silence and sleep were like twins of death.

"I won't forgive Xu Jinyang!" our father shouted again with difficulty.

Chunshan glanced at Chunshu and at me.

Chapter 19

The foundations of Zhanhui's house used to be owned by Xu Jinyang. That happened more than half a century ago. Jinyang had been hated by everybody. He became a ringleader of bandits carrying bayonets and guns after he came back from another province. One day he cleaved an eight-month-old girl named Choumei with his long knife. The upper part of her body was impaled on bamboo and the blood pouring from her mouth overturned a bamboo caterpillar. The lower part was thrown away. He tested his sword with the girl and then wiped his weapon with a velvet kerchief. After many years he was executed by shooting and his offspring left Yanerpo.

Chunshan once told me that Xu Jinyang had raped our grandmother, and our grandfather disappeared after half a month. People said that he had been killed by Xu Jinyang, or he had joined the Red Army which had entered Daba Mountain. Our grandfather used to carry sacks of salt to Southern Shaanxi, and he came to know the Red Army when he passed by Wanyuan. He did not return after twenty days and might never return. Our grandmother had a bath in folium artemisiae argyi water, wore clean clothes, burned some paper, and then hanged herself. She was 22 years old. One of her two sons was 5 years old and the other 3. Our grandfathers and grandmothers died when they were young. Our father and his younger brother had no relatives; consequently the brother soon starved to death while our father relied on fruits and meals given by other families, as well as mountain spring water to survive.

Our father was an orphan. He had never talked about his parents because he was too young when the tragedy happened or he felt ashamed. Now he mentioned Xu Jinyang. Chunshu had known about it. Mrs. Hou implied it when she quarrelled with our mother. What if our grandfather joined the Red Army and became a high official?

Several years before our mother passed away, an old man returned to Golden Town. He had a lot of medals for his bravery in battlefields. He had had a similar past as our grandfather's. He became a high official after the People's Republic of China was established. He had a new name, a new wife and several children. He did not return to his hometown until he got very old. When he met his ex, the two people were too senile to recognise each other. Her hands were not soft anymore. Her children and grandchildren were beside themselves with excitement and reported the big news to the township government and then to the county. Ran Congjing, from Ranjiawan Village and also a distant relative of that old man's, said that the latter stayed in the village for ten days and then went back to the city far away. Since then Ran Congjing's family became better-off: they could have meat every half month, be received by township and county leaders, and be provided with coupons for food and daily necessities. The villagers wished that they could have such a relative, too.

Mrs. Hou had fudged the secret past of our grandmother. Chunshan, Chunshu and Chunhong could understand a bit at that time. Mrs. Hou told the details to us after our mother died. I would not have known that if I had not been told by Chunshan. He wanted me to get more about it through my connections whether our grandfather had become a high official. He had never returned and his children and grandchildren would not come back to reconnect with their poor relatives.

Chapter 20

"Dr. Yu's words may not be true," Chunshan whispered, glancing at Chunshu and me.

"Believe it or not!" cried Chunshu.

"Remove the oxygen hose from our dad's nose if you dare," Chunshang said gravely. He knew the past between Xu Jinyang and our grandmother and also knew the former's brutal deeds. The man would be as cruel as Xu Jinyang if he pulled the hose away.

Ms. Cheng came and made aspiration of sputum for our father. Later he felt better, looked at the ceiling, and then fell asleep.

"Chunming needs a good sleep," Chunshang said to Chunshan. "He should go to Chunhong's house, have a shower, and take a good rest. Will you and Chunshu stay with our dad for one night?"

"No," said Chunshu. "Medicine can't cure a dying man. He is counting his minutes. A funeral should be prepared. The room in which the coffin is placed now is riddled with rat holes. I can't repair the room within one month if I have to finish it all by myself."

Chunshang looked sad. The night before last he asked me a question: "Did the emergence of local customs stem from poverty?"

"Which one?"

"If a man dies in another place rather than in his own home, his corpse should not be put in the central room. That means if a patient gets seriously ill, he should be carried home and wait for death. Some patient can be lucky enough to survive. Since our mom got ill because of a bad cold, she had been lying on the bed for several months, and at last she died."

I did not know how to reply. The customs had been existing and the reason was more than money. People did not think that life was precious. Someone who was working in the morning committed suicide in the afternoon by having pesticides, hanging himself, or jumping into a river. The reasons talked about by others included physical pain or bickering. He had been toiling throughout his life and his children were living in other places. He felt so empty that he would rather choose death.

However, our father was different from those men because he was eager for a better life. Chunshang asked me that question lest I should send our father home rather than let him continue to be treated.

Chunshu wanted to go and Chunshan hesitated.

"You may return and Chunming may go to Chunhong's house," said Chunshang.

I needed a shower and asked him, "Can you look after our dad all by yourself?"

"Yes, I can."

"We may stay with him for a little longer," said Chunshan. He sat down beside our father and talked with him, but the latter was still sleeping.

Chunshan poured the urine in the bag into the toilet, and then we went downstairs to have a meal.

After we finished the meal, I received a call outside. Chunshu thought that I would go, so he cried, "You should pay the bill now!"

I went to a bank to withdraw money which had been transferred to my account by my wife. And then I went back to the restaurant and paid the bill. Later we returned to the hospital. These days I had meals and then brought some food to Chunshang who had been staying with our father. He was tired and would need a good rest, too. In the ward I gave some money to Chunshang, and then I left with Chunshan and Chunshu.

Chapter 21

We returned to the town by car. Chunshan and Chunshu went to Yanerpo while I went to Chunhong's house. I did not speak to her. After I took a shower, I could feel that an ordinary life could be so good.

Her house was large and clean. Her husband and children were not at home. Qingmei would pick up Dou. Chunhong said that Li Zhi went fishing again.

Longyan Pond was the largest reservoir in Laojun Mountain. A large fish was jumping at dusk – it was cloudy and was going to rain. Li Zhi gave some money he'd had in Fuzhou to one of his buddies to buy tents, cooked meat, cakes, and a crate of beer. He ran back home and got fishhooks and would be determined to have the fish. Because it was a reservoir, he would neither use explosives nor poisons lest villages or water should be damaged or be polluted. Electric shock might not be useful for a large fish. In spite of that, he could enjoy fishing.

His mother often scolded him, but he retorted, "Fishing is a kind of sports and there are fishing competitions. If I'm the final winner, I'll give you a lot of money."

Chunhong laughed when she told me about it. Her son remained unchanged, which might be a good thing.

I had to walk through a long, bleak street before I reached the bus station today. There were middle-aged, scantily-clad prostitutes watching passengers, and they were very interested in old men: priced at 20 or 30 or even 5 yuan each time. Those old men would enjoy a wonderful moment with those women; after they went home, they told their wives or children that the vegetables today were not cheap. I wondered if those women had husbands or children. Couldn't they do a decent job? They might have no other choice and would have to suffer from poverty anyway.

I used to feel pity for them. But today my pity was gone. A life without disease or agony might be regarded as a good one. Prostitution had been existing since ancient times and it was a good job for some women.

Chunhong asked me about our father's condition, I repeated the words I'd said on the phone. I did not want to hear her complaint anymore. I gave her 5,000 yuan which I borrowed from her husband when our father was hospitalized.

"Give it to you or your husband?" I asked.

"Either," she replied. "You have several brothers and you should not pay the bill alone. Even your wife will grumble."

Li Jing was my wife. Her hometown was in Nanchong city and she had been teaching Chinese in a middle school in Chengdu since she graduated from university. She got along with her colleagues. Some female married ones older than her often told her not to marry a countryman because he would become a leech upon her to support his poor parents and relatives. One of the women was a victim and said that she should have married a man who came from a city although he might not be rich.

That was not a good subject. I chatted with Guangwen, he said that he would have to deal with a new problem in the village. I guessed that the troublemaker might be Huigoer and Guangwen would handle it effectively.

"Someone died in Lijiayan," Chunhong sighed. She called her husband half an hour ago. Li Qiantao, instead of Guangwen who was either too busy to answer it or was inconvenient, told her the details on the phone.

Chapter 22

It occurred this morning. Today was a market day in Huilong Town. Shi Shuyu, the wife of Li Baoshun, had a faster heartbeat before she sat in a boat, and worried that something bad would happen. Ten years ago she was in the same situation and a boat capsized. Five people died, three of them were villagers in Lijiayan and their corpses had been gone. Luckily, she was not in the boat. Now she was too scared to go. After she returned home, she heard her husband wailing and she was in panic. Her children had been working in other provinces, only she and her husband were living at home. She ran so quickly that she stumbled and almost fell nearby a dug-pit latrine.

She shouted and the door was not opened until a moment had passed. He did not tell her what had happened. There was no burglary, but she saw a naked woman on the bed. That woman was Yan Min whose house was close to Shi Shuyu's. Li Baoshun told his wife the truth. After she left this morning, Yan Min came and undressed herself. Meanwhile, he went to wash his body with a bucket of water. After he returned, he found that Yan Min was dead. His wife did not believe that he had cheated on her. Now she was speechless with shock. The room was silent. They had a dog named Dark. After spring came, it went outside in the early morning to search for a partner, but it could not find anyone. Today it failed again and came home downcast. The silence was not broken until Dark barked at noon. Li Cai, the husband of Yan Min, came.

Li Cai had two daughters studying in the town and he rented a house and let his mother-in-law live there to look after them. He went to the market today. This morning he came across Shi Shuyu. He sold potatoes at a good price and then returned home hastily. He had known the affair between his wife and Li Baoshun, and he would catch adultery in the act. He did not find his wife in the field, so he went to Li Baoshun's house.

Li Cai saw Li Baoshun sitting at the doorway. "What has happened?" he asked, giving a cigarette to Li Baoshun.

"You should look at the woman in the room," said Shi Shuyu. "I could recognize her when she was alive. But now she is dead."

Chapter 23

When Guangwen got there, the corpse wrapped in a blanket was placed in the central room of Li Baoshun's house. There must have been a brawl. Dark had been hacked to death. Meanwhile, Li Cai and the relatives of Yan Min were holding weapons. Yan Min's parents used to live in Wandouping Village which belonged to Lijiayan administratively later. Guangwen tried to keep calm. People usually greeted him when they saw him. But today the villagers here did not; instead, they cried much more. He realized that they needed him to be a good judge.

After Shi Shuyu called Guangwen, he asked Li Pu, the village director, and Li Qiantao, the clerical assistant, to investigate the matter. He needed water to wash up but he saw a broken vat, water flooding the area. He sat down in a stool nearby Dark in the centre of the courtyard. He took off his shirt and used it to fan himself. Li Qiantao was waiting for his order, but Li Pu had gone home to avoid trouble. Guangwen stood up and went into a small room. The things inside had not been smashed, so Guangwen used that place as a temporary office.

Chapter 24

"Let Li Cai come here," Guangwen ordered.

Li Cai stepped into the room, holding a machete.

"Are you going to kill me or Guangwen?" asked Li Qiantao.

Li Cai threw away his weapon and entered the room.

"Do you still love your wife?" Guangwen asked.

"No," Li Cai replied crossly. "I hate her."

"How long has your wife been with Li Baoshun?"

"For so many years! Both Li Baoshun and I used to work in other provinces. I transferred 4,000 yuan to Yan Min's bank account. She did not buy food for her children or for her mother-in-law. In fact she went to another city with Li Baoshun by plane!"

"She is dead and you are innocent. You don't have to waste your time here. Li Baoshun should be blamed!"

After Li Cai heard that, it all clicked. He went home.

"Let Yan Fayun come here," Guangwen ordered.

Yan Fayun was the elder male cousin of Yan Min.

"Her husband has left," Guangwen said calmly. "She came here to sleep with her lover, but she died of a heart attack according to the doctor. Li Baoshun's wife is calm. But you have smashed her household supplies and killed her dog, and you should compensate her for her losses!"

Yan Fayun's anger was lessened and left. Soon Guangwen questioned Li Baoshun.

When Li Baoshun, trembling, stood in front of Guangwen, the latter was speaking to someone on the phone excitedly. Li Qiantao gave a cigarette to him.

Li Qiantao usually put money and cigarettes, less famous than Guangwen's, into his briefcase. The latter did not receive his cigarette, but he pointed another pack. The former put one between Guangwen's mouth and lit it. The phone call was ended.

"It's so hot even before summer comes," Guangwen said lightly. "I saw a bulletin outside a court that several men would be executed by shooting."

Li Baoshun was sweating profusely and Guangwen was smoking on and on.

"You are the culprit!" Guangwen snapped.

Li Baoshun cried.

"Stop crying," said Guangwen. "It's too late!"

Li Baoshun knelt down.

"Stand up!" Guangwen ordered, watching him coldly.

"She was a charming woman ten years younger than you. But I couldn't understand why she was fond of you."

"It's my fault," Li Baoshun said sadly.

"She had never had a heart attack until she came to your house today and lay in your bed, naked."

"I found she was dead after I took a shower."

"She would not have come here if you had not told her that your wife went to the market. You've got involved with it."

Li Baoshun did not argue anymore. Last night he sent a text message to Yan Min that the next day would be the right day for their secret meeting. And the latter did what he had said.

Li Baoshun did not tell that to Guangwen, but the latter knew that through Yan Min's phone.

"Li Cai will get even with you," Guangwen continued. "He will have a corpse bound on your back for 49 days during which you must keep kowtowing without any meal or excretion. And you must carry the body even after it rots in hot summer. What's more, you and your sons will be asked to compensate, and you may be imprisoned and be executed in the Ximencao Dam!"

Many prisoners had been executed in the Ximencao Dam, a place full of reeds nearby a river. If a man swore at another one that he would be sent to the Ximencao Dam, that was a curse.

"Tell me what to do, please!" Li Baoshun implored, kneeling again.

"Set up a mourning hall and make a funeral for Yan Min," Guangwen ordered. "And take good care of her parents and relatives. Li Cai may not let her body be buried in his ancestors' graveyards, but I'll persuade him to accept her. Her children should not visit their mother in your ancestors' cemetery!"

After Li Baoshun left, Guangwen looked tired. He smoked a cigarette and then said calmly, "Shi Shuyu."

She came in and sat beside him.

"That woman is dead and you win," Guangwen said to her. "And that's what you should think about. You are a sensible, broad-minded woman. I told your husband to make a three-day funeral. That woman's family members should not prolong it because the cause of death is shameful. Make a good funeral to avoid complaints. What's more, you don't want your husband to be imprisoned. Your marriage has been 22 years and the pear tree in your courtyard has been with you. You have two children and one of them is a lobby manager, which is your blessing. Forgive and forget, which is much better than imprisonment. If your husband is asked to compensate, you will have to pay the money, too. Don't bear a grudge against a dead woman. Do a good deed for the rest of your life."

Chapter 25

That was what Li Qiantao had said to Chunhong on the phone. Guangwen would have to convince Li Cai to allow his wife's corpse to be buried in his ancestors' graveyards. That funeral would not invite guests, otherwise Chunhong would return to Lijiayan to help them. She was often invited to take part in weddings and funerals in Lijiayan, and she would just need to watch the women in the kitchen to do a good job.

It was getting dark. Qingmei and Dou had supper in Qingmei's mother's house. Chunhong bought a cold vegetable dish in sauce and cooked mung bean porridge; she and I had supper in her house. When I was watching TV, I thought about the woman named Yan Min. She must have loved Li Baoshun, so she had been with him for so many years; but she did not expect that she would die on her lover's bed. Her family members blamed her for her death.

"Are you going to have a walk?" Chunhong asked me.

"No. I'll go to sleep."

"But it's not bedtime. Chunshu should know the story between Li Baoshun and Yan Min."

"He is busy repairing his room full of rat holes in Yanerpo."

"I saw him on the street today and he declined my invitation to supper. He tried to avoid me and said that he would return to Yanerpo. His wife is there. He will tell her that he will look after our dad and then will sleep with Zhanhui."

"Chunshan will understand it if Chunshu's wife asks about it."

"Chunshan has become compliant since he got married. If he is asked by Zhuqing, he will tell her what he has been told by her husband."

I wondered if I should meddle. People said that Zhu Zhanhui was a bitch. But Chunshu did not know what love was until he had an affair with her. Chunshu and Zhuqing got married without love. Marriage would not come easy in such a poor village. Chunshu had read a lot of books which had given him eagerness and sorrow. Zhuqing took his so-called sadness as shit. She threw all his books into a fireplace after they got married. She knew that his reading would be useless. An avid reader should be employed in a state-owned company just like me. In addition, she would never speak like this: "Are you pining for me, honey?"

I should not ask Chunshu to come to Chunhong's house now.

"You are different from them," she said to me sincerely.

They referred to Chunshu, Li Baoshun, and Guangwen. Chunhong had told her husband's affair to me and my wife.

Chapter 26

More than twenty years ago, Chunhong was suffering from a toothache and was living in Lijiayan. In a summer vacation, Li Jing and I went to my hometown. We visited my father and my sisters. When we went to Chunhong's home, Li Jing was attracted by the wonderful farm land scenery so much so that she did not believe that Guangwen's home should be much poorer than mine when I told her.

Chunhong's house had been improved. Guangwen's mother had been drowned and his younger brother had been doing tofu business in Golden Town. His eldest brother and his wife had been unsociable: she had been seriously ill and had always shut herself at home. Lily was a good student but

Li Zhi was a bad one and would be expelled from school. Guangwen brought him to Golden Town and let him be looked after by Chunshang. But the boy was so rebellious that his father stopped his schooling when he was an eighth grader lest he should bring shame on the family name. When Li Jing and I visited Chunhong, her husband started to educate Li Zhi and asked him to follow the example set by Lily, by me, and by Li Jing. My wife said that Li Zhi was sincere. After his schooling was stopped, he complained, "I wanted to study hard but I was not allowed to go to school anymore." He had been unaware of his weakness.

In my hometown, guests, especially a man and a woman, should not sleep in the same bed in the host's house, otherwise a disaster would happen to the host. As a result, Chunhong and Li Jing shared one bed, Guangwen and I shared one. Guangwen fluffed up two pillows, dust rising, followed by squeals. Soon less than twenty rats were poured from the pillows. He put back chaff into the pillows and asked his wife to sew them. Through the broken threads he knew that rats had been hiding in the pillows.

"I snore," said Guangwen. "You'd better fall asleep as soon as possible." He snored at once and then I heard Chunhong moaning because of her toothache. She put some pesticides around her teeth to reduce the pain. I could not sleep at all, so I kept my eyes open.

A bulb with a dim light was hanging on the wall of a dug-pit latrine outside. Chunhong kept it on so that Li Jing and I could find the path if we needed to go to the latrine at midnight. I was thinking about something else when I watching the light. When I was a kid, I had to hold a small kerosene lamp to go to a latrine at midnight, and I must walk slowly because the light would go out in case of a wind. There was moonlight, but a kerosene lamp was used by human beings on the ground. I was a boarding student in the middle school. The latrine was far from the dormitory even though there were street lamps at night. The teachers sometimes played movies in a hall for students. After I watched *Painted Skin*, I was afraid of ghosts; *Visitors on the Icy Mountain*, of spies; *Red Bat Apartment*, of poisonous needles fired by enemies. If a teacher or a worker died, his or her corpse covered with a piece of red cloth would be placed in the hall. The cloth might fly in the wind at night and even tried to catch something like a hand. I would be riddled with fright when I recollected those things. The past was reduced either to decay or to death.

Rats walked through my face and seemed to take revenge. They stopped on Guangwen's face and smelt his eyes and mouth. He was still snoring. I used a fan to drive away the rats although they were unwilling to leave. It was my first time to share one bed with Guangwen. He had been living with Chunhong for so many years and he was one of my relatives.

He woke up when morning came. He saw me sitting on the edge of the bed and asked, "Did you have a sound sleep last night?"

"Yes."

"Oh, I did not snore."

"Your snoring was like thunder," his wife said.

We laughed.

Chapter 27

In the early morning Chunhong's toothache was eased. She woke up Lily and her younger brother. She would cut pigweed and her husband would cut firewood. He was a village party secretary and often did housework.

"Follow me to the field," Chunhong said to me and Li Jing, carrying a basket on her back. "It's a cool place."

Yanerpo was like a painting in the bamboo forest.

"Cows are mooing," said Chunhong.

We could hear the sound. There was a pond in which villagers washed their clothes and there was a stone tablet inscribed with quotations of Chairman Mao. The red paint looked dim but the words were clear: "The emperor will be useless when the revolution of the proletariat and the farmers begins." It was also known as the Stone Tablet of Quotations.

She led us into her vegetable plots. She found ten sweet potatoes in a plot. She threw away two potatoes which were being eaten by ants, went to the pond and washed the rest of the potatoes. She let us eat them. Her toothache stopped her from enjoying them herself. She looked around and told us the affair of her husband.

The woman mentioned by Chunhong used to live nearby an elementary school in the village. Her husband had been lying on the bed because of paralysis of half of his body. Students and teachers of the school had been relocated but the school had been kept for natural gas. If the walls were thickly covered with graffiti, he would have Huigoer clean them. Guangwen often visited the household nearby the school. Gradually he got along with that woman and they slept with each other. As time went by, she went into Chunhong's house and would compete with her for her husband's favour. Chunhong did not quarrel with her. When she was cooking for Guangwen, Chunhong went to her house and cooked for her husband and did housework for him.

Guangwen got so angry that one day he slapped Chunhong.

"You are a leader in the village," she explained calmly. "If you don't care for the paralysed man, I'll care for him. I am your wife and I should do the job well to bring you a good reputation. After our children come back in summer vacation, I'll tell them what has happened and I will no longer be your wife or their mother. And I'll leave that paralysed man alone; it is his fate if he is starved to death."

The next morning that woman intruded into Chunhong's farm land. Guangwen kicked her as soon as he saw her.

"Fuck off!" he yelled.

Watching the bruises in her chest, she sued him. The township government leaders had a talk with Guangwen and his wife.

"She is far beneath your wife, Guangwen," one of the leaders said. "I would not have promoted you to village party secretary if I had known that you should have an affair with the other woman."

"I'm sorry," Guangwen said.

"You should apologise to your wife."

He smiled at his wife.

"Afterwards the affair between them was ended," Chunhong said proudly to me and Li Jing.

Chapter 28

So many years had passed. Did Chunhong still feel proud of her husband?

I was picked up by Yang Jin in the railway station after I returned from Chengdu. He told me of Huigoer's troublemaking, Guangwen's lengthy discourse with Mr. Gao, as well as Guangwen's affairs. I did not know why he told me those things. Didn't he worry that I might reveal that to Guangwen? He was sure that I would keep quiet, and he should have kept those things in the dark.

Did Chunhong know about more affairs of her husband? She often expressed her mistrust to him, which meant that she had been aware of those things but pretended not to be. On the day before our father's birthday, Chunhong asked Qingmei to educate Li Zhi so that she could let him behave himself. That was from an experienced hand.

I should not pry into Chunhong's privacy, just like I could not be alone with our father. We are adults and we can't share our stories with each other like kids. We used to suffer from poverty, coldness, anxiety and humbleness. We lived together until Chunshu got married. People nowadays can't understand the feeling of separation. In the past people had to survive with clenched fists; but now they spend their days and nights with fingers typing and sliding on screens. The fist had to be separated into fingers, resulting in pain.

On the day of separation, the younger ones were listening to the complaints of the elder ones when our father was standing in the centre of the room. Kitchenware, farm land, farm tools, old accounts, each suggestion was followed by anger. The sisters-in-law's words would pour oil on the flames.

Everybody was seeking for the cruel truth. Morality was weak because everybody would have to endure the bad results. For individuals, morality might make things go athwart. Chunshu and Guangwen were like birds in another home; when they were hidden, they would not be taken seriously; in case of a wind, they would snarl and the others would have to suffer.

I did not want to ponder over those things anymore. I told Chunhong that I would go to sleep. I knew that I might not live up to her expectations; the relatives and my wife might now know that. I was living in a city. My miseries and embarrassments were engulfed in city dwellers. Chunhong saw me in low spirits and did not disturb me.

The people and the things I'd seen within these days swarmed into my dream. I called my boss the other day to extend leave and I got the approval. I expressed my gratitude to him but I knew that the company would be operated normally even without me. The sky and the earth would be still there no matter human beings existed or not.

"Did you have a sound sleep last night?" Chunhong asked me the next morning.

"Yes."

"I called Chunshang just now. Our dad is in a good condition. He had some congee at 10 p.m. last night. They had a good talk and he asked about the medical bill, and he said that he would work to earn more money after he got better."

She smiled.

"I'll go to the hospital after I have breakfast," I said.

"Chunshang asks you to rest for one more day," said Chunhong. "He can look after our dad all by himself."

I insisted.

"You may go there after lunch," she said.

"Our dad may be clouded in mind and talk foolishly, and his body shakes. I should help Chunshang."

Chunhong did not say anymore. She did not know that I wanted to see Ms. Cheng again when I was thinking about our father's illness. She talked on and on during breakfast, and her repeated topics were about our relatives and old friends.

Chapter 29

"When will you go to the hospital?" Guangwen asked me on the phone.

"I'll go there after I finish my breakfast," I replied.

"Wait for me. Yang Jin will pick up me, you, Mr. Lee, the town mayor, and Mr. Han, the deputy town chief. Let's go to the town together."

"What's the matter?" Chunhong asked after the call was ended.

I told her what I had heard on the phone.

Chunhong was not surprised. "I wonder if the problem in Lijiayan has been solved."

"He will go with us because it has been solved," I said. "And he will have his arrangements if it has not."

I would assure her that she needn't worry about her husband's work because he was quite capable of handling it.

She could understand me and then changed the subject. "Zheng Saner scolded Limin in the presence of Mrs. Hou, and she did not retort. Uncle Chenggui treats Zheng Saner well but he has never supported her when she was maltreated by her mother-in-law. So she hates her parents-in-law. Huang Ermei is an honest businesswoman. After she sold noodles one day, she found mildew on them and tried to search for the buyer. The latter did not mind that, but she bought a water gun for his grandson priced much higher than the noodles."

Guangwen called me again after I had breakfast. An opening ceremony of the second athletic meeting in Baima city would be held in Dongxuan Indoor Stadium tonight. Two pop stars and crosstalk comedians were invited for the ceremony and even one ticket was hard to get. Mr. Li had a ticket and got one for Guangwen, but Mr. Han did not have one. Guangwen told Mr. Han that I could get one. Yang Jin said that he would join it, too. So Guangwen asked me to get two tickets. He always boasted about my job title in the presence of local government leaders, and I must finish his task.

When I returned to my hometown last year, Guangwen invited local government leaders to dinner.

"You must be an honoured guest in the provincial governor Mr. Lin's banquet," Guangwen said to me deliberately.

Mr. Lin used to invite men of letters to dinner, including me. It would begin at 6 p.m., but everybody should reach the appointed hotel half an hour in advance. I got there at 5:30 p.m. Sixteen guests were sitting in the room, talking excitedly in a low voice.

I had told Guangwen about the banquet. But today he mentioned it in front of the township government leaders, who expressed their admiration for me and toasted me. They said that the dinner was set up for me and Guangwen was one of the guests. The topic was about the plight of Huilong Town.

"Dongxuan is a national-level poverty-stricken county," one of the leaders said to me emotionally. "But the natural gas discovered in Huilong

Town has not been able to lift it out of impoverishment."

I had doubted them and wrote a poem *Expressions Reflected on Wine Glasses*. After I finished it, I looked at myself in the mirror and saw hypocrisy in it, so I did not publish my poem. I talked about my participation in the banquet with the provincial governor, which was a flaunt.

But I must finish the task assigned by Guangwen. I soon called Single Braid and considered the cultural centre might be helpful. But he could not get a ticket either. His daughter was eager to go there because one of the pop stars was her idol. Ruisong came up with a solution: his wife was praised as a model worker in the county and was rewarded with a ticket; so he got it and then gave his work permit to me. "An interview will be needed," he said. "But I won't have to go there."

Guangwen and the leaders would not have to attend the ceremony so early, but all the activities in the whole day had been arranged; and one would have to be finished at night anyway if it was not in the daytime. Mr. Lee would invite me to dinner, but I declined it with an excuse of an appointment with my friends. Guangwen and Yang Jin did not tell him that our father was in hospital, and I did not say that either.

"Chunming is frequently invited by his friends whenever he returns," said Guangwen.

I got two tickets for him and he felt honoured in front of the leaders. There were more than ten villages in Huilong Town, and Lijiayan was the most important one because of its natural gas. Only Guangwen could solve problems in the village, but he had never got arrogant.

"I may invite you to dinner next time," Mr. Lee said to me. "Send Mr. Xu Chunming to his place," he said to Yang Jin.

I got off the car at the Building and Construction Authority so that I was not discovered that I would go to the hospital.

"I'm too busy to see our dad today," Guangwen whispered to me.

At 7:40 p.m., just twenty minutes before the opening ceremony, Yang Jin came to the hospital and took away the two tickets.

Chapter 30

Our father became more and more delirious. Was it hopeless? When Dr. Yu came to the ward again, he just silently nodded and went to other wards with his interns. Dr. Kang gave us words of comfort, but were they professional? I would prefer Dr. Yu's words. Dr. Kang brought numbness to us and to himself, and he came to the ward less and less. Ms. Cheng remained unchanged and did her job well, which puzzled and even agitated me. On the fourth day after I returned from Chunhong's house, the patient with pancreatic cancer felt a twinge before he went shopping. He lay on his bed and died after thirty minutes. When Ms. Cheng helped his relatives to pack his bags, she looked the same as when she patted our father on the back. Life and death were nothing new to her.

I asked Chunshang to go home, take a shower, and put on new clothes although he would rather stay with me. He was soaked with sweat and had heat rash.

Ms. Cheng made aspiration of sputum for our father again. I wanted to talk with her to enliven the atmosphere.

"There is an elderly woman who often feels hungry," I said. "She says that she must pay for each meal sent by her daughter-in-law. But where is she now?"

"She is healthy and is well treated by her daughter-in-law," replied Ms. Cheng. "She was lonely at home and her daughter-in-law was too busy to be with her. She pretended to be seriously ill so that she could talk to patients and doctors. Her daughter-in-law would not send her any meal unless she was paid so as to let her go home. The day before yesterday her son came to the ward, paid the medical bill, and carried her on his back to go home."

As soon as she stopped talking, I heard rumblings in my father's throat. I was distressed: one was a beautiful woman and the other was my dying father.

"Is Chengdu a funny place?" she asked me.

She knew the background of the patient's relatives, and she did not hope that I could give her an answer. She finished her job, threw disposable medical products into a trash can, and then walked away.

Guangwen came. Mr. Gou in a blue shirt and his assistants were standing behind him. He introduced Mr. Gou to me and he made time for visiting our father.

"This is Mr. Xu Chunming," he introduced me to Mr. Gou. I was taken as a personage and shook hands with him formally.

"Your father can be well treated here," he said to Guangwen.

"We are grateful to you," Guangwen said humbly.

They had kept in touch. Guangwen respected him and had invited him to dinner frequently.

Guangwen saw Mr. Gou out. After ten minutes Guangwen came back.

"Where is Chunshang?" he asked. "We'll invite Mr. Gou to dinner before our dad is discharged from hospital."

He gave me a cigarette. He carried a large bag containing famous liquor and cigarettes and would give them to Mr. Gou. Guangwen was a helpful man. If without him, our father could not have been hospitalized timely and he could not have been allowed to be placed in an ICU from a bed set in the corridor the next day.

"Has the matter in Lijiayan been finished?" I asked.

"Yan Min's corpse is buried far away from the ancestral graves of her husband's family.

Our father was still sleeping. He chatted with me for a while and then left. Because Mr. Gou had visited our father, Dr. Kang entered the ward frequently and spoke firmly.

Chapter 31

Chunshang slept in his own house for one night. He looked downcast when he came to the hospital. I guessed that he had been scolded by his wife again. Yumei had not recovered from her cold. Yuling would need to operate the store and plant crops. Unable to ride a motorbike, she had to retort to paying to be a passenger on one, which led her to vent her frustration onto her husband. He had been tired for one week looking after our father.

He did not mention that; instead, he said, "Zhuqing has been scolding Chunshu for having failed to do farm work timely. She thought that her husband was taking care of our father in the hospital, and that's the reason."

Chunshang did not go to Yanerpo, such excuses must have been heard by

Chunshan. Chunshan usually talked with Chunhong and then she told those things to her sisters. Chunshu was made a scapegoat for his wife's scolding: Chunshan did not look after the elderly man in the hospital, but why should Chunshu stay? Things would become difficult for Chunshu if Xiaolan knew that. Chunshu was only afraid of two people: our mother and his daughter.

When Chunshu was a teenager, he often sighed when he was reading. Our mother would spank him whenever he sighed because she considered that sighs would make him unpromising. Chunshu had been beaten the most by our mother among our siblings. What's more, he often stole rice to buy steamed meat buns. The rice had been saved by us to entertain guests. After Chunshu was badly battered by our mother with canes, our father asked him to run away at once. The dog we kept at that time could smell our family member even through a long distance. At midnight our father found Chunshu in a cave guided by the dog. After our mother died, Chunshu thought that he would fear nobody. However, as his daughter Xiaolan grew up, she was as bad-tempered as her grandmother. When she was a little girl, she was often given physical punishment by her father. After she became an adult, she often criticized her father, and the latter had to explain carefully. What's more, Chunshu had borrowed a lot of money from Xiaolan, so he was afraid of her.

"Xiaolan must know that her dad has been in the town for many days," said Chunshang.

Xiaolan had criticized her father for his affair with Zhanhui, but that turned out to be useless. She hated him and that woman. But she told Chunhong that a man would not become a victim in an affair.

Chapter 32

Our father moaned.

"Dad," Chunshang said loudly. The elderly man did not answer.

Chunshang lifted his head, fluffed up the pillow, and put the man's head down slowly on the pillow.

"Dad," Chunshang repeated.

No reply. Chunshang had to sit down in a stool. All kinds of sounds outside were like waves which had taken me away, but his words made me sober again.

"If our dad goes to another world," said Chunshang, "we'll make a funeral. But how?"

I was puzzled.

"Chunshan has talked about it with Chunhong and Chunshu. She hopes that we, the three brothers in our family, will make a good funeral, and others will say that we are united. Chunshan agrees with it and says that I may handle it. Chunshu says that he has been engaged in funeral business and he will do the things just like he has done in other families. He does a paid job for others but he will finish the funeral free of charge for our dad."

Chunshang smiled calmly just like he did when Chunshu said that he would place our father's corpse in his spare house. Money was very important to Chunshu.

When Guangwen was doing a project in Mount Lordhou, he let his elder brother and brothers-in-law join it. The project would last half a month, so they prepared a lot of food. A household was living nearby the construction site located in the border of Lijiayan. For the sake of Guangwen, they let the four men have meals with them. After the project was finished, the three men gave the rest of the rice to the host, but Chunshu carried his own rice away. After a flood occurred in spring, Chunshan called Chunshu to help his wife to plough because the farm work was too much for her. Fengjuan gave a pack of cigarettes to Chunshu and made a wonderful meal for him. But she was surprised that Chunshu should charge. If she asked Limin to help her to do farm work, it would be free. If an outsider was asked to do the farm work, the family would be laughed at.

A master had taught Chunshu to chant eulogies in funerals. Without a teacher, a learner could not sing the eulogies gravely and sorrowfully. Chunshu's master was Xiao An who came from Yanerpo. His sons resided in Changji, Xinjiang. The couple went to Changji in their seventies but came back after five years. Their sons had been unlucky. When the eldest son was driving a three-wheeled motorcycle, he was run over by a truck and died. The wife of the youngest son had eloped with the other man. Xiao An got a hernia and walked with difficulty, so he and his wife returned to their hometown. After twenty days, a man died in Yanerpo, and one of his family members had

Chunshu chant in the funeral. Xiao An, who had not recovered from the hernia, attended it with Chunshu. During the fives years of the master's absence, Chunshu became well-known in the funeral business. After the performance was over, Chunshu got paid but did not give any to Xiao An. "I, rather than he, was invited," he explained.

Xiao An was a diligent performer who sacrificed several nights' sleep, yet all his endeavors turned out to be in vain. So he cursed his disciple: "The household which he serves will be destroyed!" Nobody would invite Chunshu so as to avoid being ruined.

Later Xiao An felt worse in his hometown, so he went to Xinjiang again. When another funeral was held in Yanerpo, the family member had to invite Chunshu in spite of the curse because there was no other choice. At last the household was safe and sound. People said that Xiao An was not magical enough to make his curse come true. From then on Chunshu made a fortune.

Chunshu said that he would provide a free service for our father's funeral. Chunshang mentioned the suggestions of Chunhong, Chunshan and Chunshu, but did not mention his own.

"What's your opinion?" I asked Chunshang.

"I don't know."

"And your wife?"

"She thinks that the participants' money should come along with friendly relations, but the division of money will bring trouble because there will be freeloaders, complaints, buck-passing and even accusations. My children have not got married. I had built a house in my mother-in-law's place and had lent money to my wife's brother, which made my own siblings unhappy. Chunshan's children held weddings in other places. He has few friendly relations, should he have a share of the money?"

"It's too complicated."

"It won't be easy. A minor wound may result in a serious disease, just like our dad."

Our father had been struggling against death. When he heard our talk about his funeral, he suddenly said clearly, "I have a pain in my back, Chunshang."

Chapter 33

My sisters and sister-in-law refunded their tickets after they knew that our father was still alive. They thought that he would soon be discharged from hospital, walk with a stick and have a long life. He had gone through so many difficulties in his life and would make a miracle.

When my siblings had a family gathering during one Spring Festival, they said that our father would have a long life. Guangwen made an analogy between the elderly man and a dog he had seen in Lijiayan when all the dogs needed to be killed in the county: a badly battered dog with blood falling from its head could run as fast as it could to a mountain, never to return. The villagers said that a dog could have a rebirth in the soil, which might be true.

"Our dad's life is as tough as a dog's," said Guangwen. He was scolded by his wife, but later she understood it and smiled.

People usually consider that their parents will have longevity. But after they die, they realize that they should have carried out filial piety much earlier.

My sisters called us every day and got the same answer: our father was still breathing.

When Chunshang and I were having a nap at noon, Chunhua and her husband came. We had to care for the patient and it became a monotonous job and we were like machines but got tired. I thought about the young man who looked after his grandpa with gastric perforation. Our father was looked after by Chunshang and me. Both of us often glanced at each other and kept silent.

Chunhua and her husband carried large, green, woven bags. He said that such a bag could make a strange sound when it was touched, so it would keep its user alert. The Chinese migrant workers often use these bags for more things and for prevention of thievery. Even one worker can distinguish the sound of his own bag among hundreds of sounds.

Chunhua became thinner. When she was three years old, she would cry when she heard the sound of tapping a bowl. It was meal time but she cried incomprehensibly. She would be beaten by our mother because she thought that a child who cried when food and water were available would become unpromising. She and Chunshu were often punished physically by our mother.

"Our mom dislikes her second son and second daughter," Chunshu said one day. He thought that he would be beaten again, but our mother laughed.

She would give corporal punishment to him if she was annoyed by him.

After our mother died, Chunhua was beaten by Chunshan. We were afraid of him except Chunshu, and we trembled even when he coughed. He took delight in our fear of him and often frightened us. Now he was different from the man as he used to be. Chunhua's fear always existed; as a result, Chunshan angrily asked us to eat up each meal. We were glad about that because we were so hungry. Her trouble did not disappear until she was fourteen years old. She would have starved to death if our father had not cared for her.

When she was walking with her husband, they did not look like a couple, but like siblings. Chunying and her husband Yao Xianhe came after two hours. Xianhe, who had been a sensible production team leader in the village, did not speak or act like Guangwen. He could not know how to make his daughter less rebellious.

"Dad," Xianhe said.

Our father was still sleeping.

"Are you going to let Chunshu sing a song for you?" Xianhe added.

"You should ask him," said Chunying.

"You should often clean our father's body," said Xianhe.

"Chunming and a nurse help me to clean him," said Chunshang. "The nurse is very good."

He had never mentioned Ms. Cheng in front of me, but now he praised her, which made me feel better.

Xianhe asked his wife and Chunying to go outside. He pulled back the quilt and checked our father's body.

"Wet the towel," he said to Chunshang.

After Chunshang gave it to him, he touched it and found it was a cold one.

"You should use hot water to wet the towel," said Xianhe. "Our dad can't endure coldness when he is ill."

We usually used the cold water because we thought that our dad felt hot just like we did. Chunshang used the hot water and gave the towel to Xianhe. He cleaned our father's body carefully and removed the diaper.

"His private parts need more wipes. Give me a basin of water." He went on with the cleaning and then put a new diaper on our father's body.

Chapter 34

Fang Yun and Xianhe would stay and let Chunhua and Chunying leave. They would go by boat at 6 p.m. I invited them to dinner before they went. Chunhua could not endure having a meal in a restaurant nearby a hospital, so she said that she felt dizzy and had no appetite.

She had no car sickness but Chunying had. At the sight of a car Chunying would feel sick. When I stayed in Chunhong's house, Chunying said that she would go home by boat; I would let her sit in Yang Jin's car so that she could reach home quickly. She used to live with her foster parents in Guanmenyan and she got married in Dabaoliang; the two places were located in Mount Lordhou, and Dabaoliang was not far from Ba Valley. Chunying said that she would rather sit in a boat and get home slowly. I cared for Chunying. Her daughter Qiuyue had much more serious carsickness than her mother. Qiuyue could get along with me only among her relatives. One day I brought her into a car but after a moment she vomited in plastic bags. She yelled that she must get off the car at once. She and her mother kept vomiting, so Yang Jin had to drive them to a wharf. They rushed to a boat as fast as they could. Chunying had car sickness and train sickness. Whenever she came back from another province, she would look pale, just like now.

I persuaded Chunying to have a bowl of eight-treasure congee. She had some unwillingly and then asked, "Can our dad get better?"

"The doctors will do their best to treat him," I replied.

"I don't like him at all," she whispered seriously.

It was noisy in the restaurant. Xianhe was talking about the factory in which he was working, so they did not hear what Chunying was saying. I could understand her but I did not know how to console her.

For the first time she talked about her miseries in her foster parents' house with teary eyes. At the age of six, she was battered by her aunt after the latter had lost 1 yuan, and the little girl was taken as a thief; later she was beaten by her foster mother much more. Her aunt was the elder sister of her foster mother and had three sons and two daughters. The woman often cursed her foster mother as an infertile hen. After the girl was adopted, her aunt often yelled at her foster mother: "Your daughter calls you mom, but she is not your own! And she will go back to her own home sooner or later!"

Those harsh words made her foster mother beat her vehemently. She ran desperately into a cornfield when stones were hurled at her by her foster mother, but she was protected by corn stalks. The girl spent one night in the field. She loved corn cakes because on that night what she could hold tightly was corn stalks.

"You would be beaten by our dad even if you lived with us," I said.

"But that would be different!" she retorted.

Her foster father had died and her foster mother rented a house nearby a school to look after her grandchildren. She gave clothes, food and money to her foster mother each year; and she took her to her house in Dabaoliang during winter and summer vacations and took good care of her. After her foster mother got old, she was full of tears at the mention of Chunying.

"I should treat my foster parents with filial piety," said Chunying. But she still complained.

"You would have come home much earlier if you had not heard rats fight," Xianhe said to Chunhua.

She laughed and her husband smiled; the latter knew that his wife was unwilling to hear her past embarrassments being talked about. When she saw Chinese cabbages in another province, she thought that the cabbages should grow nearby the Qingxi River only, but how could they appear in another place far away? Only I knew that her husband had written a love letter to her; she would have been riddled with shame and anger if it had been known by others. Fang Yun would protect his wife all the time.

"Those rats would let you stay in a city, make you earn more money and see much of the world," Xianhe continued.

Chunying glowered at Xianhe and soon the latter stopped talking. She called the shots in her family and treated her husband like an errand boy.

I paid the bill. Chunhua and Chunying went to the wharf. Chunshang was in the ward with our father, and I would bring food to them.

Chapter 35

As soon as the three of us entered the ward we saw our father chatting with Chunshang.

"Our dad wakes up after we get here," Xianhe smiled.

"You've had a long journey," said our father.

"Well, you may reimburse the fare," Xianhe said jokingly.

The elderly man smiled. He hadn't smiled for a very long time..

Chunshang brought the food on the table and our father watched it eagerly. He must be hungry.

"I'll pour you a bowl of congee, dad," I said.

"I wanted to call you because our dad refused to eat the food," said Chunshang.

This was what he had told to the elderly man: he and Chunming would have kept using towels soaked with cold water to clean his body if Xianhe had not showed them the right way. The waste from his body was also cleaned by his sons. The elderly man did not want to eat more food so that his sons would not have to do such a dirty job.

"Everybody will get old," said Fang Yun. "You should make yourself strong to fight against your trouble."

Our father did not reply. I bought congee mixed with rice, vegetables and meat. Fang Yun fed the elderly man, but soon tears fell down from the latter's eyes. Xianhe tried to make him happy.

"I had a dream last night, dad," said Xianhe. "I saw a man with a grey beard. He told me that an auspicious thing was coming to me: I would visit my father-in-law who would live 100 years old."

The elderly man cried. We did not ask him why he wept. Xianhe wiped his mouth with a tissue and tucked him in. Our father became quiet when Fang Yun consoled him. He had more mouthfuls of the congee and then fell asleep.

Chapter 36

At night Xianhe bought some pot-stewed meat and bottles of liquor. We chatted happily in the ward in a low voice while our father was sleeping. At

11 p.m. Fang Yun said that he would go to sleep. Chunhua and Chunying went away with luggage, but larger bags were left in the ward. Fang Yun took sheets out of the bag and put them on the floor in the balcony for his sleep. The rest of us went on with drinking until it was 3 a.m. We did not wake up until Ms. Cheng came the next morning to make aspiration of sputum for our father. She frowned at the smell of liquor.

"Oh, I'm sorry," Xianhe said to the nurse.

"Do not drink in the ward," she warned.

I felt awkward.

"My brothers say that you have taken good care of our father," Xianhe said sincerely. "We are grateful to you."

Ms. Cheng smiled with a red hue in her face.

Our father woke up and looked around. Xianhe threw away the urine bag and then cleaned the elderly man's body. Chunshang bought some food for him. After our father had a meal and fell asleep again, we could not find Fang Yun. We thought that he went to the toilet but he did not come back after ten minutes. On the phone he told us that he went to find a job before morning came.

The county was more of a mountain city, just like Chongqing. Carriers with thick poles on their shoulders served passengers. Villagers often sold their products in this way and then went to a tea house. Fang Yun did an odd job like that.

At 4 p.m. Fang Yun came soaked with sweat. Xiaolan let Qingmei look after her children and visited her grandpa. When Chunhong got to the hospital, Chunhua and Chunying had left, and my wife had not arrived.

"Is my grandpa seriously ill?" asked Xiaolan.

Chunhong glowered at her to stop her from speaking much more. Our father could not hear anything when he was sleeping.

"You don't have to carry heavy things as an odd job," Chunhong said to Fang Yun.

Fang Yun smiled awkwardly.

"You are rich," Xianhe said to Chunhong. "But the poor must work hard to earn more money."

Fengjuan came. She neither greeted us nor put down her luggage.

"Our dad is a dying man!" she cried, watching him.

Chapter 37

Fengjuan could not understand the electrocardioscanner, but she could judge based on her experience. In the village, when a man was lying on the bed weakly, if a visitor cried just like she did, the family member would wail because he would die soon. It was said that a man's throat would make a sound before he died: say goodbye to the world. It was also said that the sound was falling. When we were chatting in the ward, she said those words as soon as she saw our father.

Such a thing reminded me of our mother's death. I thought that she was still alive. On an autumn night, she got up and sat beside the fireplace. Our father stood behind her, put his hands on her shoulders and his knees against her waist to support her. Mrs. Hou came and had a chat with our mother.

"She is dying!" Mrs. Hou suddenly cried.

Our father held our mother in his arms and wailed. She was looking pale and died soon. She did not speak her last words to her husband and children.

Her funeral lasted four days. The third day was sunny. Chunshan asked me to watch her coffin to keep the light on and to keep a cat far away from her body. If the light was off, her soul would get lost in the underworld and could not get reincarnated soon. If a cat jumped on her body, the corpse might sit up. I saw sweat on her nose at noon on that day. The yellow paper was too narrow to cover her whole face: eyes covered, mouth and nose not.

After many years I could understand the meaning of the sweat. At that time I thought the difference between a dead person and a living one was to eat food or not. Chunshang holding chopsticks ran towards the coffin and cried, "It's time to have a meal, mom!"

She was silent. He would throw himself into her arms but the coffin was too high to be reached by him. Our father was anguished: he used to be an orphan, and his younger brother died at the same age with Chunshang.

Our mother was still breathing that day, but she was buried alive later by us.

Most of the villagers might be dealt with in the same way. A corpse should not be placed in the central room, so the patient was carried home early. Would it be buried alive?

Chapter 38

Chunshang let Fengjuan watch the electrocardioscanner and the oxygen hose. She silently put down her bag. She believed her instinct rather than medical equipment. Death was like a sound and it could be sensed even without eyes. Death and life were also smells. She was shocked by our sulk. She looked agitated and her face was like a shadow. That was different from the woman as she used to be.

"When did you buy the ticket?" Chunhong asked Fengjuan, giving a stool to her. "How many hours? You should have told us much earlier."

"Our sisters did not tell us, either," said Chunshang.

"Our dad's soul is wandering a long distance," said Chunhong. "He has never been to a remote place but has suffered quite a lot."

"You did not have any water on your way," Chunhong said to Fengjuan. "And your lips are parched."

Fengjuan gulped down a glass of water and would refill it.

"Take a rest," said Chunhong. "There is a kettle."

After Chunshang refilled the glass, Chunhong said to Fengjuan, "The glass does not want to be held by your hands full of scars."

"Oh, let me touch your delicate hands," Fengjuan said jokingly. And then she touched her face.

Fengjuan became cheerful again.

Chapter 39

My wife Li Jing would arrive in the city after half an hour. Chunhong would take her, Fengjuan, Xiaolan and me to the town. She would let us enjoy a wonderful meal.

A lot of private cars were parked in a square nearby the railway station. The car owners would drive passengers to their destinations. They often shouted like this: "Sit in my car if you go to Dongxuan!" After you sat in his car, you would have to wait much longer because the driver would need more passengers. If you sat in another car, you would be put in the same situation. It was time-wasting.

"Are you sitting in a car?" I asked Li Jing on the phone.

"Yes. It will go after the driver picks up two more passengers."

"You may choose a chartered car. Our relatives are waiting for you. You may stay in Chunhong's house for one night after you visit our dad."

"You don't have to wait for me."

I knew that she would not pay more money. The fare of a chartered car was 160 yuan but she could pay just 40 yuan for herself if she shared one car with other passengers. She had been worried about expenses since our father was hospitalized. She said that she would go back tomorrow morning and would not go to Huilong Town with Chunhong.

Today was Friday. She made a shift change with one of her colleagues. She had said that she would return the next Monday morning, but she changed her mind without a reason.

Yang Jin would have to pick up Guangwen from village to town. Chunhong said that someone had put poisons into Qingxi River. The dead fish alarmed everybody and the county government leaders would arrest the culprit. There was no monitor in the village, so it would be difficult to search for the suspect. Guangwen and his colleagues were busy investigating the matter. As a result, Chunhong had to take a bus. The transportation would be stopped at 6 p.m. each day. Li Jing might reach Chunhong's house if she could take a chartered bus; otherwise it would be troublesome. Chunhong asked me to tell Li Jing on the phone to let her stay for the weekend, and she might go on Sunday.

I knew she was worried about money. She had transferred 80,000 yuan to my bank account: the first time 30,000 yuan, and the second time 50,000 yuan. After the second time, she said to me: "Please ask your three brothers to repay the money they have borrowed from us, so that we can continue to provide medical treatment for our dad."

Chunshan had borrowed my money for his son Sixi, and it was in complete disorder. Chunshang had no money to repay and Chunshu was always in arrears. What was more, I did not want to trigger a conflict when our father was lying in a hospital bed.

My wife would rush to go back because of money, but I would rather keep my relatives in the dark.

Li Jing had been praised by my relatives. She was an urban girl but did not dislike the dirty rural areas. A man from Yaqueliang Village nearby Yanerpo went to university several years later than me. He got married with an urban girl. After they came to the countryside, she saw courtyards full of chicken manure; the pigpen was also the latrine, and a pig would put its nose close to her buttocks when she was squatting. She got so annoyed that she yelled and left at once. Another man from Laojun Mountain had not returned to his hometown since he became a political committee member. His parents visited him in the city when they were alive. After they returned, they boasted that they had a good daughter-in-law. But later they cried and told the truth: they were detested by their daughter-in-law: the chopsticks and bowls used by them would be thrown away by her as soon as they left; and their son gave some money to them on the sly.

But my wife was different from those women. She took good care of our father when he was staying in my house in Chengdu; I gave our father 3,000 yuan each year, in fact it was paid by her; whenever I returned to my hometown, she would bring clothes to our father. I did not know if she regretted having married me, but she had endured the unhappiness. Chunshang and Chunying regarded her as an elder sister. I would rather keep her image in front of my relatives because she was praised the most by our father and by Chunhong.

I had to tell a white lie to Chunhong that Li Jing had got a bad cold. She said that I and my wife would stay in a hotel.

Chapter 40

Xianhe called Guangwen: "Are you in the county? Fang Yun and I are in the ward with our dad. We may have dinner together someday." And then he told our father's condition to him.

After the call was ended, Xianhe continued, "Guangwen is searching for the man who has put poisons into a river. But he is in a rather quiet place, and that is strange. If a serious event occurs, the village leaders will not report lest they should be scapegoated for that. Guangwen must be having fun somewhere. His life is worthwhile."

"He is much smarter than all of us," said Fang Yun.

"Yes, indeed," said Xianhe.

When Dongxuan was rated as a national-level poverty-stricken county many years ago, the local leaders set off firecrackers and invited village leaders to attend a banquet. At that time Guangwen had a low rank but sensed that he should not attend it. He said that he had loose bowels, which was used as an excuse. When the then village party secretary visited him, he went to the toilet twice within five minutes. The leader soon left. Later the matter was investigated by the provincial leaders. Many officers were demoted but Guangwen was promoted. For the households enjoying the minimum living guarantee in Lijiayan, Guangwen did not choose his poor relatives or foster children. They thought that they should have had the right and they were disappointed. Later they found that they had got much more benefits from Guangwen. Power was indeed useful.

The other leaders brought benefits to their family members and relatives as much as possible. If they had minor injuries, they could be rated as the disabled and enjoy benefits. As a result, they were often cursed by villagers. By comparison, the villagers in Lijiayan supported Guangwen. Trust was important and powerful.

Chapter 41

Li Jing came. I went downstairs to meet her. She, carrying a bag and wearing a pink dress, ran to me as soon as she saw me. I found strangeness in her during her absence. The strangeness made her charming, which was different from the curiosity out of seduction of the other women. My wife's charm was affection, much deeper than intimacy. I held her heavy bag full of clothes and skin care products. She planned to stay two days here, but she changed her mind.

I took her to our father's ward in the third floor. My brothers and brothers-in-law greeted her, she talked to them and then walked to our father.

"I'm Li Jing, dad," she said.

He was still sleeping.

In the past, our father would rush to meet Li Jing whenever she came. "My daughter-in-law Li Jing comes to see me," he said proudly. When he was in Chunhong's house or in Yanerpo, he would always care about her. My son said that his grandpa's friendly greeting remained unchanged. Li Jing had a younger brother who worked in Chengdu. After their parents retired, they sold their house in Nanchong and went to live with their son. Now our father's children came to visit him, and he was saying goodbye to them.

After my wife and I had dinner, we went to the Pahsien Hotel. If Ruisong booked a room for me, he could get a 40% discount because the Hotel was a business partner of the television station in which he was working. If he knew that Li Jing was here, he would invite us to dinner. I had had to decline my friends' invitations since my father got ill, and they could understand me. A couple left family affairs behind temporarily and enjoyed their moment in a hotel room, which was a wonderful thing. Even though I stayed in the best hotel, I could not have such a feeling again.

"My brothers are short of money," I ventured.

"When will they become rich?" my wife asked.

I did not know how to reply.

She had told me that she would be glad to answer my sisters' calls for good news, but she was unwilling to answer the ones from my brothers: either about money or trouble.

"Your sisters should pay the medical bill for your dad, too," she added.

"A daughter will become a guest to her own family since she gets married," I explained. "And that's the local custom. A guest may help you but should not pay the bill."

Local parents would feel sad at their daughter's wedding, so they would rather have a son.

We took a shower by turns. Before I spoke again, she interrupted: "I might not have married you if time had been able to go back to twenty years ago."

"Do you regret it?" I whispered, pressing my body against hers on the bed. "You have married a promising man!"

"Even Guangwen earns much more money than you do!"

I tore off her bath towel.

She giggled and then said sadly, "I got my younger brother's call before I reached the railway station today. My mom is hospitalized because of a car accident."

Disasters came one after another.

After a moment of silence, we made love violently and crazily, mixed with shadows of pain and death, and with nothingness and misfortune.

Chapter 42

"The patient should have Human Albumin Solution for his energy," Dr. Kang suggested. "Try one to see the result. It is unavailable here. If you agree, I'll contact The First People's Hospital in the county for purchase."

Scarce and valuable medicines in all the hospitals of Dongxuan had been monopolized by The First People's Hospital. It sold the medicines to the other hospitals at a price of 130 percent.

"The Human Albumin Solution is 500 yuan per piece," Dr. Kang added. "You and Mr. Gou are friends. It can be sold to you priced at 480 yuan. You can decide if you use it or not."

"Will we use it?" Chunshang asked me.

I did not answer him at once.

Fang Yun and Xianhe had left, only Chunshang and I were in the ward.

"Can our dad be cured?" I asked Dr. Kang.

"We'll do our best to rescue him," he replied lightly.

I controlled my anger and then Dr. Kang went to another ward. I threw banknotes of 500 yuan at Chunshang crossly and asked him to give it to that doctor. Chunshang picked up the money in a sulk.

I went downstairs. When I was sitting on a bench and smoking, I got a phone call from my wife who went home three days ago.

My mother-in-law broke a shin bone and her pain was going on. She got high retirement pay but she worked as a part-time driver with a second-hand three-wheeled motorcycle within the city. Some passengers lived in the suburbs and she had to drive a long way to pick up them with the fare of 5 or

8 yuan. What's more, she collected waste products along the way and stored them in her house, which angered her son and daughter-in-law. After she fell asleep, her daughter-in-law threw them into garbage cans outside on the sly lest neighbours should ask her why she had had so many waste products.

Her injury was caused by herself. Three-wheeled motorcycles were banned and she was hit by a cross-country vehicle when she was driving without any passenger on the wrong side of the road.

Li Jing's younger brother and his wife were working in a machinery manufacturing company and they were having a tight schedule to complete a huge order from a French company. Li Jing was teaching the grade-three high school students, and our son would take the college entrance examination soon. We were in a very stressful situation.

"How is our dad?" Li Jing asked me.

I replied concisely, smoked three cigarettes and went upstairs.

In the corridor of the second floor, I saw a woman in her thirties rushing to a doctor.

"Please save my son!" she cried, kneeling.

"We are looking for a donor," the doctor said, trying to support her to stand up.

"Several months have passed. If you can't find a one, you can use my kidneys although his father's are not suitable!"

The doctor did not want to repeat but the woman kowtowed desperately. I walked away fast.

Chunshang was sitting on the ground, holding the banknotes of 500 yuan.

"You should give the money to the doctor now," I said.

"It'll be useless to use such expensive medicine," Chunshang sighed.

I snatched the money and walked into the doctor's office. After half an hour, a vial was brought to the ward. Ms. Cheng transfused it into our father. She glanced at Chunshang and me and then walked away. I watched the medicine entering our father's body drop by drop. I felt assured although he was still in a coma.

Chapter 43

Yesterday Chunshang called Chunshan and Chunshu, so they came the next morning. Chunshang had been worried about sending our father home too early, but now he changed his mind. We had a long talk outside the ward.

"What's your opinion?" Chunshan asked me.

I knew our father was still breathing but I did not know if the expensive medicine could work in his body.

"If it is late …" said Chunshu.

"It's going to rain," Chunshan added. "And it will last half a month if it rains." He glanced at me.

The roads in Yanerpo had not been hardened, even drizzle could make the roads muddy. Such a good driver as Yang Jin could not take our father home smoothly. If he died from falling off a car rather than from his disease, it would become a laughing stock. What was more, a shed would easily collapse in heavy rain. If he died halfway, his body should not be placed in the central room, and a shed should be established. But where could I get sufficient, durable waterproof cloth timely? If I could not finish the great task for our family, I would bring shame on my family name.

"Chunming pays the medical bills for our dad," said Chunshang. And then he told the medicine priced at 500 yuan to our brothers.

"We should have shared the expenses," Chunshan sighed in embarrassment. "I'm poor and I have an unpromising son. Swallow's current boyfriend Ren Dayou is as bad as Sixi and had been freeloading on her, but she is unwilling to break up with him. Sheng Jun has stopped doing pyramid selling and he had left that woman from Hebei province. She had induction of labour and the baby could not survive. Sheng Jun went to Zhejiang province and wanted to be with Swallow once again, but she avoided him. So he went to meet my wife, knelt and made an apology. She scolded him and had a long talk with Swallow, but it did not work. She warned that she would cut off the relation with her mother if she asked her to be with him again. Sheng Jun is not good enough, but is much better than Ren Dayou. Swallow and Sheng Jun have a son, but she is stubborn."

Chunshu got annoyed and realized that Chunshan was talking about those things to him on purpose. Hongquan and Bihua were living in Suzhou and working in different companies; they were rich and would buy a car. What was more, everybody knew that Xiaolan's family made a fortune. According to Chunshan, the rich one should pay the medical bill for our father and the poor one should not.

"You say Sixi is unpromising," Chunshu argued, smoking. "No man in our family lives in the house bought by his father-in-law except your son."

Chunshan did not retort.

"What should we do next?" asked Chunshu, smoking. He would take our father's body home today, otherwise he would be too busy to come to the hospital.

Chunshu glanced at everybody.

"I'll listen to Chunming," said Chunshang. He called Chunshan and Chunshu yesterday but changed his mind now. Chunshu glowered at Chunshang.

I did not say anything. "I'll call Guangwen," said Chunshang.

"He will let our dad continue to be hospitalized because he and the president of the hospital used to be classmates," Chunshu argued. "You pay the money and he can earn the money."

"If our dad snuffs it," Chunshan retorted, "it'll be difficult for us to contact a driver who is willing to take his body home. And that's what Guangwen says."

Chunshang called Guangwen at once and told him what was going on in the ward. After the call was over, he said, "He suggests that we should hold on and our dad may make a miracle, just like Dr. Yu said."

We became silent. I gave them cigarettes.

"I'll go back after I finish the cigarette," said Chunshu. "And you?"

Chunshan gave a forced smile silently.

"Our dad may become paralyzed," Chunshu added. "He is old and has been in a coma for too long. He may become a vegetable, just like Pighair Chen!"

Chapter 44

Pighair Chen came from the lower section of Huilong Town. He operated a store collecting pig hair. His true name had been forgotten. Two years ago, one day he rushed into a tea house run by Shang Zhongbing and shouted: "Come out, Bingwazi!" But soon he fell down on the ground. The owner would have got involved if no customer had sat in the tea house playing mahjong. Bingwazi was the nickname of Zhongbing.

Everybody knew that Shang Zhongbing and Pighair Chen had been enemies. Pighair Chen had had an affair with Zou Juhua, Shang Zhongbing's mother. Such a thing should have been kept secret, but Pighair Chen spread the news that Zou Juhua was his woman. Shang Guo, Shang Zhongbing's father, had been enduring that for more than ten years, and died when his son was 16. The boy was determined to kill Pighair Chen. After thirty years, Zou Juhua had been dead for five years, and the knife had been placed there quietly.

People said that Pighair Chen was Shang Zhongbing's father biologically although Zhongbing looked like his mother. They would rather believe that the adultery was true. As Shang Zhongbing grew up, he treated Pighair Chen as a stranger, and the latter did not go to his tea house. But one day when he went to meet him, he soon fainted. Neighbours said that Pighair Chen would tell the truth to Shang Zhongbing and would recognise him as his own son before he died. However, Shang Guo's spirit stopped him from doing that, at least he had called him father for so many years.

Pighair Chen had never got married and had an adopted son when he was 50 years old. The original name of the adopted son was Huo Jiu, and his name was changed to Chen Jiu after he had a foster father. Jiu was just four years old when he was adopted, and now he was 23. Shang Zhongbing got nervous when he saw Pighair faint and vomit blood. One of the customers called Jiu and told the details to him, but the customers did not mention "Bingwazi" so as to protect Zhongbing. They had owed Zhongbing. The income of a tea house included consumption of tea and 30% of the money that the customer had got in playing cards or playing mahjong. Some of them even borrowed money from Zhongbing after he lost all his money, but it was like usury.

Chen Jiu called an ambulance. When he was waiting for it, he cleaned the floor and apologised to Zhongbing. Pighair was in a coma and at last became a vegetable. Since then he had been lying on the bed for two years like a corpse. When his friends visited him and called his name, his chest was puffing up and his throat was rumbling. He desperately wanted to say something, but he could not.

Jiu had been taking good care of his foster father that the room in which he had been sleeping had no foul smell, and that there was no bedsore in his body. A small hole was made in Pighair's throat because he could not swallow; Jiu made food into liquid and injected it into his throat. The room should be set at a proper temperature to avoid infection and an air conditioner had been operating day and night. Power failures frequently occurred in hot summer because of excessive electricity consumption, Jiu would sit beside the bed and keep fanning him for the whole night.

Jiu had a girlfriend before his foster father got ill. They would have held a wedding, but they had to postpone it. That woman had taken care of the patient with him for six months, and at last she said, "I can't do it anymore and I'll break up with you. I know I owe you, and I would become your wife in the next life." Jiu cooked a wonderful meal in the kitchen silently. After they had their last meal together, he said, "You must have a happy life from now on; if not, you will owe me." He saw her out and then went to the kitchen to cook food for his foster father.

Chapter 45

"Can you do just like Chen Jiu has been doing?" asked Chunshu. "You should think about it, Chunshang. Our dad is willing to live with you only and he has been favouring you. You should not let your brothers look after him by turns after he becomes a vegetable. I won't look after him."

Chunshan cleared his throat.

"Even if our dad keeps lying on the bed like Pighair Chen," Chunshu added, "it is torment and also a sin! Few vegetables can be treated as carefully as Pighair. Yuling is not Chen Jiu and she won't do such a job even Chunming gives her 100,000 yuan each year!"

Anger and sadness were mixed on Chunshang's face.

"We'll take our dad home after we finish the cigarettes," I said.

Everybody including myself felt relieved at once.

Chunshang told our decision to Guangwen and hoped that Yang Jin could take our dad home. Later his facial expression indicated that Guangwen got angry. Chunshang said that Yang Jin would not come here. Chunshan and Chunshang glanced at Chunshu who was looking at the street. And then they looked at me who was thinking about our father.

The decision was made by me. Our father might recover if he could be treated a little longer. But if we could not find cars to take him home, he might survive and live 100 years.

"I've told this to Mr. Gou," Guangwen said to me on the phone. "Our dad can be sent home by a car arranged by the hospital priced at 800 yuan. The driver is Mr. Wang. He is sending another patient home and will reach the hospital half an hour later. Write down his phone number and he will contact you." When he told me the number, I repeated it and it was remembered by Chunshan.

I threw away the cigarette and went upstairs. I saw Ms. Cheng at the doorway and she would add medicine and make aspiration of sputum for my father.

"Do not leave your dad alone in the ward," she said.

"Thank you very much," I said sincerely.

She was surprised and then went into the ward.

He was lying on the bed, closing his eyes and opening his mouth a bit, and his pillow was put a little lower. After Ms. Cheng's operation, he was breathing calmly and looking much better. I stifled my eagerness to call him and I held his hands with syringe needles and adhesive tape. I was afraid of being alone with him when he was awake; but now I wanted to be with him as long as possible.

My brothers came into the ward. I released my grasp from our father's hands. The liquid medicine was like the fleeting time drop by drop. Time was neither a good thing nor a bad thing. We were waiting for the call silently.

"You'd better pay the medical bills now," Chunshu said to me. "We can leave as soon as the car arrives."

I did not reply because I would not go with them. After a few minutes, I received the call from Mr. Wang.

"You'll carry our dad's body into the car," I said. "And I'll pay the bills." I left the ward at once to avoid watching the medical tubes being removed from his body.

"The patient numbered 00033428 needs to be discharged from hospital," I said to a girl in the office area. "The ward will be cleaned and a car is waiting outside."

"Tell me the bed number and the name," she said.

I told her.

"The car to be sent by the hospital?"

"Yes."

She typed on a computer and then bills were printed.

Soon I saw our father lying on a stretcher being carried into a car by the workers arranged by the hospital. The adhesive tape rather than the needles was left on his hands. He was smiling and was free; he might be eager to go home. I soon looked away. Chunshan was holding bags of our father's belongings.

"Hurry up, Chunming," said Chunshan. "The driver is waiting for us."

"I've paid the bills," I said. "You can go now and I'll contact other drivers after I finish the rest of the matter."

They ran to the car and Mr. Wang drove off.

Chapter 46

I was sitting on a bench, smoking and thinking about the matter. Guangwen had said that he would invite Mr. Gou to dinner before our father left hospital, that could not happen. I was feeling that our father was still lying on the bed in the ICU in the third floor. I ran to that ward and stopped at the doorway: it was full of new people; they were surprised to see me and would greet me; but they chose to ignore me when they found that I entered the wrong ward. I saw a young patient with a wan face lying on the bed.

I thought that I should meet Ms. Cheng again before I left here. Dr. Kang walked past me too quickly to hear me speak. He entered the ward in which my father stayed just one hour ago. I searched for Ms. Cheng but I could not find her. I waited for her for a while because I thought that she might go to the toilet. Later I saw a wall covered with pictures of the nurses marked with their names. I saw the name Cheng Fangbing but the nurse in the picture was a middle-aged woman, not Ms. Cheng. Did she wear the wrong work clothes? No nurse in the pictures looked like her.

Part Four

Chapter 1

At noon I reached Chunhong's house, she was alone at home. I took a shower. As soon as she put my clothes into a washing machine, she got a phone call from Yuling.

"Our dad is dead," she said.

Chunhong burst into tears.

"Chunshan called me after the car started," she said, weeping. "I waited for him at the bridge. Qingmei's mom is living nearby that bridge and I don't want to see her. She has been sad since her husband passed away. Her house was closed and she might go to her hometown to plant crops. Today there were few cars. When I saw the car marked with The Third People's Hospital, our dad could hear me and grasp my hands. But he left us too soon!"

Neighbours greeted her and said, "Your dad was a kind-hearted man, so your relatives were willing to see him through a long journey. He chose to go to another world without hesitation so that his children and grandchildren would worry no more."

She called her husband.

"I know," Guangwen said on the phone. "I'll go back tomorrow after I finish important tasks. I've told this to Lily. Bring cigarettes to me."

She put cartons of cigarettes into a bag and said, "Let's go, Chunming."

Her voice was like a person who had a bad cold. Our father's hospital discharge was a prelude to his death. Without "Ms. Cheng" making aspiration of sputum for him, he was choked to death. His body was sent to Yanerpo.

Chapter 2

Chunhong and I walked past the riverside road. An egret, which I had seen, flew into the sky. It was the only creature left in the river. She asked Qingmei on the phone to look after Dou at weekend, and then called Xiaolan if they would go with us; if they did, they might let Qingmei take good care of their children. Xiaolan said that her husband was still working and they would decide after he got off work. Chunhong and I rented a motorbike at a fork road.

The motorbike owner wiped the seat with a towel. He asked us to sit behind him: me in front of Chunhong; the lighter one at the back. I saw the river rippling in the wind along the way.

"Do you know who the driver is?" she whispered to me.

The driver laughed. "Chunming may not recognize me."

"He is Maer, the son of Zhu Zhanhui."

He was like a dim shadow in my mind. I could not recognize the younger generation of Yanerpo. I was a guest here now and I would be treated as a stranger if I returned after several years.

Maer had been able to sing dirges since he was a child. At the age of nine he went to a funeral with his mother in Qingping. After he went back, he could sing laments. At that time funeral music had not been adopted in Yanerpo. The villagers thought that was an interesting thing. However, after those tunes were used in funerals, they regarded Maer's melodies as a jinx. His parents often beat him because of that, but the boy would sing dirges even in weddings. At the age of 13 he was hit by a stone when he started his singing in the mountain. It was a warning to him, but his habit was still with him: he was like a silkworm and his melodies like silk, and he would feel bad if he could not sing. Now his habit had been gone. Even Mrs. Hou was no longer a gossiper. They used to bring news to the village but their sparks became dullness.

"Hold my waist tightly, Chunming," said Maer. "Do not touch my hands." The motorbike was climbing a slope. I did what he told me, and Chunhong held my waist tightly for safety. There were steep turns.

"You may drive slowly," said Chunhong.

"Don't worry," said Maer. "I can drive safely." He spoke to us at ease when he was driving fast.

After Maer drove past Guaizaoping, he asked, "Is Chunshang there?"

He knew that our father had passed away. The villagers could easily know all kinds of news. Did he know the affair between his mother and Chunshu?

I watched those houses with courtyards. Maize was hanging on the beams on which squirrels were jumping. That reminded me of Tan Ruisong's hometown in Fengming Mountain. There were lots of men who could go into caves freely, and they were like the squirrels although they had no wings. Chunshang's house was located in one of them, but I did not know which one was his. I felt sad. An unsurfaced road was right ahead, and it would be a difficult ride even if the road was hardened. Maer had to stop and he was soaked with sweat. Chunhong got off the motorbike first, I was supported by him to get off. His sweat had an extremely strong odour.

"What's the fare?" asked Chunhong.

"It's free," Maer replied. He took out a Bafine with a white cover, the cheapest one, and he looked at me in embarrassment. I received the cigarette and asked him about the fare.

He lit it for me and got on his motorbike.

"I'm sorry," he said. "I did not take you to your destination." He drove off.

The fare was just a perfunctory remark. Chunhong had had so many free rides; what was more, Maer's mother had had an affair with her second brother. To anger her or to treat Zhanhui well or to treat Maer kindly? It was complicated.

Chunhong and I were taking a rest, surrounded by wonderful scenery. The two halves of an earthworm were finding each other, but were also like two repulsive magnetic poles. Trees, clouds, chirps … our father could not enjoy them anymore.

Chapter 3

The road was full of twists and turns. Chunhong and I saw a motorbike carrying two large bags when we were at the second crossing.

"That's Liu Xianwen!" she snapped.

He came from Laojun Mountain and worked as a funeral geomancer. Several years ago, whenever our father got ill and returned to Chunshang's house, he would say to Chunhong on the phone: "I'm back luckily, otherwise Liu Xianwen would be invited."

He was driving towards our destination and he must have been invited by Chunshan or Chunshang to conduct our father's funeral. The bags were full of robes and instruments. He would wear a Taoist's robe and chant Buddhist scriptures.

"Why are you so angry?" I asked Chunhong.

"He has been walking around my house since our dad got ill," she replied crossly. "And he even asked me if our dad got better. He has been waiting for his death!"

He would take his five disciples to each funeral. He could get 300 yuan each day, and a disciple of his 150 yuan and would give 50 yuan to him. What was more, he would demand red envelopes as many as possible. He, who might hear her swearing at him, smiled at us and continued his driving.

I had met him long before. He was a senior high school student when I was a junior middle school student. At that time his name was Liu Dong and was much more brilliant than Chunshu. Villagers said that he would be admitted to a prestigious university in Beijing. He used to live in Baihuaping, a place much higher than Yanerpo geographically. When I was cutting grass during summer vacations, I often saw him pass by Yanerpo. I gave way to him and saw his figure fade away. I regarded him as a hero. However, he failed in the college entrance examination. He restudied year after year, and even his younger sister's dowry was sold to be used as his tuition fees. He failed again and again, so he had to choose to be a farmer. I did not know when he changed his name and worked as a funeral geomancer.

His motorbike was tens of meters ahead of us. The road was riddled with hard objects and mud, which made the driving difficult and dangerous.

"Throw your bags to us!" Chunhong shouted loudly. "We may carry them for you!"

"Don't worry!" Liu Xianwen answered. "It'll be OK after I drive through this section!"

He kept driving; if he stopped, he could not restart the engine.

He was familiar with the path because he had been invited to conduct so many funerals. In fact, the roads around were as bad as this one.

For the sake of the road, I should not have written poems. Instead, I should have done my best to be promoted to a high official to build a new road for the villagers. Ruisong said that he had gone through the helplessness without a privilege. The government leaders in the town and county said that smooth roads had been built across the village, and Dongxuan had been commended by the provincial leaders. I was unable to build the road for the villagers. They took me as a hypocrite who had cut from old ties. Even Chunhong thought that I might become a monk.

The motorbike finally removed itself from mud. Dirty houses and graveyards could be seen. Eight plum trees were growing in front of the graveyards; some of the plums were mature.

"We may pick some plums," said Chunhong.

This was Poplar Terrace and the people here knew Chunhong. One of the women, who was using the toilet in a pigpen, heard Chunhong's voice and said, "Is he your third brother? You may pick the best plums." She peered at us through a gap in the fence.

"Thank you," said Chunhong. She picked several plums and put one into her mouth without washing it. It was sweet and sour, and such a taste could only be had in the mountain. That woman was still in the pigpen and asked, "When will your dad's funeral be held?"

Guests would express their condolences to the relatives of the deceased man on the night before the funeral. That woman would attend it.

"I don't know," Chunhong replied. "Liu Xianwen may know it after he checks the date."

Chapter 4

There was an elementary school ahead. Flowers and grass had been growing since the school collapsed. The words "Study Hard and Aim High" had been left in front of the grass. We saw six motorbikes carrying heavy bags passing by fast. They came from Yanerpo and had been doing business in the streets, including Maer.

They greeted us and their motorbikes were loaded with bags full of funeral products including firecrackers, incense and hell bank notes. Chunshan had bought some, but a lot of them would be used during the funeral.

After a few minutes another motorbike carrying more things came. At first we did not know who the driver was, but he greeted us and gave me a cigarette.

"Oh, you are Dayou," said Chunhong.

"Swallow and I would visit our grandpa," he said. "But we got the news that he had said goodbye to us. We went to the town by bus and rented a motorbike to Yanerpo. She is there now but I went to Guaizaoping and drove Uncle Chunshang' motorbike. He never locks his motorbike. I saw both of you in Maer's motorbike just now."

"Thank you," said Chunhong.

"You are welcome. I love driving motorbikes but I can seldom use it when I'm working in the factory."

"What have you bought?"

"My dad asked me to buy oil, liquor and other things. Some of them are put in barrels in the street and I'll fetch them tomorrow."

"Take your time."

He drove off as fast as he could.

"He is a sweet talker," said Chunhong. "He has not got married with Swallow, but he calls her relatives ingratiatingly." Sixi, Li Zhi, and Sheng Jun came into her mind. Ren Dayou was handsome and smart.

She called Qingmei to bind the chickens to be sent to Yanerpo the next day, and then she called Li Zhi. He went fishing again for a large fish. He had been staying beside a reservoir for three days and got a crucian and mosquito bites and ant bites. He had left home early this morning, so his mother did not know that.

"I'm in Eaglebeak Rock Reservoir in Mount Lordhou," Li Zhi said on the phone. "It's farther than Longyan Pond."

She scolded her son so much so that she forgot to tell him the most important thing after she hung up the phone. She called him again.

"Your grandpa has left us," she said gravely.

"Oh, I'm sorry," he replied. "But my dad, my uncles and my wife did not tell me."

"Go back to the town as quickly as you can! And help Qingmei to bind the chickens!"

"My brothers will work together to hold a funeral for our dad," she said softly. "Chunshang and his wife can't handle it because they are inexperienced and can't afford it. If the funeral is held by one family member, I should not give the chickens to him, otherwise people would say that I favoured him, which would be troublesome." She looked tired.

Weir Pond Trench, half a mile to the village, was a place for villagers to do the laundry, wash grass, feed cattle, and commit suicide. With the drum beats, Liu Xianwen's disciples came much earlier than their master.

Fields and steep slopes were right ahead, so motorbikes could not go any further. They were parked on the lawn, and the bags were carried by men. Our ancestors' graveyards were located thirty metres to the Weir Pond Trench. A mound was covered with grass beside our mother's grave. She had been waiting for our father for decades.

Chapter 5

The gate was opened and cypress twigs wrapped in pieces of white cloth were hanging on the beam. Chunhong and I stepped into the mourning hall and saw our father's feet. His body was placed on the door plank and his face was covered with a piece of yellow paper. He was still breathing this morning but now he was dead. His soul had left him and the black hat and blue hessian clothes made him look grave. His body was wrapped in seven layers of clothes with the marks of the past. His timeline seemed frozen and his life had been complied into a book of memories.

Chunshang had prepared his clothes and a black-and-white portrait of his in plastic package. The picture was placed above a table on which a bowl of rice and a bowl of cooked cured meat were put. Several sticks of incense were inserted into the meat beside a portable light. The picture caught fire half an hour ago and only eyebrows were left. Nobody knew how it began; perhaps our father disliked the picture. I pondered whether he found satisfaction in his appearance after he left the world. Death resembled such a powerful object that I knelt down and wept.

Chunshan and Chunshang supported me to stand up.

"You have done your best," Chunshang said sadly. "And our dad won't blame you."

I thumped his chest and I could not understand why I should do that.

Chunhong removed the paper from our father's face which had a metallic grey. With an open mouth he was eager for fresh air which was ordinary to others but precious to him. When a man understands that an ordinary thing can be extraordinary, he has been enlightened or he is a dying man. I covered his face with the paper, which seemed to separate death from life. Each of his arm was placed on each side of his body; his hands and legs were bound with black ropes. I could not know its meaning but I could see the solemnity of death. Both anguish and death were grim. His left leg was shorter than his right one even though he was wearing shoes. His hands were as wan as his face, and the backs of his hands were swollen because of excessive infusion, which I had not found under the adhesive tape. He had been tormented and should have been sent home much earlier. He had suffered too much so as to keep himself breathing a little longer. Villagers would rather send a tormented patient home rather than continue his useless, grievous medical treatment. Hell bank notes had been put between his fingers neatly, which seemed that he would scatter them on his way to another world.

When I watched a movie in an open-air cinema, I would run to the area behind the large screen. The content was the same although the direction was not.

I had written a poem about a dead man who entered Hades and had to be trained every day.

"Turn right!" the Commander ordered.

He made mistakes because he had not learned the thinking in hell: the right in the underworld was the left in the upper world. He was punished to do 100 push-ups. The Commander asked him to number off, he counted one, two, three and so on; but he made mistakes again because he should have counted from negative number. Now he could understand that he should transpose things when he was in hell, and that would be correct. Even when he became confused about the difference between right and wrong, he found that could be acceptable. I should have read the poem for our father. He and my relatives knew that I had been working in the provincial capital, but they did not know about the details; because if I told them that I was an editor of pictorials, they would not take it as a good job. What's more, I would feel ashamed of myself if I told them that I was a poet. Poetry was my secret both physically and spiritually.

Limin had been often invited by villagers to emcee weddings and funerals, and he would act like an efficient, candid general director in those events. He would host our father's funeral, too. He greeted Chunshan and asked Chunhong and me to sit outside the courtyard.

"We can manage by ourselves," she said.

Chunshan and Chunshang went outside.

Chapter 6

Liu Xianwen concluded that the auspicious day for our father's funeral would be on the 22nd day of the fourth lunar month according to geomantic omens and the Eight Diagrams (eight combinations of three whole or broken lines formerly used in divination). Today was the 13th day, and we would keep busy for the following 9 days. Artisans making funeral products would produce a tower-like house with paper as our father's dwelling place in hell. If the paper-house was poor, our father would be laughed at there: "When Xu Chengxiang was alive, he was a victim of poverty and raised seven children, and one of them was working in the provincial capital. But now he becomes a wretched ghost!"

Four meals would be provided for the staff each day during the funeral. The fourth meal was at midnight. Meat was a must in each meal. A pig would be slaughtered on the eve of the funeral. All the cured meat provided by three families should be consumed within the eight days; if insufficient, the men would go to the town by motorbike and buy more.

Before lunch and the midnight meal, everybody (including women) would be provided with a packet of cigarettes; if not, the participants would make trouble: give no tea water or let bowls of meat fall from their hands deliberately. The family members of the deceased man should buy or borrow the things to be needed in the funeral and hire workers. The relatives must kowtow, including children. You should be pulled up by others or you should finish your kowtows before you could say something.

Xu Xing's mother died many years ago. He asked for help from Wang Qingguang to send the message to his relatives. Wang Qingguang would have to walk across the village to tell others. Xu Xing knelt down and thought that he would be pulled up by Wang Qingguang, but the former had to kowtow four times because the latter did not support him to stand up. In early Ming Dynasty hundreds of years ago, it was required that the man must kowtow four times for the living one, and three times for the deceased one. However, the rule was changed in the areas around the Qingxi River: four kowtows for the dead man. Wang Qingguang battered Xu Xing with his fists after he finished his kowtows. As a result, Xu Xing had to lie on the bed during my mother's funeral and his wife Zhu Zhanhui dealt with all the problems. The subject had been on and on. Villagers said that Xu Xing should not have made four kowtows and criticized Wang Qingguang for his inflexibility. But the rule must be abided by.

Chunshan and Chunshang could understand it, but Chunshu could not. When Chunhong and I stepped into the mourning hall, Chunshu was measuring the door to paste paper of elegiac couplets. He was wearing glasses although he did not usually. He was focusing on his job that he did not notice us, and he would rather consider and write the couplets by himself than ask me to do it. When one of the villagers invited Chunshu to write couplets for his dead father, he looked at me and hoped that I could write for him because he thought that I had much more education than Chunshu. Chunshu wrote these words without asking me: "A Brilliant, Virtuous Doctor Buried in Good Soil." The deceased man had worked as a barefoot doctor for forty years, and those words were in good handwriting. I did not know who had taught Chunshu such good handwriting.

Chapter 7

After Chunshan and Chunshang went outside, Chunhong squatted and checked the ever-burning lamps and neatened the wicks, which seemed to reassure our father's soul. Swallow came. She was still a charming girl. She greeted her relatives and then put her hand on her grandpa's head.

Before we came here, Chunhong said to me, "Lily and Swallow are the most considerate children among the younger generation in our family." But soon she realized that she had a slip of the tongue.

"Weisheng is still a child," she added.

She thought that a child should be forgiven no matter what he had done.

But he was 18 years old and would take national college entrance examination soon. Weisheng had been pampered by my wife's parents since they retired and started to live in Chengdu with him.

"Swallow is a filial girl, but Xiaolan is not," Chunhong continued. "Swallow comes to see her grandpa through a long journey. Xiaolan is living in the town but she would rather play mahjong than come to the mourning hall with us."

"Only the first generation can carry out filial duties," Chunhong sighed. "The second, third, and fourth generation can't."

Only Swallow had the filial piety among the younger generation of our family.

"Are you tired?" Swallow asked me and Chunhong. "Dayou would pick you up but he had to unload the things. My mom told me that my grandpa had left us."

Fengjuan cooked lunch today and had it with Chunshu, Chunshang, and their wives. After our father was carried home from the hospital, he was put on the bed which he and his wife had shared for twenty years and in which he had slept alone for thirty years. Yuling heard a rumbling from our father's throat, and then found that he was dead. She yelled.

Chunshan rushed to set off firecrackers. According to the local custom, the dead man's children were not allowed to clean his body, otherwise his soul could not be pacified. Mrs. Hou had been cleaning female corpses while Magpie male ones. Chunshan went to see Magpie while Chunshu set up a wooden bed frame to place our father's body.

"When Magpie was doing his job," said Swallow, "Uncle Chunshang put clothes on my grandpa's body. As soon as he carried him on his back, my grandpa's head fell on Uncle Chunshang's with a thump."

She giggled but Chunhong glowered at her.

"Oh, the shoes have not been properly put on my grandpa's feet," Swallow suddenly exclaimed. She took off his shoes and put them on his feet again.

Chapter 8

Chunshan and Chunshang carried a table into the mourning hall for the funeral geomancers' chanting. The table was not stable, so Chunshang found a tile to stabilize it. Chunshu said the rooms were plagued with numerous rat holes, however, in reality, there were just six tiny openings. In fact, there were just six small holes.

The funeral geomancers holding two benches entered the hall. Liu Xianwen was flanked by four disciples. A booklet *Gratitude* was put on the table. They started their chanting.

"The deceased man is escorted to Hell…"

I imagined the scene. Were the black ropes the shackles on our father?"

The scene was much more horrible than death. Everybody is a sinner and will need to atone for his sins in hell. Is death a sin? The shoes were properly put on our father's feet. I saw Chunshu pasting the couplets: "It's a pity that our virtuous father could not live 100 years, but he will always be remembered by us."

Chapter 9

In the evening guests arrived amid firecrackers. The guests who came in daytime were very close relatives. The youngest sister of our mother was still alive, but we were strangers now, and she would not come here.

Before Chunshang's wedding, Chunhua went to Qingping Town to buy a blanket. One day in late autumn she came across the youngest sister of our mother who was living next to the store. The elderly woman was sitting in a cane chair in front of the door, holding a bowl of medicine.

"She looks healthy," Chunshu once said. "But she says that she has been ill. The medicine seems to be a blessing to her."

We did not know who many difficulties she had gone through. The medicine was cold, but she was still holding the bowl.

"Do you still remember me?" Chunhua asked the elderly woman.

"You are Chunhua," she replied impatiently.

Her voice reminded her of her mother's voice.

"Your bowl of medicine is getting cold," Chunhua said on the verge of tears.

"I can't recover soon."

"Chunshang will get married on October 28. Will you go to Yanerpo to attend his wedding?"

"No. I don't owe you."

She poured the medicine onto Chunhua's new shoes. Since then we had treated that woman as a stranger. But now we wished that she could come here. We had no elderly relatives except that woman and her husband. It was like peeling an onion, layer after layer, and at last, it was our turn. We had been eager to be protected even after we got old. We did not want to grow up rather than be afraid of death. We missed childhood even though heat, coldness and hunger were with us. The door would be opened and the future would be right there. If the elders were gone, our childhood would be gone, too.

Chapter 10

Chunhua and Chunying together with their husbands and children came. Two cushions had been put in front of our father's coffin. Children and adults kowtowed successively. Meanwhile, villagers talked who was the sincerest one.

"Chunhua and Chunying are much more pious than their husbands in their kowtows," Mrs. Hou said.

"The husbands are genuine, too," Xianhe retorted.

The villagers whispered that Mrs. Hou was still a gossiper. Fang Yun and Xianhe looked like prayers. Zheng Saner glanced at her mother-in-law. Chunhong came to the kitchen and chatted with her in the afternoon.

"Mrs. Hou seldom scolds Uncle Chenggui now," said Zheng Saner. "She plays her grandchildren off against their parents."

Mrs. Hou could hear those remarks and ignored them.

"Chunying has been crying so hard," she said. "But Chunhua cries less."

If you did not cry, people would say that you were unfilial. Chunhua got angry at once.

"Use a funeral kerchief now," said Fengjuan.

A quarrel was avoided. Fengjuan wrapped the kerchief around Chunying's head, and did the same to her children. I had covered my head with it much earlier. Chunying held my hand and walked into a quiet place through a long distance until gongs became unclear.

"Trust me!" she cried, grasping my shoulder.

I was puzzled.

"That day I told you that I disliked our dad, but that was untrue!" She wept.

Chapter 11

Everybody greeted Guangwen when he, soaked with sweat, walked into the courtyard. Yang Jin drove him to Weir Pond Trench. It was 9 a.m., but it was scorching. Guangwen wiped away his sweat and entered the mourning hall.

Guangwen gave everybody cigarettes. The men making funeral products and the funeral geomancers came from other villages, but received the cigarettes, too. Guangwen was well-known in Yanerpo. A chair in a shady area had been prepared for him. Half of the courtyard was cool.

"How about the dead fish in the river?" one of the men asked Guangwen. "There's a large fish looking like a human face!"

"That's just a rumour," Guangwen replied.

"If it were like a man's face, it should be a human being," said Wang Qingguang. "The fish was still alive after its flesh had been removed."

"Don't believe that!" Guangwen ordered.

"Has the fish been poisoned to death?" asked Limin.

"Our village has been investigated," Wang Qingguang said crossly.

"We should not be inspected," Magpie retorted. "But you, Qingguang, should be inspected. You might be the culprit."

Villagers in Yanerpo seldom joked to Wang Qingguang who would take banter seriously. But Magpie often made fun of him. Magpie's true name was Jiang Qiang and he was a cheerful man. He often teased and annoyed Wang Qingguang; after the latter lost his temper, the former was still giggling.

"I don't know why you are so cheeky," Wang Qingguang retorted. "Think about your dad!"

Magpie's father used to swear: "My eyes will explode if I tell a lie." And soon his eyes blew up. That was shame and agony. Even Mrs. Hou did not mention that unless she was cornered.

My brothers used to persuade Magpie to stop teasing Qingguang.

"We will reap what we sow," said Magpie. "My dad should not blame God."

"At least I have a wife and children," Qingguang argued. He derided Magpie. No woman would marry Magpie because of his father's shame. Magpie might have retorted that Qingguang had no son but had three daughters who had married far away. In fact, Magpie would say: "I have my own destiny."

Chapter 12

The listeners wanted to know the details about the culprit.

"The natural gas company should be blamed," said Guangwen. "One of the gas pipes leaked and polluted the river."

A villager said that the river rushed upwards several feet high one night. The listeners lost their interest in the subject; but the arrest of the culprit would be interesting.

In the past, prisoners would be shamefully shown to everybody on a market day. The ones under sentence of death and serious criminals would be sent to Ximencao Dam. Zeng Cai, who came from Laojun Mountain, and Xia Shuguo, from Mount Lordhou, were taken to five towns and the county to be watched by everybody, and at last they were taken to the Ximencao Dam to be executed by shooting. Zeng Cai was the husband of Xia Shuguo's younger sister. They had been engaged in kidnapping and selling hundreds of women: the females would be raped by turns before they were sold. Few prisoners were executed by shooting now. Zhang Dachao was imprisoned but he was not treated in the same way as the prisoners used to be. People said that his accomplice jumped into a river and he was arrested by the police.

"What's your name?" one policeman asked.

"I am Zhang Dachao!" he cried as loudly as he could.

If a man committed a crime locally, rumours about him might be known; if in another province, information about him would be unknown until a cinerary casket was taken home by his family members, and the truth would not be told to villagers. The caskets could be frequently seen because of accidents. The other day one casket was taken to Yaqueliang. When the man was joking with his colleagues, bits of wood flew into his throat, and he died after he was sent to the hospital. There was another man who came from Yefeng Village. When he was installing a lamp bulb, he fell into a crawler belt and his body was flattened after he came out of a roller.

A cinerary casket was as quiet as soil. The story of the soul resting in it was told in another place and had little to do with his hometown. An on-looker might feel disappointed when there was no prisoner to be watched by everybody, but there was much more than that.

"What should we do next?" asked Limin.

"I'll question the leaders in the natural gas company," said Guangwen. "During the years of gas exploitation, fruit trees in Mount Lordhou have been fruitless, pigs infertile, yields of crops and vegetables decreased. Even humans may not be able to have children."

The listeners got shocked.

After the two mountains were prospected, the natural gas was discovered in Mount Lordhou only. Meanwhile, Laojun Mountain was cursed. When Guangwen mentioned the polluted river, the listeners thought life in the Laojun Mountain was much better. However, the villagers in Lijiayan would be compensated with a lot of money, so the listeners envied the villagers living in the Mount Lordhou.

"Will the villagers protecting forests be provided with subsidies?" one listener asked.

"You have been provided with the money for more than ten years," replied Guangwen. "You used to cut down trees at will, but you can't now. The natural environment has got better and better, and natural disasters have become less and less. You should be grateful to the authorities."

"We have known nothing about the subsidies until recently," said Limin. "The village leaders have got the money for protecting the forests."

Guangwen glared at him and did not speak. The leaders were living in other areas, but Guangwen should not gossip about his colleagues.

The man making funeral products lived in Houziyan Village. The subsidies had been embezzled by villager leaders, and even the roads had not been built.

"What if the leaders are offenders in corruption?" he asked.

"Guangwen is a good leader!" Limin argued.

"Everybody in Huilong Town knows that! I mean the leaders in my village! If our village leaders are bad, we will think badly of our nation. If good, think well of it."

"Yanerpo and Lijiayan are like two nations!"

Later they said that they hoped Guangwen could be chosen to be the village party secretary in Yanerpo.

Bang! Limin's son was tuning up a loudspeaker. The instrument was owned by Liu Xianwen and it was put in Chunshan's spare room. When villagers in Mount Lordhou heard dirges, they knew that someone had died in Laojun Mountain, and vice versa.

Liu Xianwen whispered to Limin and the latter rushed to Chunshan's room.

"Weaksight, Xu Xing, Crap, Stone!" Limin yelled. "Take thick sticks and ropes, and go to Weir Pond Trench to carry the freezing coffin!"

The funeral music went on.

"The names are interesting," the man making funeral products smiled.

Weaksight, a nineteen-year-old man, got his name because of his visual defect, and he had never been employed by any company. Crap's mother gave him such a name because she thought his name might bring good luck, and he believed in his fate and was not greedy. Stone was Limin's son; the boy had often got ill since he was born, so Mrs. Hou gave him such a name and hoped that he could grow tall and strong. Crap's father died many years ago. In harsh winter, the leaders in people's commune asked men with questionable family backgrounds to carry firewood so that the leaders could work beside a fireplace. At that time Crap was a little boy, but he could carry a large pile of firewood barefoot and walk through heavy snow. He became a butcher after he grew up, and he could slaughter a fat pig easily.

The freezing coffin store had been operated by Liu Xianwen in the town.

Just like Mr. Gui had a set of kitchenware for rent, Liu Xianwen had a set of funeral devices for rent, too. Those things had been carried by truck to Weir Pond Trench, which meant that Yang Jin was not the only good driver in Huilong Town.

Chapter 13

Dayou came, holding a barrel of oil in his left hand, a barrel of beer in his right hand, with a large plastic bag around his neck. He had gone to the town three times today, and he would go to Chunhong's house to bring chickens, cylindrical fireworks, and bottles of mineral water. The cylindrical fireworks would be set off on the eve of the funeral and each bottle of mineral water would be given to each guest before each meal. In the past villagers had spring water through pipes connected with reservoirs. Now people would rather buy bottles of mineral water in supermarkets to show their superiority.

Dayou soon left to finish more tasks.

"Have some plums," said Chunhong. "Dayou picked them in Poplar Terrace."

The large bag around Dayou's neck contained plums. Chunhong took me to the kitchen which was set in Chunshan's house. The old houses of Chunshu and Chunshang were used to boil water, to store sundries, and to accommodate the staff and guests. On the eve of the funeral, the performers invited by relatives would keep working and would also need a rest.

Chunhong looked around and found nobody standing nearby, she whispered to me, "Dayou is hardworking."

Female relatives and other women were busy in the kitchen while cooks were making dishes. Mrs. Hou was making a fire and black ash could be seen on her face.

After Swallow and Qiuyue finished washing plums, Swallow gave some to everyone in the kitchen.

"Where are my two aunts?" asked Swallow.

"They must be having fun somewhere," Chunhong replied.

"I know where they are," said Qiuyue, holding a basin. "Uncle Chunming will join us."

Qiuyue's parents said that she was a rebellious girl, but she was less bad-tempered when she spoke to me. I often visited her and her younger brother in the school if I did not have a tight schedule in my hometown. She sweetly introduced me to her classmates and teachers, which seemed that I was the only uncle to her. She and her brother were not good at studies, but that did not matter. Other kids would arrive on the eve of the funeral, but they asked for leave at once to help adults. She was a charming girl with a lachrymal mole.

Qiuyue stumbled and fell because the heels of her shoes got stuck in the cracks on the ground. Swallow tried to pull her up, but she fell, too, because she stepped on slippery plum pits. The two girls' new clothes and new shoes were covered with mud. People in the kitchen including Mrs. Hou and Swallow laughed.

"Don't worry," said Swallow. "I have other clothes and you may wear them, and I'll wash the dirty clothes."

After Swallow stood up, she found blood pouring from her ankles. Qiuyue did not get hurt, but she needed help. I would help her to stand up.

"Don't pamper her!" cried Chunhong.

Qiuyue threw herself into my arms, watching Chunhong sadly.

"She must be peevish now," said Mrs. Hou.

"She wants to be taken good care of," said Zheng Saner.

"Do not dote on a child!" Mrs. Hou retorted.

When Qiuyue changed her clothes, Swallow picked the plums on the floor. There was a pigpen under the floor. The smell of pigs could be smelt usually, but today could not; because a funeral would be held.

"The pigs are eating plums," Swallow laughed. Some plums had fallen into the pigpen. "What if their teeth are hurt by plum pits?"

"Doctor Liang Boer will cure them," said Chunhong.

Liang Boer was a dentist in the town and had been frequently visited by Chunhong over the years due to her recurring toothaches.

Swallow rewashed the plums and gave good ones to me and Chunhong, and kept some for Qiuyue. She had the smallest one. She cleaned the dirty areas in her clothes with a brush soaked with water in a basin, and then she poured the water outside. Chickens under walnut trees squealed.

Qiuyue came out with new clothes, held the plums and gave the dirty clothes to Swallow.

"You should wash your own clothes, Qiuyue," said Chunhong.

Qiuyue was eating a plum silently.

"She is a guest," said Swallow. Even Fengjuan supported Qiuyue.

Before Swallow scooped water from a vat, a cook shouted, "Don't do that!"

Too much water would be used in the kitchen and pipes were connected with a pond outside. She had to go to Weir Pond Trench to wash the clothes.

"My mom and aunt are in the kitchen," said Qiuyue.

"You should have told me much earlier," said Swallow. "And the cook would not have yelled at me."

The cook Pu Gen smiled. He was invited from another village and he could make good use of food materials for a large number of guests and he was praised by his employer. But he was bad-tempered: he would yell if the materials were not provided according to his requirements. Even if his parents were in the kitchen, he would shout. He called the shots in the kitchen.

Swallow put the dirty clothes in a basin and went outside. Qiuyue, taking my arm, went to Weir Pond Trench, followed by Chunhong. Mrs. Hou and Zheng Saner had no topic to talk with each other in the kitchen.

Chapter 14

When we were walking leisurely, I said to Qiuyue, "You should be less impetuous when you are speaking to your parents, and you should listen to them."

"I don't want to be educated by them," she retorted. "They did not look after me after I was born, and they will feel ashamed of themselves if they keep me under strict control."

"Your parents have to work in another province and earn more money for you and your younger brother. They wear cheap clothes but you wear good ones."

"I can wear cheap clothes, too!"

"You should understand that they have been working hard to support you.

You are so beautiful that which parent doesn't want to take you by his side? but they can't."

She looked at me with sadness.

"Your brother is not as peevish as you," I added.

She laughed. "He is much more petulant than a girl, and he becomes a sweet-talker when he is with our parents."

"Why is he petulant?"

"They buy cheap clothes for him, but buy brand-name ones for me."

Chunhong and Swallow stopped to wait for us, so we hurried up.

"Dayou has been treating Swallow well," Chunhong said to me. "He has been unable to work for several months since he got hurt in his hands. He is not an idler. But Sheng Jun called me the other day and he wanted to be with her again. I scolded him but I should not meddle in his business."

"Dayou is much better," said Qiuyue. "And he is handsome."

"You don't know about the whole thing," said Chunhong.

"Dayou can take good care of me," Swallow explained. "But Sheng Jun can't. I must work hard to survive. When I was doing pyramid selling, I was anxious although I looked happy. If I were with Sheng Jun again, he would criticize me that I had cheated on him."

"How dare he say that? He has cheated on you!"

"He argues that men are different from women."

Chunhong did not know what to say. Most of the men in the world, including Guangwen, had said the same thing.

"Be careful after you become a stepmother," Chunhong added. "People will always talk no matter how well you treat your stepchildren."

"I know," said Swallow.

Our ancestors' graveyards were surrounded by bamboo forests. When Swallow was washing clothes, we walked into a shady area.

"When did you come here?" asked Chunhong.

"Much earlier," Chunhua replied.

"We are talking about our dad," said Chunying, glancing at Chunhua. "Whenever I returned to Yanerpo for the Spring Festival, he would always wait for me. It lasted even when I was 10 years old." She was on the verge of tears.

My sisters began to talk about the past.

"Chunying was adopted by another family," said Chunhong. "And our dad said that he would take her home after one year. My aunt lived near that family. She said that the girl had been taken good care of, so he did not take her home."

Chunying became sadder.

"In October after our mom died," Chunhong continued, "our dad went to cut firewood and I brought food to him. When he saw me, he let me have the food because I looked too thin. I had the congee. At that time we only had two meals a day. He often escorted me to school and he would hide himself behind a tree and would not leave until I went far away."

In the forest we could hear the funeral music. The man who had cared for us most died.

Chapter 15

"Silence for the man who has left us…" Chunshu chanted.

Each of us was holding three sticks of incense. Guangwen, the man in the front, was holding a rod wrapped in white paper. We were walking around the coffin amid drums and chanting. Our father was lying in a transparent freezing coffin without yellow paper on his face.

"Kowtow!" Liu Xianwen chanted. He repeated three times and we kowtowed three times.

The process lasted for nearly an hour; we were soaked with sweat and Guangwen could hardly stand up. Chunshan and Chunshu were busy, so Guangwen became the man holding the rod in the front. We were wearing kerchiefs in our heads but he was wearing a piece of hemp cloth for mourning in his head and a long gown. The gown was borrowed from Liu Xianwen and it had been worn by too many men. Guangwen held on even though others might relax a bit.

Except Guangwen, we were standing freely. Xiaolan came this morning. Qiuyue squatted tenderly so that her clothes would not be dirtied and the incense would not fall on her. Huatian kowtowed piously. He kicked Qiuyue's ankles when she did not kowtow, and she tapped on his face.

"A mosquito!" he cried.

The others laughed. Guangwen glowered at us and then moved slowly. My sisters continued to guffaw.

"Look at Guangwen," Chunying whispered to me.

What I could see was his fat buttocks covered with white cloth.

The funeral geomancers laughed, too. After the drums ended, we felt relieved.

"You are not serious!" cried Guangwen, holding the freezing coffin. "Kowtow for King of Hell, for Bodhisattva, and for atonement!"

Chapter 16

Guangwen vented his anger. He complained that we did not listen to him about our father's hospital discharge. We called him and he arranged a car to take our father home. Last night when Chunshang talked about our father's death, Guangwen argued, "You wanted him to die as quickly as possible."

All of us were there. The grudges among family members for decades would explode during the funeral of a parent. If there was a terrible quarrel during a funeral, the members would have ill luck. To avoid that, Chunhong said to her husband, "You must have drunk too much!"

Guangwen remembered that he was accepted by our father even though he was rather poor thirty years ago.

"Even Mr. Gou felt a pity for our dad," he cried resentfully. "A patient with a cerebral haemorrhage can be cured. He might have survived if he had not been taken home."

"The car was arranged by Mr. Gou," said Chunshu. "He knew what was going on."

"He is the president of a hospital," Guangwen argued. "And he respects the decision made by the patient's family members."

Zhuqing pulled Chunshu's sleeve, trying to stop him from saying more. We could understand why she did that: such a matter should be taken on by all the sons of the family, not by himself. He should not offend Guangwen; what was more, he had borrowed money from the latter. The three sons could not afford a funeral, so they borrowed 6,000 yuan from Guangwen. They would have borrowed from me, but I had paid the medical bills for our father.

"You have overthought, Zhuqing," said Guangwen. "I've lent you some money and I don't know when you will repay. We do know each other. You will smile after I lend you the money, but soon you will criticize me."

He hit the nail on the head. Just before he lost his temper, Limin came.

The subsidies were mentioned in the morning, so Limin wanted to know much more. The village leaders in Yanerpo would rather keep the villagers in the dark. The office building of the town government was eye-catching. A banyan was planted in the courtyard in which artificial hills, goldfish, various plants and flowers could be seen. Long stone staircases would be a difficult job for the elderly. Two walls in the hall were covered with signboards of various departments. The staff were busy but visitors did not know what they were busy with. Limin wanted to ask Guangwen about the details. Guangwen's mood changed at once.

"We should take things seriously from now on," said Chunhong.

Chunhua and Chunying looked at each other and stifled their laughs.

Chunhong would rather the funeral geomancers listen to her because she found they were doing their job perfunctorily. Liu Xianwen soon realized that and he stepped out of the mourning hall, pretending someone calling him. Guangwen walked outside, followed by us. Tables were placed in the courtyard and more guests would come here. The guests would play mahjong before and after meals. Even Chunshan and Chunshang would join the players when they were not busy.

Guangwen would rather play mahjong with town government leaders and bosses in tea houses. Winners would not care about losses, but losers would be calculating. Striking a golden bell once would be much better than beating a bad drum repeatedly. If there was no golden bell, you would have to use a bad drum.

Chapter 17

Chunshu had never played mahjong. He used to be a bookworm; if he did not read, he would sleep. During these days he had been busy writing couplets and funeral orations. He would write as required by guests and would chant. If he wrote a funeral oration for a guest's deceased parent or relative, he should use proper wording; after he finished, he would be provided with 30 yuan and a packet of cigarettes. Today he wrote elegiac addresses for our father, he would have cigarettes but no money. He had finished nine addresses, eight of them would be used by Guangwen's adopted children who had come here and would come again on the eve of the funeral; the last one would be used by my friends in the county.

I had to tell my friends what had happened, and later they drove here. One car ran into a rice seedling bed. A woman asked my female relatives where the restroom was, they were puzzled. Swallow explained, "There are latrines." As soon as she led the woman into a latrine, flies and mosquitoes rushed at her.

Tan Ruisong and Single Braid knew the rules in rural areas. They would pay for funeral orations, I said that I would handle it. Single Braid gave a packet of cigarettes to me. It was a cheap one and I gave it to Chunshu. When he saw that the cigarettes were much better than he had smoked, he said no more. I stayed with my friends when Chunshu was writing an oration. Later he chanted in the mourning hall and we were standing nearby solemnly.

Single Braid did not attend it. "I had a dream one night," he explained. "I saw a man shitting along the way. He stopped shitting when I was standing in front of him. A man in the cultural centre told me not to attend any funeral within one month."

After the chanting was over, Ruisong said, "The funeral oration is remarkable."

"It was written by Chunshu," I said.

"Wow!"

Single Braid looked at me and I could understand him: he should have given much better cigarettes to Chunshu. He took pictures of the couplets and said, "Did your brother write them?"

"Yes," I replied.

"Your family has men of letters!"

Ruisong gave me an envelope containing the funeral money. As soon as I accepted it, he said, "We have to go now."

I would not let my friends have meals with my relatives. The tableware was dirty and the guests were not as clean as those who came from cities. Some of the guests had never come to the mucky rural areas. Swallow whispered to me that the two women got shocked at the sight of the latrine. I should not let them suffer from dirtiness anymore.

I saw my friends outdoors although my relatives tried to stop me. Guangwen gave cigarettes to them and we followed them. Limin told through a loudspeaker that villagers would carry ropes and thick sticks to get a car out of a field.

"The county government leaders should have valued you and should have made a new road in your hometown for your sake," Ruisong whispered to me.

Others did not hear what he was talking. I was an unimportant poet. We returned after my friends drove off, and I caught a glimpse of my true hometown reflected in their eyes.

Chapter 18

My three sisters shared one funeral oration. Li Zhi with his wife and child, Lily and her husband, Chunhua's son and daughter-in-law would arrive tonight. Guangwen told Chunshu about the funeral orations for guests. He might choose Chunhong to say this, but he insisted. Guangwen gave two packets of famous cigarettes to Chunshu, but the latter did not receive them at once.

"Qingmei will bring more," said Guangwen. He put the two packets into Chunshu's pocket, and lit one cigarette for him.

Chunshu would keep busy until the funeral was over. He chanted with a microphone, "Silence for the man who has left us…"

If the chanting could be recorded, Stone would just need to play it, but Chunshu would rather sing with his own voice.

"Every time I sing," said Chunshu, "I'll improve the words and melodies." Those skills had been taught to him by his master Xiao An.

Chapter 19

At 11 a.m. my three brothers and the cook talked about the pig which would be consumed on the eve of the funeral. Such a pig of 330 pounds could only be provided by Zhu Zhanhui. Xu Xing might tell this to his wife, but Chunshan suggested that Chunshu should tell this to Zhanhui because there would be discounts and money might be paid to her later. Chunshu gladly called her.

But Zhanhui wanted the highest price fluctuating from 7.5 yuan per 500 grams and 7.2 yuan per 500 grams. "I'll need money," she said. "And I'll sell it if you don't buy it now."

There was no fat pig in other villages now. Zhanhui knew that only her family could provide such a large pig.

Before lunch, Chunshan told this to me and Chunhong.

"Chunshu got so angry that he could not light a cigarette," said Chunshan.

"She is a leech upon Chunshu," said Chunhong. "He tries to satisfy her, but she is ungrateful! It serves him right!"

When Zhanhui was having affairs with Baohan, Xueqin and Zhenxun, she treated them as her servants. In one spring, Zhenxun ploughed her farmland and then his own. After he came back from the field, his nine-year-old son put the bull out to pasture, but the animal had got so tired that it could not stand firmly and fell off an escarpment. Luckily the boy threw away the rope timely, otherwise he would have died. Zhenxun would borrow a bull from Zhanhui, but she refused with an excuse that her bull needed a rest.

"You are doing useless work for that bitch!" his wife scolded him.

He thought he had been treated worse than an animal by her. He punched her in the chest so much so that she had to keep bending for one month, but she did not learn the lesson of ingratitude.

Chapter 20

Zhanhui came in the afternoon. School was over much earlier on Friday and owners of motorbikes were waiting for customers outside the school gate. Zhanhui's son Maer could not do business this afternoon because he would have to drive his mother and his son. Even Tian was a free rider on Maer's motorbike. Three or four people could sit in one motorbike and the driver could go.

Tian greeted his grandpa. Zhanhui would not have come here early if she had not had to sell her pig. Chunshan led Tian to kowtow in front of our father's coffin. Chunshu knew that Zhanhui was here.

"Look at Chunshu," Chunhong whispered.

We were taking a rest and Chunshu was smoking a branded cigarette. He covered its brand mark with his fingers lest others should discover: they were smoking cheap cigarettes. He talked with men producing funeral products and then glanced at the mahjong table. He had been focusing on his own business during these days.

"Chunshu is much happier than Xu Xing when Zhanhui is here," said Chunhong. "I thought that he had become annoyed."

Tian greeted us after he walked out of the mourning hall. He was a good boy and also academically brilliant. Whenever Chunshan lost his temper because of Sixi, he snapped, "Sixi is so bad that I'd rather let Tian become worse than him. Fight evil with evil!" Tian smiled when he heard this, and he often consoled Chunshan. When Chunshan called Sixi, Tian said on the phone, "You should behave yourself, dad. You have parents and a son." Chunshan often told this to others emotionally.

"Your grandparents will depend upon you, Tian," said Chunhong, holding him in her arms.

"I'll always be a good boy," said Tian.

"Do you know when your dad will return?"

"I don't know. And my grandpa doesn't know either."

"What's in your pocket?"

"The plums given to me by Aunt Qiuyue. She picked them in Poplar Terrace."

Qiuyue was picking plums when others were walking around the coffin. Chunhong asked Tian to wash the plums.

"Oh, you look unhappy, Chunhong," said Zhanhui.

Zhanhui was living in her old house. She and her family members stayed in their new house for three months during which they had been invaded by snakes day and night. In addition, bamboo rhizomes often entered the house and the occupants dreamed that they entered their mouths and eyes. It was said that the dreamers would become dumb and blind in the next life.

Xu Xing would worry about the next life, but Zhanhui was worried about her current life. She chose to return to her old house so that she would have more time to be with the livestock. In addition, she often heard a girl crying at midnight in her new house. She had known the shocking news that Xu Jinyang had killed a little girl. Before she died, she laughed instead of crying; she cried after she was split in two; and she had been weeping for decades. The dead girl had been wailing because of Xu Jinyang. Zhanhui's new house had been built on the foundations of Xu Jinyang's old one; as a result, she often heard the girl crying.

Chapter 21

Zhanhui was looking at Chunhong sadly.

"Why are you so downcast?" Chunhong asked. "Join us."

I wanted to let her sit down, but since I was standing, she stood too.

"Is your husband here?" Zhanhui asked Chunhong, tapping her on the shoulder.

Now everybody could hear Guangwen snoring and they laughed. Chunshu, standing in front of the man who was crafting funeral products, cast a glance at Zhanhui.

"Chunshu looks handsome when he is wearing glasses," she said coquettishly.

"Oh, I'm no longer young," Chunshu sighed.

"But you are much younger than the Narrow Rock," one man said.

There was a well-known Narrow Rock in Huifeng Ridge of Laojun Mountain. It was 10 meters high and there was a narrow path beneath it. In addition, there were two obvious marks in the shape of testicles. According to the legend, the marks had been left by Chang Kuo-lao as a result of sitting on it for countless years. In Chinese mythology, Pengzu lived 800 years and Chang Kuo-lao 27,000 years. Chang Kuo-lao had spent 5,000 years measuring the growing length of the millennial Rock.

"They are immortals," Chunshu laughed.

"You are gaining weight, Chunhong," said Zhanhui.

"I've been busy with my dad's funeral," Chunhong said. "But I've put on more weight."

"He passed away in his eighties, which is a blessing to your family." Zhanhui greeted Limin.

"I hope that you can do us a favour," said Limin.

"But I haven't been invited," said Zhanhui.

"I invite you now," said Chunhong, ready to kowtow.

"Oh, that's too much for me."

"I can make four kowtows for you if you want me to do it."

That reminded her of Wang Qingguang. Many years ago, Xu Xing made four kowtows for Wang Qingguang, followed by trouble. The two men were playing mahjong and did not hear the women's talk. Tang Qun, the wife of Wang Qingguang, carried chickens, eggs, bean curds, and cured meat to visit her youngest daughter who had a baby.

"Your son and your husband have been earning money for you," said Chunhong. "You are having a comfortable life."

"I don't believe that my husband can win in playing mahjong!" cried Zhanhui.

"Oh, I win today!" Xu Xing laughed, slobbering.

He was smoking tobacco with a long-stemmed Chinese pipe, just like most of the elderly did. The pipe contained a smoke tube, with copper-plated iron in the head and a bamboo tube in the middle. He drooled when he was gripping the pipe with his teeth.

"I hate that!" Zhanhui cried, looking at him.

He wiped his mouth with his hands and then grasped mahjong tiles.

"Oh, that's disgusting!" Zhanhui yelled.

That was how Zhanhui greeted her husband. Someone called out Limin's name before he could arrange an odd job for her. He ran so fast that he nearly bumped into his father.

Uncle Chenggui was like a silent snail now and was wearing cotton-padded clothes and trousers even in hot summer. When he was standing or sitting in a place, he would be like a statue and there was sorrow, puzzlement, or emptiness on him. He moved himself towards the mourning hall of our father and watched his picture, and then he kept sitting on a stone roller for several hours. He had been with his shadow and would be left alone after the shadow was gone because of in the evening or the dim light. It seemed that his shadow had been sitting there.

Now I could understand Uncle Chenggui much better. You can't comprehend a man fully when he is alive, and what you can catch on to is the situation similar to yours; the different one is his secret.

Uncle Chenggui had been preoccupied with his secrets quietly and he did not wake up until others shouted that it was time to have a meal. Young people supported him to sit beside a table, and then he finished his meal silently without any interest in other's talk. He became the eldest man in Yanerpo after our father died. He was not afraid of death; instead, he was eager to see that a curtain could cover up everything after death. Tan Ruisong once told me that humans were living with the times; if one's era was gone, his heart would be gone with the era although his body was still alive, which was the reason why eternity was much worse than death. He said that he would rather turn himself into a fool because being stupid could make him survive all the time.

Chunshu tried to watch Zhanhui when he was talking with others, and he wanted Limin to arrange an odd job for her as quickly as possible so that he could enjoy staying with her. Such a person should be invited, which was good manners.

But Zhanhui was relaxed. "I can make eight kowtows for you, Chunhong," she said, looking at Wang Qingguang.

"Have a seat," said Chunhong.

She sat beside her and talked about Wang Qingguang's family affairs in a low voice.

Chapter 22

The three daughters of Wang Qingguang did not marry too badly. Many years ago he got nervous and bad-tempered when he could not have a son. His eldest daughter married a man who worked in a brickyard, and later she introduced her two sisters married men who worked in a lime factory.

Afterwards Wang Qingguang often boasted that his family members could benefit from state-owned companies. In fact, the brickyard and the lime factory were collectively-owned enterprises. The lime factory went into bankruptcy, within less than half a year after the youngest daughter's marriage, resulting in six months of unpaid salaries. The brickyard went out of business within one year. Everybody knew that.

"Wang Qingguang thought that others had been kept in the dark," Zhanhui said with derision.

What Zhanhui wanted to tell most was that the husband of Wang Qingguang's eldest daughter had strangled his aunt. The culprit had been still at large. He would be executed by shooting if he was arrested, and he dared not return home even if he contacted his family members. The eldest daughter of Wang Qingguang had had to live alone.

Zhanhui said this in a low voice but she could work off her anger. Since Wang Qingguang badly battered her husband she had never forgotten that.

"Gratitude can be always remembered but hatred can't be dispelled easily," Chunhong sighed.

Zhanhui cared for her husband although she had cheated on him again and again. Chunhong and other villagers of Yanerpo had never heard of the killing. Wang Qingguang often boasted that he had great family wealth, but everybody would turn a deaf ear to his bragging. After telephones became popular in the village, he was gradually ignored.

"You'll need to wash dishes in the following days, Zhanhui," said Limin.

"I don't want to do that," she said. "What are Mrs. Ye, Mrs. Jiang and Mrs. Zheng doing?"

"They are in the kitchen," replied Chunhong.

"Join us to roast meat!" Zhuqing yelled.

We wondered if Zhuqing had known about the affair between her husband and Zhanhui. Chunhong once said that Zhuqing would not make a scene if she did not know that her husband had given eggs and money to Zhanhui.

"Don't burn your meat!" Zhanhui replied loudly. And then she said to Limin, "I'll go to the kitchen."

"You'll need to sell your pig on the market day, so you may do an easy job now.”

Women would rather be chosen to help cooks during weddings and funerals. It was not cold in the kitchen in winter, but it was stuffy in hot summer. A woman should work cleanly and efficiently in the kitchen.

“I’ll chat with you later,” Zhanhui said to Chunhong. And then she said to me, “I’m sorry that I’ve taken your seat.” She walked towards Chunshan’s room and then went to the courtyard holding a barrel of pigwash.

“Zhanhui can make pigs fatter by using the pigwash,” Chunhong said to me. “She is smart. Chunshu and Chunshang don’t keep pigs. And the leftovers are too much for Chunshan’s pigs. Xu Xing cuts greenfeed for pigs but does not carry a barrel of pigwash home. He may be too embarrassed to do that. But Zhanhui can do things willfully.”

Chapter 23

“Qiuyue has fallen over!” Tian shouted.

The funeral music was going on loudly, but Chunhong and I could hear Tian’s voice.

“Where is she?” I asked.

We saw Qiuyue walking normally.

“She is all right,” said Chunhong.

“I saw her… he…”

Dayou came, holding a large plastic bag of plums. That’s the man whom Tian mentioned. Did he pick plums with Qiuyue?

Dayou quickened his pace when he saw us but Qiuyue was walking with a limp. I did not help her lest Chunhong should say that I doted on her.

“Qiuyue got off the motorbike before I stopped,” Dayou explained. “She nearly fell.”

“Nearly?” Qiuyue retorted. “My ankles hurt!”

“Dayou is very busy today,” said Chunhong. “You should not have let him drive you to pick plums.”

Qiuyue did not argue but watched her sadly.

“Don’t worry,” Dayou consoled her. “I’ve been to the town just twice today.”

Qiuyue held my arm and she was still watching Chunhong sadly. She tried to hide herself.

"I've brought chickens here," Dayou added. "They were blind and they did not eat the food on the ground unless their heads were pushed downwards."

"You were efficient," said Chunhong. "Where did you store them?"

"I've kept them in Uncle Chunshang's empty pigpen. Dad says that there is sufficient meat and the chickens will be killed on the eve of the funeral."

"When you went to my house, who opened the door? Li Zhi or Qingmei?"

"I did not go upstairs. Swallow called Li Zhi and Qingmei was waiting for me outside. The chickens were strung on a rope. After Qingmei lifted the iron grating, I pulled the rope upwards hard. It was heavy."

"I'll wash the plums," Dayou added. "You can have them soon." He looked at Qiuyue and then he went back holding Tian's hand.

Chapter 24

We saw Zhanhui holding an empty barrel.

"What has happened to Qiuyue?" asked Zhanhui.

"She has fallen down," Chunhong replied. "But she is OK."

"I have medical plasters. You may use them. My husband had a low back pain last month, and he recovered after he used two plasters."

"Will you use them?" Chunhong asked Qiuyue.

"No. I dislike the smell."

"You don't have to use them."

"Qiuyue is such a beautiful girl," Zhanhui smiled. "I can bring you plasters if you need them."

Her house was located on a slope full of red stones and with some amaranth thirty meters away from here. Cactuses and blue stones could be seen on the roof to exorcise evil spirits. I thought Chunhong would decline, but she said, "Chunming and I haven't visited your house for twenty years."

That was a big surprise to Zhanhui. "Let's go now," she said warmly.

"I won't go there," said Qiuyue.

"You should stay in a safe place," said Chunhong. "We will walk around the coffin several hours later."

Zhanhui's house looked tidy. It must have been cleaned by her; her husband could not do such a good job. Chunhong watched the pigpen after she stepped into the courtyard. I realized that she came here for the pig. Zhanhui brought sunflower seeds and would prepare glasses of water for us.

"We are not thirsty, we…" said Chunhong.

The pigs gave loud farts; they must have had a delicious meal.

"Are you keeping fat pigs?" Chunhong asked deliberately.

"Only one," replied Zhanhui. "I would have sold it on the next market day, but Chunshan said that he would need a fat pig for his father's funeral."

In fact she had received the call from Chunshu, but she said that it was called by Chunshan on purpose.

"You won't fleece us," said Chunhong.

"Oh, our two families have got along," Zhanhui said ingratiatingly.

"The price?" Chunhong asked.

"Well, let's go to see the pigpen."

There were four pigsties and one cattle house. Two pigsties were empty, one was used to keep two piglets, and the fat pig was living in the largest one. After the host entered, the bull was quietly regurgitating food but the pigs got excited. The piglets squealed sadly because they could not have the delicious meal; but as soon as they saw the two strangers, they stopped crying and watched us curiously. The fat pig was mature. It wanted to have more food, but it did not shout. It was so fat that it had to walk with difficulty and that it could not wag its tail. It was like a large ball of meat without fur. After a few days it would go to a courtyard driven by a bamboo spar and would be slaughtered by its female owner. Unawareness could be sometimes be a form of mercy.

Chapter 25

Qinglian and her younger brother arrived by foot and mud could be seen on their clothes. Yuling came out of the kitchen and supported the two children into the mourning hall. They did not kowtow but leaned on the freezing coffin and watched their grandpa's body. Yuling tried to pull them to kowtow, but she failed.

"Xu Chengxiang loved Qinglian and Zhaohui," said Mrs. Hou. "They often helped him tp drink water at midnight. Qinglian allowed him to have only one cup of liquor each day and she would take away the cup if he wanted to have more. If Yuling took away the cup, he would say that she did not treat him well. In places like Yuling, daughters in law are treated just like daughters. He should not have complained so much."

"The adults are good," said Zheng Saner. "So their children are good."

Yuling was on the verge of tears.

"Even Yuling is crying for Xu Chengxiang," Mrs. Hou added.

Yuling consoled her children. Meanwhile, Lily with her husband, and Li Zhi with his wife arrived. Lily had been crying along the way and Li Zhi gave cigarettes to others just like his father did. Qingmei gave a bag with three cartons of cigarettes to Guangwen. He did not care if the branded cigarettes were discovered by others, and Qingmei's behaviour followed Chunhong's example.

"Did Li Zhi take away my cigarettes?" asked Guangwen.

"He took away the cheap ones," replied Qingmei.

"OK."

"Qingmei looks like a young girl," said Limin.

She wore no makeup for her grandpa's funeral.

"She is a good daughter-in-law," said Guangwen. "And she is much better than my son."

Limin knew through the talks between Chunshan and others that Guangwen had made his cigarettes into grades. The cigarettes Guangwen smoked should not be smoked by his son.

"You did not let Li Zhi bring your cigarettes here?" asked Limin.

"If my wife is not at home," replied Guangwen, "Qingmei will open the cabinet. If Li Zhi is at home, he will act like a robber."

"You have a good son but you are such a stern father. He is very lucky to be born in your family and he should enjoy all the good things."

"I'll be with Dou," Qingmei said to her father-in-law. "She is calling me."

"The son of Ho Laosan has gone nuts," Limin added after Qingmei left. "But that's not caused by taking drugs."

Whenever Li Zhi was mentioned, people would talk about the son of Ho

Laosan to make Guangwen and his wife feel less worried.

"By what?" asked Guangwen.

"By syphilis," replied Limin. "It can make a man go crazy."

Mrs. Hou used to curse someone that his ancestor had died from syphilis because he had slept with prostitutes. The patient's body would be rotten gradually, and Mrs. Hou's description terrified others. Everybody fears something and the most serious one is to watch his own body rot. The body is closely related to a man's feelings. When a person is hungry, his body will feel it at once; if he makes a fortune, he will have good food and clothes as gifts to himself. Even taking a bath can make his body feel comfortable. If he watches his own body decay little by little, he will go crazy.

The secrets told by Mrs. Hou were very remote. Syphilis is both a disease and a fate. All kinds of life are endless ethnically and memorially. Syphilis will wake up from its long sleep. Cholera, plague, schistosome, swine flu, famine and wars will hit human beings sooner or later.

It was said that leprosy had disappeared, but Guangwen's sister-in-law had been suffering from it. He did not believe that the son of Ho Laosan should be a syphilitic.

"Nonsense!" he cried, looking shocked. It seemed that syphilis was worse than drug addiction; the former was like a ghost.

When Guangwen thought about Li Zhi, he vowed to draw a sharp line between him and his son when the funeral was over. He was determined to deal with all the problems in the village and had never made a pledge. However, he would swear concerning the education of his own son.

Chapter 26

In the evening Ziguo appeared. His elder brother Ziqiang and his wife and children did not come.

"Where is your brother?" asked Chunhua.

"He will be here tomorrow," replied Ziguo.

"But why? They said that they would come here today. The funeral orations will be made after supper."

Ziguo did not reply further. When Dayou gave cigarettes to others,

Swallow introduced him to Ziguo.

"Your M-shaped hairstyle is cool," said Dayou, watching Ziguo.

It might cost 700 yuan. Qiuyue laughed, but others did not lest Chunhua should overthink.

"What are you laughing at, Qiuyue?" Chunhua asked.

The girl's laughter was triggered by Dayou who was one of the guests, so Chunhua smiled.

But Qiuyue looked sour at once because she disliked being questioned. She could ignore Chunhong's nagging but could not bear Chunhua's questioning. After Qiuyue left, Dayou found it dull, so he walked away holding a bottle of mineral water.

"Ziqiang and his wife are having a quarrel at home," said Ziguo.

The couple's "home" referred to the one in Huilong Town. Ziguo would go to Anping's parents' house and pick up the two children – her parents did not rent a house in the town. Their grandpa would receive them after school and then would go to Yanerpo. They lived in the upper reaches of the river, more than four kilometres to the town.

Before they set off, Anping said to Ziqiang, "Your parents don't visit their grandchildren after they have been in the town for a long time."

"They will visit my grandpa," Ziqiang argued.

"Your parents don't like their granddaughters! I have no son!"

The couple bickered.

"When my husband was looking after the elderly man in the hospital," Chunhua argued, "I visited my granddaughters. After he came back from hospital, we had dinner with Anping's parents. They must have lied to her!"

"Chunhua and her husband stayed at my house for several hours with their grandchildren," Chunhong explained.

"They are gossipers!"

Chunhong pinched Chunhua's hand when she saw Mrs. Hou coming over.

"It's your fault!" cried Chunhua, flinging off Chunhong's hand.

When they went to Chunhong's house, Chunhong mentioned that a daughter-in-law should be paid for looking after children. Chunhua got angry and considered that Chunhong had started all this. Anping was jealous of the payment, so she picked a hole.

"Just forget about it," said Chunhong.

Mrs. Hou walked towards them.

"What are you quarrelling for?" Mrs. Hou smiled.

"We are sad," replied Chunhong.

"Chunming, Chunying, Lily and Yuling are sorrowful," Mrs. Hou added smilingly. "They cried, but you didn't."

Chunhua's chest heaved.

"Are you with Shanrui again, Ziguo?" asked Mrs. Hou.

Before Ziguo made an answer, his mother cried, "He will keep single for the rest of his life, and that's not your business!"

"I've never said that!"

"You must have cursed him!"

Mrs. Hou got speechless.

Since Ziguo was jilted by Shanrui, he had had many blind dates, but all of them failed. At last no woman would be with him, which worried Chunhua very much.

"You have been laughing at others in your life," Chunhua snapped. "And you are disliked by everybody!"

"I am your elder," Mrs. Hou retorted. "And I care about you."

Mrs. Hou had gossiped that someone's ancestor had got syphilis; that someone's husband had secret lovers; that someone's wife had an affair with another man; that a new bride could not have children or would hurt her husband.

"Human beings would be extinct if you cared about others," Chunhua added. "A good person may not have a long life. You'd better become a bad one if you want to live much longer."

Chunhua thought about our mother who had died early because she had been a good woman. By contrast, Mrs. Hou was still alive – the latter knew what Chunhua meant. Mrs. Hou was too old to retort.

Chapter 27

Limin saw his mother and Chunhua boiling with fury. It might be inconvenient for him to ask why, so he smiled at them and walked towards

Chunshan's house.

Later Chunhong said to me, "Chunhua's harsh temper can hurt others and herself. Mrs. Hou has been a gossiper and also been a neighbour of ours for decades. Even though we want to have a quarrel with her, we should bury the hatchet for the sake of Limin."

Limin got along with all of us. When his mother and our mother were enemies, he could still smile at us. After he got married, his wife treated us well.

Limin had two children: Stone and his younger sister Raindrop. Chunhong and Chunhua often looked after the two kids. When the male villagers were building the Longyan Pond, Chunhua took good care of Stone and Raindrop when Chunhong and Zheng Saner were busy. When Chunhua was cutting grass, she would find fruits for the two kids; after they returned home, she would feed food to them – such a thing was precious when people were in poverty. Raindrop loved bright clothes, but the clothes lost their colours after they were washed. Chunhua taught her to add vinegar into the basin when she was washing green clothes, add alkali washing purple clothes, and add salt washing red clothes. In addition, Chunhua carefully taught her various knitting methods. After Raindrop got married at the foot of the Mafu Ridge rich with natural gas just like Lijiayan, she earned a lot money by selling embroideries to the staff in the gas company. Mafu Ridge had a much more complicated landform than Lijiayan, so foreign experts were often invited for assistance. They loved Raindrop's embroideries. A German expert would buy a large embroidery of cranes dancing with 12,000 yuan, Raindrop sold it to him at 10,000 yuan.

Chunhua respected Limin. Chunhong explained, "Chunhua gets angry with Anping, not Mrs. Hou. Anping complains that she isn't treated well by her parents-in-law who should look after their grandchildren. Anping can't have a happy life after marriage. Her own parents are not demanding. If I were her parent and her in-laws were neglecting their grandchildren, I would not accept them into my care; if they came and treated themselves as guests, that would anger me much more."

Chapter 28

"Dinner time!" Limin exclaimed in a loudspeaker. "Hurry up!"

"Just a moment!" cried Xiaolan. She was having a winning hand.

"Stop playing mahjong!" Zhuqing ordered.

"I've lost more than 200 yuan and I must win!"

Limin repeated and mahjong tables were used as dining tables. Women were busy serving the dishes. Uncle Chenggui was sitting on a stone roller. Chunhong wanted to support him to stand up, but she asked Swallow to do it lest Zheng Saner should feel sad. Swallow and I supported Uncle Chenggui towards the dining table. He looked much older and marks of senility could be clearly seen on his face.

"Oh, it's you, Chunming," he said excitedly. "Are your wife and son here with you? How long is it from Chengdu to our village?"

Swallow sat beside her aunt, and I beside Uncle Chenggui. I put delicious dishes into his bowl, and he tried to eat up. People were talking about mahjong.

"Dinner time!" Limin said in the loudspeaker once more. "After the meal is finished, memorial essays will be read and the family members of the deceased man will walk around the coffin again." He said those words three times.

Qiuyue, Dayou and Tian were walking slowly towards the dinner tables.

"Enjoy the meal now," said Swallow.

Chunhong glanced at Swallow and then at Chunying and Xianhe. Chunying asked Qiuyue to sit on a bench. Nobody would take away excessive bottles of mineral water. "Does anybody need some water?" someone might ask. He or she would put up his or her hand, and a bottle of mineral water would be given to him or her. Qiuyue had to sit beside her parents although she was unwilling. Dayou was sitting next to Swallow.

After we finished the meal, Guangwen whispered to me in the courtyard, "Stop Qiuyue from staying with Dayou. Tell that to Chunying and Xianhe. Dayou is Swallow's boyfriend, but Swallow is too foolish to see that Dayou favours Qiuyue."

Did I overthink? Qiuyue was just a teenager and Tian was with her and Dayou. I would be too embarrassed to tell that to her parents. What if something bad happened? The root of the bad thing should be removed as early as possible.

But I should do the task assigned by Guangwen. I watched the courtyard. Women were pouring leftovers into barrels and Zhanhui was clearing the table. After a moment she walked away, carrying two barrels filled with leftovers. They washed the dishes on the tables. The tableware would be placed on each table and be covered with nets when it was not used as a mahjong table. All the tableware had to be put on two tables and would be handed out to guests before each meal. As a result, women had to do much more work, but the mahjong players complained that they were tardy. The two groups swore at each other. A woman angrily poured dishwater on a man and a bowl broke. After Limin heard the sound, he rushed to inspect as soon as possible even though he was in a lavatory, and then he scolded the woman; at last she had to compensate for the broken bowl with one taken from her own kitchen.

I saw Xianhe and Chunying in Chunshu's kitchen while Chunhong, Chunhua, Lily and Qiuyue were there, too. When I was standing at the doorway, I heard Chunhong's speech: "An immoral woman is much more serious than an immoral man. If a man is neither a thief or a robber, he will not be criticized even though he sleeps with different women. If a woman has an affair with a man who is not single, she will bring shame on the family name." Chunhong insinuated that Qiuyue might become such a woman. If the matter was mentioned bluntly, it would become serious.

I did not have to do the task assigned by Guangwen, and I felt relieved. Soon Xianhe joked to others. Qiuyue, closing her eyes and leaning on her mother's thighs, had a red hue on her face.

Chunhua was surprised to see me.

"I saw our dad last night in my dream," she said. "He was carrying a basket of potatoes, standing at the doorway. I asked him to enter, but I suddenly woke up because I realized that he had been dead."

"You are so sad," said Chunhong.

Villagers said that if you saw your dead parent or relative in your dream, that meant you were so sad that they frightened you to release you from grief. Chunhong tried to dispel Chunhua's displeasure before the meal.

Chapter 29

"The family members of Mr. Xu Chengxiang go to the mourning hall please," Limin said in a loudspeaker again. He used the word "please". However, there was a power failure suddenly.

We had to light candles because of no power restoration. Xiaolan shouted that we should use the candles as loudly as her mother did. Chunhua wanted power outage to last longer. Ziqiang and his wife and children had not arrived, which might anger our father's soul. The electricity was still off after twenty minutes, but Limin standing in the courtyard yelled. We walked outside.

"Will the memorial ceremony be held tomorrow?" asked Chunhua.

"No," replied Guangwen. "I'll have a meeting tomorrow morning, and Yang Jin will pick me up. And I'll have to deal with many problems in the town."

Chunhua had to accept it and then she complained that Ziqiang had been controlled by his wife. In fact, she did not know whether Anping would come here tomorrow or not.

Holding two candles, I walked into the dark mourning hall. We stood around the freezing coffin, and each of us held three sticks of incense. I provided the light source for Chunshu who was standing in the front of the team with a booklet in his hand.

"Today is April 16th of the lunar calendar," Chunshu said solemnly. "The children and grandchildren of Mr. Xu Chengxiang will hold a memorial ceremony for him. He has three sons-in-law: Li Guangwen, Fang Yun and Yao Xianhe; he has three daughters: Xu Chunhong, Xu Chunhua and Xu Chunying (Lian Ying); he has three sons: Xu Chunshan, Xu Chunshu, Xu Chunming and Xu Chunshang; he has five grandsons: Li Zhi, Fang Ziqiang, Fang Ziguo, Yao Huatian and Xu Weisheng; he has two granddaughters: Li Lily and Yao Qiuyue; he has two granddaughters-in-law: Yang Qingmei and Fu Anping; he has one grandson-in-law: Yu Peiliang; he has three great-granddaughters: Li Dou, Fang Min and Fang Yuan. He has more grandchildren, granddaughters-in-law, and grandsons-in-law."

"Mr. Xu Chengxiang and his wife had taken great efforts to raise their children," Chunshu chanted sorrowfully. "The father had to bring up the kids after Mrs. Xu passed away. He would strain to get rice when his youngest daughter just several months old needed nutrition. With tears and difficulties, the father must hold on. Through hardships the daughters grew up. The eldest daughter married a man who lived on the other side of the river; the second one married a man who lived in Huanglingtan; the youngest one was adopted by the family who lived in Guanmenyan and they prospered in Dabaoliang. They had done all in their full strength for survival in spite of poverty. His daughters and sons-in-law have taken his advice and have got better and better."

Chapter 30

The power was restored the next morning. With burning candles, the participants, including Chunshan, Chunshang and Yuling, kept playing mahjong until midnight. How much the candles would cost?

"The money has been squandered by them," Zhuqing complained to her husband.

"Xiaolan has been playing mahjong, too!" Chunshu retorted.

"She is a guest. Are Chunshan and Chunshang together with their wives treated as guests, too? Yuling should not have worn eye-catching earrings on our dad's funeral!"

I saw that, too. But Yuling had covered her earrings with a kerchief.

"It's not your business," Chunshu argued. "You may wear earrings if you want."

"I'll wear them if you buy them for me," said Zhuqing.

"You will be too embarrassed to go outside if you wear earrings."

"I'm a married woman and I can wear them!"

"You were lucky that you could marry me."

"I've been waiting for my good luck."

"What are you talking about?" asked Zhanhui.

Zhuqing loudly told her about the conversation between her and husband just now.

"I'll need a funeral oration for Mr. Xu Chengxiang," Zhanhui said to Chunshu.

Zhuqing was surprised. The funeral oration should be provided by the relatives and good friends of the deceased man, but Zhanhui did not belong to them.

"You don't have to provide one," said Chunshu.

"Do you grade your guests?" asked Zhanhui. "Can't I express my condolences to your dad?"

"I'll write one for you."

"How much?"

"A high price."

"I'll pay for it."

When she took money out of her pocket, she deliberately showed her sexy buttocks in her stretch pants.

"It's free," said Zhuqing, glowering at Zhanhui.

"Really?" Zhanhui asked Chunshu, ignoring Zhuqing.

"Yes," said Chunshu. He wanted to end the conversation as quickly as possible.

"Thank you," said Zhanhui. And then she said to Zhuqing, "Bookworms can make knowledge into money. Your husband would have been employed in a state-owned company if you had not burned all his books."

Zhanhui glanced at me. Thirty years ago, before morning arrived, Zhu Qing burned all of her husband's book while preparing pig's food, in order to do her farm work at the earliest opportunity. Pigs might feel that the food that day had a smell of printing ink, but they could not know that the books had made souls cry at midnight. When I wanted to borrow a book from Chunshu one day, he said that his wife had burned all his books. Afterwards he stopped reading and villagers thought that he was getting better: they considered that reading was just for being admitted to a good university, but Chunshu's reading was not for that purpose, so he was regarded as an idler. He was a cold fish because he used to be a bookworm. But Chunshu had never argued for that. It had been Chunshu's agony, and he had told it to Zhanhui only.

Zhuqing could not understand Zhanhui's intention, so she, patting her on the shoulder, said, "At that time even firewood was in shortage. Pigs would have been hungry if without his books."

Chapter 31

We did not know if Chunshu wrote an elegiac address for Zhanhui, and she did not chant in front of our father's coffin. What would people talk about? Even our father might think why Zhanhui expressed her condolences to him; but he would not be shocked because he would always find a good excuse. Zhanhui's deed might remind our father of one day in spring a few decades ago.

Xu Guo, the father of Xu Xing, ran to the slope full of red stones to search for food, but he fell off the slope. Such a thing happened to many villagers. Our father returned from the town, holding a bottle of cough syrup which could cure our mother. At that time she was suffering from oedema. People said that Recovery Powder, made of wheat bran, bean flour and granulated sugar, could cure oedema, hepatitis and emaciation. Our father holding 0.5 yuan went to the street. A man told him that the Recovery Powder could only be bought in Beijing with a special coupon. When he was sitting in the street like a beggar, he heard someone say: "Buy a bottle of cough syrup in the hospital."

After he got home, he saw a man falling to the ground; but he ignored that man because he would rush to cure his wife.

He suddenly felt that he was pulling backwards by someone. "Go away!" he shouted. But he walked back and saw that man was Xu Guo. Our father unscrewed the cap of the bottle of cough syrup and he could smell the sweetness. Xu Guo might be dead, and the Production Team would handle it.

Xu Guo moaned. Our father considered that he might cry at the thought of his wife and his sick son (Chunshan). He watched the sky and would search for Bodhisattva who could hear and see even the faintest cry. What he saw was the blue sky. He turned over Xu Guo who had been the only man in Yanerpo to join the army during the Korean War. Xu Guo was having a facial spasm and there were red stones on his teeth. He poured the syrup into Xu Guo's mouth. Xu Guo survived at that time although he died after a few days. Xu Guo's offspring attended our father's funeral, and our father's soul might feel glad. However, our father was in the underworld. If a soul in the nether world was happy, the living human beings would get into trouble.

Chapter 32

After breakfast, Liu Xianwen led us to fetch water. Water wells in Yanerpo had been located in the bamboo forests in the west. Villagers now would get water from a weir. One of his disciples took bamboo shoots and leaves out of the water and found it had become dark. After drums Liu Xianwen chanted: "Amid light, rivers, and air, all the living beings …" and then joss paper was burned, drums were beaten, and he repeated his chanting. It was 11 a.m. after the water was fetched. As soon as drums were stopped, Li Zhi said that he would return to the town.

"Nobody is at home now," said Chunhong.

"But I'll return and take a look," said Li Zhi.

"Your dad has gone back, and you don't have to."

"He's eager to play mahjong."

"He'll have a meeting and deal with the problems in the village."

"Do you know the date?"

"Today is Saturday!" Dou yelled.

"I don't believe those leaders have to work today," Li Zhi added. "They returned to their own houses yesterday afternoon. My dad will play mahjong with them in the town."

"You should stay here," his mother ordered.

"You scold me that I'm an idler. But now you stop me from doing useful things."

"There is no treasure in your house."

"You will take Dou to school tomorrow afternoon, or you may return on the morning of the day after tomorrow."

"Qingmei can look after her!"

Qingmei was playing rock-paper-scissors with Dou nearby.

"Qingmei will leave after the funeral is over," said Chunhong. "You will pick up Dou during these days."

"But what will she do?"

"Kowtow for your grandpa."

"Would my grandpa come back to life if we made 10,000 kowtows for him? That's superstition!"

"Watch your tongue!"

Li Zhi left. His mother had never been able to educate him effectively. Ziguo would leave, too.

"You should have hitchhiked in Yang Jin's car this morning," said Chunhong. "You will have to pay for a ride in a motorbike."

"I can always get a free ride," Li Zhi retorted.

What Li Zhi said was true. He called four friends and soon they drove to Weir Pond Trench by motorbike; Ziguo could sit in one of the motorbikes. Chunhong called her husband, but her three calls were not answered; at last, his mobile phone was turned off. Chunhong sat there sadly. She often turned a blind eye to her husband's deeds, but she did not know why she became stubborn today.

"Li Zhi and Ziguo annoy me," Chunhong said to Chunhua. The listener smiled.

"I'll go with Li Zhi, mom," said Ziguo.

"Be careful," said Chunhua.

"Li Zhi would have stayed here if Ziguo had not decided to leave," Chunhong complained.

"Li Zhi will go, so Ziguo will follow him," said Chunhua.

Chunhong did not say anymore. Meanwhile, Xiaolan yelled on the mahjong table.

"Xiaolan is a player of mahjong, not a mourner," said Chunhong. "Her husband and children will arrive on the eve of the funeral."

"Guibing is busy and his parents look after his kids," said Chunhua.

"We are busy, too!" Chunhong retorted. "Can he earn all the money during these days? He is not filial!"

Chunhua did not argue. Ziqiang and his wife and children had not arrived; Ziguo had come here but soon left. Chunhong's husband and son had left.

"You have five family members," Chunhua added. "But we have only two."

Chunhong did not want to bicker with her.

Chapter 33

The drums were beaten in the mourning hall, and we would walk around the coffin again. Guangwen, Li Zhi and Ziguo had left, but Dayou joined us. Dayou, following Swallow, was wearing a funeral kerchief and a black armband. The black armband did not belong to the local funeral custom. If the buyer of supplies was also one of the participants of the funeral, he would be provided with a black armband. When he was driving a motorbike, the flying armband might hook a branch, and it would be dangerous. In addition, when he was buying things for the funeral, he might be fleeced by the shop keeper. The funeral kerchief was very long, and one should wrap it around his head for several layers in a good shape so as to help the deceased person to go through a huge river in hell. After the kerchief was taken off, there was no suitable pocket to keep it. By contrast, it was easy to use a black armband with a pin and easy to pocket it.

Dayou kowtowed seriously. After Guangwen left, Chunshan and Chunshu became busier, so I had to stand in the front of the team, holding the stick. I held on even I felt tired, and I might be laughed at by others because my buttocks were being watched. Sweat fell into my eyes and I must persevere in what I was doing.

"You should put away the hemp thread lest Swallow should step on it," Dayou said to Qiuyue.

"It's not your business," she said coldly.

"How dare you speak to Dayou like that?" Chunhong snapped. "He is your brother-in-law!"

Dayou was 30 years old but Qiuyue was just 16. Dayou had looked at Qiuyue seductively twice: the first time occurred when he said that he would wash plums yesterday afternoon, and the second time during supper; the two moments were discovered by Chunhong.

Now I could understand why Chunhong became stubborn today: those moments reminded her of her husband. A man is always lustful. She hated such a defect and she got angry with Qiuyue: the girl should not take a fancy to her brother-in-law.

After drums were stopped, Liu Xianwen and his disciples chanted: "Amid the sun, the moon, the flowers, and the river, kowtow now!"

The procedure was repeated. After it was over, we walked out of the mourning hall with exhaustion.

Ziqiang with his wife and children came, followed by Huchuan, the son of Swallow, holding a jar of liquor for his grandpa. He ran to his grandpa's house, put the jar at the door, and went to find his mother. When Swallow was wrapping a funeral kerchief around Xiaolan's head, her legs were held by her son.

"Oh, it's you," said Swallow. "Have you kowtowed to your great-grandfather?"

"Be quick," said Xiaolan. She was eager to play mahjong.

When Swallow and Huchuan got to the mourning hall, Ziqiang with his wife and children were kowtowing on the cushions.

"Go to see your great-grandfather," said Swallow.

"You'll go with me, mom," said Huchuan.

"Are you afraid?"

She had to walk toward the freezing coffin with his son, and he was preoccupied with his mother.

"Kowtow to your great-grandfather," said Swallow.

The boy grasped his mother's arm and cried. Swallow had to kowtow again, holding her son. But she had kowtowed repeatedly until she fell to the ground. The guests laughed.

"The boy is thin and strong," said Mrs. Hou.

"Why are you crying?" asked Swallow.

"Uncle Ziqiang told me when I was buying fodder with my grandma," replied Huchuan. He cried that his mother did not visit him timely after she returned, and she did not tell him about the death of his great-grandfather.

"You are not on holiday," said Swallow, holding him in her arms. "And I should have you come here on the eve of the funeral."

She asked her son about his grandparents and about fruit trees and livestock, but she did not mention his father Sheng Jun. Huchuan wiped away his mother's sweat with his hands.

"Why are your hands full of dirt?" asked Swallow.

"We fell from the motorbike," Anping explained. "Look at the blood in my hands. Ziqiang carried his two daughters in one motorbike, a driver from Mount Lordhou carried me and Huchuan in another one. But the driver had bad skills even on a smooth road."

Perhaps the driver was inexperienced.

"Did you pay for the driver?" someone asked Anping.

"No," she replied. "We were lucky that we could be safe and sound!"

"Oh, a free ride indeed!"

Before Swallow talked with Anping, Huchuan pressed her head lower so that she could not speak to others. He wanted her to speak to him only.

"Wash your hands in the kitchen, Huchuan," said Swallow. "Did you greet your grandma?"

Chunhong and Chunhua were sitting on chairs in the courtyard.

"Bad luck!" Chunhong exclaimed.

"Indeed!" Chunhua said. She held her two granddaughters in her arms. The two kids did not inherit their grandma's beauty in her youth.

Chapter 35

Chunshan and Dayou carried one table into the courtyard; it was borrowed from another courtyard. Huchuan holding his mother's legs greeted his grandpa and nearly cried. She consoled him and walked towards Chunshan and Dayou. The table was not stable, so Chunshan went to find a pad.

"Say hello to Dayou," Swallowed said to Huchuan.

The boy did not know that Dayou was his mother's boyfriend, and he looked grave. Chunshan got a firecracker which could not explode and used it as a pad. Huchuan greeted his grandpa, but the latter soon went to help others after Limin called him.

"I'll visit my parents," said Dayou.

"I'll go with you," said Swallow.

"Stay with me, mom!" cried Huchuan.

"You will stay here with Tian," said Swallow. "Tian!" Nobody answered.

Qiuyue came back and said Tian and Huatian were catching bamboo partridges.

"You may join them, Huchuan," said Swallow.

The boy put his head between his mother's knees.

"I'll go to Cotton Infertility with Dayou," Swallow added. "And I'll be back soon."

Qiuyue glanced at Dayou, and the latter walked past Chunshang who was playing mahjong. Swallow whispered to Huchuan, and then the boy cried; she blushed and found Dayou gone. Swallow called Dayou again and again, but it was not answered by him. She got so hurried that she pushed Huchuan on the ground accidentally. She would take a shortcut but the boy would catch up with her.

"Stop!" she ordered.

The boy kept running and lost one sandal.

"You may go to Dayou's house after the funeral is over," cried Chunhong. Later Fengjuan said the same to Swallow.

Swallow pulled Huchuan into a courtyard. "I dislike you!" she snapped.

The boy was too scared to hug his mother. She ignored him. He picked up a fan on the stairs and moved carefully behind her and fanned her. He was sobbing.

Chapter 36

Chunhong called Li Zhi, but he did not answer it. He was sitting beside a bank with his buddies and was answering a call from Sixi. He and Ziguo went back to the town because they did not want to kowtow frequently; what was more, he received a text message from Sixi that he would reach Huilong Town in the evening and would take a rest and go to Yanerpo the next morning.

"If I came back alone," said Sixi, "I would kowtow for my grandpa at midnight and even walk to the mountain if there was no motorbike." His girlfriend Shen Xiaofei came with him. She was a city dweller and had had a long, difficult journey from Harbin to Huilong Town with him by plane, by train, and by bus.

Sixi asked Li Zhi to wait for him in the town and would stay in Li Zhi's house for one night. Sixi worried that his aunts and uncles would get angry with him, so he told Li Zhi and Ziguo to keep it secret. In addition, Sixi called Li Zhi to book a reservation in a steakhouse.

"My girlfriend loves steaks," said Sixi. "I've been with her for so long that I love them, too."

"Harbin is a charming city," Sixi added. "It has Gothic architectures, tall beauties, Russian shopping malls, international concerts and freshly brewed coffee."

After the long phone call was ended, he saw missed calls from his mother.

"Mom," he said softly. His mother scolded him on the phone, but he was calm and would talk to her tenderly. At least he was much better than Sixi.

"Sixi will come back," he added.

"When?"

"Sixi says that he is about to get on the plane," said Li Zhi, and he was scolded by his mother again.

Sixi never told the truth to his family members. When he was in his hometown and was asked by an acquaintance, "When did you come back?" he said that he returned this morning; in fact he returned yesterday evening. In addition, he often boasted that he had a very good life in another city. When he mentioned that he met a successful businessman in the West Lake, in the beginning, he said that man was Mr. Zhang, but he immediately said that man was Mr. Wang. The listener did not mind that. Sixi said that honest people were too foolish.

"You should have stayed to kowtow to your grandpa," his mother yelled. "Guibing is earning money so he can't come. Your dad has turned off his phone. You must go to the town government now to see if he is having a meeting!"

"Even if I go there, I can't change anything."

"You must do it! Otherwise I'll skin you!"

Li Zhi could not be treated softly by his mother although he was eager to.

Chapter 37

"After the call from Li Zhi's mother was ended," said Ziguo, "he took 1,900 yuan from his pocket."

Last night Li Zhi asked his father to give him some money with an excuse of using it for Dou; his father yelled at him. At that time Limin was with Guangwen and laughed. The latter gave a wad of banknotes to his son. He did not count the banknotes, now it was counted.

Li Zhi gave 600 yuan to his buddies to cook lunch in a restaurant: chicken blood soup with cabbages, stir-fried chicken giblets with chili sauce, and stewed chicken with potatoes; the chicken should be simmered and six bunge pricklyash leaves should be added.

"You have good cooking skills," said Ziguo.

"Call Qin Kuan to cook good steaks, Dangshen," Li Zhi added. "The customers will arrive at 8:30 tonight."

Li Zhi and Ziguo went to Huang Ermei's store. Li Zhi could ask Yang Jin where his dad was, he did not want to go to the town government. If he could be allowed to fish in the rockery pond in the courtyard of the town government, or if a billiard table could be provided there, he might go to that place. It would be a difficult job to step on the 99 stone staircases.

"Dangshen told me to cook steaks," Qin Kuan called Li Zhi. "Is that true?"

"Yes."

Qin Kuan felt assured because he did not want to waste the beef or the gasoline in his car through a long journey.

"Qin Kuan does not believe your buddies," said Ziguo. "You should have called Qin Kuan."

"Let them do it," Li Zhi smiled. "They often consume in the restaurants on account under my name, and Qin Kuan does not believe them."

"You'll pay the bills?"

"It depends. Most of the time I do. Sometimes I don't, so Qin Kuan calls me."

"I dare say that Sixi called me in the junction of the carriage in the train," Li Zhi added. "He told his girlfriend to take the plane, but later he told her that he couldn't get two tickets, so they would take the train and enjoy the scenery along the way and he would write a poem for her."

"He must be out of pocket now," said Ziguo.

"If he were rich, he would travel first class by plane! Women can be easily deceived. When I was in Fuzhou, I met new friends and I knew they were swindlers just like Sixi. They sleep with many women and con them of a lot of money with various excuses. Women love sweet talk. They could have uncovered those swindlers by making phone calls occasionally and refraining from any emotional and financial involvement with any man for a period of six months. The impatient frauds can't wait for half a year. But women would rather indulge in their sweet dreams."

"I wish I could do that," said Ziguo, thinking about Shanrui. If he could have kept her in sweet dreams, she would not have left him.

"You should not have brought her to our hometown," Li Zhi explained.

"Sixi will bring his girlfriend here," Ziguo argued.

"They will be here for our grandpa's funeral."

"Poverty can be clearly seen."

"Half of the powerful and wealthy men come from poor rural areas. A cunning confidence man can tell some true things in his words so that his listeners can trust him."

"Sixi is such a man."

"The crafty swindlers are like us: wear a good mask!"

Ziguo did not say anymore because he knew that Li Zhi was always richer than him. Li Zhi felt hurt when Sixi said that he knew nothing about the architecture in Harbin.

"Sixi boasted that he had slept with a lot of actresses and had sent their pictures to me," Li Zhi added. "But I have never seen them on TV. They may perform in bars and they are ugly and fat. I dare say Shen Xiaofei is fat, too."

Shanrui was a fat girl and Ziguo did not think thin girls were attractive.

Yang Jin's car was usually parked in front of Huang Ermei's store, but it was not today. Li Zhi and Ziguo entered the store.

"You don't wear a black armband for your grandpa," said Huang Ermei. She gave him a bottle of mineral water taken out of a freezer.

Li Zhi and Ziguo put the black armbands into the trunk of the motorbike when they were in Weir Pond Trench. Li Zhi acted like a good boy in front of the elders which had good relations with his parents.

"I'd taken it off before I came here," said Li Zhi. "I should wear it only in the mourning hall. This is the son of my second aunt."

Huang Ermei gave a bottle of mineral water to Ziguo, too, and gave a packet of good cigarettes to each of them. During these days Chunshan let buyers go to Huang Ermei's store on account for a good price, for good quality, and for good relations between Guangwen and Yang Jin, and their wives.

When Li Zhi was having water, he wanted to ask where Yang Jin was, but he did not ask. His car was not here, so his dad must have gone to the town for fun. He thanked Huang Ermei, smoked two cigarettes in the street, and told his mother on the phone that his dad was having a meeting.

Chapter 38

Chunhong felt assured and then tidied her funeral kerchief and would walk around the coffin again. Liu Xianwen and his disciples stepped into the mourning hall again after they took a rest outside the hall. They struck chime stones and chanted scriptures. Stone had installed loudspeakers in the hall, so the chanting could be heard across the mountains.

"My legs hurt," said Chunhong.

"Mine, too," said Chunhua. "Anping took my two granddaughters to catch bamboo partridges, followed by Qingmei and her daughter."

They began to talk about their daughters-in-law.

Chunhua would have told Anping that she and her husband had visited their granddaughters and had dinner with their grandparents. Anping was good-tempered these days. In the past Anping called her mother and served her, but she looked cold; but this time she called her mother cordially. She guessed that Anping smiled at her after she knew that she had visited her kids. But Chunhong did not think so.

"Did Ziqiang quarrel with Anping?" asked Chunhong.

"She often scolds him," replied Chunhua.

"But he dared to quarrel with her yesterday. A husband should educate his wife well. A daughter-in-law is not your own daughter. If she calls the shots, she will turn her parents-in-law into punchbags. Qingmei used to be bossy to me. When Dou was still a baby, she shat on the sofa. Qingmei threw tissues at me. Li Zhi got angry and battered her. She would have been beaten to death if I had not thrown the used tissues at him to stop him. Afterwards she became submissive. If a son can't control his wife, she will bully her parents-in-law."

Chunhua got speechless because she had never heard of that before.

"Anping is a good daughter-in-law," Chunhong consoled her. "Now a daughter is much better than a son. Lily is much better than Li Zhi."

Chunhua considered that parents should look after their own children, and she did not complain that Anping had no son. Thirty years ago, Chunhua carried Ziguo on her back and did heavy farm work before she could make a full recovery after childbirth. She did not have her parents-in-law or her father look after the baby.

A daughter could have a husband easily. A son must buy a house in the town before he could get married; even though he had a house, he might not have a wife. That reminded Chunhua of Ziguo's marriage.

"I love my granddaughter Dou," Chunhong added. "My husband wants a grandson, but Dou makes me very happy. Some babies have congenital diseases. You have two lovely, healthy granddaughters Fang Min and Fang Yuan. What's more, Fang Yuan is clever."

Fang Yuan could be much smarter than an adult. When she visited Chunhong's house, Qingmei asked, "Who is Fang Yuan?"

"I am Fang Yuan, the only one."

"Is Fang Min your elder sister?"

"Yes."

"She is Dou's sister, not yours."

"Fang Min would have lived with Dou if she had been her sister."

"You saw two dogs yesterday, but they did not live together."

"I'm a human being, not a dog. If my grandma hears our talk, she will hold a knife in front of you."

Qingmei showed a knife to Fang Yuan, but the little girl did not flinch.

"My grandma will use the knife to peel potatoes," Fang Yuan said calmly.

When Fang Min had fun with Dou only, Fang Yuan had fun by herself. Dou shared delicious snacks with Fang Min only, Fang Yuan did not get angry and minded her own business. One day Fang Yuan and Chunhong could not take a boat or a motorbike to go home. Chunhong lost her temper when they were walking. Fang Yuan consoled her, "We step on the road, it does not shout. And we should not shout, either." The little girl did not let her grandma carry her on the back.

Chunhua was very glad that Fang Yuan had been praised as a clever girl. She favoured Ziguo between her two sons. She loved her two granddaughters, and took good care of Fang Min who was seldom praised.

When Chunhong praised Fang Yuan, Chunhua said that Fang Min was thoughtful and brave. One night she heard someone sighing outside, she got so terrified that she woke up the two-year-old Fang Min. The little girl got up, stood on a stool and looked through the window with a flashlight. After a moment she said, "Three small monkeys are leaning on the wall."

The monkey could entangle a bull all over with its milky white filaments from its belly; the filaments could be tightened under the sunshine and could entangle the bull to death. It could pant and sigh. Chunhua closed the window and went on with her sleep.

Limin walked towards the two women. "You are chosen to cry in the mourning hall, Chunhong," he said.

Chapter 39

Weepers would be hired for the funeral and they would not come until the eve of the funeral. Before that day, the offspring of the deceased man – usually a female – should cry her heart out in front of the coffin to tell the whole life of him. Joys were not to be told but miseries and contributions were. Happiness was not ignored intentionally because delightful things were few throughout one's life. Happiness was like sand between fingers or like firecrackers that everything would become quiet and dark after the fleeting glamour. Happiness was selfish and had to be owned secretly; but agony could be sharp. Anguish meant suffering and sacrifice.

A female family member of the deceased man would keep crying for agony until she was pulled to stand up; if someone was standing beside her but did not pull her, she would have to keep crying day and night. In addition, the wailer should not stand up until she was pulled many times; after she was pulled to the doorway, she would struggle to throw herself onto the coffin again. When the wailer was standing outside the mourning hall, she would keep crying for further 30 minutes before she could speak to others. The wailer should let others hear her hoarse voice to show that she had cried hard; and she should try to speak hoarsely if her voice was normal.

That was how the offspring of the deceased man should cry. A weeper would set up a tent outside the mourning hall, kneel down on a cushion, and tell the whole life of the deceased man with a well-trained, crying voice. The participants might make things hard for the whining offspring of the deceased man: when someone refused to pull the wailer to stand up, the latter should strain to cry and cough, and even pretended to faint. The two people might be on bad terms for many years.

Now the offspring would not have to cry. If the host wanted to hold an impressive funeral, he would ask one of the female family members to wail. However, some would not cry for the deceased man but for herself: her miseries caused by the man when he was alive; what's more, she would curse the dead and the living; at last the mourning hall would be left in a mess.

Chapter 40

Chunhong was surprised after she knew that she had been chosen to wail.

"Oh, I don't know how to do it," she said.

"But you'll have to do it," said Limin.

As the eldest daughter of our father, she should be the wailer. "When?"

"Soon," replied Limin. "Liu Xianwen and his disciples finished reading *The Earth Store Sutra* just now, and you will wail."

"I'll turn the microphone up to full volume," said Stone.

"Oh, I won't use the microphone," said Chunhong.

"A microphone will make your voice go far away," said Limin.

"Xu Chunhong will begin her whining soon," said Stone.

Mrs. Hou, Zhanhui and Zheng Saner came out of the kitchen at once.

Stone strapped the microphone to the bench under the freezing coffin and then said to Chunhong, "You will kneel here and whine."

Zhanhui pressed Chunhong's head lower so hard that her funeral kerchief fell to the ground. Zheng Saner picked it up at once and wrapped it around Chunhong's head.

"I know the steps," said Chunhong.

Zhanhui went to the doorway and mahjong players gathered in the mourning hall. The wailing was a diminishing spectacle.

Chunhong knelt down, one hand holding the coffin and the other the ground. Chunhua and Chunying were standing beside me.

"Chunhong is doing well," said Chunying.

Chunhua smiled.

"Can you do it?" asked Chunying.

Chunhua shook her head. Meanwhile, no tears fell down from Chunhong's eyes.

"Hurry up," said Fengjuan. "We are busy."

"You may do her job," said Mrs. Hou.

"If a daughter-in-law is chosen to cry," said Zhuqing, "Fengjuan should do the job."

"A daughter-in-law should wail if the deceased man has no daughter," Fengjuan explained.

Anping and Qingmei glanced at Fengjuan with respect and panic.

"You may teach my mother-in-law how to wail now, auntie," said Qingmei.

"You are driving away my upcoming tears, Qingmei," said Chunhong.

Onlookers at the doorway laughed.

"Do not tease her!" Mrs. Hou said loudly. "We should laugh or cry as the situation demands. A man's fury and a woman's wailing can exhaust him or her. I have whined seven times in my life, and it took me 15 days to recover from each hard crying."

We did not know when she had each crying. Since she married in Yanerpo, she had not returned to her hometown in Dahuozhai again. We had never heard that she had gone to a place to attend a funeral. When Limin's grandpa died, she had not become engaged to Uncle Chenggui; before her mother-in-law died, she tore at her daughter-in-law's mouth; as a result, the daughter-in-law could not cry in her funeral if there was one.

"Father ..." Chunhong shouted.

It was not sobbing, it was laughter. Others laughed, too.

"Watch your manners!" Mrs. Hou ordered.

"You should allow weepers to do the task," the man making funeral products said to Limin. "You are making things hard for Chunhong and you also stop weepers from earning money."

"I'll take your advice," said Limin. And then he said to Zheng Saner, "You may pull Chunhong to stand up now."

"Are you going to wail or not, Chunhong?" Zheng Saner asked loudly. "I'll help you to stand up if you don't cry."

"Nobody wept for her dead mother before," said Mrs. Hou. "Now she should cry for her dead father."

Zheng Saner did not argue although she wanted to, and she let Chunhong continue her job.

Chapter 41

Chunhong became quiet and her body seemed to be covered with a blue light, which was serene sadness.

"Father!" Chunhong yelled. Everybody felt as though blue droplets were seeping into their bodies.

She began her long wailing: "Father! Your birth was remote but your death is right here. Your life is riddled with miseries. You became an orphan 70 years ago. How did you grow up? Which house were you standing nearby when you were surrounded with the smell of a delicious meal? When firecrackers were set off, did you know that it was the Spring Festival? When our second uncle was lying in the soil quietly, he would be much better than you. If I could be born decades earlier than you, I would rather be your mother; but God had decided that you would be our father. You had seven children. After our mother passed away, you had to raise us all by yourself. You had gone through difficulties, had been treated with scorn, and had sacrificed yourself for your children. We are grateful to you. You had been our father for decades, but you had never been Xu Chengxiang for yourself. It's a good name, but it did not bring good luck to your life. You are in heaven now and your spirit will always be with us. Life and death, live and cry. I miss you now! Are you feeling cold? (thumping the freezing coffin) We are parentless children now, but you and our mother have become immortals!"

On our father's birthday, Chunhong said to him, "I won't cry if you go to another world someday." On his funeral, she kept wailing and she was too weak to stand up even when she was pulled by Fengjuan. Chunhong began the next section of her wailing in her hoarse voice. Later I could hear words about train, theft, hunger, Xinjiang, belly, Lily and hair. Chunhong and her husband had never mentioned their life in Xinjiang. And I heard another word: shooting.

Fengjuan grasped Chunhong's shoulder and pulled her backwards, but Chunhong struggled to throw herself onto the coffin again.

"You may stop now," Fengjuan whispered to her sorrowfully. Fengjuan's voice could be heard by everybody through a microphone. Chunhong continued her wailing. It was about her life and agony.

Fengjuan returned around and smiled although tears were still in her eyes.

"Help Chunhong now!" she said loudly to Zhuqing, Yuling and Zheng Saner.

The women including Zhanhui entered the hall and helped Chunhong to stand up.

Chapter 42

Chunhong kept crying and she was accompanied by her relatives. When Lily was sobbing, her husband Peiliang was also sad. He had always been taking good care of her. One day Chunhong went to Zhoucheng to visit Lily. When she and Lily were having a walk, neighbours said to Chunhong admiringly, "Your son-in-law has been doting on your daughter!"

"Bring a bottle of mineral water to your great-aunt, Huchuan," said Swallow. The boy rushed to take a bottle from a table and ran towards his mother as fast as he could. Swallow gave the bottle to Chunhong, but she did not take it. Lily held it and poured some water on her mother's face to wash away her tears.

"Don't waste water!" Chunhong yelled.

"Oh, you still have a clear voice, auntie," said Xiaolan.

Others laughed but they seemed to blame Xiaolan. She realized that she had said something wrong, so she added, "We must save water as much as we can during the funeral. Cheer up, auntie!"

"Tears come into your belly, not from your eyes," someone said to

Xiaolan.

"My grandpa is thrifty and enjoys having fun," said Xiaolan. "I'll save water and play mahjong, and my grandpa will be very glad. He blesses me to win."

"You can give the money you've won to your grandpa," another one said.

"He does not need that now. Oh, you owe me 40 yuan."

Xiaolan was lucky this time. The gongs to walk around the coffin again rang.

Chapter 43

It was lunch time. Swallow, holding chopsticks, was watching trees although did not know their names: pines, cypresses, oriental white oaks, five-leaved chaste trees, silver birches, and chestnut trees. There was no wind or bird now. The whole place was surrounded by mists of sadness, so birds would rather fly away.

A yellow dog looked around and then it had eye contact with Swallow. "Hey, where are you from?" she asked. It ran towards the west.

"Oh, I thought it came from Cotton Infertility," she talked to herself.

Dayou did not come back even it was 3 p.m. She felt too awkward to call him because she knew that he disliked Huchuan. The boy wanted to be with her every minute, and the three people could not get along. Chunshu chanted the funeral orations again, Zhanhui carried two barrels of pigwash home, and Xiaolan lost all the money that she had earned in the morning. One of the chickens kept by Wang Qingguang pecked at a firecracker. The chicken flung it off with its mouth and it ignited the cigarette butt thrown away just now by the man producing funeral products. Bang! The chicken ran away angrily and seemed to curse the firecracker and the smoker. Everything was going on.

Swallow called Dayou at last. He was not in Cotton Infertility.

"When and why did you go to the street?" she asked.

She listened. "Why are you so angry? I'm not your punchbag!" she said those words fawningly.

"Swallow is submissive to Dayou," Chunhong sighed. The sorrow that she expressed during wailing in the mourning hall was gone now. Swallow did not hear what she said, and she holding Huchuan by the hand walked towards her. The latter watched her with concern.

"Dayou borrowed Uncle Chunshang's motorbike and went to the street," Swallow said happily. "And he'll come back soon."

After a moment Dayou returned with his own son. He had made an agreement with his ex that she would keep taking good care of their son until she had a new boyfriend, and she would let Dayou raise the boy all by himself so that she could marry again. Dayou had not seen his son since he came back from Zhejiang. Huchuan reminded him of his own son Ding.

"This is Ms. Swallow," Dayou introduced her to Ding.

"Hello, Ms. Swallow," Ding said timidly, putting his head between his father's legs.

She squatted and was ready to hug Ding when Huchuan was still grasping her sleeve. Huchuan released his grip and stood behind her silently when she reached out her hands to Ding.

"This is your elder brother, Huchuan," she said, holding Ding in her arms.

Huchuan did not say or do anything.

"A child can perceive his enemy like an animal," Chunhong whispered to me. "Swallow has never held Huchuan in her arms!"

Dayou gave cigarettes to the men.

"Oh, it's a new brand," said Xianhe.

"Let me see," said Qiuyue, holding a cigarette, and then returned it to her father.

"Sometimes I smoke good cigarettes," said Dayou, blushing.

"Did you use the borrowed money?" asked Swallow.

We knew who had lent the money to him. Dayou had to cover up his embarrassment and hastily changed the subject.

"A disaster has happened in the town, Uncle Chunming," Dayou said, watching me seriously.

"What?" everybody got shocked.

Part Five

Chapter 1

Thousands of years ago, a Banese general named Tuofu made a military coup. According to Single Braid's research, the then capital was located in Ba Valley nowadays. Since then Dongxuan had been riddled with rebels. Wang Chuan was born in a landlord family in Qingping Town. In the 18th year of the Republic of China he returned from his overseas study in Lomonosov Moscow State University, and later he organized social activities against the imperial rule. Dongxuan suffered from famine in the seventh year of Tongzhi Period of late Qing Dynasty and refugees had to steal food from granaries. More than twenty people were arrested and seven of them were sentenced to death. Local scholars wrote letters to let the prisoners be pardoned. However, the seven prisoners were shot to death. Four heads were connected with neck skin and three flew away and one of them jumped beside a river and gripped a dead fish with his teeth. The family members of the rest of the prisoners died, were sent into exile, or were maltreated. In the national examination the next year, the local scholars wrote the details of the tragedy at the expense of their promising future. That was shocking news in Dongxuan historically.

Dayou said that villagers who used to live in Bijia Mountain made trouble in the town. They were asked to be relocated into a residential quarter in Zhongba Town 17 kilometres upstream. It was a new building named Happy Home. Seepage could be seen after they lived in the Happy Home for half a month. Occupants reported the problem to the town mayor and said that they would rather go to their hometown.

"The walls can be dried!" the town mayor snapped. "Hold on and things will get better and better. If you are asked by leaders from the city or from the province, you should say that you have a good life in the Happy Home."

"Even the quim can't be happy," one of the dwellers grumbled.

Everybody including the town mayor laughed.

Several years ago, Mr. Lu, the Secretary of Provincial Committee of the CPC, visited Kaiyang County. He greeted an elderly woman and asked her if she was having a happy life.

"Even the quim can't be happy," she said with a local accent.

Mr. Lu could not hear those words clearly, so he asked others about it.

His staff got shocked and one of them, the deputy secretary general, ventured, "She says that her life is getting better and better."

Mr. Lu got excited.

The matter brought two results: if a leader from the province came to visit a city or a town, arrangements must be made beforehand. The deputy secretary general at that time was Feng Quan who used to be the village party secretary in Huilong Town and who had ridden the high horse in front of Guangwen. Feng Quan was promoted to deputy head of Phoenix District of Baima city, to head of Phoenix District, to deputy secretary-general of the Municipal Committee, to deputy mayor, and to executive vice mayor. The town mayor required that the villagers should speak well of everything the local government had done.

Chapter 2

Villagers living in Bijia Mountain had heard of that, and they were determined not to be relocated to another place. Meanwhile, the county government was resolved to establish a new town in the vicinity of mountains. One day the village government officials asked all the villagers to attend a meeting. During the two hours, their houses were demolished. The village committee was located in a detached courtyard, so the people inside the room did not hear the rumblings.

The villagers sat in the rubble, too sad to wail. Ruisong once said that modern people were unable to laugh or cry. The villagers could not sit there for too long because the land had been expropriated by the government, but they must do something.

There was a steel-framed bridge named Qingxi River Bridge 40 meters wide and 300 meters long in the town. It was built twenty years ago and was connected with thoroughfares along the banks. The road on the other side of the river led to three neighbouring counties. People could go across the river to reach Baima and Chongqing. The villagers of Bijia Mountain put a barrel of dynamite and scores of gas cans in the middle of the Qingxi River Bridge. The county government leaders called the police nervously, and soon the villagers catapulted kindling materials into the centre of the Bridge.

"The Bridge split in two in the explosion," said Dayou. "The villagers invaded the town and killed everybody they saw."

Xin Hongcai told Dayou about that. Xin Hongcai had become the director of grain supply centre before he was 30. At that time he was an influential man in Huilong Village, not a town yet; and he frequently gave negative comments to the grain on purpose. People had to give vegetables or eggs to him to fawn on him when they were selling those things, and they cursed him after he left. Now he was an old, healthy man, but he became soft-hearted and often visited his daughter in the county after she got married.

Dayou came across Xin Hongcai after the latter returned from his daughter's home. He started to tell what was going on in the county after Dayou lit a cigarette for him. There were more and more listeners.

"I saw Junfang and her husband on the bus," one of the listeners said. Junfang was Xin Hongcai's daughter. The couple went to the town for a shelter.

"Killings are everywhere," Xin Hongcai said with teary eyes for those dead innocent people. "Flee for survival."

Chapter 3

The news became the subject in the courtyard. The man who made funeral products took a break to smoke, but he should do a lot of tasks. The mahjong players were talking about the incident exaggeratedly.

"I should have gone to the county today," said one man.

"You can go now," said Limin.

That man laughed.

"If all of dwellers in the county are killed," said another man, "house prices will drop sharply. And we can buy one house at a very low price and live there."

"House prices will be much higher if all of dwellers are dead," said a third man.

"Why?"

"The county will be owned by the villagers of Bijia Mountain, just like a state-owned enterprise becomes a collectively-owned one."

"It'll be the same," said Wang Qingguang. The incident reminded him of the factories which had not paid the wages for his sons-in-law for a long time, and he was rather angry about their bankruptcy. If what Zhanhui had said turned out to be true, his first son-in-law had been a killer. He was upset now.

"I will never live in the county," said Xiaolan, holding a mahjong tile. "Because it will be ill luck!"

Peiliang's parents lived in the county. He soon called his mother but got no answer, and then he called his father and the latter hung up the phone. He continued but got the same result. "I'll need to go to the county," he said anxiously.

"Let me call them," said Lily.

The guests became quiet and would listen to the conversation. Lily's mother-in-law received the call.

"Your dad could not use the phone well," she laughed.

Everybody could hear her laughter. Peiliang snatched the phone and asked his mother why she had turned off the phone. He was usually calm but he lost his temper now.

"The phone battery died," she explained.

"What's going on in the county?" Peiliang asked.

"It's weird. The walls and the ground are being cleaned with high-pressure water guns. Cars are not allowed to go today."

"You should buy crates of instant noodles and of bottles of mineral water, and hide yourselves at home."

"OK. Is the funeral going on well? We were not told about your grandpa's hospitalization, so we did not visit him."

"Lily and I did not know about that until our grandpa left us," Peiliang said loudly as a cover-up.

The phone call was ended.

"Your mom is unaware of the killings," said Magpie. "Your parents live in the suburbs."

Magpie had been helping us during the funeral. He usually went to the county to buy paint so that he could do a good job for his employer. One day he came across Guangwen when he went to the county with Chunshan. Guangwen said that he visited Peiliang's parents just now and would go to the county party committee which would lead the local leaders to see the Rising

Sun New Village. The residential quarter had been built much earlier than Happy Home and it was the new rural model created by the county. The villagers could operate happy farmhouses for customers' relaxation. After Guangwen left, Magpie asked about Peiliang's parents' residence, Chunshan replied and mentioned the stiffness of Peiliang's father, the two men laughed.

"To remove all traces of blood," Magpie explained.

Everybody agreed with it. Humans' blood should not appear in the street because it might be the symbol of something bad.

Chapter 4

My friends in the county did not tell me about such a serious thing. They often told me even trivialities, but this time they became silent. Perhaps they would rather leave me undisturbed for my father's funeral. But I worried if they could be safe and sound. I took a shortcut. It was a mound above which an apricot tree was growing. I grasped a branch and climbed the tree. Nobody could watch me. I walked eastwards along rice fields. The scenery was peaceful and wonderful, and even the air was sweet.

I nervously wondered whom I should call. At last I called Ruisong who could know a lot of things in the television station. It was not answered, so I called Single Braid.

"I'm in Baili Canyon," said Single Braid. Bad connection.

Baili Canyon was the most remote area in Dongxuan county, and it bordered a county in Chongqing. The situation in that place was harsher than that of in Wanyuan Mountain. It took three days for a farmer to go to the farmland. He usually set up a shed nearby the field and waited for the harvest. He returned after six months with tattered clothes and long hair.

Weeding drums came down: sing and beat a drum to invigorate oneself during farm work. "Listen to my melodies. Locusts are found in the crops. We pray that the insects will disappear. The best singers will be invited to this place…" Single Braid did not hear the melodies when he went there many years ago. Now he could hear and would stay there.

"I want to hear the melodies from each stone there," said Single Braid. He was usually quiet, but he would keep talking on the subject he was interested in. I did not tell him about the shocking news in the county. It seemed that he had not known about it. His parents, wife and children had been living there. I guessed that they kept him in the dark so that he could concentrate on his work. There are two kinds of wisdom: awareness and unawareness; sometimes the latter can be much wiser than the former. The fat pig kept by Zhanhui did not know that it would be slaughtered soon, and it could enjoy the last hours of its life. The news brought by Dayou might be his own or Xin Hongcai's imagination.

Chapter 5

I could see our mother's graveyard from the place I was standing in. Our grandma's graveyard had been relocated into the cemetery hill of our ancestors. After our father lived in Guaizaoping, Chunshan cleaned our mother's only. Chunshu and Chunshang had never cleaned it. Our grandma's was full of bamboo rhizomes, yellowwood, willows, red vines, or snakes. These tombs were unrecognizable, but a new one would be set up here. Chunshan would clean it before spring thunder came the next year – the deceased man's soul would be disturbed by the spring thunder, and bamboo roots and saplings would grow. Our parents' tombs would be deserted after many years.

But that was not a sad thing. Those memories should not become a burden on us. Ten years ago I went to Ukraine with the delegation of Chinese poets. The locals said that they had an obligation to remember their ancestors of seven generations. If you came across a child and asked him or her some questions, such as "Who are your parents?", "Who was your father's father or your grandfather's father?", "What kind of man were they?", "What did they do for a living?", "How did others think of them?", if the child could not answer them, his or her parents would be criticized.

At that time I felt embarrassed. They could remember the seven generations. Nowadays we are the offspring of human beings of the first generation; an individual cannot exist now if without one generation. We have our ancestors' blood even though we may laugh at the strange pictures of them.

Chunshu chanted the funeral oration sorrowfully and funeral geomancers started to recite scriptures. Those words could be clearly heard: "The Great

Mother and the Great Father created everything. Pan Gu created the universe. Six children were born. Fu Xi taught people the things about marriage, Shen Nong taught planting crops, and Xuan Yuan taught clothes making. After the world and human beings were created, immortals were asked to deliver sermons on right and wrong, and to save sinful people."

Chapter 6

Li Zhi said that his dad was having a meeting, which was true. Today was Saturday. Leaders went to the county and all the government organs in villages and towns should work harder because they were worried about petitioners who were so slippery that they would go to the provincial government in Chengdu or higher government offices in Beijing.

On the day when our father left hospital, Mr. Han, the deputy town chief, took the man named Qin Yuan to the town from Beijing. Qin Yuan, also known as Qin Dagun, had been living in Peartree Village nearby Laojun Mountain. Many years ago Qin Dagun had a grudge against the family planning staff in the village. When they found that his wife had been hiding herself in a cave, so they played a waiting game in a forest nearby the cave. After half an hour, Qin Dagun came out of the cave furtively holding empty bowls and dirty clothes. He put the bowls and clothes into the grass and went down the mountain carrying a basket. As soon as his wife walked out of the cave and was about to pee, the family planning staff pinned her against the ground. After seven years, Qin Dagun would claim justice. He said that a man named Jing Xiaopeng touched his wife's breasts and private parts after he pinned her down. Seven years had passed, and the marks had been gone even though there were some. Jing Xiaopeng might brush against those areas accidentally. But Qin Dagun insisted that Jing Xiaopeng had sexually harassed her and had smelled his fingers after he touched her. That was bullshit. What's more, Qin Dagun said that the family planning staff killed the chickens kept by him and cooked them. Now he wanted fairness.

However, Qin Dagun had no evidence. As a result, he went to higher government offices in Beijing. After an officer swiped his identity card, he told him that his case would be accepted within two months – he would have talks with local village and township government leaders, but it could not be solved. He became a persistent petitioner. Residents became tenacious petitioners, too. The unfinished building with the pit excavated by the property developer was the evidence that they had been deceived.

The petitioners also included township workers. The newlyweds Long Yunqing and his wife Peng Rui worked in the forestry station. One day Peng Rui went to the town and did not return. Her husband called the police and said that his wife had been kidnapped. The case was not solved. After three years she came back. In fact people knew that she had eloped with a man from Jiangsu province and had a baby. When that man came to Dongxuan and saw her on the street, he was attracted by her voice and beauty; and he invited her to dinner, sweet-talked to her, and bought a lot of jewellery for her. She went to Zhejiang with him and became his secret lover; later she got pregnant and was treated well by him. However, after she gave birth to a baby, she was not allowed to look at the baby and even did not know if it was a boy or a girl; the baby was taken away and she was left alone. She had to return home with some money at last.

She became jobless after she went home. Long Yunqing asked for an explanation and had to follow Mr. Huang, the then secretary of party committee in the town day and night. One day Long Yunqing visited Mr. Huang. The former sat on a sofa and snatched a cigarette from the table although the latter was in a sulk.

"I know what you were doing last night and three days ago," said Long Yunqing, smoking and crossing his legs.

Mr. Huang made tea for him hurriedly and fawningly. The next day Peng Rui resumed her job.

However, Peng Rui disliked Long Yunqing and divorced him after a few years. Two years after divorce, she remarried the director of river transport station whose wife had died. Long Yunqing petitioned the township government leaders again: Peng Rui had cheated on him and had lived with another man for three years, and she had left her post without permission. Such a woman as her should not have her job resumed. Mr. Huang, who had dealt with this, had retired. What's more, such a case should be treated seriously. Long Yunqing went to higher government offices in Chengdu and boasted that he would go to Beijing. The township government leaders got so worried that they told Peng Rui's current husband to bring Long Yunqing under control, otherwise he would be scapegoated for the bad result.

On the twenty-eighth day of the twelfth lunar month (just two days before the Spring Festival) the year before last, a call about the petition from Beijing reached the provincial government, and then reached the city government, and then the county government, and then the government in Huilong Town: the petitioner must be taken home at once from Beijing. The call was just like the biting wind. It was so short that the name could not be heard clearly. Most of the township government leaders had gone to the city, and only Mr. Song Nian, the deputy secretary, was left. He was asked by the secretary to go to Beijing with two strong assistants. The petitioner must be taken home and be closely watched, otherwise he would go to Beijing again.

Song Nian was not an influential leader. He treated people so humbly that he was not treated by them importantly. What's more, he was a slovenly idler in the office. Now he was asked to wear a suit as a good image for the local government. The cars had been used by the other leaders, so the secretary called Guangwen. The latter asked Yang Jin to send Song Nian to Chongqing, and Song Nian would go to Beijing by plane to save time. Guangwen usually accompanied the important leader, but he would not do so to Song Nian.

After Song Nian and his assistants reached Beijing, they saw a couple from Yaqueliang Village: Sun Jiushan and Yong Qin. The couple had been working in Beijing for so many years. Their hometown was next to Yanerpo and there was no construction project or demolition. What was the reason for their petition? They did not say anything about it. Song Nian could not get an answer, which lessened his excitement. He would just need to finish the task.

After the first month of the lunar year was over, villagers in Yaqueliang said that Sun Jiushan and Yong Qin could not buy tickets, so they came back with the excuse of petition. They could take the plane and it was a free trip.

Song Nian was a thrifty man and he was disliked by his colleagues in the era of consumerism. He had to return by plane because he must hurry up to have a reunion dinner with his family members. He could have bought tickets from scalpers, but the date would be after the fifth day of the first lunar month. If he had bought those tickets, he would have stayed in Beijing for one more week and would have spent much more.

More and more people did what Sun Jiushan and Yong Qin had done. As a result, the township government leaders had to send more staff and spend more money so as to take those people home no matter where they were. The huge costs nearly made the township governments go bankrupt. Guangwen once told me that the situation in Huilong Town was much more serious: the township government leaders had to give 1,000 yuan to each regular petitioner each month to avoid long trips and bad track records. There were six regular petitioners and they asked the leaders to give them more money.

Chapter 7

But those things were made pale by comparison when higher government officials visited Dongxuan. Even though you picked them up, you had no chance to speak to them, and they did not care about who you were. But you would lose your job if you made a mistake when the big shots were in Dongxuan. But some villagers were so bold that they might stop those leaders' cars. To avoid that, the roads must be heavily guarded and the villagers were asked to stay at home. The villagers had never seen such a spectacle and they would be eager to see it, so measures must be taken to refrain from any trouble. Yesterday afternoon village party secretaries were asked by government leaders of Huilong Town to keep track of the villagers. Guangwen was not asked because they knew there was a funeral for his father-in-law. There had been no petitioner from Lijiayan, but today he must attend a report-back meeting.

Guangwen should keep a close eye on Huigoer who had been living far away from neighbours just like Li Baoshun. Huigoer was lying on the bed when Guangwen knocked at the window. Huigoer's house was similar to Chunshu's: a room with a window. Huigoer did not hang curtains when he was sleeping in that room. Without curtains he would feel like sleeping with all the villagers in the same room. He was aloof because he treated others like trash.

Huigoer was sleeping stripped to the waist. It was chilly in the early morning, but he was not covered with a quilt. Guangwen kept knocking at the door and then heard Huigoer's loud farts. Meanwhile, a magpie was chirping along with its tail wagging.

"Fuck!" Guangwen snapped.

Huigoer could hear his voice. He jumped out of bed and opened the door quickly.

"Oh, I thought you would be busy with your father-in-law's funeral, Mr. Li," he said.

As soon as Huigoer saw Yang Jin standing beside Guangwen, he realized that Mr. Li would soon arrange a task for him: to be a troublemaker. He knew what to do.

Many years ago, Guangwen asked Huigoer to make things hard for Lu Qing in the Moon Village. When sand excavation ships owned by Guangwen and Ho Laosan were working in a river nearby the Moon Village, Lu Qing argued that the river belonged to the Moon Village and he even poured coal-tar pitch into the iron sieves. One day Ho Laosan pointed at Lu Qing and told Huigoer about it. At that time Lu Qing and his wife were planting sweet potato seedlings, Huigoer was smoking a red-covered Bafine cigarette and looking around. After the couple finished their farm work, Lu Qing walked in front of his wife. Suddenly Huigoer blew his nose on Lu Qing's wife, and then he rubbed his hands on her breasts. She yelled, but Huigoer did not remove his hands from her body. Just before Lu Qing hurled a hoe at Huigoer, the former immediately recognized that the latter was the notorious man in the village. Lu Qing stopped.

"Hurl it at me if you dare!" Huigoer shouted.

The woman ran and Huigoer chased after her, and then he continued to touch her breasts. Meanwhile, her husband was too scared to move. Huigoer cursed him and then he left.

Huigoer thought that he did not finish the task, but Guangwen gave food and wine to him. From then on Lu Qing did not meddle in the sand excavation again.

Chapter 8

Huigoer thought that he would get some benefits soon. Guangwen sat on a bench and asked Yang Jin to sit down. Yang Jin blew off the dirt from the bench, but Guangwen sat down without Yang Jin's step.

"Cook breakfast for us," Guangwen said to Huigoer.

Yang Jin looked at Guangwen in astonishment. Just now Guangwen declined many villagers' invitations to have breakfast with them. Huigoer's house was such a pigsty that there had been no visitor for so many years. He did what Guangwen said. The kitchen was next to his bedroom, and the two rooms were his home. He spoke to Guangwen softly and shyly when the latter talked with him. Yang Jin got speechless.

"There is cured meat in your home," said Guangwen, looking at the meat with a smell of white mould.

Huigoer poured hot water into a basin and removed the mould from the meat with vegetable sponge. A delicious smell was permeating the air when the meat was being grilled.

If there was no visitor, Huigoer would eat it just after he grilled it for a few minutes. But today the meat was sizzling. He fried the meat with potato slices, and then fried hot pepper. He would make soup with Chinese cabbage, but Guangwen said that he did not have sufficient time.

"Only two dishes," Huigoer said awkwardly.

Guangwen sat beside the table which was covered with filth and hair. Huigoer was soaked with sweat, so he used a dirty towel to wipe his body; and then he used the towel to scrub bowls. At last he poured liquor into the bowls.

After a few days Yang Jin said, "I nearly vomited at that time!"

He did not drink at all that day because he would drive, but Guangwen drank up the liquor without any frowning or disgust. Yang Jin respected Guangwen because even such a man as Huigoer did not feel self-abased in front of him.

After they had breakfast, Guangwen gave 100 yuan to Huigoer.

"Why do you give me that?" asked Huigoer.

"It's for you," said Guangwen.

Huigoer did not take the banknote, which surprised Yang Jin once again.

Huigoer had never refused anything given to him. He had not invited a guest to his house for decades, but today he treated the village party secretary for the very first time, and he would feel embarrassed to receive the money. Guangwen could understand him, so he put back the money and began to smoke.

"When will you attend the meeting?" Yang Jin asked anxiously.

"At 11 a.m.," Guangwen replied. "We'll leave ten minutes later."

It dawned on Yang Jin that Guangwen stayed at Huigoer's house to stop him from making trouble outside.

Yang Jin knew that a senior officer would arrive at the county at 10 a.m., and Guangwen would stay at Huigoer's house to watch him. He could have delegated the task to Li Qiantao, but instead, he chose to handle it by himself. It was his duty, which could not be understood by the people who were not dutiful.

Guangwen was walking on the street when his wife called him the first time, was having a meeting the second time, and was giving a speech the third time.

Chapter 9

Guangwen returned to Yanerpo the next morning. Yesterday when they were reporting, they received a notification that the senior leader could not arrive at Dongxuan timely, and the attended time would be extended and there would be another notification of the exact arrival time. The meeting had to be over and the village party heads returned to their villages. Villagers had gone to different places although the villages were still there geographically. The village party heads would go to the street in the town and visit some households who used to live in the village. There had been no petitioner from Lijiayan, but Guangwen visited all the households who had relocated in the street and he declined their invitations to dinner. And then Yang Jin drove him to Lijiayan.

According to the schedule of the senior leader provided by Tan Ruisong, Guangwen would stay in Lijiayan until 4 p.m. He did not return to his home in the town last night. Li Zhi, Ziguo, Sixi and his girlfriend Shen Xiaofei stayed in that house. Sixi appeared at 8:15 p.m. After he and Shen Xiaofei had a shower, Li Zhi called his buddies together with Guibing and his daughter to go to the steakhouse. Guibing and his daughter had the dinner for one hour and then returned, and the rest of the people enjoyed themselves for two more hours. Li Zhi's buddies would sleep in his house, but Sixi said that he would chat with his cousins. They could understand him, so they left. After Xiaofei slept, Sixi told his life in Harbin to his cousins. They did not stop chatting until early morning came.

Chapter 10

Funeral geomancers chanted scriptures, led the offspring to walk around the coffin many times, and greeted gods who brought the dead man's soul to the nether world. Our father would report to the King of Hell and cancel his number: 00033428. It used to be his admission number which I thought to be a good one, but it became his death code. Our father would have a new identity card in another world led by gods, and he would hold a banquet for them to express his gratitude to them. Chunshu made a large pile of joss paper, and Liu Xianwen wrote magic figures and letters on each piece. Each god had 49 pieces of paper.

There were two reasons why Liu Xianwen could become a master. The first one was about a funeral geomancer named Tong who used to work with Liu. During one operation, when Tong saw Liu's shadow falling into the coffin, the former shut the coffin at once to conceal Liu's shadow in it. The shadow was a man's spirit, if it was buried or smothered, the living man would become a fool and Tong could do all the funeral business in the areas around the Laojun Mountain. After the coffin was closed, it could not be opened again. Otherwise, the dead man's phantom would come out of the coffin on the seventh day after its burial, eat his own family members, and scourge the village. Liu Xianwen showed the whites of his eyes but soon he calmed down; he strained to wield his hands and seemed to pull his shadow out of the coffin little by little. He fetched a piece of bean curd and a kitchen knife. He smashed the bean curd with the knife and then hurled the weapon into a stone column outside the mourning hall. The knife could not be pulled out. As a result, Tong's skills were destroyed. Afterwards he left his hometown and became a beggar. Liu Xianwen did not teach the method to his disciples although they were eager to learn it, and they tried to fawn on him. The second reason was that he could write magic figures and letters on a piece of joss paper. Those things had magical power, so the gods would accept them. But if they were written by other funeral geomancers, they could not become magical.

Liu Xianwen in a Taoist's robe was chanting incantations and writing on joss paper. His vigorous handwriting resembled Xiao An's and could surpass Chunshu's.

"You have inherited the handwriting from the ancient calligraphers," I said with awe.

"People say that we are superstitious," said Liu Xianwen. "But I take it as traditional culture. Even Confucius said that we should hold a good funeral for our parents. A dead man needs a ceremony, too. Both funerals and good handwriting belong to traditional culture."

His smile reminded me of his past. He used to be a very smart boy but he failed in the national college entrance examination. He would not have become a funeral geomancer if he had gone to university. But who would chant incantations for my dead father if he did not do the job?

In my opinion, a man chooses his occupation because he is needed by others rather than he wants to do it. Your marriage is not determined by you but by your children. Destiny makes that. People either dislike their marriage or blindly believe it, but they ignore kismet. Liu Xianwen had been a loser in the examinations but he became a funeral geomancer because he was chosen to escort the dead men's spirits, including my father's. I was grateful to him.

The joss paper would be burnt. Chunshan got a metal bucket and he said that it had been used to store ammonium nitrate dynamite when Longyan Pond was built. Liu Xianwen used it as a burner. Chunshu put a blue string on the head of the bucket. When Liu Xianwen and his disciples were chanting scriptures, Chunshu ignited one piece of joss paper and threw it into the burner. The process was repeated. At 3 p.m. it was over, and it was lunchtime. After it was finished and tableware was washed, and before the guests played mahjong, Sixi and Shen Xiaofei came.

Chapter 11

Shen Xiaofei's appearance made the courtyard shine, which seemed that a glorious event was going on. Li Zhi once said that Shen would be an ugly woman. But on the fifth day of our father's funeral, she brought beauty to the solemn place. Death was not about ugliness, not about loss, not about sadness. I could feel that although I was not the deceased man. I thought that the nurse called Ms. Cheng could not impress others just like Shen Xiaofei did. An ordinary human being could not feel something deeper if he was not on the spot. Ms. Cheng was like a dream I had in the hospital, and it could not exist in the reality.

Shen was wearing trousers and a green scarf. The coldness brought by a northerner could turn summer in the south into spring.

Swallow held Sixi's bag. Xiaofei taking Sixi's arm walked into the mourning hall while he looked much older. Chunhong shouted that Sixi returned. After Sixi and his girlfriend kowtowed and stood up, he yelled with teary eyes, "Where is my funeral kerchief?"

Fengjuan brought two kerchiefs at once. Chunhong wrapped one around Xiaofei's head and Fengjuan around Sixi's.

"Xiaofei looks like a landlady when she bends," said Mrs. Hou.

A few decades ago, there was only one landlady in Yanerpo. She was Yang Tongshu, the mother of Crap. Mrs. Hou felt humiliated in front of Yang Tongshu. Yang had never fought back or argued whenever Mrs. Hou cursed her. Yang's daughter died at the age of three. Mrs. Hou said that her daughter would marry White in the nether world, Yang nodded silently. White was a bullock kept by Xu Weifeng. His son pissed in the grass, so White could not distinguish the smell of poisonous weeds when it was devouring the grass. Piss and blood raged in its stomach, it yelled three days and three nights in agony, and it died one week earlier than Yang's daughter. Mrs. Hou felt mortified towards Yang's silence. When landlords and landladies were punished many years ago, many people spat at Yang, threw shoes at her, and kicked her. Magpie's father beat her before he became blind. But Mrs. Hou had never done such a thing. Crap was the only one who respected Mrs. Hou in Yanerpo because she did not bully his mother when she was targeted by others. But he did not know that Mrs. Hou did not want to feel embarrassed again. Silence agitated her. When Chunhong was awkwardly wrapping a funeral kerchief around Xiaofei's head, others laughed at them, but Mrs. Hou did not laugh.

Chapter 12

Funeral geomancers needed to take a rest. Sixi and Shen Xiaofei were in the mourning hall. Sixi was standing beside the freezing coffin, watching his grandpa's body and crying. There was a red hue on Xiaofei's face. Our father's spirit would look at his grandson and his charming granddaughter-in-law so that it could boast in front of other ghosts.

My sisters were standing in the area with a circle of darkness left by the burner outside the mourning hall.

"Sixi is such a hypocrite," Chunhong whispered, watching him crying.

She had called her son and asked why he did not come here with Ziguo and Sixi. Li Zhi told her about the dinner and chats last night in details.

"Sixi should have kowtowed for his grandpa last night or this morning," Chunhong added. "He pretends to be sad. Crying is useless."

"You cried so hard in front of our dad's coffin," said Chunying.

Chunhong glanced at her angrily but the latter did not notice that. Qiuyue pushed her mother's face towards Chunhong's, but Chunhong looked calm at once.

"What are you doing?" asked Chunying.

Qiuyue did not reply. She had been watching Shen Xiaofei since the latter appeared, and she had a sense of inferiority at the sight of Shen's charm. Others would avoid that, but Qiuyue faced it: she kept watching Shen.

Sixi wailed leaning on the coffin. Shen Xiaofei put one hand on his back and whispered to him.

"He wants his grandpa to stay," said Chunhong emotionally. That reminded her of Hongquan who did not say when he would return.

"He feels sad for his grandpa," said Swallow.

Chunhua smiled meaningfully.

"The sight of his shedding crocodile tears makes me sick!" Chunying snapped. She still remembered that she had been deceived by Sixi to get involved in pyramid selling. People may forget how miserable they were when they were suffering from bad things, but Chunying would never forget that.

"Do you agree with me?" Chunying asked me.

I smiled silently. That reminded me of a basketball game. When a commentator was talking about a player good at using deceptive movements, I received a text message from Sixi. He told me that he had been busy giving lectures on marketing and would invite personages to a ceremony in Xiangyang city, Hubei province. I did not reply because I did not believe him. Sixi was just like that basketball player. If Sixi had been born in the Era of Warring States, he might have become a lobbyist. Now he could travel across the country, enjoy his good life, and have a girlfriend with his sweet talk.

Chapter 13

Tian was rubbing at Chunying's legs. Sixi had not met his son since he came back. Tian was watching his father and Shen Xiaofei and he blushed. Sixi did not tell his girlfriend that he had a son living with his parents and a daughter with her mother.

"Don't call your dad too early," Chunying squatted and whispered to Tian.

The clever boy could understand her at once and nodded.

"You are a good boy, Tian," said Chunying.

Before she wanted to say that he was much better than Huchuan, she did not say it when she saw Huchuan standing behind Swallow. Huchuan had been less close to his mother since she hugged Dayou's son, and he was unwilling to take her hand. Chunying had been adopted by another family, which was a like a scar in her heart. She knew that she must be independent and disliked being weak.

Chunhong pulled Tian into her arms and the boy clung to her.

"Stop crying, Sixi," she said.

When Sixi hit his head on the freezing coffin, he was pulled back by his girlfriend.

"May our grandpa rest in peace," Xiaofei said softly.

Sixi, supported by his girlfriend with her hands, walked out of the mourning hall. When he saw Tian and was about to hug him, the boy flinched.

"I'm your dad," Sixi said.

His words surprised us. Tian looked at Chunhong and she said, "Greet him now."

He rushed into his father's arms. He kissed his son and, pointing at Xiaofei, said, "She is your mom."

Tian had never met his biological mother, but he could see her pictures each year. He was so familiar with her face that he realized the young woman in front of him was not his mother, but his father asked him to call her mother.

"Mom," Tian said shyly. He grasped Xiaofei's legs and wanted to be hugged by her.

"Don't make Miss Shen feel tired, Tian," said Fengjuan.

"Miss Shen is Tian's mom now," Chunying explained.

"Let your mom take a rest, Tian," Fengjuan added.

Fengjuan wanted to get Tian out of Xiaofei's arms, but the boy grasped her neck.

"I'll stay in my mom's arms," he insisted.

"Don't make her too tired, Tian," said Chunhong. She had to ask Sixi to come here.

After Sixi introduced his girlfriend to us, he gave branded cigarettes to his male relatives. Sixi watched Tian and the boy got off Xiaofei's arms. But soon he asked her to carry him on her back. She squatted and let Tian lean on her back.

Huchuan was watching them while others laughed at them.

"Will you let me carry you on my back?" Swallow asked Huchuan tenderly. The boy did not answer her.

Chapter 14

After a moment Tian had to get off from Xiaofei's back and go to school.

Zhanhui was soaked with sweat after she carried several buckets of pigwash to her home. She asked Tian to go to school and then she whispered to Xu Xing. We could guess that she asked her husband to drink less and smoke less but carry more buckets of pigwash to their house. But he went to cut grass, but pigs disliked the grass and they became thinner, which was discovered by Zhanhui after several days.

Chunshu glanced at Zhanhui in a sulk when he saw her whispering to Xu Xing. She got worried when she could not find Chunshu, and she got surprised when she saw him standing at a distance. The two people looked calm when they saw each other.

"Hurry up, Tian," said Zhanhui. "Maer is waiting for you in Weir Pond Trench." She looked away to avoid eye contact with Chunshu. Chunhong was watching all this.

The kids would go to school, but there was only one motorbike.

"I should not carry four kids in one motorbike," said Dayou. He was not doing business and he should not take risks. He was using Chunshang's motorbike and he would have to carry three kids but he was unwilling to take Huchuan. Huchuan did not want to go with him and he cried when he heard that his mother would take her to the street with Dayou. Huchuan had not cried for a long time.

"You may go with me, Huchuan," said Qingmei.

Li Zhi remembered that his daughter would go to school, so he had a motorbike driver take her and her mother there. Ziguo told Li Zhi to arrange two motorbikes because his nieces would go to school, too. Anping and her daughters sat in another motorbike, just a moment later than Tian.

Chapter 15

The whole village became quiet, which was liked by adults. The funeral music could be heard after noisy kids went home. This was a funeral. Chunshu's sorrowful chanting made us focus on our father lying in the freezing coffin again. The crying relatives dwindled and the courtyard resembled a bleak place even amid gongs. Laughter was needed although it would not be proper. Guangwen was walking with a funeral stick and it seemed to be his third leg when he was moving forward. Nobody laughed. Peopled got tired, and they needed company and solitude. The desolateness was with the living.

The participants did not laugh because there was a special guest. Before we walked around the coffin again, Chunhong asked Xiaofei not to join them.

"Xiaofei should join us," Guangwen argued.

"I'm afraid that she may get tired," his wife explained.

"I can hold on," Xiaofei said calmly without any body language. And then she stood behind Sixi, but he let her stand in front of him so that he could look after her. Sixi was watching her during the process. Before we kowtowed, he put his hands forward and seemed to use his hands as pads for her knees; but he could not because he was holding sticks of incense. Before we stood up, he helped her up to her feet by holding her arms.

We had been familiar with Sixi's intentional deeds. When Ran Qing came to Sixi's home, he treated her like a baby. Even when she was stepping on a threshold, he stopped what he was doing and rushed to help her. He also took Kang Furong home when he was having a relationship with her. It was a severe winter in Yanerpo. Water should be heated up all the time and the fireplace would be kept burning except sleeping or going out. Before Kang Furong washed her face, Sixi added some cold water into a basin of boiling water. He put a towel soaked with warm water on her face. But he had never treated his own son so carefully, and he seldom thought about his daughter. Sometimes he looked at her pictures in his mobile phone and said, "My daughter is so beautiful." And then he put his phone aside.

Chapter 16

Supper was delayed. When we were waiting for supper, Chunhong told us what Li Zhi had told her. Sixi had talked about those things to Li Zhi and Ziguo.

"Xiaofei's parents should have taught her how to see men," Chunhong explained. "Women can't tell whether a man is a good one or a bad one unless they have met a lot of them. I feel pity for such a good girl as Xiaofei who has been deceived by Sixi!"

"He must have told all the things to her," said Chunying.

Chunhong moved her neck nervously. I saw her doing this when Sixi was doing his utmost to please Xiaofei. Chunhong considered those deteriorating deeds could be commonly seen in men. Chunying felt the same way because she had been raising a daughter, too. The girl was with us.

A girl's parents wanted a good son-in-law.

"One of my colleagues in Guangdong had an elder brother," said Chunying. "He was the curator of Ningyang County Cultural Centre in Sichuan province and had a charming, talented daughter. After her graduation from university, she became a secondary school teacher in Deyang. After six months she had a boyfriend. She told her parents that she would go home with her boyfriend. At that time they did not have mobile phones, so they could not have a picture of his. With mixed feelings they expected that their daughter would get married and have children. When the father reached the railway station, he saw a short, scrawny man standing beside his daughter."

"In disappointment her father took her luggage from that man's back," Chunying continued. "Her boyfriend worked like a servant, but that was how he deceived her. She was a pampered girl. When she was alone in a new place and met a man who could look after her like her parents did, she fell in love with him. But her father disliked that man."

"They went to a hotel so that the father could avoid meeting his friends," Chunying continued. "He would feel embarrassed if his neighbours saw that he should have such an ugly son-in-law. The next day he asked that man to leave, and he thought that his daughter would forget him soon. But the love between her and that man grew stronger and stronger. Her father got so depressed that he got cancer after one year and died after several months, and her mother died less than two years. That's terrible!"

Qiuyue stood up and walked towards a sycamore tree slowly.

Chunhong glanced at Qiuyue and then watched the sky. "It was going to rain according to the weather forecast during our father's hospitalization," she said. "But it did not rain. God will let us hold a good funeral for him. But the bad thing is coming. Parents should educate their daughters well."

Chapter 17

Limin said that supper was served. Whiteness was permeating the air. It was not the light, but the smell. The guests enjoyed the delicious meal.

The man making funeral products said that he wanted thick chilli sauce. Zheng Saner walked out of the kitchen holding a bowl of thick chilli sauce, and then she saw her father-in-law who was still sitting on a stone roller.

"Will you have supper, dad?" she shouted.

He seemed to suddenly wake up from his memories, and I rushed to support him to stand up.

"Let me help him," she said to me.

She supported her father-in-law by grasping his shoulders and walked towards the table.

"You won't sleep unless you have supper!" she yelled.

"All of us will except Xu Chengxiang," Magpie laughed.

Human beings' joy and sorrow could be related with food. Our father was neither happy nor sad now, because he needed food no more. Zheng Saner returned to the kitchen after her father-in-law sat down. Cooks and assistants were still busy in the kitchen, and they could not have a meal until the guests finished.

When Sixi and Xiaofei were sitting at the table under the glare, I thought of my friends who came to see me the other day. I did not let them stay and have dinner with my family members because I was worried that they might dislike my dirty hometown. Was I too obsessed with my hometown? Did it still exist? My parents had gone to another world. Chunhong said that a woman had no hometown. I was not a woman, but it was like a fast train with whistles and vibrations left.

Would Xiaofei feel disgusted about using the dirty tableware and watching the guests' yellow teeth when she was sitting with Sixi under the light? Would he be worried about that? I wished that she could marry Sixi and become one of our family members, but he was far beneath her. When I thought about my relatives, I hoped that one of them could have a new, extraordinary life through his or her hard work. But nobody could make it come true, even Lily could not.

After Lily lived in Zhoucheng, I visited her during my business trip. There was no book in her house because she had burned all her books before she graduated from university. The burning of textbooks had become a crazy event in universities. Later the authorities required that the students should not be forced to buy textbooks. As a result, the excited students just took their mobile phones into the classroom. If the teacher asked the students to mute their phones, they would let their mind wander without taking notes.

"You should take notes," the teacher ordered.

"The students had to go to the library to look up a piece of information," one of the students explained, "but now we can use the Internet."

"You must take notes! After the term is over, your notebook will be included into your credit hours!"

The students of the previous term sold their notebooks to the younger ones. The student could buy one and change the name. After the class was over, the teacher would continue to write his or her academic papers; if without them, he or she could not have a professorship even though he or she was a good teacher. The names of all the students could not be remembered by the teacher, to say nothing of recognizing their handwriting. Lily would take notes seriously and she was just a good student.

But that was enough. Life does not need insistence; no persistence, no compromise. Meanwhile, life does not need indifference; if you are indifferent to many things, you will forsake your rights in your life, which may become an excuse of idling away your life. Sufferings and hardships are tricks made by idealism, and the civilization based on them can kill vigour.

In my relatives, Sixi was an adventurer in cities, but he was not capable enough to enjoy the good life there. An overnight millionaire did not know how to use his money. Ziguo did not know how to get along with such a good, rich girl as Shanrui. There were many young people like them in my hometown. That was a new kind of urban-rural gap, which could not be eliminated by drinking bottles of mineral water in a city instead of drinking mountain spring water in the countryside.

Chapter 18

Qiuyue was thinking about something else when she was having supper with us. She had been watching Shen Xiaofei silently since the latter appeared.

Dayou did not return after he sent his son to the town, which was related to Sixi and his girlfriend. He did not know Sixi but from Lianwazi he had known about the bad things he had done. As a result, he felt that he was much better than Sixi. When Fengjuan said that Dayou was a lazy worker in the factory, he was scolded by Swallow who told me and Chunhong that he had hurt his hands, but he retorted that he had surpassed Sixi. What's more, Dayou felt a much stronger sense of superiority when people complained how bad Sixi was. But when he saw Sixi, he was impressed by his appearance and eloquence. Sixi bent in the mourning hall, but he looked like a charming, mysterious man when he gave cigarettes to the men in the courtyard.

There had been a legend across the river: a dissolute man returned home after he had left and been forgotten by others. He became such an imposing man that he was regarded as a great adventurer. The killer Xu Jinyang used to be such a man, but villagers refused to say that they had admired him. They cursed him and mentioned his opinion on death penalty before he was executed.

The sinful Xu Jinyang joined the army led by Liu Xiang against Japanese invaders and later against the liberation army, and the army which he joined was stationed in Shandong province. After he returned home – it was said that his father had got seriously ill or he would carry out a secret task, he was arrested by Wang Chuan who was controlling Dongxuan. Xu Jinyang, tied to a post with shackles on his hands and feet, was shown to everybody in an ox cart and then was sent to Ximencao Dam for execution. That happened two years after the victory of Chinese resistance against Japanese aggression.

"It's a dull thing to use a gun," Xu Jinyang said to an executioner. "But it's exciting to use a bayonet. The pleasure of killing is about the feelings in your hands. I dislike the high-altitude bombing made by Japanese invaders, because I can neither see the fright nor the blood, and I can't smell the dismemberment or the burnt body. Those killings are useless. The pleasure of killing should be driven by sins. The deeper the sins, the excited the pleasure. When you use a bayonet, your hands can feel the struggle of the skin and the bones, and the weapon can become stronger and you sharper. And you can understand what your right is. And you will …"

He died after gunshots. People still cursed Xu Jinyang after he died, but in fact they admired him.

Many villagers had gone to remote places and they became beggars, criminals, or heroes. Some had travelled across China, a villager in Houziyan had run a restaurant in Japan, one in Yaqueliang had worked in a construction team to build roads in Sierra Leone. All of them would die after many years. There were less and less heroes, and people became mediocre. However, the curiosity for the ancient mystery went on and on.

Dayou treated Sixi as a hero when he saw him for the very first time. A hero needed either a great career or a beauty. But such a man as Xu Jinyang had lost his life although he had been successful.

Dayou piously received the cigarettes given by Sixi. The former was watched by the latter, but they did not speak to each other. Dayou stifled his eagerness to greet him. Afterwards there was no communication between them. After Sixi knew who Dayou was, he looked aloof; but Dayou pretended to be indifferent. They met each other by chance. If Dayou had had supper with us, he and Sixi would have ended up sitting back to back.

Chapter 19

Chunhong said that she would go to sleep after supper. We would not have to walk around the coffin again in the evening.

It was a difficult task to sleep whenever we returned to our hometown. My brothers could not provide sufficient beds, even quilts stank of dirt, mould, and rats' urine. Iron plates were make-do beds and the quilts would make you feel stuffy when you were sleeping at night. But when you turned over and stretched your legs, you would feel so cold that you would wake up. Before kids went to school, my male relatives and I went to find beds in Limin's house and Qingguang's. Tonight several people could share one bed.

The beds in the attic of Chunshang's house were quiet. The funeral music and chanting would be stopped at midnight. Chunhong asked Swallow to find Xiaofei and tried to find a good bed for her. Chunhong, Xiaofei, Chunying and Chunhua would share one bed. Qiuyue was rebellious but would cling to her mother during bedtime.

"I've told your aunt (Zheng Saner), Qiuyue," said Chunhong. "You and Lily will sleep in her house."

Qiuyue was grasping her mother's arm.

"You, Chunhua and Xiaofei will sleep in the room of Chunshang's house," said Chunying. "Lily, Qiuyue, and I will sleep in Zheng Saner's room."

"Chunhua may go there," said Chunhong. "But you will stay with us."

Chunhong, Chunying, and Xiaofei went to the toilet in the courtyard. That was what a woman should do before she slept at night. There was a chamber pot under each bed, but it was for men, not for women. If the urine was not poured off, the pungent smell could be unbearable.

Sixi turned on the lighting on his mobile phone for those women, but Chunhong was using a flashlight.

"Bring Xiaofei's bag here," said Chunhong. "And let her wear new clothes. Her current clothes are full of dirt."

Chunhua and Qiuyue were quiet. Chunhua wondered why Chunhong refused to let her sisters sleep together. Meanwhile, tears fell down from Qiuyue's face.

"Xiaofei won't feel cold if she sleeps between you," said Sixi, giving the bag to Chunhong.

After they entered Chunshang's house, Chunhua said to Qiuyue angrily, "Why are you crying? Ask Lily to come here. We should sleep now!"

Chapter 20

Moths rushed towards bulbs and died because of high temperature, and their bodies were trampled. These insects were attracted by the light, and they struggled and died after the light went out. In the early morning chickens swarmed to peck at the moths so much so that they could not crow.

Two women stepped on the dead months when stars could still be seen. One of them walked towards the mourning hall. She kowtowed twice but got shocked when she heard someone snoring. The other one came and soon found the sleeping man was Liu Xianwen who watched the coffin as his duty and friendship to the deceased man and could have a sound sleep in the mourning hall rather than in his own house. The two people kowtowed once more and then left.

They walked hand in hand in the darkness on a dirty road, and their footfalls were muffled by clouds of dust. One household was living in a wooden house and its sole occupant was Magpie.

Chapter 21

Magpie used to live in his old house next to a bamboo forest nearby Zhanhui's new house. It was unbelievable that such a talkative man as him should live in an isolated place.

When he was building his new house in a rock basin, he invited a geomancer to inspect the surroundings. The geomancer looked around with his one eye which often shed tears, put a handful of earth into his mouth, spat it out, smelt it and threw it away, and rubbed his hand on his trousers.

"I should tell you something," he said to Magpie. "And it'll be a serious one."

"You may go now," said Magpie, giving 10 yuan to him. "I'm busy."

"I must tell you because you have paid me. Do you build the house for yourself?"

"Yes."

"A married woman will remarry you within 3 months."

"I'm glad that you tell me good news."

Magpie was going to remove the bark.

"You are destroying your good luck," said the geomancer. "You are building a house on barren soil. The woman is the soil. When I was chewing the soil, I could smell the scent of a woman. If you don't stop now, the scent will be gone. And the dream of having a wife will not come true, and you will have no children."

The geomancer left.

Magpie kept sitting on the tree and did not go to sleep until evening came. The next day he invited the mason Wang Qingguang, the carpenter Xu Chenggui, Limin, and Chunshan to saw the wood. Chunshan said that Magpie had been headstrong because of his father Jiang Xingfu.

More than twenty years ago, a four-year-old boy fell into a river. Xu Huijun jumped into the river and tried to save the boy. But he got entangled in those branches which had been soaked into the water for years. At last the boy drowned. Sun Pingliu, the son's father, claimed that his son had been pushed into the river by Xu Huijun. People got puzzled because the two families had got along: Xu Huijun often gave prey to Sun Pingliu and had dinner with his family members; Sun Pingliu visited his father-in-law who castrated animals and gave half of the reproductive organs to Xu Huijun.

The two families had a terrible fight. Leaders in the Production Team, Production Brigade, and People's Commune had to mediate in the dispute. The director in the People's Commune had a private talk with Sun Pingliu about his confrontation with Xu Huijun. Others did not know the details of the conversation. Afterwards the two families left Yanerpo and the aforementioned conversation remained a mystery.

The director also obtained an oral confession from Xu Huijun, and the latter denied everything. As a result, a witness would be needed and he was Jiang Xingfu, Magpie's father.

"When I was cutting firewood," said Jiang Xingfu, "I saw Huijun washing sweet potatoes in Weir Pond Trench. Later I saw Liuping's son having fun nearby the Trench. But he fell into the river accidentally, far away from Huijun. It was impossible that Huijun should push the boy into the river."

"You should be responsible for your verbal evidence," said the director.

"I will lose my eyes if I provide false evidence," said Jiang Xingfu. His eyes exploded at once.

The director was a materialist and considered that Jiang Xingfu's words would be the key to approaching a conclusion on the case. But later the director made a meaningful remark about it: "The truth may not be fairness." Sun Pingliu had to accept the director's advice and buried his son. But villagers, including Magpie, would rather believe in God's will that Jiang Xingfu had given the false evidence. Magpie had never asked his father about it. Now he refused to accept the geomancer's suggestion, which seemed that he would atone for his father's wrongdoing.

Chapter 22

When the two men reached the Weir Pond Trench, they turned on the lighting in their mobile phones to avoid snakes. But they turned it off when they were standing in front of the rock basin. The road was slippery, so they walked hand in hand. Magpie could wake up easily at midnight. If Chunshan farted when he was walking in the mountains at night, the next day Magpie would complain that his loud farts made him sleepless. But Magpie was still sleeping when the two women entered the oriental white oak forests. After spring thunder came, the trees would be gradually covered with mists of greenness, surrounded by chirping birds and running animals with fragrance permeating the air. In autumn the forests would be clad with golden leaves amid autumn winds, and in winter bare boughs right up to the sky.

Now the oriental white oaks had thick foliage. Strangers walking in the darkness would feel like being in a horrible place and would regard this place as a vulgar one although it was worshipped by the locals. Corpses had been buried deep in the woods, which horrified the villagers. Countless children's dead bodies had been stored in large clay pots and been put beneath rocks.

Cui Xuehua, the mother-in-law of Zhanhui, saw a clay pot shaking as soon as she went into a forest to cut grass. Suddenly a skull protruded from the pot. She continued to cut grass fearlessly to ensure her cattle had full stomachs. Her husband had died from hunger, so she considered that the skull must be hungry, too. She went back home and brought a bowl of rice, joss paper, and sticks of incense, which would become the food of the ravenous ghosts. Gradually the skull returned to the pot. When she told this with a pronounced stutter to the villagers, they got speechless with fright. People in Yanerpo knew that she came from North Korea.

One of the two people was thinking about the skull and his or her parents as well as his or her marriage if he or she could grow up. They chose a shortcut far away from households. They kept moving forward through the branches and vines, and might stop when they suddenly heard strange sounds, but would continue after the sounds were gone. They squatted when they heard a bird squealing, and after a moment heard a river roaring. A flare tower could be seen. Morning came and they sat on a rock for a rest.

"Do not hate him or us."

"Let it go."

They were Chunhong and Xiaofei. The latter would leave.

Chapter 23

Before Chunhong slept last night, she wanted to send Xiaofei away the next day. She did not know if Xiaofei would leave or not, but she would do what she should. Chunying told us the details.

Chunhong asked Xiaofei about her parents. Xiaofei had been raised by her grandparents since she was born. Her parents had been doing business at home and abroad. Their house had always been full of containers, and Xiaofei had never known about the things inside.

"Did Sixi meet your parents?" Chunhong asked Xiaofei.

"No."

"Did your parents say that they would buy a house for you?" Chunhong asked again after a moment of silence.

Xiaofei considered that it was required by Chunhong or by Sixi's parents, so she felt awkward.

Funeral geomancers were chanting scriptures. The sounds could be heard in diffident places, but they became murmurous in the attic.

Chunhong thought that Xiaofei misunderstood her, and she did not tell what she had known from Li Zhi because those words might not be true.

"It's not an easy job for your parents to earn money," said Chunhong. "Young people should have a clear estimation of themselves before they make a living. Your parents provide you with a better-off life in your twenties, but that comes at the expense of your toughening. You must do what you should."

"Well stated," Xiaofei said calmly. But her hands parted before she clapped.

"My daughter refused my financial support before she got married," Chunhong added. "And she and her husband bought a house with their own money."

"Chunhong was a liar at that time," Chunying said with scorn.

"I feel the same way," said Xiaofei.

"How about Sixi?" asked Chunhong.

"I haven't told this to him. But he will think the same as I do about it."

"Did he tell you that he had got married?"

"Yes."

"Are you willing to be a stepmother?"

"I feel pity for Tian. His mother died when he was less than three months old."

Chunhong glanced at Chunying. The latter was shocked to hear a tale about herself.

"You were talking about Chunying. When she was less than three months old," Chunhong explained, pointing at Chunying, "her mother died. But Tian's mother is still alive. The other day she sent clothes to him by express delivery!"

Chapter 24

Xiaofei got stupefied and Chunhong would tell the truth to her anyway.

"Sixi's ex was Ran Qing," Chunhong explained. "When she was carrying his baby, he had a new girlfriend. Ran Qing had quarrels with him, and he asked her to have an abortion and would divorce her. She gave birth to a son and she divorced him when the baby was less than six months old. She was so sad that she had to forsake the baby when he was in the suckling period. She called him Tian and hoped that he would become a good man."

"Since then Tian has been living with his grandparents," Chunhong continued. "But he could not have breast milk, so he kept crying. He was missing his mother and refused to have milk powder. There were some of her clothes left with her smell. His grandma dipped the clothes into the milk, and Tian had it, and that's how he grew up. Sixi has been sponging on his parents. Tian had to have rice soup sometimes. He is an academically brilliant boy, but he will need a lot of money for higher education. His grandma has been working in another city, and she did not return until his great-grandfather got ill."

Xiaofei cried.

Chapter 25

"Sixi had a new girlfriend Kang Furong," Chunhong said. "They had a daughter named Rong. After the girl was one month old, he left her mother when she was sleeping one night. He did not possess a marriage certificate with either of the two women. What's more, Kang Furong's medical report showed that there was a tumour in her head. Their house had been provided by Kang Furong's parents. They got angry with their daughter, and they asked her to register a marriage certificate with the baby's father. But such an irresponsible man as Sixi ran away."

Xiaofei stopped crying and she seemed to listen to a stranger's story.

"Did Sixi tell you about his education background?" asked Chunhong.

Before she answered, Chunhong continued, "He had not finished his junior middle school education, had engaged in pyramid selling, had swindled others, and had received a court summons because he did not pay the overdue balances for his mobile phone."

When Chunying told this to us, Chunhua snapped, "You should have told a different story to Xiaofei!"

Chunhua considered that Sixi would have no girlfriend if Xiaofei left.

"You have a daughter, too!" Chunhua continued. "Qiuyue may be deceived by a man!"

"I will console her," Chunying retorted.

"I suggest that you should leave now," said Chunhong. "People will laugh if they see you leave in the daytime. But I will escort you to the bus station."

"I'll go now," Xiaofei said with a nod.

The funeral music and chanting stopped, but mahjong players went on.

"We'll set off after the guests leave," said Chunhong.

After half an hour she walked out of the attic with Xiaofei. The latter kowtowed in front of our father's coffin. Chunhong escorted her to a fork at the bridge, and Xiaofei got on the bus. Chunhong soon returned to Yanerpo by motorbike.

Chapter 26

The morning was quiet. When Chunhong came back, she saw smoke emanating from the kitchen and men making funeral wreaths and funeral geomancers striking bronze drums which symbolized a memorial to the dead while heard Chunshu chanting a funeral oration. Others had not got up but Chunying did not fall asleep until early morning came: she had been worrying about how Sixi and his parents would react after they knew that Xiaofei had left.

Chunhong walked into the kitchen from the courtyard and asked where

Chunshan was. Her sister-in-law said that he was busy collecting water pipes, and then she waited for him. After he came back, she led the couple into the courtyard. The three people took seven or eight steps and stopped, one in each stair, Chunhong at the front, the brother at the back, and the sister-in-law in the middle.

"This is for Tian from Xiaofei," Chunhong said, giving 1,000 yuan to her sister-in-law.

The woman flinched in the face of the banknotes.

"We haven't given money to her," Fengjuan said, blushing. "My husband would intend to give some to her after the funeral was over; and it might be improper if she did it before we did it."

We had worried that Xiaofei would dislike Tian after she knew that she would become a stepmother, Chunshan and his wife had grown more anxious. However, Xiaofei cared for Tian, hugged him and carried him on her back, gave pocket money to him, and even let him call her mother.

Chunhong turned around to cover up her teary eyes. The sun cast patchy rays over her face through the leaves. She lowered her head, lifted her sister-in-law's apron tenderly, and put the money into her purse.

"Xiaofei has left," she said. "I asked her to leave because she deserves a much better man and a much better life."

Chunshan and his wife got shocked.

"I escorted her to the street," Chunhong added. "The 1,000 yuan should be given to Tian."

In fact Chunhong provided the money.

Before Xiaofei got on the bus, Chunhong gave 2,400 yuan to her. The young woman was unwilling to take the money.

"You'll think the banknotes are insufficient if you don't accept them now," Chunhong said firmly.

Xiaofei could understand her. "Give 1,000 yuan to Tian and I'll take the rest of the money."

"You may use more money during your journey," Chunhong added, giving additional 400 yuan to Xiaofei. "You should find a man of integrity to be your boyfriend. Don't be deceived by such a man as Sixi again. There are too many sweet talkers and swindlers. And you should investigate the company that he is currently employed by.”

“I’ll take your advice,” Xiaofei said with teary eyes.

Chunhong worried that Sixi might appear, so she let Xiaofei go at once.

Chunhong did not tell that to Chunshan and his wife. He cleared his throat and his wife blushed.

“Xiaofei left at midnight,” said Chunshan.

“Sixi is far beneath her,” said Chunhong.

“Sixi told me that he and Xiaofei had been operating an online store when you were sleeping last night,” said Fengjuan. “He said that he could earn nearly 2,000 yuan each day. He has changed himself.”

“He told Li Zhi that he was a planner,” Chunhong retorted angrily. “But he told Xiaofei that he had been doing business with Israelis. He is still a swindler!”

Fengjuan did not argue.

“Xiaofei may know about his business,” said Chunshan.

“You are his dad,” Chunhong yelled, “but you don’t know what he has been doing! Last night Xiaofei told me that she had never seen the men who were doing business with Sixi because he was too busy. Sixi was and is a liar! Even her parents have never mentioned buying a house for them and they have never met Sixi!”

“Does Sixi give you some money?” Chunhong asked Fengjuan.

“He will before he leaves.”

“He is still a freeloader! He returns to his hometown with Xiaofei’s money!”

Sixi’s parents looked embarrassed.

“What will he do?” asked Fengjuan.

“It’s his business,” said Chunshan.

Fengjuan rubbed her hands in her apron. The scars in her hands began to heal, but dark areas would be left. She would have to tell this to Sixi because she was his mother.

They walked into the courtyard, opened the door and saw Sixi with dishevelled hair and a dirty face trotting outside.

Fengjuan had given the 1,000 yuan to Sixi, and he went to find Xiaofei. His mother did not tell him why she had left, and he did not expect that he was betrayed by his relatives. During Xiaofei's stay in his hometown, he had been with her except bedtime. He worried that Mrs. Hou might be too talkative and that his female relatives might say something to Xiaofei, but he did not believe that Chunhong should be one of them because he had been taken good care of by her.

Sixi thought that the poverty in his hometown had frightened her away. After Chunying got up, she told it to me and Chunhua. Others did not know that Xiaofei had left and Sixi went to search for her.

At lunchtime, when Limin saw Sixi and his girlfriend were not at the table, Chunhong explained, "Xiaofei goes to Harbin to deal with an emergency in her family."

"What's it?" asked Zhuqing.

"I don't know," Chunhong replied, shaking her head.

The dishes were served. The guested enjoyed the meal so much so that the topic about Sixi and Xiaofei was stopped.

Chapter 27

At 3 p.m. a miniature mansion made by bamboos for our father was established. Swallow was attracted by the mansion while she was excited to see Dayou back. A picture of a hunter on horseback shooting at a running sika deer with an arrow was shown on the right wall of the delicately carved mansion. There was a door in the left wall. In front of the courtyard there was a stone tablet of deity and a tall tree full of fruits under which tea was being brewed. One kid was standing on the shoulder of the other, trying to pluck fruits.

"Oh, my grandpa will live in such a grand mansion after he goes to another world!" Swallow exclaimed.

Colourful pieces of chrome paper on the walls were printed with computers, TV sets, refrigerators, cars, weeding machines, swimming pools, tennis courts, and golf courses.

The man making funeral products should meditate for 30 minutes before he put necessary things on the miniature mansion. In his mental world he could see the afterlife of the deceased man. I wanted to have a talk with Mr.

Zhao who came from Houziyan Village and made funeral products. But he received the money from Chunshan as his hourly pay, walked through the alley outside Mrs. Hou's house, and went home. It took him more than three hours to walk from his house to Yanerpo.

The picture of promising future made us less worried about our father's afterlife.

"My grandpa has never ridden a horse," said Swallow. "And he has never used a computer or played golf."

"Zhu Yuanzhang, the first Ming Dynasty Emperor," said Liu Xianwen, "had been a mother wolf in his previous life, had bitten calves to death and fed abandoned babies. After she was reincarnated into a man, he lived like a beggar before he became an emperor."

"My grandpa will be with my grandma again in the afterlife," Swallow continued. "But she had never seen those things."

Liu Xianwen smiled and went on with his work. The branches and flowers were made by iron with copper plating. He loosened them a bit for comfortable use.

"You should stop talking," said Chunhong.

Swallow went into the mourning hall and said, "My grandma had never seen the things such as computer or golf, grandpa. You should teach her after you can use them well."

Chapter 28

After Liu Xianwen put a wreath around his head, he asked Chunshan to provide two tables to be used as altars in front of the miniature mansion.

The guests were still playing mahjong on the tables except the one with tableware.

"Stop playing mahjong, Xiaolan," Chunshan ordered.

The tables were carried to the miniature mansion.

"Xiaolan gets a good hand," Zhuqing whispered to her husband.

She laughed when she saw me standing behind her. "Oh, we should worship our father in front of the mansion. Xiaolan is obsessed with playing mahjong!"

Chunshu held Liu Xianwen's dark robe. It was put into a bag when it was not worn. Stone laughed at the robe which looked like a pig's bladder. The robe was patterned with eight diagrams and a circle of whiteness could be dimly seen.

Liu Xianwen stood on the table and asked his disciples to give him a flag and a sword. The sword had an iron hoop with ox horns, Taoist seals, and a wood-carving deity. He jumped while chanting and wielding his robe. The exterior of the robe was black but the interior was red which was the colour of blood and death. Clangs and flourishes of the sword lasted for 30 minutes amid Liu's chanting. He closed his eyes and opened after a moment. The ceremony was over. He took off the robe and he was soaked with sweat.

After he smoked a cigarette, he took a scroll written with "Absolution with Vajra" from Chunshu's desk. He held the scroll in his left hand and pointed at the scroll several times with the sword in his right hand, whispering. After a moment he stopped. Chunshu could understand the procedure and had prepared adhesive paste. Liu Xianwen pasted the scroll on the façade of the miniature mansion and put on his robe again. We would worship the mansion amid drums and gongs.

Magpie cleaned the courtyard. Fengjuan provided woven bamboo mats for us as kowtowing cushions. Chunshu was burning joss paper in a bucket. The wads of the paper should be equal to the age of the deceased man. There were three pieces of paper in each wad: the uppermost piece stood for heaven, the bottom one for earth, and the middle one for the man. My relatives argued about the age, or the wads. Chunshu burned the wads according to his consideration. At last nobody counted the wads.

Amid drums and gongs, Liu Xianwen and his disciples chanted passages from *Hellbreak Incantations*: "The place is surrounded by mountains. Golden rays can purify sins. Ghosts are gone with lotuses and deities employ their power." They also chanted passages from *Styxbreak Incantations*: "There is a river in front of Hades. The man has suffered from raising his children, and they should save him from the fire." There were more scriptures and we should keep kowtowing while we should chant: "Absolution with Vajra".

We should have 999 kowtows totally and we took a rest after we had 80 kowtows. It was much more toilsome than walking around the coffin, and we felt like being in Hades. After we became exhausted, Liu Xianwen asked us to do it the next morning.

Chapter 29

At dusk Sixi came back. We thought that he had gone to Harbin and would never return.

His new hairstyle took away his gloom this morning, and we were surprised to see him.

"What has happened to Xiaofei?" asked Zhuqing.

Sixi had been unaware of the white lie made by Chunhong, so he replied calmly, "She will return to Harbin and I'll go there after my grandpa's funeral is over."

Zhuqing's son-in-law, son and daughter-in-law had not come, so she did not say more.

"She goes alone," said Zheng Saner. "Aren't you worried about her?"

"I've bought a soft sleeper ticket for her," Sixi said softly.

My sisters and I asked Sixi about the details.

"She was waiting for me in the railway station," Sixi explained. "She knew that I would go to see her, and she cried as soon as she saw me. She hugged me and hoped that I would forgive her. She thought that she would never meet me again. I asked her to leave, and I'll go to Harbin after my grandpa's funeral is over."

Chunhong stifled her question but she looked relaxed after a whole day of anxiety. She should tell the truth to Xiaofei and she also felt pity for Sixi's parents. Chunhua considered that Shanrui would have stayed with Ziguo if she could have been as affectionate as Xiaofei.

"You should behave yourself, Sixi!" Chunshan snapped.

"You should be a down-to-earth man and take good care of Xiaofei from now on," Fengjuan said.

"I've been hardworking," Sixi argued. "And I'll tell you the processes after I succeed." He gave cigarettes to his father and to me.

Chunshan ran outside as soon as he heard Limin calling him. The dinner was served and we enjoyed the meal. Chunhong asked Li Zhi on the phone to come to the funeral site the next morning.

Chapter 30

But Li Zhi appeared at noon the next day with a plausible excuse. Li Zhi went to the railway station with Ziguo and Yang Jin to pick up Li Jing. Yesterday my mother-in-law left hospital in plaster and sat in a wheelchair. Li Jing had asked for leave but had to extend it so as to worship our father in front of the miniature mansion. Our son would soon take the national college entrance examination. He was too busy to see his grandpa, and the latter would forgive the former. Guangwen asked Yang Jin to send Li Jing to Weir Pond Trench, and he would need to tell something to Yang Jin. Li Jing arrived at 2 p.m.

Li Zhi, Ziguo and their buddies went to the mountains for sightseeing. In the town they could only see dirty rivers. They had been eager to have a much better life in a city, but they were villagers who relocated in the town. Meanwhile, their parents could not afford a house in a city.

A town was not a city even though it might be illusively taken as a city. The son of Ho Laosan had been chained up and sometimes yelled as marks that he used to be a carefree human being.

People said that the son of Ho Laosan was a drug addict and a syphilitic because he could have sex with women when he was high on drugs. Carnal pleasure was dirty and tantalizing. Even noble women were filthy inside. He was a seeker of lust and he did not stop until he could not do it anymore.

That was nothing new in a city. People could be familiar with each other if they lived in a town for one year. Familiarity might not be a good thing.

Li Zhi and his buddies kept themselves far away from sex and drugs, but they enjoyed themselves in the mountains: fishing, camping, or riding motorcycles. They could drive much faster than Yang Jin and they loved drag racing. The more dangerous, the more alluring.

Four motorbikes came that day. Li Zhi and Ziguo sat in the backseat of two motorbikes. They drove crazily. After they finished smoking, Yang Jin had not appeared.

Chapter 31

Chunhong accompanied by her husband and I waited for Yang Jin. Guangwen was clear about Yang Jin's schedules and called him every five minutes. After we smoked a cigarette, Yang Jin came.

Li Jing was carrying the bag which she used when she went to see our father in the hospital. The bag looked bigger because she looked thinner, but she had been unaware of that.

"You have lost weight too quickly," she said to me. "And you have a lot of grey hairs."

Was it serious? She used to pull my grey hairs out when I was working in the study in my house in Chengdu.

"You look like an elderly man!" Chunhong exclaimed.

Both of us were in the same situation.

Our parents can protect us when they are alive. After they pass away, we must protect ourselves and take on more responsibilities. We can learn that the cliché about life is true as we get old.

Chunhong and her husband received two large bags of sunflower seeds and a carton of branded cigarettes from Yang Jin. Guangwen asked Li Zhi and Ziguo to kowtow at once. The worship of the miniature mansion established for our father began in the afternoon, we could hear gongs and chanting. Stone had bound a loudspeaker on the post. The sounds of Fang Yun and Xianhe could be heard from it, and they might be indistinct sometimes.

"I won't have them," said Li Zhi, holding the bags and the cigarette.

People laughed. Li Zhi's friends greeted his parents and then returned to the town by motorbike.

"Be careful!" Chunhong cried.

"OK," they replied.

Guangwen talked with Yang Jin about buying a house in the county. Guangwen would buy it after the funeral was over, but Zhang urged him and would choose another buyer if he did not buy it soon. Guangwen had Yang Jin do it. Now I realized that a lot of Guangwen's money had been deposited in Yang Jin's bank accounts. The income of sand excavation had been deposited in the accounts of Guangwen and his wife. Yang Jin would need to pay the earnest money to Zhang and get a receipt.

Chapter 32

"I can't walk anymore," said Guangwen.

Our legs ached and we desperately needed a rest, so we sat on rocks.

Chunhong asked about Li Jing's mother and our son.

"Weisheng gets picky about his appearance," Li Jing complained.

Weisheng often looked at himself in the mirror after he returned home from school. His bedroom walls were covered with posters of NBA stars; the more he compared himself with them, the more he got dissatisfied with his face. He did not study in the school in which his mother was teaching. He went to school by bike every day. After evening study in the classroom was over, he returned home at 10 p.m., and he did not stop watching himself in the mirror until his mother shouted at him. Now he had under-eye bags and he insisted that his eyeballs had protruded 1 millimetre.

Li Jing laughed. She said that her son measured his own shadow. That reminded me of my puberty. When I was in the middle school, I was dissatisfied with my appearance, my family background, and my gender. I wished that I could have a rich father and that I could become a girl. At night when I heard others snoring in the dormitory with 60 occupants, I tried to pull my penis backwards and felt like it being gone, but it soon bounced to its original position. I would have had a transsexual operation if I had known about it.

However, the fact could not be changed. I was always a humble man. Now I'm often invited to give lectures in universities and arts groups on poetry which can build life upon words, and I'm worshipped by listeners and I often write my signature for them. At that time, the real me is squatting in a corner. The corner is a symbol of my space and time and also a mark in my poems.

My gloomiest moments came before the national college entrance examination. I felt pity for my son, and I would have lost my temper if I had been at home. But my wife tried to console our son. A mother always boasted that she had a charming son. One day her colleagues visited her and were attracted by Weisheng.

"Oh, your son is much more handsome than your husband," she

exclaimed.

Weisheng had never compared himself with me because I was not a good reference object. His mother's efforts became futile and he doubted himself much more. My wife encouraged our son and told him that virtue and talent were much more important than appearance. As a result, he considered that he should use something else to cover up his ugly face.

"I just leave him alone," said Li Jing. "I asked him to stay in his uncle's house and visit his grandma. But he would rather stay at home all by himself and he will feel much better."

Chapter 33

Chunshu was chanting funeral orations. We stood up and then we were received by our female relatives when we walked past Zhanhui's house. Dayou went to buy things.

Firecrackers would be set off when a new guest came. My wife did not know that and I had not told her. When she greeted her female relatives, I led her to kowtow in front of our father's coffin. The paper covering his face was shaking.

"Look! He is breathing!" my wife exclaimed.

That reminded me of the sweat on our mother's nose during her funeral. I was an adult and I knew our father would be dead anyway when he was lying in the freezing coffin.

"A refrigerating machine is working in the coffin," I whispered to my wife.

"The paper should be removed." She cried.

"Xu Chengxiang's daughter-in-law is crying for him!" Mrs. Hou said loudly. "But Daizhen was not lucky."

Daizhen was our mother.

Others regarded her as a hammersmith because she hammered us whenever we misbehaved, and also because she often had terrible quarrels with Mrs. Hou. The latter was crying for Daizhen now. Stone shouted at his grandma, just like his father and his younger sister did. They treated others kindly and worked hard, but they often yelled at their family members.

Stone married a woman who came from Kaiyang county. It was next to Dongxuan, but the locals became skilful workers after they grew up. They resembled the Banese offspring and they were taken as the gypsies in Daba Mountain by anthropologists. They did not care about buying a house; instead, they focused on finding their way. Stone and his wife had been working in Henan province. He returned to Yanerpo to deal with some matter and he would leave after our father's funeral was over. We had been neighbours for decades and he always remembered that he had been raised by Chunhua.

Raindrop, the younger sister of Stone, earned money by selling embroideries and gave some to her parents, and her husband often quarrelled with her. She and her brother were independent-minded and honest. Zheng Saner told Chunhong that Mrs. Hou would play Raindrop and Stone off against their parents. Mrs. Hou would lose if it was true.

Chapter 34

Yuling asked Li Jing to have lunch. Li Zhi and Ziguo were not hungry, so Li Jing had lunch alone. My two sisters and I were sitting beside her. Later Qiuyue came, sat beside me, and watched my wife. She looked at the girl in surprise.

She had not seen Qiuyue for many years.

"She is the daughter of Chunying," said Chunhong.

"Oh, you are Qiuyue," my wife exclaimed, putting a small piece of cooked potato into her mouth. The girl chewed the potato with her chin on my shoulder.

"Both of you are doting on her," said Chunhong. "Do you pamper your son?"

"No. My husband wanted a daughter. After Weisheng was born, he was unwilling to buy fermented glutinous rice for more breast milk. When Weisheng learned to play the piano, his dad would beat him if he did not play well."

My wife put meat into Qiuyue's bowl, but the girl cried.

"What has happened?" Li Jing asked with concern. "Does a beautiful girl often cry?" she added, pointing at the lachrymal mole on Qiuyue's face. And then she wiped her tears with a tissue.

"Let Qiuyue be your foster daughter," someone in the kitchen said.

"You did not cry for your grandpa," said Chunhong.

Li Jing asked the girl if she needed more meat, the girl shook her head, leaving her tears on my face.

Swallow brought more dishes on the table.

"Does your brother return?" Li Jing asked Swallow.

"Sixi!" Fengjuan yelled.

Sixi ran outside and greeted my wife. He was calling someone and did not hear our talk.

Gongs again. We would kowtow again. My wife gulped down her food.

Chapter 35

Dayou said on the phone that he would sit in Guibing's motorbike to return after the latter finished his job. Guibing did not know Dayou in the past, but he became an acquaintance of his after Dayou had bought things frequently in the street. Dayou said that he would buy seasoning, the cooks said that there was sufficient seasoning but he would let Dayou buy more lest it should rain.

"It won't rain," said Zhuqing.

Dayou could stay in a hotel for one night and would return the next day. At that time Guibing would finish his work.

"Guibing does not have to come here," Guangwen said to Zhuqing. "Our father has so many children and grandchildren."

Only Xianhe was chanting "Absolution with Vajra". He was sitting in the fourth row and his loud voice could not be propagated by the loudspeaker.

"The kids will misbehave if Guibing is not at home," Zhuqing argued.

"Guibing told me on the phone that his mother would look after the children," said Xiaolan.

"Did they hear me say those words?" asked Guangwen.

"You always say good words," said Zhuqing.

"Do not let the leaders hear that," said Guangwen.

The village leaders came here in the morning for the sake of Guangwen and me. We had a chat although I did not know them. They played mahjong arranged by Limin, and they laughed and enjoyed themselves.

Swallow did not know how to reply Dayou.

"He should return after he finishes his task," said Guangwen. "And Guibing won't have to share one motorbike with him."

"They are not as rich as you!" Zhuqing retorted.

Guangwen gave branded cigarettes to his colleagues, and they received them lightly. Villagers would receive them humbly and watch the words and patterns on the external packing. His colleagues played mahjong in a way which Guangwen disliked.

The leaders left after one hour and Limin and Chunshan saw them out. They respected the leaders who condoled our father and gave him wreaths.

Wreaths had never appeared in Yanerpo before our father's funeral. My boss let me buy a wreath for my father and the expenses would be reimbursed. But that was not popular in Yanerpo. Chunshang insisted that we should use a wreath, and then he asked Dayou on the phone to buy the best and the largest wreath for our father. Later Chunshu wrote "May Xu Chengxiang Rest in Peace." That was the first wreath for our father.

The company in which I had been working was located in Chengdu, so the villagers admired the wreath but they also complained that I had not built a road for Yanerpo. That was a humiliation.

News spread fast. The township government leaders had their assistants send wreaths to our father and the next day the village leaders in Yanerpo did the same thing.

The village leaders were going to leave. Limin and Chunshan made futile attempts to persuade them to stay, so the two men saw them out. After they returned, Chunshan yelled, "I dislike Xu Bing!"

When Xu Bing worked as the village party secretary, he sent a court summons to Chunshan.

"I thought it was a university admission notice or an enlistment certificate," Xu Bing said with scorn. "But it's a court summons to your son Sixi!"

Chunshan would lose his temper at the thought of that.

Chapter 36

Dayou and Guibing shared one motorbike and, carrying bags of seasoning, returned at the noon the next day. Swallow told Dayou that he should come back yesterday and there was sufficient seasoning. She was not a liar. Dayou glared at her and then put the seasoning into the kitchen when Guibing was kowtowing.

"You are stupid!" the cook Pu Gen shouted, throwing a plastic bottle of vinegar on the ground.

He asked Dayou to buy Sanhui Vinegar, but the latter bought Baoning Vinegar.

"Baoning Vinegar is much more expensive than Sanhui Vinegar," said Limin. "You don't have to get so angry."

"I've been using Sanhui Vinegar to cook dishes," Pu Gen retorted. "Baoning Vinegar will ruin my cooking skills!"

"It's just vinegar," Limin argued. "Nobody can distinguish the taste."

Pu Gen got annoyed. He had been working hard to provide meals for all the guests, and he felt humiliated by Limin's words.

"Baoning Vinegar has grain as the principal raw material and has traditional Chinese medicine as the yeast," Pu Gen explained. "But Sanhui Vinegar has herbs and spices as the yeast. They have different combinations."

"But it's just vinegar," Limin added. "You may make do with it. And the bottle of Baoning Vinegar can't be returned."

"You should have invited Shen Pangwa to be your cook!" Pu Gen shouted.

Shen Pangwa was another famous cook in the village. When the son of Ran Congjing who came from Ranjiawan got married, Ran Congjing considered that he should hold a grand wedding ceremony for his son although he was one of the distant relatives of his second grandpa who had been awarded with a lot of military medals and who had remarried and who had not come to Golden Town again. Ran Congjing invited two cooks for the ceremony: Shen Pangwa and Pu Gen. The two cooks treated each other like a foe.

When stewed pork with sweet potato flour was cooked in the afternoon the next day, the confrontation between the two cooks began. The procedures included: put balls of stewed pork with sweet potato flour into soup with a large spoon, remove one piece of firewood, adopt moderate heat and cook for 20 minutes, and then put cabbage leaves into the soup. However, after it was cooked for 19 minutes and 30 seconds, Shen Pangwa put the cabbage leaves into the soup. Pu Gen, who did not look at the watch but knew the time clearly, cursed Shen Pangwa. The two cooks quarrelled terribly. Pu Gen hated making do with dishes.

"Which cook will you choose?" Pu Gen asked Ran Congjing.

The employer tried to make peace, but Pu Gen left without asking for pay.

Now the villagers whispered that Pu Gen was too stubborn. Limin knew Pu Gen's character and admired him although he had to ask someone to buy a new bottle of vinegar.

Chapter 37

Just before Swallow touched Dayou's feet, he pushed her hands away. She tried to support him to stand up, but he refused. He sat down on a rock.

"How are Dayou's feet?" Chunshan asked Swallow.

"They have been swollen and he can't ride a motorbike!"

Someone was needed to buy things and carry tables and desks. Chunshang was busy. Who could do Dayou's job?

"Pu Gen should be responsible for that!" Limin yelled.

Pu Gen was too preoccupied with cooking dishes to hear the talk. Chunshan went to Chunshang's old house and put the bottle of Baoning Vinegar there.

"I'll find an empty bottle of Sanhui Vinegar," Chunshan said to Limin. "And I'll put the label on another bottle. Pu Gen can't distinguish the taste!"

"He is demanding!"

When Limin heard Pu Gen chopping meat loudly, he realized that the latter would discover the vinegar.

"I'll use the vinegar tonight!" Pu Gen roared.

Chunshan got an empty bottle of Sanhui Vinegar.

"Pu Gen can smell the differences between the two kinds of vinegar," said Limin. "If he quits, Shen Pangwa won't come here to help you."

An employer should pay 30 yuan for each meal to a cook. 50 meals would be held for the funeral, and the cook should be paid with 1,500 yuan. In fact, the cook would charge more for each meal every day, and Shen Pangwa was such a cook. However, Pu Gen was unlike him: he would receive the money given by his employer and would never charge more.

"Dayou will have to buy another bottle of vinegar in the market," said Chunshan.

"He has got hurt in his feet and should take a rest," Swallow argued. "Sixi can ride a motorbike, too!"

Chunshan saw the bottle be thrown at Dayou, but it was not serious. Swallow protected him.

"Sixi!" Chunshan yelled.

"What's the matter?" asked Sixi, glancing at the courtyard.

"Dayou may go after lunch," said Chunshan, watching him walking down the stairs.

"Return the bottle of vinegar," said Limin.

It had been bought in Huang Ermei's store. Chunshan said that the vinegar could be used. Sixi did not understand what he should do. He walked into his room and did not come out until the worship began.

Chapter 38

Lunchtime was late. Liu Xianwen asked his disciples to do the ritual again. Guibing participated in it but some did not appear. Guangwen was having a nap and his wife taking a rest, too. Chunhua had hypoglycaemia and her heart began to palpitate when she felt hungry. She used to cry to cover up her palpitations when she was a child. Now she felt uncomfortable, so she sat down beside Chunhong.

Chunhong asked Chunhua to have some crispy meat and flour gluten balls in the kitchen, but Chunhua would never be bold to eat food without permission. Chunhong took some flour gluten balls from the kitchen, but Chunhua was too shy to receive them.

"Fill your empty stomach," Chunhong ordered.

Chunying laughed when she was kowtowing. Chunhua snatched the balls and rushed into the mourning hall.

"She will share the food with our dad," said Chunhong.

Qiuyue was sitting under a sycamore tree with her chin resting on her knees. She had been gloomy since Xiaofei left.

"Bihua and I will soon get off the train," Hongquan said to Xiaolan on the phone. "We'll sit in our son-in-law's car if he is still at home."

"He can't drive to the mountains," said Xiaolan. "Dayou will pick you up. He is Swallow's boyfriend."

After a moment she called Dayou.

"That'll be good," said Chunhong. She said this for Swallow while she was glaring at Qiuyue.

"Dayou will buy a bottle of vinegar," said Swallow. "And he can pick up Hongquan and Bihua."

It was nearly supper time when they arrived at Weir Pond Trench.

Chapter 39

Moths flew and died under the light. People laughed and played games amid the funeral music.

Swallow was waiting for Dayou, Xiaolan for her younger brother and his wife, and Lily for her friend.

"I haven't danced for many days," Xiaolan complained, putting down mahjong tiles. "Backache again!"

Firecrackers were set off. Chunshu and his wife greeted new guests. Swallow held Bihua's bag which had been carried by Dayou along the way. Hongquan was talkative and Dayou treated Swallow softly.

"I haven't seen you for ages," Lily said to Bihua, holding her hand.

The two young women walked towards the mourning hall. Bihua was much more charming than Lily, but the latter had never had a sense of inferiority in front of her or Xiaofei. Lily could get along with beautiful women. Bihua had been leading a more settled life since she married, and she had never realized that she was much more attractive than Lily.

Bihua and Hongquan entered the mourning hall and kowtowed. Later they had supper. Sixi greeted them and gave cigarettes to Hongquan. The younger generation of our family laughed and drank when they were having a meal.

"I've been to Singapore, South Korea, United Arab Emirates, France, African countries, and I can speak Swahili language," Sixi boasted. "The Africans love buying second-hand cars from the Japanese, and they don't paint the cars. The stores are closed at the weekend in the African countries. People go to church and we can drive a car or sleep on the street."

I remembered the foreign words mentioned by him. When I had a meeting in Chengdu, I asked professors studying African literature about those words, they said the words were right.

"Can you return from Africa riddled with wars?" Li Zhi asked doubtfully.

"The wars are triggered either by resources or by poverty," Sixi explained. "Europeans regarded West Africa as a dark continent. They could go to Eurasia and American continents and could communicate. But people could not enter Africa because they were stopped by tropical rainforests. But East Africa seldom has wars."

Li Zhi and the other listeners did not continue the subject. Hongquan was interested in earning money, not wars.

"The company in which I've been working has acquired two firms," said Hongquan. "The company in which Bihua has been working has become a large one. Both of us have had driving licenses and bought cars. We planned to drive to Yanerpo, but it would be a very long journey."

Xiaolan glanced at her husband and then at me and her female relatives. Hongquan had borrowed money from us to buy a house in the town but he had not repaid us. Now he was too excited to notice Xiaolan.

"My wife can earn 10,000 yuan each month," Hongquan boasted. "And I can earn much more than she can."

"You are bragging," said Xiaolan.

"More liquor!" Hongquan shouted.

"The boss of the company in which Bihua has been working is one of my friends," Hongquan added. "A boss usually chooses his friend or a trustworthy person as his accountant. We are better-off now. My father-in-law should not have made things hard for me before our wedding!"

"You have drunk too much, Hongquan," said Xiaolan.

Bihua smiled. Her parents were satisfied with their son-in-law. Her father decorated their house after their wedding. Her brother bought materials but the cost of labour was saved.

Sixi failed to surpass Hongquan. Hongquan's income, house, and living conditions of his parents were much better than Sixi's. Sixi was making repeated actions of flicking cigarette ash with one hand, and putting the other into his pocket, which seemed that he was afraid of coldness.

Chapter 40

Zhanhui came to the courtyard after breakfast the next morning. Today was the eve of the funeral. She sent the children to school, and went to the village by sitting in Maer's motorbike. Maer would take care of the children during the daytime and would take them to the funeral site once school was over.

Today Zhanhui's pig would be slaughtered, so she must inspect the site. She scolded her husband that he did not give sufficient food to the pig. Meanwhile, Xu Xing and Chunshang were carrying a table.

"I fed the pig leaves every day," Xu Xing explained with a smoke pipe in his mouth. Zhanhui asked Xu Xing to let the pig have pigwash frequently, but he did not do it. What's more, the pig shat everywhere. As a result, Zhanhui hurled abuse at her husband. He started to slobber and his saliva fell on his wife's clothes. She angrily snatched the smoke pipe from his mouth and threw it on the ground.

Chunhong, holding a basin of dirty clothes, heard Zhanhui yelling. She considered that Zhanhui had lost her temper excessively. What's more, the couple should not quarrel in the house of the deceased man.

Zhanhui would greet Chunhong usually. But now she was too furious to notice Chunhong.

"How can we sell a thin pig to Chunshan?" she shouted.

"Is that true?" Limin asked, with soap foam on his head.

"It's a serious matter!" Zhanhui argued.

"Just do as agreed."

"But there must be a transaction."

She was unwilling to sell the pig now. There was no agreement on buying a pig from her.

"Chunshan!" Limin shouted.

Chunshan was cleaning leaves and water pipes to smooth the path from Longyan Pond to Yanerpo. He did not hear Limin calling him, but Chunshu came out.

Chunshu pricked up his ears when he heard Zhanhui's voice, and he did not expect that she should come here today.

"How much has your pig lost weight?" Chunshu asked.

"I haven't weighed it," Zhanhui replied angrily.

"Your pig loses 5 pounds each day, and that lasts four days, 20 pounds. If your pig is 100 pounds, it will be calculated as 120 pounds." He went into his room at once.

The affair between Chunshu and Zhanhui was ended after our father's funeral was over. Chunhong said that it was such a good thing that Chunshu could clearly see how cold-blooded Zhanhui was.

"How much weight should my pig be calculated?" asked Zhanhui.

The skilful butcher Crap appeared wearing a dark leather apron and carrying a basket with various cutters and an iron bar. He made a cut in the pig's foot, put the iron bar across its body expertly, and blew at the cut. The air flow made the pig's body bulge so that its hair could be easily removed after its body was boiled. At last he used a rope to bind its mouth.

"You and your wife will carry the pig here," Limin said to Xu Xing.

"You have a cauldron, Chunshang," Limin added. "Is it usable?"

"Yes."

"Boil the cauldron."

"Will you do me a favour, dad?" Limin said to Xu Chenggui. "We are very busy today."

"It's my pleasure," Xu Chenggui replied. He seemed to wake up from his dream.

He fetched water from the kitchen with a bucket. Chunshang lit the firewood and asked him to be careful. The elderly might burn their own clothes, their houses, or themselves. Those things had frequently happened in other places.

Chapter 41

The pig was slaughtered now. Zhanhui thought that she should have fed it more pigwash, so she vented on her husband. Xu Xing pushed the pig forward with a bamboo spar, followed by Zhanhui. The pig could feel the upcoming danger, so it stopped walking. Xu Xing beat it but it remained motionless. It wanted to turn around, but it could not because of its heavy weight. If it fell down and died, its price would be decreased sharply. Zhanhui pinned it against the ground. It panted and could not open its eyes. The pig and its owners slipped, and it desperately fought back against its owners. Crap shouted at the pit and it became quiet. Xu Xing battered the pig until blood could be seen on its back.

I used to see how a butcher killed a dog. One day it wondered through fields of rape flowers so sadly that it went mad, and it would bite anybody who got close to it. The butcher silently waved at the dog, and it ran towards him. He raised its head softly and pierced its throat with a knife. He wiped the knife on its back, and it fell down. It did not shout. Its last piss was mixed with its blood. I had also seen the castration of a bull. A gelder sprayed a mouthful of clear water on a bull's back. He smashed the bowl and patted its buttocks. It spread its hind legs and he began to cut off its testicles. It endured the pain motionlessly until its testicles were removed and the wound was stitched. Wild foxes could bring cats under control. If a wild fox chose one cat, it would brush against the cat with its tail, and the cat would follow the fox. When the cat enjoyed a wonderful meal, the fox was just taking a rest. After the cat excreted waste matter, it would eat and drink again; after a few hours, it excreted again. When the cat's stomach became clean, the fox would eat it alive.

After Crap shouted at the pig, it was like the cat controlled by the wild fox. Xu Xing kept battering it until it could not resist anymore.

The pig looked fat when it was standing in the courtyard. Xu Xing and his wife were also there.

"Its weight may be 407 pounds," said Crap.

The pig was bound on a bench and weighed. The total weight was 431 pounds, the bench 20 pounds, and the pig 410 pounds. Crap was an experienced butcher indeed.

Chapter 42

I walked towards the mountain alone. My wife was reading in Chunshang's old house. She was an avid reader in the school, at home, and even in the subway. I kept her inconspicuous.

"Uncle Chunming is afraid of watching slaughter," Li Zhi laughed.

I quickened my steps. Chunhong was busy in the courtyard.

In our childhood, butchering pigs was a festival related to the happy life. Nowadays people, especially the younger generation, nearly forget the festival because they can have pork every day. After Mr. Zhang, the secretary of the County Committee, was dispatched in Dongxuan, he created plazas for singing folk songs and revived traditional festivals, including the "Pig Festival".

After the pig screamed, it was killed with a long knife. Its blood poured into a basin with salt when it was struggling and yelling. Pig blood curd could be cooked into a delicious dish.

I hoped that its squeals could be ended as soon as possible and it could die at once. Its fear would be gone with its death. Fear was much more terrible and undignified than death. Its screeches made me uncomfortable. Yelling could arouse people's feelings. Fish would not shout when it was killed, and we would not feel pity for it. Watching the slaughter of a pig reminded the middle-aged and the elderly of their childhood memories. But it was meaningless to the pig and to me who was hiding myself. If it had a meaning, it could show my feebleness and hypocrisy.

Chapter 43

I had discussed this with Tan Ruisong.

"Homo sapiens created the concept of goodness against stronger genes," he said. "Time was fabricated against stronger spaces. Goodness targeted evilness. Each male ejaculation was not for the creation of life. The sperms were like a country with a rigorous social structure and division of labour. The industrial workers in the sperms fused with the egg to begin the process of fertilization, and the police killed enemies. Human beings, animals and plants did not adopt monogamy; adultery and rape existed. There were sperms of other countries in a womb, so the police would wipe out the antagonists. Killings had begun even before a life was formed. Whether life was torture, consumption or elimination of another one, it was not related to goodness or evilness. Homo sapiens could obey or break genes. Obedience to the evilness would be bad for maintaining or ruling the population. As a result, goodness was fabricated, too. A concept would become material and powerful after it was formed, which was the competence and sorrow of the homo sapiens. But cyborgs, which will replace homo sapiens, have no feelings, no sex, no agony and no fear. Religion, philosophy and art regard death as the starting point for thinking. If the subject of death collapses, all kinds of concepts will be ruined. Even medicine will be destroyed, especially Western medicine which takes a human being as a corpse for dismemberment and study. No death, no life; goodness and evilness, right and wrong will become ineffective. And art will become useless."

"I think my mom had the foresight to fell the banyan tree," he continued. "A seer does not need to have too much knowledge. A person of foresight can lead the later generations to comprehend and speak. My mom was an illiterate but could understand heaven and earth. I'd read a lot of books and had written poems and novels, but heaven and earth turned its back on me. So I don't think culture is a good thing. The culturally trained people have lost their sagacity, sensibility and foreknowledge. I'm getting old but I've enhanced my appreciation."

He smiled at me. When he saw my calmness, he said seriously, "Do you know why you feel that you are a hypocrite? Because you are a perfectionist. Perfection only exists in limitations and you should understand them. Self-importance may become a laughing stock. When one is regarded as a genius, that means most of the people at that time are too ordinary. Historians can write history in a simple but profound manner."

I remained silent because I did not agree with his opinion. I was always a humble man.

"You may be too soft-hearted," he added. "And that may be turned into hypocrisy. Authenticity and strength are socially praised. That is to say, one should be relentless. In *The Story of the Stone*, it becomes dull after Wang Xifeng dies. She is tough-minded compared with those weak-minded characters. She is like sunlight. No sunlight, no life. So you must get tough with yourself. I can give you traditional Chinese medicine prescriptions, and you may cook food with white turnips. After you have them for 5 days, you will feel stronger."

I should not have engaged in that discussion with him, nor should I have told my female relatives that I was afraid of watching slaughter.

Chapter 44

I saw Chunhong talking with Swallow when they were washing clothes in Weir Pond Trench. They were looking for me who was hiding myself behind a sour jujube tree and sitting on a haystack. I returned after I smoked several cigarettes.

Crap and others were cleaning the intestines of the pig. He squeezed out the shit and then turned the intestines inside out with a club. The boiling water which had been used to remove the pig hair could get rid of the faecal odour.

The pig's weight was 410 pounds, and Chunshu calculated it as 432 pounds for Zhanhui. The pig shat after it was weighed and before it was killed. Zhanhui refused the price.

"432 pounds," said Yuling. "The total weight of the pig and the bench. She won't charge more."

"I'll pay the price of the excessive 20 pounds."

Zhuqing took the side of her husband and gave the money to Zhanhui. Everybody had heard Zhanhui yell at her husband, and had seen the pig shit. Chunshu and his wife looked proud, but Zhanhui was too embarrassed to return the money.

The three brothers shared the rest of the price of the pig.

"Chunshu has done the right thing," Guangwen said to Chunshan and Chunshang. "Zhanhui would not have sold the pig if Chunshu had not fixed the price."

Chunshan and Chunshang agreed with him.

Zhanhui returned home soon. Limin said that it was lunchtime, and Xu Xing did not care about that. Limin used a loudspeaker to let Zhanhui have lunch with everybody, but it was useless. She did not appear when the dishes were served. Before Chunshan called her, Fengjuan said that she would go to find Zhanhui who had been looking after Tian. Fengjuan found her house locked and knew on the phone that she had gone to the market.

Chapter 45

After lunch we worshipped the miniature mansion again. Liu Xianwen counted that we would finish having 999 kowtows after we made 103 ones.

The last worship went through the motions. Chunhong went to Chunshang's pigpen to slaughter the hungry and weak chickens which had been brought there from her home. In Chunshang's old house Guangwen had to record the gifts and money brought by the guests while Magpie accepted the money and told the figure. There was a bag around Magpie's neck holding the money.

On the eve of the funeral the guests arrived to express their condolences and give gifts and money to the family relatives of the deceased man. That was the custom in Laojun Mountain. The figure and the name should be recorded on the spot. If two guests had the same name, the village should be written; if they came from the same village, his family relationships should be written.

Fang Yun and Xianhe were too busy to worship. Without Xianhe the ceremony was quiet and even the funeral geomancers were chanting in low spirits. We had not kowtowed 50 times, but Liu Xianwen stopped beating drums. We did not finish 999 kowtows and the rest of the ones would let our father stay in the Styx a little longer.

Chapter 46

It was stuffy in the afternoon. Men guessed if it was going to rain, but they saw blue sky. But we hoped there would be no rain tonight because it was the eve of our father's funeral.

More guests came, including Dayou's parents and Qingmei's parents. Most of them were strangers to me. Dayou's parents greeted others kindly, Sheng Jun's mother did not come, but she asked others to bring gifts. Ten large tables were placed in the courtyard and there were 40 seats. Totally four rounds of dinner would be served separately as the guests arrive in succession.

Limin said in the loudspeaker that dinner would begin. The guests wanted to enjoy the first round of the dinner. After each round was finished, women put the used tableware into the large iron basin beside each table. The tableware had not been cleaned well before it was used again. Mahjong players could have the meal in situ. Each guest was standing closely behind another one so that the he could occupy a seat as soon as the former one finished eating. Meanwhile, the guest had to eat as fast as he could.

The guests could put meat and dishes into food bags and take them home. The participants did it in the past, but now they seldom did it unless they kept pets. The villagers preferred lean meat to fat meat. The pig kept by Zhanhui was too fat. The guests only ate the lean meat.

Dark clouds were gathering in the third round of the dinner. Limin shouted in the loudspeaker and asked everybody to hurry up. There was a smell of rotten eggs in the air. Limin could not see what was going on in the courtyard but he knew there was going to be a storm. Meanwhile, chickens were running towards the courtyard. Limin kept yelling in the loudspeaker.

Chapter 47

An artistic lion dancing team was much louder than Limin's shouting. The team sadly danced for the man in heaven. The guests felt pity for the deceased man although they were eating ravenously. Three men and three women in red were playing the suona with sorrowful melodies. The sorrow came from the earth and the grain. A man wearing a plastic mask of a monk's face touched the lion with a horsetail whisk. He raised his hands and seemed to wipe away the lion's tears. After a moment the lion began to dance happily amid cheerful melodies from suona players.

Firecrackers were going on. Clouds of dust enshrouded the whole place. The smell and the dust were a part of the local culture in weddings and funerals, and the participants enjoyed it. After the suona players stopped, two old men panting came out of the lion costume. Bang! A martial lion dancing team came, jumping and running. After half an hour, the wailing team and the funeral dancing team gave their performances. It was so impressive that the guests admired the deceased man Xu Chengxiang who had a son working in the provincial capital and had a son-in-law who worked as a village party secretary.

The performers were the adopted children of Ho Laosan, Yang Jin, and Guangwen. Li Chengzhong, one of the children, did not come but his mother came. Huigoer was also one of the participants. The guests got annoyed at the sight of Huigoer; a young man whispered to an old man to avoid being overheard by him, "Keep yourself far away from that man. He is a trouble maker." But the hard-of-hearing old man could not catch him.

The new guests worshipped at once. Huigoer did not because he thought that he did not belong to them. Guangwen and Limin came to greet the new guests.

Limin gave cigarettes to the guests. The green-covered Bafine would be given to cooks, funeral geomancers, men producing funeral products, men carrying the coffin, village leaders, and men from cities; the white-covered Bafine to ordinary workers and guests. Limin knew that he should protect the cigarettes because he was trusted by the family relatives of the deceased man. He was carrying two bags with the two kinds of cigarettes: the green-covered Bafine in the left and the white-covered Bafine in the right hand. To avoid the obvious differential treatment, he pretended to throw away the cigarette case but could not find a suitable place, so he put it back into the bag. "Oh, there are much more," he talked to himself. After the firecrackers stopped, he was tired of repeating those words. When he gave cigarettes to Huigoer, the latter did not receive them.

"I smoke the red-covered Bafine," said Huigoer.

"Those leaders are smoking," Limin said after a moment of surprise. "And you should choose one."

"Give me one more cigarette," Guangwen said to Limin. The latter lit it for the former and then glanced at Huigoer.

Later villagers said that Huigoer participated in the funeral without giving any gift or money. He explained that he did not receive the 100 yuan given by Guangwen when the latter and Yang Jin had breakfast in his house; so the 100 yuan could be regarded as the participation fee. He had realized why Guangwen and Yang Jin had breakfast in his house that day.

Chapter 48

It thundered and then it poured down. People rushed to clear the table, but soon they were soaked with sweat. Men took off their shirts and the guests were surprised to see the fat Yang Jin. People laughed when it was raining cats and dogs.

When I was watching the rain, I was pulled by Chunhua into Sixi's room. He was watching his phone and Chunying was sitting in the bed.

Before the door was closed, Chunying said to me, "Chunhong has gone too far!"

I was shocked. The problem was about the gifts and money.

Chunhong said that she would give 10,000 yuan, but Chunhua and Chunying were not as rich as her, so they would give 5,000 yuan. To repay a kindness, the 5,000 yuan would surpass the total sum given by my brothers. Chunhong said that her sisters could pay according to their financial abilities. For the sake of a good reputation, Chunhong did not want to become a laughing stock because of the gifts and money about our father's funeral. In other families, relatives would take away the excessive payments as agreed. Chunhong insisted that she should pay 10,000 yuan, but her sisters strongly disagreed with her.

"Chunhong gives monthly payments to her daughter-in-law for looking after her grandchild," Chunhua complained. "Now she asks us to pay more."

"She is so demanding that nobody accompanies her to the graveyard in Yanerpo," said Chunying.

I had thought that my sisters had been grateful to Chunhong. In fact, they had had a grudge against her for a long time.

"We haven't been able to earn much money since the Spring Festival,"

Chunhua said angrily. "But we'll have to pay a lot this time."

"Xianhe was hospitalized in February to treat gall stones and stomachache," said Chunying.

"Fang Yun had to work hard although he moaned in agony at night because of backache," Chunhua argued. "And we did not go to hospital.

"You were eager for money."

"You are rich and you can give 20,000 yuan."

Chunhong and Swallow came when they were quarrelling.

Chapter 49

People outside the door could not hear the talk inside when it was raining heavily. The two sisters looked at each other meaningfully and then smiled at each other.

"What's up?" asked Chunhong.

"It's about Sixi," replied Chunying. "He has been watching his phone since Xiaofei left."

We knew that Sixi must be contacting Xiaofei.

"It poured down during our mom's funeral," Chunhong said sadly. "And now it's the same situation."

"My grandma has let it rain to take my grandpa away," said Swallow.

"But she does not think about her children and grandchildren."

Meanwhile, there were insufficient beds for so many guests. The rain seemed to understand Chunhong's sadness, so it stopped after twenty minutes.

"Resume your seats!" Limin shouted.

The courtyard became clean but the guests rushed to go home for their own fields. Ho Laosan was the first one to go so that he could anchor his sand excavation vessels; and soon Dayou's parents, Qingmei's parents, and the villagers of Lijiyan left.

"Huigoer wanted to stay," said Chunshang. "Guangwen winked at Li Qiantao, and Li grasped a piece of plastic cloth and covered his head and Huigoer's head with it. Li grabbed him by the shoulder and walked away. Yang Jin will pick up Guangwen tomorrow because the muddy road tonight isn't fit for driving."

Chunshan sighed that too much food would be wasted. Pu Gen was disappointed that few guests could taste the delicious dishes cooked by him. Before the second round of the dinner was finished, he had a quarrel with Limin.

"The guests dislike fat meat, Pu Gen," said Limin. "You should have sliced the meat. An employer will have a good reputation for providing good meat during the dinner."

"A good cook should make delicious dishes even though the materials are not good enough," Pu Gen argued. "People enjoy the streaky pork and steamed meat cooked by me."

He ate the steamed meat and streaky pork disliked by the guests, but they regarded that as his promotion of his cooking skills. He was sad. He hoped that his dishes could be liked by everybody, but the guests ran after it rained.

Limin asked all the assistants to have dinner. Cylindrical fireworks would be set off after dinner. The days that the corpse had stayed at home would be the times that the fireworks would be burnt. Totally nine cylindrical fireworks would be ignited and there were 20 fireworks in each cylinder. The night sky was full of brightly coloured fireworks.

Chapter 50

After the last firework was set off, the wailing team set up tents outside the mourning hall. After a man put a cushion in the hall, a woman knelt down on the cushion and wailed.

"Dad…" she had known about our father's life from Chunshu, so she told his life stories when she was wailing. She was indeed a weeper and had professional colleagues.

"That sounds weird," said Chunshang.

"Why?" I asked.

"The man she is crying for is not her father."

I was watching her heart-touching performance. She took wailing as her career.

She paused when she mentioned the marriage between our father and our mother.

"The relatives?" one of her colleagues asked.

As soon as Limin gave him a red envelope, she came out of the tent.

The dancing teams and the wailing team gave their performances and took a rest by turn, which lasted the whole night. The male and female performers shared one or two beds provided by the relatives of the deceased man. The performers of the artistic lion dancing team were middle-aged and old men, and the rest of them were the young. They pissed on the ground when chamber pots were full.

The courtyard became quiet when the two male and four female dancers began to work. The men were wearing black clothes and the women wearing see-through dresses. The leading dancer was a female who covered her nipples with things like adhesive bandages. She was a thin woman with large breasts. Everybody was watching her excitedly.

I found Magpie and Yang Jin were attentive watchers, and I could hardly believe that Yang Jin should be deeply attracted by her. After several months, Yang Jin divorced his wife and began a relationship with that female dancer,; then we could understand how seductive she could be.

Chapter 51

The coffin would be sealed. Chunshan and I took one last look at our father. Li Jing wanted to put a book of my poems into his coffin so that he could know what I had been doing. He had been unaware of my occupation before he died, and he got worried about me when he found me smoking worse cigarettes than Guangwen.

"He can recognise your name," said Li Jing. "And he will be glad to know that you have been doing a decent job."

I had never done that before and I would never do that.

My poems might be understood by King of Hell. I had seen his statue in the Hall of the Son of Heaven in Fengdu county of Chongqing city; the King of Hell was a gentleman. My poems were not about a deity or its statue. As a result, the King of Hell might get angry if he read my poems, and he might let my father suffer more if he knew that they were written by me. My father could not understand those verses and he would get much more worried about my job.

"Your children and grandchildren say goodbye to you, Mr. Xu Chengxiang," Liu Xianwen chanted loudly. "Forget your life in the human world and start a new life in heaven."

After he finished, Limin gave him a red envelope. Liu led his disciples to open the cover of the freezing coffin.

Our father's face looked rosy. Sixi cried, leaning on the coffin, followed by Swallow. Dayou tried to pull her back because he thought that her crying would be embarrassing. His muscles could be seen in his sleeveless shirt.

Sixi glared at Dayou and found his clothes unsuitable for the funeral. After Dayou pulled Swallow towards the door, Sixi had a fight with Dayou. Bang! The men in our family tried to separate them. Swallow supported Dayou out of the mourning hall.

"Sixi and Dayou are naughty boys!" Chunshan snapped.

The farewell to the deceased man was over.

Chapter 52

The wooden coffin was placed on two large benches and its cover was put vertically nearby. "The coffin is good enough for Mr. Xu Chengxiang's spirit," said Liu Xianwen. "Deities will lead him to become an immortal in heaven."

Limin gave a red envelope to Liu Xianwen. Liu's disciples carried the corpse and put it into the wooden coffin. Large piles of joss paper were used as his pillow. Chunshu put square wads of joss paper to tightly fulfil the gaps in the corpse and in the coffin. No paper could be pulled out. Our father's portrait was placed in the wall made of hell bank notes. The piece of paper which had been adopted to cover his face now was used again.

Before the coffin was closed, Liu Xianwen thoughtfully used his fingers to count the relatives who he deemed unsuitable for participating in the process: neither see nor hear it, otherwise he or she would have ill luck. Chunshan, Chunying, and I should avoid that, so we walked out of the mourning hall. However, I heard the dismal sound of closing the coffin, and I wondered if they could hear it.

It was still dark and everything was unrecognizable. Chunying was touching my face while I heard Chunshan crying sadly. He had been calm during our father's stay in hospital and the days after his death. Chunying and I consoled him, each of us holding one of his hands.

The long nails with the symbol of longevity were being hammered into the coffin.

"Let's return to the courtyard at once," said Chunshan. He would make sticky rice paste to seal the space between the cover and the coffin body.

Chunhong, Chunhua, Swallow, and my wife were consoling Dayou who was sitting on a stool and leaning on a bag full of maize husks. During the funeral Sixi had been loafing but Dayou had been busy.

"Sixi has gone mad!" Swallow exclaimed.

Sixi could hear that but he was focusing on his phone. I wondered why Dayou did that in the mourning hall. Did he dislike watching Swallow crying with Sixi? Was he too agitated at that time?

Sixi's crying might be his pretence. People could understand deception through one's deeds. The differences between thought and action would produce the fraud. We could see through Sixi. Even though Dayou married Swallow, he would still be an outsider.

"It's Sixi's fault," I said to Dayou, patting him on the shoulder.

I saw Qiuyue lying nearby.

"You should sleep in the bed to avoid getting a cold," I said to her.

"I've told her many times," said Chunhong. "But she did not listen to me."

A lock of her hair was on Dayou's right arm. Chunhong glared at Chunying.

"Now you should do what your aunt and uncle have said!" Chunying ordered.

Qiuyue remained motionless. Chunying had to put a coat on Qiuyue's body, and Swallow did the same to Dayou, removing Qiuyue's hair from his arm.

Chapter 53

Morning came. A lot of things could be clearly seen, including the roller basins under the sycamore trees. Villagers had used the rollers for rice, sugarcane, and wheat flour, but the rollers had been deserted. They would have been neglected if there had not been debris of firecrackers. Villagers were using machines to produce flour and mini-tillers for ploughing. Old things were disappearing or had been gone, including our father. Trees and the light of the early morning sun could be seen, and soon clouds would come out.

Gongs again. Except Sixi, Dayou and Qiuyue, we went to the courtyard. The coffin would be moved to the courtyard from the mourning hall. Liu Xianwen waved a flag and then instruments rang. He whispered with his eyes closed, suddenly he opened his eyes and ordered, "Rise!"

Four men put ropes around the coffin and two long, thick poles across the ropes. They shouted and carried the coffin amid Liu Xianwen's incantations, followed by burning of joss paper. Limin gave a red envelope to Liu Xianwen. Liu waved the flag again and then the carriers moved towards the door.

The coffin was put on the two large benches and a long, crimson flag was used to cover the coffin. Liu Xianwen splashed water with a bottle of mineral water on the flag totally five times; each splash was meaningful, such as blessing his children. Chunshan, the eldest son of our family, was prostrating himself during the process. Afterwards Limin gave another red envelope to Liu Xianwen. Chunshan put sticky rice paste, which included sorghum and which looked like the colour of the coffin, to seal the seam crossing. His hands were full of the paste and he had to wash them. Gongs again. It was time to carry the coffin outside.

Chapter 54

Sixi, Dayou and Qiuyue were standing among us and thinking about something else. When the men carried the coffin on their shoulders, we knelt for them and also for the deceased man; if they changed a position halfway, we would kneel again. The path to our ancestral graves was not far and there would be no change of shoulder-carrying position. We moved amid drums and gongs. Chunshan was wearing the mourning clothes in the front of the team and holding a basin, Chunshu holding a long narrow flag with the symbol of longevity in another world, Chunshang and Fang Yun holding wreaths, Xianhe, Peiliang, Hongquan and Dayou carrying the miniature mansion made by bamboos, and Sixi putting his hands on the mansion. The teams of wailing, funeral dancing, and lion dancing followed us. Three men and one woman were playing the suona with the melodies of *Sacrifice* and *Death March*.

Puddles had been cleaned. Clangs could be heard when the carriers stepped on the residual water. The road was not slippery. Two large benches had been placed on the path to the bamboo forests. Magpie and several women were standing nearby with hoes in their hands. In the past only men dug a graveyard, but now even Mrs. Hou joined the work team because of an acute shortage of assistants. According to the best moment for good geomancy given by Liu Xianwen, they started the digging last night.

We knelt when the coffin was put on the benches. Qiuyue did not kneel so as to keep her clothes clean. The ground was full of dirty leaves.

We stood up after the coffin was placed stably. Chunshan smashed the basin on a rock.

"Let's smoke," said Guangwen. He gave cigarettes to the male participants.

Chunhong removed the bamboo leaves from his trousers, and used clean ones for wiping.

"I'll change clothes after I go home," said Guangwen, patting himself on the knees. He did not stand firmly and nearly fell into the graveyard.

Others stifled their laugh.

"You'll have good luck," said Liu Xianwen.

We did not know why it would be good luck, but the funeral geomancer said so.

"Our dad shows me the good foundations of the graveyard," Guangwen smiled.

It was a good, square graveyard with a central axis written with lime. Our mother's graveyard was located in the east and our father's in the west, separated by old tombs. That was perhaps because vegetable fields were located in the east and uncultivated land in the west. A dead man's body should not be buried in the vegetable fields. Our mother might be unhappy: she had never seen her parents-in-law or their ancestors, her mother-in-law's graveyard had been placed here but her father-in-law's had been missing. She had been buried here for decades and been waiting for her husband, but now her husband's graveyard was far away from hers.

Liu Xianwen scattered earth into the graveyard, symbolizing that the deceased man's offspring would have a promising future. And then the men slid the coffin into the graveyard.

"Now the coffin is sealed," said Liu Xianwen. "The spirit will go to heaven. It will meet the Great Father in the east and meet the Great Mother in the west."

Limin gave him a red envelope to Liu, and then the latter adjusted the position with long sticks for good geomancy. Even a minor mistake would bring bad geomancy.

"Bless your children and grandchildren, Mr. Xu Chengxiang," Liu Xianwen added.

Limin gave him another red envelope.

"Your children and grandchildren will become rich and powerful," Liu continued.

Limin gave him a third red envelope.

"Very good," said Liu. He put away the long sticks.

Fengjuan gave Liu Xianwen a basin of rice. He asked us to stand with our backs against the graveyard and hold our clothes, and he would stand in a high position and scatter the rice to us. He or she would become wealthy with more rice in his or her clothes.

I walked away, followed by my wife and Guangwen.

"Let them become rich," he said. His wife glared at him and then held her clothes solemnly.

"More rice, more wealth," Liu Xianwen said loudly, scattering the rice.

Limin gave him a fourth red envelope.

"OK," said Liu.

When the men were backfilling the pit, Liu Xianwen chanted, "May you rest in peace, Mr. Xu Chengxiang. Bless your children and grandchildren with good health and good fortune."

Limin gave him a fifth red envelope.

Chunshan had to carry more earth to make a good graveyard, followed by Fang Yun, Xianhe and Ziqiang. Chunshang burned the funeral products and Magpie set off firecrackers. Sizzles and smoke were the last gifts to our father.

Part Six

Chapter 1

After spending a month in my hometown, I could feel that city life was much better. When I was a new comer in the city, I thought that I would have countless opportunities. However, after I became a wily old bird, I knew that everything should be operated in its own position, otherwise it would be destroyed. I could go anywhere except vital government places and military zones, but only five places were related to me: the company in which I had been working (the editorial office, No. 5, Baihua Road); my house, No. 8, Yinsha Road; my parents-in-law's house nearby a bridge; Huaxiang Middle School in which my son had been studying; and Dongpo No. 1 Middle School in which my wife had been teaching.

Before I left my hometown, Chunhong gave me a lot of food such as pickled mustard roots, allium chinensis, thick broad-bean sauce, pork preserved with salt, and rapeseed oil. Without having a shower, I visited my parents-in-law. My mother-in-law was in high spirits although she had to sit in a wheelchair. She was sad about her money when she heard the policemen's words. Now she enjoyed using her wheelchair to move here and there. She asked me about my father's funeral, and let us go home to have a good rest. As soon as we left, she cried that we should bring American ginseng to Weisheng who would soon take the college entrance examination. My father-in-law took them out of the refrigerator and gave them to my wife, and then he slammed the door to avoid his wife's nagging.

My parents-in-law did not notice my grey hair which had grown during the one month. They still regarded me as a young man because my head had not been fully covered with the grey hair. When I walked past a garden, I saw people playing chess and gaudily-dressed old men standing in two groups and singing old songs conducted by an old man wearing white gloves. The other elderly men were doing bodybuilding exercise and talking about national affairs. In one alley two pairs of lovers were locked in embraces.

The next day I went to work and I was greeted by my colleagues, just like I were working yesterday. Nobody noticed my grey hair and nobody asked me about my father's funeral, and I did not go to my boss's office to reimburse the expenses of buying wreaths. There were books and letters on my desk.

Single Braid sent me pictures that he had taken in Baili Canyon. He had hundreds of aborigines wear homespun embroidered vests, carry waist drums and perform the nearly lost dancing. He must have bought the clothes and drums for them, and he had given 200 yuan to the local dancer. He had frequently financially supported the culture he needed and had spent the money that he had earned from doing business on the cultural undertakings.

Life went on although my mother died in my childhood and my father died when I was a middle-aged man. Now I was worried about my son's national college entrance examination. I could not revive my father even at the expense of a lot of money, kowtows and tears.

My son was rather serious during the days of the examination. He had told me that he came from one of my sperms, but he was good at mathematics, not Chinese language and literature.

"You could not have been able to do math problems if you had not been born by me," his mother argued.

"I will have a promising future," he retorted.

My wife laughed. She appreciated that his son approved of his father.

My son was admitted to a second-tier university. He would have been admitted to a first-tier one if his marks were a little higher and then we might hope that he could study in a prestigious one. Everything returned to normal.

Chapter 2

I visited my mother-in-law again with my wife and my son, and she could walk with a stick. After I returned home, I sent an email to Single Braid and told him that his works would be published in the magazine. I wanted to write a poem for my father. When I was in the metro yesterday, I heard a woman talk on the phone: "Mr. Huang will come at noon, dad." Her words saddened me because my father had been gone. Others had told me that people would feel anguished at one moment after their parent died. After one of my friends lost his father, he did not have painful emotions at first; but one day when he was driving, he burst into tears suddenly. I had not seen my father in my dreams during these days although I had been eager to see him.

I was riddled with disappointment. When I was a new poet, I thought that

I had found the key to a new world with my creation of words. But I came to understand that art could be used to interpret the world rather than reshape or foresee it. In addition, the interpretation would be futile. The complexity existed in the things which had happened, just like the deaths of my parents. I could provide a correct or an incorrect interpretation for that. The future would be simple. My father had died and I could not see him anymore, which was irreversible.

My poem was about vastness, including people living or dead. My son had been luckily chosen among countless sperms. Just like Tan Ruisong had said, an individual must live in the tide of the times and in different worlds: your joy or anxiety came from the other self which was having bad things in another world. The two selves could not meet each other.

I wrote more than 90 lines and I smoked when I felt tired. I found too much sorrow and clearness in my poem, but I wanted ambiguity. It had been misunderstood but it was not a bad word. People preferred answers to solutions. I was trying to find an answer. When I could not write a good poem, I felt that I would not be able to write again. The distress had always been with me.

Chapter 3

Swallow called me suddenly. "Dayou is having an affair with Qiuyue."
She found that on his phone. She had never checked the information on his phone before. When he was having a shower today, the phone rang.
"Swallow."
"I'm here."
"Don't you want to see me?"
"No."
They have been decorating their house which was located beneath the teahouse in the stilted building in Suwan. The house was provided with beds, but no tableware, no kitchenware, no furniture, no electric appliances. They would leave after they got a marriage certificate. Swallow did not hold a wedding when she was with Sheng Jun. But now she would hold one with Dayou after the Spring Festival.

To buy the house, Dayou's parents gave 20,000 yuan, Chunshan and his wife 10,000 yuan. Swallow paid 115,000 yuan, but both her name and Dayou's were written in the property ownership certificate. Her parents could not give more money. Guangwen was rich enough to buy a house for her daughter, but Chunshan was poor. In addition, Dayou's parents refused to give more money, so Fengjuan had to give another 10,000 yuan so that Swallow could buy furniture. When Dayou was having a shower, Swallow was putting cloth cover on the sofa.

"Don't you want to see the good things?" the voice in the phone asked.

"My phone is much better than you although it's cheaper than you," Swallow retorted.

"This is good news."

She saw the message from Qiuyue on WeChat.

"Honey, what are you doing?" asked Qiuyue.

Another message soon: "I'll go to see you if you don't answer me now!"

After her grandpa's funeral, Qiuyue did not want to live with her parents anymore, and she made a fake identity card (19 years old) and a fake high school diploma and went to work in an electrical appliance factory in Huainan city, Anhui province.

A third message came: "Oh, you are having a shower. Why does it take too much time? Does she punish you to kneel? I'd rather that she can read the messages between us, and she will know it."

Swallow got shocked and she was regarded as an enemy by her younger sister. Qiuyue had been bad at her school work, but she could use meaningful words in the messages to Dayou. The messages in the phone were overwhelming.

Chapter 4

Dayou and Swallow had been using the same password on their phones since they began their relationship. He wanted to change it one day, but he was worried that he might be doubted by her. In fact she had harbored suspicious about him, making it a challenging task for him to gain her trust. Today he put his phone on the table when he was having a shower to show that he was loyal to her, but she found him out. He could control Swallow who was like a clear river, but he could not control Qiuyue who was like a burning fire.

Dayou called her name but she went outside. She phoned me jokingly but she went to Chunhong's house with teary eyes.

Chunhong realized that Swallow had been made the scapegoat for Sixi's sins. Dayou had deceived Swallow in the way that Sixi had deceived girls. Nothing was fair in the world.

When Swallow was crying, Chunhong phoned me but she did not curse Qiuyue. It would be useless to tell this to Chunying. Chunhong had told Chunhua that Chunying and her husband had been protecting their children blindly without distinguishing right from wrong. Chunhua laughed and did not get herself involved in it. "I don't know."

Chunhong did not call Chunying or Chunhua, but she called me and then her husband. At that time Guangwen did not play cards but he hung up the phone. He was talking with Qian Wen in Yang Jin's store. Above the store there was a windowless attic full of sundries with the smells of vinegar, soy sauce, and salt. Guangwen did not turn on the light. Qian Wen had borrowed usurious loans from Guangwen, but the former was unable to repay the capital and interest. The latter said that he would have to adopt other measures to solve it.

Guangwen returned home after twenty minutes and knew what had happened. Swallow had stopped crying and did not answer Dayou's calls.

"Turn off your phone!" Guangwen snapped. "Otherwise I'll smash it! You can live in my house as long as you want. Ignore Dayou!"

After Swallow stayed in Guangwen's house for four days, she went to meet Dayou.

Dayou came to the riverside road for three nights in a row and sent messages to Swallow.

"I'm downstairs."

"I'm at the doorway."

"I put my phone on the table to let you see the information in it. Qiuyue kept bothering me, but I seldom answered her. I did not want to hurt her because she is your younger female cousin."

Swallow did not know who had sent more messages to the other, and she thought that she perhaps had misunderstood Dayou.

And then he sent messages about his miserable childhood: "I had never been loved by my parents and I was brought up by my grandparents, but my grandpa died when I was still a child. I had to earn school fees all by myself doing odd jobs, and I nearly croaked after I fell off rocks. I got married but divorced. My ex was a bad-tempered woman; but in fact, she had cheated on me. I have been able to have a new life since I met you. If you want to leave me, I won't complain at all and I will live alone. God bless you!"

The ice in Swallow's heart began to thaw.

The next morning Chunhong cooked mung bean soup to calm Swallow down. Swallow usually went to the kitchen to help Chunhong after she got up, but this morning she was gone. Chunhong realized that she must be with Dayou again and she had left at midnight.

Chunhong called Swallow but the phone had been turned off. She told this to her husband, he did not say anything but went on with his sleep.

At 11 a.m. that day, Swallowed called Chunhong and told Dayou's miseries to her.

"Does he love you or sponge off you?" asked Chunhong.

"I should not forsake him," said Swallow.

"You are over-kind and you should not cry in front of me again. You'll pay the piper if you are with Dayou again!"

Swallow cried and Chunhong was waiting for her reply. But Swallow hung up the phone. On the same day she and Dayou got a marriage certificate.

Chapter 5

During my father's funeral, I asked Liu Xianwen about the things after death. "On the first day after death," he said, "his spirit goes to the ghostdom. But he goes back to his home in the human world, and then he goes on with his journey. On the second day it goes to Chickens' Ridge; if he killed chickens when he was alive, his spirit will be tormented by chicken ghosts as retaliation. On the third day it goes to Dogs Mountains; if he killed dogs when he was alive, his spirit will be bitten by dog ghosts. On the fourth day it goes to

Fengdu Town – City of Devils, also the motherland of the deceased man. On the fifth day it looks back at the place where he used to live as a human being. On the sixth day it walks through the Abyss Bridge and has the Water of Oblivion. On the seventh day it reaches the House of Hell and will be questioned by the Governor of the Nether World. During the seven days after death, a lot of joss paper will be burnt for the deceased man so that his penalties will be reduced. The trial by the Governor will last for 21 days. On the 21st day after death, large piles of hell bank notes will be burnt, too, to nourish the fatigued spirit of the deceased man. The first seven days and the 21 days are important, but the 35 days are much more important. The spirit will realize the death of its body on the 35th day and it will lament its death. The realization of death is equal to the realization of life. At noon of the 35th day the spirit will be sentenced by the Yama in the Five Halls who is stern and who likes daughters. On that day, the daughter of the deceased man should host a ceremony to reduce the sins."

Two days before the 35th day, Chunhong asked me on the phone if I would return to Yanerpo. She thought although I am a son, I've gone further away than my sisters, so I'm almost like a daughter to my father. Ten days ago I was invited by a university in Yunnan province to give a lecture, so I was too busy to return to my hometown.

Chunhong had to prepare for the ceremony. Chunhua and Chunying went outside. She cooked food for the ceremony in Chunshan's house. He let his wife stay at home to help the relatives. Yuling helped Fengjuan, too. Chunshang said that he should go to work but he was tardy.

Chapter 6

We held another ceremony on the 42nd day after our father's death. Chunshan let Chunshu, Chunhong, and Chunshang to prepare a third one on the 49th day, also the last section. Liu Xianwen would be invited again to beat drums and chant.

However, Sixi called his father unexpectedly.

"I'll buy a house with Xiaofei," he said. "The total payments will be 820,000 yuan. Her parents will pay 700,000 yuan, and I'll pay 120,000. I haven't signed a contract with the Israeli businessman, but I'll soon. I'll need to borrow money from my relatives."

Later Chunshan called me and would borrow 60,000 yuan from me and it would be much better if I could lend him 120,000. I was speechless with shock. He said that he would borrow from Chunhong and would let me provide the rest of the money. He immediately stopped preparing for the ceremony on the 49th day after our father's death, and he went to see Chunhong.

He went to Suwan and stood outside the building in which Swallow had bought her house. The temporary occupant was Dayou's mother who worked as a baby-sitter and also looked after her grandson Ding. The boy's biological mother was having a relationship with another man. Chunshan got angry as soon as he saw her clothes hanging in the balcony.

"I told you not to come here," his wife said.

The house was bought with Swallow's money and she had given the key to her mother-in-law without telling this to her parents. She treated Ding like her own son but Huchuan like a stranger.

"Swallow wanted you to live in her house," said Fengjuan, "but you would rather live in your old one. A house will become a ghost place if there is no occupant for a long time."

What goes around comes around. Her son's house was bought by his girlfriend and there was deception. It was said that if one was sinful, his or her family member would be punished.

"Don't forget our task today!" Fengjuan warned.

Both Chunhong and her husband were at home. Before she lent money to her sister or brother, she would tell it to her husband. Chunshan received the cigarette from Guangwen, just before the former spoke, Guangwen gave several packets of red-covered Bafine cigarettes to Chunshan.

"Sixi will buy a house soon," said Chunshan. "And he will get settled."

Guangwen got surprised but soon he realized that was Sixi's lie again. After Xiaofei left during our father's funeral, Sixi could not meet her in the railway station because she had been gone through convenient transportation. He had a new hairstyle and returned home and told a sham to his parents and relatives.

"Where is the house located? And the price?" Guangwen asked.

"Sixi will have to pay 120,000 yuan," Chunshan replied.

"He is always a liar!"

And then Chunshan mentioned the Israeli businessman.

"You are Sixi's parents and you should judge his words," Guangwen retorted angrily. "If Xiaofei's parents could provide 700,000 yuan, they would make a down payment on the house. What's more, the deal with the Israeli businessman would bring more money."

"Sixi said that they would never buy a house if without the total payments," Fengjuan said after a moment of silence."

"Don't buy the house," Guangwen snapped. "Sixi told Li Zhi and Ziguo that Xiaofei's parents had been worried about the money."

"I feel pity for Xiaofei. She is determined to be with Sixi."

"Even her parents don't care for her."

"But she has cried so sadly that I care for her."

"When did she cry?"

"Sixi asked me to borrow money from you and Chunming. And then Xiaofei said to me sobbing on the phone and she called me mom. She said that her parents would become heartless if without the money to buy a house."

"Are you sure that woman was Xiaofei?

"Another girl?"

"Yes."

"But I could recognize Xiaofei's voice!"

"Sixi could hire a girl and asked her to speak like Xiaofei! I can call her now to confirm this!"

But nobody had Xiaofei's phone number.

"I won't lend money to you this time!" Guangwen cried.

"Xiaofei would be a good daughter-in-law," Fengjuan said, lowering her head.

"There are much better girls than her," Guangwen retorted. "Would you feel pity for a girl who could not become your daughter-in-law?"

Tears fell down from Fengjuan's cheeks, which surprised Guangwen.

Fengjuan had been a long-suffering woman, but she burst into emotions when she visited our father in the hospital. Chunhong said that Fengjuan looked like another woman at that time. Nobody knew when she had changed herself. Her life became harder and harder, and a bad thing would become the last straw. Luckily Swallow and Dayou got married.

Chapter 7

Chunhong kept silent. She had had a talk with Xiaofei and was much more doubtful now. But her doubts were taken away by Fengjuan's tears.

"What if it's true this time?" Chunhong ventured.

"But that has been loathsomely repeated!" Guangwen shouted. He slammed the door and left.

Chunhong knew that her husband would lend the money to Fengjuan.

"I can lend you 40,000 yuan at most," Chunhong said to Chunshanand his wife. "I have an unpromising son. His dad has never treated him with a high hand although he has yelled at him frequently. Both Li Zhi and I won't live in the hometown. The young people treat their hometowns with scorn."

"You have a house in the county," said Chunshan.

"The redecoration just begins. It is a second-hand house and I'd rather live in the town full of friends. And I won't let Li Zhi live there. He should be further educated. Parents should be responsible for their children's incapability and should help them when they are helpless. And I should think about my granddaughter. You may borrow 20,000 yuan from Chunming at most. He has paid all the medical bills for our dad, and he will pay for the costs of building a new graveyard for our ancestors. What's more, his mother-in-law has got ill and his son will go to university in Tianjin in September. Those things will cost a lot of money."

Chunshan and his wife nodded. I lent 10,000 yuan to Chunshan. My wife disagreed if I lent 200,00 yuan to him.

"We give the money to them," Li Jing said. "They won't repay us." And then she left.

It was 9 p.m.

"I can have a walk with you," I said.

"Leave me alone," she said.

Both she and Chunhong had got involved in the trouble of their relatives.

Li Jing was in a sulk because the money she had earned with her hard work would be squandered by a freeloader. She had never bought expensive clothes for herself.

Chunshan transferred 50,000 yuan to Sixi's bank account.

Chapter 8

After a few days, Xiao Fei, the youngest son of Xiao An who was the master of Chunshu, met Sixi in Wuhan. When Xiao Fei was living in Yanerpo, his wife eloped with a man who had lived in the areas around the Qingxi River. In order to find his wife, he gave gifts to each household, and later he was invited by them. Sixi, who was just a little boy at that time, was at home when Xiao Fei was invited by Chunshan to dinner. Xiao Fei now worked as a waiter in the Two Rivers Restaurant in Wuhan, and he could recognize Sixi at the sight of him, but the former did not greet him because the latter was rude.

One man and three women went to the Restaurant with Sixi. They had three bottles of the famous Kweichow Moutai. A woman with colourful, erect hair like antennas on her head and with crimson lipstick was sitting beside Sixi. She poured the whole bottle of Moutai into a large goblet, put a drinking straw into the goblet, and sucked the straw. Half of the liquor was left. And then she threw herself into Sixi's arms and licked his earlobes. Both the middle-aged Xiao Fei and the five customers disliked each other. The customers liked young, handsome waiters, but those men were unwilling to wait upon others. Xiao Fei wanted to say hello to Sixi, but the latter was surrounded by women.

After three days Xiao Fei met Fang Yun. After our father's funeral, Chunhua and her husband went to Hubei province: they went to Jingzhou before to Wuhan. Fang Yun tried to find an odd job during the break time in the construction site. He heard someone calling his name when he walked past the Two Rivers Restaurant. That man was Xiao Fei. They had often chatted with each other in Yanerpo. Fang Yun used to live in a river. If there was a torrential flood upstream, the section downstream would cry. When the red moon was connected with the water glow, it was like thousands of hairy hands protruding from the river. Those were fantastic stories to the villagers. Xiao

Fei had led his brothers to explore and live in Xinjiang. Xiao Fei and his father became homesick, but they would rather talk about the negative side of their hometown.

Xiao Fei and Fang Yun had lunch together. The former spoke ill of Yanerpo after he had some liquor, but Fang Yun did not want to hear that. The negative judgements on his hometown showed his loneliness. Xiao Fei could feel it, so he changed the subject and mentioned Sixi.

Fang Yun did not believe that. On the day when Xiao Fei came across Sixi, Chunshan told Fang Yun on the phone that Sixi would buy a house in Nangang District, Harbin; the first house he liked would cost 820,000 yuan, but he had 750,000, so he would have to buy a cheaper one. Xiao Fei was sad about Fang Yun's doubt. Xiao Fei and his three brothers went to Xinjiang and operated cotton fields. He went to work in another place after his eldest brother had an accident and his father got ill. Xiao Fei could not find his wife anymore; perhaps she had a much better life with another man. But he could remember all his fellow-villagers clearly, even though Sixi was still a child when he met him for the first time.

Fang Yun could not understand Xiao Fei, so he called Chunshan.

"I'm drinking with Xiao Fei," said Fang Yun. "He said that he met Sixi in Wuhan three days ago. What has happened?"

Chunshan phoned Sixi at once, but his calls were not answered.

After half a month, Jiang Hua in Fuzhou called Guangwen. "Is Xu Sixi your wife's nephew?"

"Yes. What's the matter?" Guangwen was playing mahjong. He asked Jiang Hua suspiciously although he was unwilling to answer the phone call.

"He wanted to borrow money from me for a project in Fuzhou," Jiang Hua explained.

"Do not lend any money to him! He is a liar!" Guangwen shouted, throwing a mahjong tile hard. It nearly fell on the eye of Mr. Han, the deputy town chief.

"I doubted him and I only gave him 2,000 yuan. I did not know how he found me. He told me the family relations between you and him, and he looked like a beggar."

Guangwen told that to his wife after he returned home.

"A liar is always a liar!" he roared, pushing a tea cup hard on the table.

She wiped the tea liquid silently with tissues. From then on, we took Sixi as a dead man.

Chapter 9

A poet said: "A man dies yet he still lives on."

He did not refer to Sixi, but several mysterious men. The fish in the Qingxi River had been poisoned again.

This was the third time. The first time happened ten years ago and the second time several months ago. The culprits were still at large.

"The second time was caused by natural gas leakage," Guangwen explained. "But the official conclusion was just like the first time, an unsettled question."

The two old cases happened in the stream segments below Huilong Town. This time even Golden Town got involved in it. Both fish and creatures that ate fish died. The egret disappeared and a bull or a cow who had the river water either croaked or had convulsions, foaming at the mouth.

Mr. Zhang, the secretary of the County Committee, yelled at the local senior leaders: "You must arrest the culprit within 10 days!"

After the second accident happened, the local leaders just went through the motions. But this time any suspect would be questioned in the township government office.

Wang Qingguang of Yanerpo and Huigoer of Lijiayan were questioned. Wang Qingguang got angry; after he knew that he was in the same group with Huigoer, he got furious. Mr. Hu from the criminal investigation team of the county questioned the suspects in Huilong Town.

"You work in a state-owned institution," Wang Qingguang argued. "But you can't clearly understand the distinction between right and wrong. You should not have been swayed by an old bachelor!"

"We don't arrest you," said Mr. Hu. "But you must answer my questions." He did not know who was the old bachelor.

Wang Qingguang suspected that Magpie might be the snitch. Magpie once said that Wang could easily poison the river. But Mr. Hu's words did not prove that Magpie was the informer.

"Why do you ask me to sit here?" Wang Qiangguang snapped. He hurled abuse at Mr. Hu.

"You were chosen by random selection of the local police station," said Xu Bing, the village party secretary of Yanerpo.

"There has been a suspected murderer in your family," Mr. Hu explained. "All the suspects and ex-convicts will be questioned, including their relatives."

Now everybody knew that the husband of Wang Qingguang's elder daughter had killed someone. Afterwards he became silent and weak.

Chapter 10

The investigators left after five days and the culprit was still at large. It was not reported on TV and the walls outside the court in the county were covered with bulletins about swindlers, rapists, robbers, human traffickers, and murderers. But the poisoning in the river was not mentioned. What's more, a flood took away all the evidence. People in Huilong Town gossiped on the matter. Wang Qingguang and Huigoer were still in the village. The family members of the convicts in the past were still at home, such as the relatives of Zeng Cai and Xia Shuguo. The ex-convicts such as Zhang Dachao was questioned, but now he was sitting in the Congee Restaurant from morning to night. The idler Yaqiong, who had lost her son because of her gambling, was also questioned. But she either went to another place or shut herself at home for several days. When she walked on the street, she talked to others madly that she had seen guests sitting around more than 60 tables on her son's wedding and seen her beautiful daughter-in-law who called her mother sweetly.

There were changes. Billboards were hanging on the road: "If there is no water, within a few days your lips will be gone, your gums will be blackened, your nose will become smaller, and your eyelids will be dead." People said those words were bullshit. It would rain anyway. Mr. Gui, who used to teach geography before retirement, found that his knowledge would be very useful. He was being careless about his business of renting his tableware to villagers.

"Only fresh water can be used," Mr. Gui explained. "And there is only

3% of fresh water on the earth. The 3% is ice mostly, and 90% of the ice is located in Antarctica. The water in lakes and rivers accounts for only 0.036% and the rain for 0.001%. The water mentioned in the billboards refer to the usable fresh water. There is abundant seawater, but it can't be used. We are far away from the ocean but we are living around the Qingxi River. If it becomes poisonous, all of us will die."

People respected Mr. Gui. But day after day, everything was safe and sound. Meanwhile, people were eager to see who was the culprit. Everybody was busy with farm work in summer and with harvests in autumn, and people gradually forgot the poisoning in the river. They idled away time by smoking, talking, and playing cards. Gossips were everywhere but nobody could find the source.

Chapter 11

Chunhong went to Huang Ermei's store.

"What are you thinking about?" Chunhong asked.

Huang Ermei, standing at the door, was surprised to see her but soon she let her sit in a clean plastic stool. Both of them held a handful of sunflower seeds.

"There is something about the culprit who has poisoned the river," Huang Ermei whispered.

That reminded Chunhong of Huigoer. He yelled after he was questioned and returned to Lijiayan, and he felt wronged. Guangwen tried to calm him down, but Huigoer retorted, "Someone wants to put me into prison. If I can't get any benefit, I won't be scapegoated for the poisoning!"

Guangwen would intend to give a bag of red-covered Bafine cigarettes to Huigoer, but now he dropped the idea. He asked Li Qiantao to let all the villagers have a meeting in the playground. Guangwen made a speech: "The river should be protected from rubbish or poison. No clean river, no wonderful mountains. The river resembles the heart and eyes of the mountains. The dirty and poisonous river will be hated by everybody. What's more, a wicked person will be punished by a much more wicked one."

The listeners looked at Huigoer with scorn. After Guangwen made a blueprint for Lijiayan's future, he went on with the subject about Huigoer: "Huigoer has been questioned, but we should not regard him as the culprit. If an innocent man is investigated, we tend to think that he has done something wrong. If anybody among us is questioned, is he or she the criminal?"

After the meeting was over, Guangwen was invited to lunch by Guangli. Just before the lunch began, Huigoer appeared and apologized to Guangwen. The latter let him have the meal with them, and Huigoer treated him ingratiatingly. Guangwen thought that petty favours would be effective on that man.

That afternoon Guangwen went home without going to the tea house.

"What has happened?" his wife asked.

"Huigoer should stop making trouble." He did not say anymore.

Guangwen would be sentenced if Huigoer had poisoned the river. Mr. Zhang, the secretary of the Party Committee, took stricter measures: an official would be expelled.

Afterwards Huigoer was still disliked by everybody although he was no more taken as the culprit. But now Chunhong got worried about the matter again.

Chapter 12

Chunhong felt that her husband's leadership had fatigued him. When he was living in the village, there were frequent knocks at the door at midnight: a villager's daughter-in-law had taken pesticides, a cow was having a difficult labour, someone saw his grandpa living in luffa stems in his dream and he wondered if he should build a miniature mansion and burn it for the spirit ... Guangwen had to rise and would either promptly respond or visit the villager's house holding a flashlight. After he lived in the town, he had to answer countless calls. When he was playing cards, he was unwilling to answer his wife's call, but he rushed to answer the villager's. When the caller worked in another province and got hurt or died, he or his relatives would phone Guangwen.

The funeral arrangements of Yan Min were not difficult because she was one of the local villagers. Guangwen would be formally dressed when he went to another province to deal with a problem. He could get back 50,000 yuan when the victim thought that 30,000 yuan could be reclaimed. The wounded man was sent to hospital and the medical bills would be paid by the troublemaker: he would have died if without Guangwen's persuasion. However, there were millions of villages in China, and Guangwen sometimes was looked down upon by men in other provinces.

Chunhong had been worried about her husband. The leadership could bring benefits, but they came at the expense of his toil. She did not value the leadership like Chunshu did.

"You will know the obvious differences between having power and losing power after retirement," said Chunshu.

Chunhong did not know how to retort. After our father's funeral, she did not receive the chickens given by villagers and by her adopted children. She considered that a good reputation would be much more important. Chunshu divided people into the smart and the stupid, and she divided people into the honoured and the dishonoured. Her husband would lose his good reputation if he was dismissed from his post, and all his hard work would turn out to be shameful. What was more, he would not resign his position. He considered that a leader, regardless of rank, should serve the people. An official's resignation showed that he had problems. The higher the better, and that's the way for leadership. A failure halfway would become a laughing stock. Meanwhile, Chunhong thought that her husband was as headstrong as Swallow. Such a rogue as Huigoer should be left to stew in his own juice and Guangwen should not have helped him again and again. If Huigoer had poisoned the river, Guangwen would get involved in it. However, Huang Ermei told another story.

Chapter 13

"The three dead men from Lijiayan who had been bound with stones and steel wires and been poured into the bottom of the river are now discovered," said Huang Ermei.

The shell of a sunflower seed choked Chunhong. She coughed it out after a long moment, blushing.

"Who has said that?" Chunhong asked anxiously.

"People are talking about it," replied Huang Ermei. "Mr. Feng, the then secretary of the Party Committee in Huilong Town, is now promoted to deputy mayor of Baima. That thing had been done secretly, but how could it be known by others?"

"This is far away from Fengdu Ghost Town, and the spirits of the three dead men could not return through a long journey."

"But there is something more behind it. You should ask your husband to be careful. Good luck can't last long. He is a lucky man, but sometimes he goes too far that he offends others, and someone may throw a rock at him."

Chunhong realized the importance of the matter and left. As soon as she returned home, she could see a shelf full of good wine. She asked her husband on the phone to come home. He did not play cards, and she started to put away the bottles of famous wine. Chunshan once told her that the clay jars could be left in the living room, and the famous wine should be put in the bedrooms. There were two closets in the room in which our father used to sleep. She took the things out of the closets and placed the bottles of wine in them.

Chapter 14

After Guangwen entered his house, he found the place had lost its grandeur, and he even felt that it was not his house.

"Chunhong!" he shouted.

She was in another room far away from the living room, so she could not hear her husband's voice. He watched the wall before he could hold a cigarette and felt that his house had been burglarized.

Thieves reappeared although they used to disappear. They targeted rural areas because urban areas were full of monitors. Barber Sun lost his camera the other day. It was bought by his grandson Sun Jun priced at more than 100,000 yuan. The students in the university in which Sun Jun had been working chose him as a top professor through votes, and he was rewarded with 500,000 yuan, so he bought a Hasselblad digital single-lens reflex camera for his grandpa who had never used such a precious one. The elderly man covered it with a piece of red cloth and touched it before he slept every night, but it was taken away by a burglar.

A fat pig kept by Li Chengzhong was also taken away by a thief. His house was located nearby a road. One day his mother visited neighbours and his father did farm work. Later Chengzhong's father helped a middle-aged man to hustle a crying pig onto a plank connecting with a small truck.

"I've bought it in the Cypress Ridge," said the man. "The pig jumped from the plank. It would have run to the forest if it had not broken its leg. Thank you very much."

After he drove away, Chengzhong's father returned home and found the empty pigpen. He slapped himself hard across the face because he had helped the thief to take away his pig, and he should have recognised the pig's yelling.

After Guangwen thought about those things, he called his wife but he was startled by the ringing of her phone on the shelf.

Chapter 15

Guangwen disliked being scared by himself. A man can discover his own life after he hates something. The clay jars contained good wine. The famous wine could not be recognized if without a brand or an attractive package, but Guangwen enjoyed a glittering life. In addition, his wife tried to hide the bottles of famous wine, which made him feeling like being a thief. Embarrassment followed bad memories. Even Monkey King felt miserable when he saw the six-eared macaque named by Buddha. Monkey King was lucky and was supported by Buddha. But who could help an ordinary human being like Guangwen? Those memories came back to him.

Thirty years ago, he and Chunhong went to Xinjiang to search for a distant relative – his father's younger male cousin Huang Zhong who tried to make a living in Xinjiang in childhood and did not return. His relatives thought that he had died. After Guangwen was in high school, his uncle (his mother's eldest brother) received a letter from Shihezi and the sender was Huang Zhong. The uncle asked Guangwen to reply to Huang Zhong's letter. At that time people might be lifted out of poverty by a distant relative. In the letter Guangwen wrote about family affairs and about his happiness to receive Huang Zhong's letter. Afterwards Huang Zhong wrote to Guangwen frequently. His own son was also in high school and in the same grade as Guangwen. Huang Zhong asked him to send examination papers to his son. Guangwen sent the papers with answers by mail after examinations were over, but it was difficult to pay the postage. A student could buy an ordinary dish with 0.03 yuan, and the leftovers were poured into buckets. Even the smell of rotten leaves was delicious to Guangwen. After he sent papers to Huang Zhong, he was unable to obtain the the rotten vegetables he desired; sometimes he ate rice only, and at other times, he had to endure hunger.

After one year, Huang Zhong asked in another letter if Guangwen had received the 10 yuan in the previous one. Guangwen did not receive it, so he asked the student in charge of general affairs about it, and knew that each letter was firstly received by the care teacher and then went to the addressee. Guangwen doubtfully asked the care teacher about it, and he said that the letter had been given to the student in charge of general affairs. The ten yuan could support him for many months! He frequently speculated the student in charge of general affairs had torn open the letter and had taken away the 10 yuan, and he even madly imagined each leaf was like a bank note, and each blast of cold air was like the hand which had stolen the money.

Guangwen was too embarrassed to tell Huang Zhong that he had not received the money, but he expressed his gratitude to him, and he sent more examination papers to him by mail. The papers at the beginning usually had full marks, but the later ones had low marks, so he tampered with the names. Huang Zhong did not write to him after he graduated from senior high school.

Guangwen wrote more than ten letters to Huang Zhong within the next few years but got no reply. In spite of that, he still remembered Huang Zhong's kindness and believed that the latter would provide him with a good job if the former went to Xinjiang. Huang Zhong once told Guangwen that he could go to Xinjiang and help him to operate farms after he graduated from university. Xinjiang was rich with cotton and sweet grapes, and one could have more than two hours of the daytime and watch sunset glow even at 10 p.m. In fact, Guangwen had been agitated by the ten yuan so much so that his studies became worse and worse and failed to be admitted to a university. But he thought that he would become useful anyway if Huang Zhong could give him an opportunity, so he went to Xinjiang with his wife although they did not hold a wedding.

The young couple found Huang Zhong's residence in Happiness Road, Shihezi according to the address on the letter. Huang Zhong had been living there for a long time.

It was their first meeting. Guangwen could feel that Huang Zhong and his wife treated the two uninvited guests arrogantly, and they wanted them to leave at once. Guangwen did not know why the poor orphan Huang Zhong had left his hometown, but he could see that Huang Zhong did not miss his hometown at all. Many years ago he wrote a letter to his fellow-villager because his son needed much better education resources.

Huang Zhong's son was two months younger than Guangwen.

"Where is my cousin?" asked Guangwen.

"He has been living in Beijing since he graduated from Peking University," replied Huang Zhong.

"Will you take me to the farms?" Guangwen asked, blushing.

"No. They are in the military reclamation area and I can't take you there."

Guangwen soon realized that he was useless because he had neither a bachelor's degree nor good skills.

The young couple stayed in the middle-aged couple's house for three days. On the fourth day Huang Zhong's wife looked aloof, and the young couple felt like being beggars. After the meal, Chunhong wanted to do the dishes, but Huang Zhong's wife refused that. She let Chunhong do it during the first two days.

When the middle-aged couple were not with the young couple, Chunhong whispered to her husband, "It will be too shameful to stay longer."

"But we have no money to leave."

He had to borrow money from Huang Zhong in his wife's presence. She stood up angrily and tipped over an enamel cup printed with the Xingjiang Construction and Production Corps. She went into the bedroom and did not come out.

Guangwen told Huang Zhong that he was in difficulty.

"I'll find a truck to Ili tomorrow," Huang Zhong said coldly. "You can hitchhike and will have jobs after you reach there."

He did not lend Guangwen any money. It dawned on the young man that the ten yuan had been a lie. He should not have wronged the student in charge of general affairs; two classmates had been admitted to the university, and he would have become the third one if he could have studied harder.

Chunhong felt terrible when she heard the long journey. Her husband glared at her and then agreed to Huang Zhong's request.

At midnight, Guangwen whispered to his wife, "Huang Zhong gives us 300 yuan in private. Let's go right now lest his wife should discover."

She used to carry 45 pounds of corn and green beans together with a large piece of preserved meat to visit Huang Zhong. Now she had a very light bag with some clothes. The young couple soon left the house. However, she had to stay in that city for another 6 months and her husband for three years. In addition, she went to see Huang Zhong all by herself to repay the money twice: the first time to repay 0.4 yuan and the second time 10 yuan. They used the 0.4 yuan for the journey from downtown to railway station. Huang Zhong said that he had sent 10 yuan to Guangwen. At that time she was a poor, pregnant woman, and she had to swallow saliva when she felt hungry. After many years had passed, she came to believe that her daughter's short stature was a consequence of the hunger she had endured. During those days of hardships, she had been pining for her husband and she had been maltreated by her mother-in-law. The distress was that she could not share with anybody what had happened to her husband.

Chapter 16

After several months I visited Guangwen in a special place and then I went to Huilong Town to see Chunhong. She told me their life in Xinjiang.

"I should not have put away the bottles of famous wine," she sighed after a long moment of silence. "Whenever my husband comes home he will touch those bottles. He does not want to show off, but he needs a sense of security because he can't forget the miseries caused by poverty."

She shook her head, looking far away.

She had been worried about her husband and her children. Since Guangwen came back from Xinjiang, he had become cheerful and talkative; but only his wife knew the reason. He often played cards so that he could try to blot out something, and he would lose his temper if his wife said too much. She considered that one's life would become meaningless if he was engulfed with sufferings. She had to tell this to our father and he said that Guangwen would become a promising man. Her griefs came from being a wife and also from her memories of our mother, but our father could not think of those things because he had been protected by his wife.

Chunhong was different from our mother and her husband was different from our father. She was determined to make Guangwen better and better: he became a village party secretary and was greatly supported by villagers.

Li Pu, the village director, was much older than Guangwen and did not call the shots. But the young people would covet Guangwen's position. The clerical assistant Li Qiantao wanted to be a leader, too. What was more, he took charge of the financial affairs of the village and he could do something crafty if he wanted to bring Guangwen down.

"You should be careful about the people around you," Chunhong warned.

Her husband was sitting there silently.

He had been a victim of suspicion and hatred, so he was even unwilling to doubt Huigoer. He trusted Li Qiantao and he did not believe that he should be surrounded by enemies.

"You should not be swayed by the gossip," he said. "Ermei says that mistrust is the cause of a problem."

Afterwards Chunhong often chatted with others but failed to get any implication. Her husband did not get it, either. Even if there was any, it would be soon replaced by a new subject.

Chapter 17

Any topic would travel fast in a town and life would be too boring if without gossip. The new topic was about the old Blacksmith Zhang. He had worked in freighters from 15 to 24. At the age of 24, he went with his employer and travelled through long rivers and saw the impressive Chaotianmen Wharf in Chongqing. Afterwards his vision was widened. His shipmates often teased women washing clothes or vegetables by the riverside, the women retorted sharply when they could not endure those dirty words anymore. But

Blacksmith Zhang was a sissy and he could only cry when he was mistaken for a girl by coworker and raped at the age of 17. Since he came back from Chongqing with a beautiful woman, he turned over a new leaf. He was taught by a master and later he worked as a blacksmith. He was still energetic after decades of forging. He started to make kitchenware because of dwindling farm work, and the kitchenware was very marketable in restaurants. However, he gave up his old business after he made iron chains for Ho Laosan's son.

One day Ho Laosan carried rusty machetes and two large piles of pig iron and asked Blacksmith Zhang to produce chains. The final product was more than two meters long and weighed 33 pounds. Blacksmith Zhang would not have done such a job if he had known that the chains would be used on Ho Laosan's son. He thought that a human being should not be chained up no matter how bad he was, and he considered that he had committed a sin. Since then he had been killing time, yet he walked swiftly and appeared to be in a rush to accomplish something urgent after consuming his daily quote of tea. His store was now full of bagged food. Every day men carried those things away for free. Sufficient food was put in the four rooms, and each of them was much larger than that of in Guangwen's house.

Later people knew that it was not for free. You should pay beforehand, for example, pay 10,000 yuan and you would get 20,000 yuan the next year, and you might withdraw the money or keep it in his bank account, and you would get 40,000 in the third year. If you were worried about that, you could carry away the food from his store worth 10,000.

Was it true? Someone had got the money. Nobody had carried all the food worth 10,000 to his own house, but he could take some. He could get 20,000 yuan the next year anyway. It was said that Blacksmith Zhang had a relative in the county and the relative had an acquaintance in the central government. Huilong Town was boiling with excitement because the people-benefit project would be much better than the lottery.

Chapter 18

Pighair Chen died when the news about Blacksmith Zhang spread. He was so lucky that he could be well looked after by the kind-hearted Chen Jiu.

Two days before he died, he yelled when he was visited by his friends and blood streamed out of his mouth and nose. Chen Jiu had a doctor examine him and the doctor said that death could set him free.

"You may leave as you wish," Chen Jiu cried, kneeling in front of the bed. "I'll go to work and get married, and your grandson will visit your graveyard."

Pighair Chen still shouted. His foster son let all his friends come here, but he kept screaming.

"Does he want to meet Shang Zhongbing?" Chen Jiu whispered.

Pighair Chen became quiet at once.

Chen Jiu realized that man wanted to see his own son before death. But it would be a difficult job to let Shang Zhongbing see him. The man lying on the bed screeched again. Chen Jiu went outside and came back after 15 minutes. Nobody knew if he had met Shang Zhongbing whose tea house was full of card players, and nobody would ask him if they had seen each other.

"I'm your biological son, dad," Chen Jiu whispered, holding his foster father's hand and kneeling in front of the bed. The man died.

People said that Chen Jiu had sacrificed his life to look after his foster father. His girlfriend waited for him for one year after she left him, but at last she could not wait anymore and got married with another man.

Everybody in the town helped Chen Jiu to hold a funeral for Pighair Chen. Some provided food and others provided free service, including Mr. Gui's kitchenware, funeral geomancers' chanting, dancers and drum beaters who had performed in my father's funeral. The leading dancer used to learn Sichuan opera in a city, but the opera troupe went bankrupt before she could learn it well. Later she made a living in the town. On the eve of Pighair Chen's funeral, she danced wearing a green see-through dress. Her name was Jiao Yan, the daughter of Pockmarked Jiao. The girl was charming although her mother was not.

After the funeral Chen Jiu went to work in another province, and people went on with their own business. Guangwen's new house in the county was being decorated and it was watched by Peiliang's incommunicative father. Guangwen was so worried about his house that he often inspected it. One day he sat in Yang Jin's car. After a moment the car was parked at the kerb. "Jiao

Yan will hitchhike," said Yang Jin. "She has business in the county."

He opened the door. As soon as Guangwen saw Jiao Yan, he remembered her and then he glanced at Yang Jin.

Chapter 19

Chunhong received calls from Chunhua, Chunying, and Swallow. They asked about the same thing: how to invest money with Blacksmith Zhang?

"How did you know that?" Chunhong retorted.

"People are talking about it," Xianhe said loudly on the phone.

Chunying got angry with Chunhong who had asked her and Chunhua to provide 10,000 yuan as gift money during our father's funeral and who had insinuated that Dayou and Qiuyue might have an affair. At last, Swallow and Dayou got married, but Qiuyue dropped out of school. Chunying considered that Qiuyue might have got better and better in her studies if Chunhong had not said those things. After our father's funeral was over, Chunying went to Guangdong and did not call Chunhong again until she heard about the investments operated by Blacksmith Zhang.

Chunhong went to Blacksmith Zhang's store for more information. His corpulent wife poured Chunhong a cup of tea but she declined it. After Blacksmith Zhang made a long speech, Chunhong had a general understanding of his business.

She told this to her husband after she got home.

"Money can bring more money, but can also bring more trouble." Guangwen said doubtfully. "You should tell your sisters to be careful."

Chunying and Swallow could understand her, but Chunhua got impatient because she needed a lot of money for Ziguo's marriage. She considered that Shanrui had left Ziguo because of poverty, and he could not have a new girlfriend with the same reason. The mother should do everything she could to make her son prosper.

Chunhua wanted to get 100,000 yuan with the investment of 50,000 yuan, but she also worried that she might lose all her money. She asked if Chunying and Swallow if they would do this.

"I've checked the information on the Internet," said Swallow. "It's like pyramid selling. The early participants will get more money and the later ones will lose all his money. What's more, how could Blacksmith Zhang have a friend or a relative in the central government?"

But Chunhua got so worried day by day that she looked gaunt.

"We can let Ziguo operate a company," said her husband.

"We only have 70,000 yuan in our bank account," she retorted, pinching his arm as hard as she could.

"We may run a cannon factory in empty houses across a ditch from neighbours. The people in Qingping Town and Huilong Town usually go to the county to buy cannons. We will make a fortune if we can sell our products in one town."

She considered that Ziguo would be able to have a girlfriend if he could be a boss.

Her husband soon called me. "I'll need your help."

I'd never helped him and he asked me to support him this time anyway.

I was excited to hear that he would operate a factory. Guangwen once complained that nobody in our family could become a boss. But I was disappointed when Fang Yun said that he would run a cannon factory.

"An explosion in a cannon factory in Henan province killed nearly 20 people several months ago," I explained. "A woman living nearby the residential area in which my house was located lost her life in a cannon explosion on the Lunar New Year's Day. She had sold cigarettes but she got cannons before the Spring Festival. However, when children were playing fireworks in the street, sparks flew into the store. Bang! An old woman saw a child's hand in her basket and she fainted.

The listener became silent.

"When one has bad luck," Fang Yun said lightly after a moment, "he can't avoid the bad result anyway."

It seemed that I gave a performance just now. I told him the truth exaggeratedly.

"Will you apply for a business license for me?" he asked.

I thought that he would borrow money from me and I was not in a good financial condition. I would prefer my relatives to borrow money from me rather than assign me to interact with people, because it would be much more complicated to deal with people. The prerogative mentioned by Tan Ruisong would hurt the one who needed assistance.

"Did you ask Guangwen?" I said.

"No. It should be handled by a county government." He knew what Guangwen could not do.

"OK. I'll do my best."

I seldom said no to my friends and relatives. I did know the upcoming trouble, but I could not refuse them. I could not slam the door. Even a stranger walked past my house, I would close the door softly after he left. That's politeness.

Chapter 20

The wind from the crevice of the door made me shudder. I felt that I was useless. A bird squealed at me but it flew away when I looked at it. I wished that I could fly like a bird. It would be confronted with more dangers than a human being would, but the latter always wanted more and more. That reminded me of an old song about a man who hankered after delicious food, beautiful women, good horses and farm land, higher official position and the throne, and longevity." I was not ambitious but I had been struggling.

I called Guangwen after I calmed down.

"A dun is much more troublesome than a debtor!" he shouted on the phone.

When I was puzzled, he continued, "Is that Chunming?" I realized that he referred to someone else just now.

"Are you busy now?" I asked.

"What's up?"

I told him the matter mentioned by Fang Yun.

"He is stupid!" Guangwen snapped. "Cannons are forbidden in the county, and soon in the town. Who will buy the cannons? Such a factory will need a lot of machines and raw materials. Where can he buy them?"

Fang Yun must have had a talk with him about it, but he failed to persuade him.

"I should mind my own business," said Guangwen.

He had never spoken like that. Perhaps he had been be let down frequently, or his relatives would not listen to him anymore.

Chapter 21

After a few days I received a call from Fang Yun.

"Ziguo and I got off in Baima city before we returned to our hometown," said Fang Yun. "We saw an advertisement on the local radio-television newspaper for free to celebrate the 25th anniversary of its publication. It was the thing we needed. The factory is located in Changsha and there is an agent in Dongxuan. I contacted the agent and he said that the whole set of the machine would be priced at 68,000 yuan and he would apply for certificates."

I told Guangwen's words to him.

"He did not want to help me!" Fang Yun snapped. "He said that the operation of the factory would be prohibited if there were insufficient licenses. He has done so many illegal things but he is still the village party secretary!"

I was surprised to hear that. When did my relatives become fretful? Fang Yun transferred 48,000 yuan to the agent's bank account.

The agent was Ho Quan. Fang Yun met him before he paid, and the latter went to Fang Yun's hometown and said the place would be very good for the factory. Ziguo, who would be the boss, signed the contract which had been prepared by Ho Quan. There was no table, so they made the plum tree as a table to write their signatures. Ziguo was Party A and Ho Quan was the representative of Party B and he took away two pictures of Ziguo's to apply for certificates. After one week Ziguo received the parts but they were rusty. Ho Quan said that they had been caught in the rain. Fang Yun skilfully assembled the parts. After he fueled the machine with diesel, it screeched and moved slowly, but soon it stopped moving.

"What has happened to the machine?" Fang Yun asked Ho Quan on the phone.

"I'll need the residual payment."

"You should repair the machine and give me the certificates."

"Wait for me."

Ho Quan did not appear after five days.

Fang Yun contacted the manufacturer of the machine according to the phone number on the contract.

"How did you buy it?" the person in charge asked.

"I've paid Ho Quan 48,000 yuan," Fang Yun replied. "And he has been dealing with the matter."

"Who is Ho Quan?"

"He is one of your agents."

"You should ask him about it."

Fang Yun had to call Ho Quan again.

"I haven't received the 20,000 yuan from you yet," replied Ho Quan. But he did not appear.

Later Fang Yun told me the matter on the phone.

"You should call him every day," I said.

"I call him nearly 20 times each day."

"Call him 100 times each day!"

"OK."

After three days, he told me that he hadn't met Ho Quan.

"Where does he live?" I asked.

"I don't know," Fang Yun replied.

"You should not give him the residual payment if he does not show up."

"He has conned me of 48,000 yuan and he will not return the money to me for the 20,000 yuan."

"You should call the police."

"I can't get my money back even though I report the case."

I knew that honest people would not call the plice to avoid trouble, unless they were driven to desperation. The honest people I was referring to were not the general populance. I never considered the general populance as a single category.

"Tell him that you'll call the police," I said.

Chapter 22

"I'll call the police, too!" Ho Quan shouted on the phone. "You haven't given me the residual payment according to the contract! I'll send you to prison!"

Later Fang Yun asked me to phone Ho Quan to threaten him.

I called Ho Quan many times but his phone had been turned off. At last Fang Yun had to go to the police station. After two days Fang Yun called me. "A middle-aged policeman took notes coldly. I'll need your help."

He hoped that I could contact the leaders in the police station, and the problem could be solved. I started to touch a cigarette and then I smoked it. Before it became ashes, I looked far away and thought about my hometown. I used to travel across the Qingxi River with my friends in Dongxuan and Baima. It was dark outside but we felt bright inside. We had a wonderful time. But now I must finish the difficult task required by Fang Yun. I had to use all my connections and chose Tan Ruisong.

"I'll need your help," I said to Ruisong on the phone.

He was surprised but calmed down after I told him the problem.

"The 48,000 yuan is very important to your brother-in-law," he said. "I have no friend in the police station. What's more, there is a serious case. Chen Shuliang has been kidnapped and the ransom is 50 million yuan. If the ransom is above 2 million, the victim will be killed even though the ransom is paid. He had a double bachelor's degree and also studied in a police academy and in an architectural college. He is a zillionaire but he treats his friends and alumni stingily."

And then he talked about all kinds of meetings. The most boring one was the classmate party, just to show off. The middle-aged participants did indecent things. Several days ago about thirty people held a classmate party in Ximencao Dam. A woman put a balloon in her buttocks and she held a telegraph pole with her hands, and a man in his forties stood behind her and thrust the balloon until it burst.

"That's too dirty!" Ruisong exclaimed. "It's much dirtier than the Fuzi Lane! But they laughed!"

I had to get back to the point. "Chen Shuliang will not pay the ransom," I said.

"He is a miser," said Ruisong. "But he had donated 10 million yuan to the county government and another 10 million yuan to the police station to save his mother. By contrast, the 48,000 yuan is too small and it's not about saving a life."

I became silent and I did not reply to Fang Yun.

Chapter 23

One day in July Yuling visited our father's graveyard. It was just an ordinary day, but she was a serious participant.

She bought a pig's head and a large bag of incense and joss paper in the town. She returned to Yanerpo and cleaned the house without any occupant for three months. She cooked the pig's head until its colour changed. She put a small quantity of salt into the pot because our father had died from a cerebral haemorrhage and should not have too much salt. The salt had been put in a white porcelain jar, and lard had also been put in the jar.

Four dogs and two cats had been kept in the courtyard since our father's funeral was over. The cats had been given by others: one was kept by Chunshan and the other by Limin. Afterwards the rats raged in Zhanhui's house, and she had to buy rat poison. However, her chickens died. Four dogs came from unknown mountains and they would make their new owners prosper: two were kept by Wang Qingguang, one by Chunshan, and one by Limin.

Later Wang Qingguang and his wife left Yanerpo and lived in their daughter's house. They had two daughters, and villagers guessed that they lived with their elder daughter to protect her. Her husband had been at large since he killed someone. She had to raise her child all by herself and she was often threatened by the relatives of her husband. As a result, the two dogs were kept by Limin. Mrs. Hou and Zheng Saner said that Limin was unwilling to keep the dogs which had been kept by Wang Qingguang. But Limin said the dogs treated Wang Qingguang's house as their own.

But Limin could not give sufficient food to the dogs. They scrambled for the pieces of fried tofu thrown by Yuling. One grey dog bit the other two dogs and ate the tofu all by itself, and they had to hide in a corner. The dogs and cats should not eat salty food because it could cause hair slip, illness and death.

Yuling continued to cook the food with moderate fire, and stopped when meat became tender. She brought rice, Chinese cabbage, and garlic sprouts from Guaizaoping. And then she cooked rice. She liked the crisp rice, but it would be served for her father-in-law, and she did not want to be discovered by others. Fengjuan came. Yuling thought the comer might be Mrs. Hou. She did not want to meet anybody. Chunshan and his wife were busy with farm work, and she would carry a bucket of manure.

"You may have a meal in my house," said Fengjuan.

"I'll need to cook in the house," Yuling replied, "otherwise it may become damp."

"I can cook for you now."

"No, thanks. I can manage it."

Fengjuan carried a bucket of excrement and left.

Yuling washed an enamel round plate, which used to be a part of her dowry, and put the cooked pig's head in the centre of the plate. A half bowl of rice soaked with soup was put nearby. She walked outside holding the plate and a red plastic bag containing incense and joss paper hanging on the two fingers of her right hand. She was followed by the dogs who were attracted by a human being rather than by the delicious food. The dogs that did not eat the fried tofu got along. Dou used to call the female dog among them White. Just before Yuling reached the graveyard, she yelled at the dogs. They stopped to sit or stand, watching her going into the bamboo forest.

She burnt the incense and then the candles to let the deceased man know that his offspring visited him, and the candles would light the way for the spirit. And she burnt the joss paper piece by piece. The paper should not be moved when it was burning, otherwise the other spirits would loot it. She did not set off firecrackers lest others should know that she visited her dead father-in-law unexpectedly.

"Dad!" she cried, kneeling. "I'm here to see you. You are a good man and you should be rewarded by King of Hell. I hope that you can use your power to protect your children and grandchildren from bad people and bad things."

And then she went back, followed by the dogs. She had no appetite now, and she threw the dishes into the henhouse. When she looked at the thin dogs, she tossed the rice at them. The animals enjoyed their food. When the grey dog tailed her, she yelled at it. She left the place alone.

Chapter 24

Any news could travel fast in the countryside. Since the industrial revolution, the spirituality of heaven and earth had been existing in rural areas. Soon villagers knew that Yuling visited her father-in-law's graveyard, and soon it was known by Chunhong.

"She should have treated our dad well when he was alive," Chunhong said irritably. "Chunshang is not a good man either!"

Yuling wished that the spirit of our dead father could protect her husband from the other woman who used to be one of the classmates of Chunshang in junior high school.

She came from a city. When she was twelve, her father was appointed as a leader to support the local development initiatives in Tibet. Her mother would stay with her father and she would let her daughter continue her studies there. When they entered Erlang Mountain, the girl had high altitude sickness at an elevation of about 2,000 metres, and she would not endure anymore when they reached their destination Ali at an elevation of above 4,500 metres. Her parents made the decision to have her aunt (wife of mother's elder brother) take care of her. The aunt had a house of three rooms in Huilong Town of Dongxuan county. She had been living alone and used one of the rooms as a tea house. The girl felt like being a forlorn wanderer on the night when her mother left her. She lived with her aunt for three years until she graduated from junior high school. After many years her aunt's house was washed away by floods.

At that time villagers' children lived in the dormitories of the school, but some students lived with their parents. Kids would buy steamed bread on the street if they did not have breakfast at home, but she bought meat-filled steamed buns. After she ate them, delicious smells lingered in her mouth and attracted her classmates. She blew towards her classmates' faces and they guffawed; but soon they felt that she made fun of them. She considered that her classmates did not have the meat-filled steamed buns, so they got annoyed. The next day she got more money from her aunt, and the situation lasted for many days. One day her aunt tailed her and knew why.

She gave steamed buns with meat stuffing to her classmates: she bought 9, gave 7 to them, and she ate two.

"Your parents have been working hard to give you sufficient money!" her aunt snapped. "And you must be thrifty!"

The girl cried because her classmates disliked her no matter how hard she tried to please them. She came from urban areas and she was treated by them as an outsider. After three years, her new classmates in the city treated them as an outsider, too, because she came from rural areas. Since then she had had a sense of insecurity.

Chapter 25

People soon knew why Yuling visited her father-in-law's graveyard: her husband had been away from home for three days. She went to Chunhong's house and cried. Chunhong still remembered that she had treated our father badly. Yuling covered her face with the towel given to her by Chunhong.

Yuling stopped crying when she heard Chunhong scold Chunshang loudly on the phone. She went into the bathroom to wash her face, the towel, and her earrings. After she put on the earrings again she went to the living room.

"I'll go home and do farm work," she said.

"You should stay in my house until Chunshang comes to see you," said Chunhong. "Let your children have meals here."

Yuling helped Chunhong to do housework. After she finished, she said, "I'll go home."

Chunhong took four pieces of large meat covered with plastic wrap from the refrigerator.

"You may give two pieces to your elder sister and keep the rest," said Chunhong.

After Yuling left, at dusk that day Chunshang went to Chunhong's house. He was scolded harshly by her. He smoked five cigarettes and then left. Later Chunhong called me and told me about the matter. We were curious to know why Chunshang had fallen in love with that woman.

Yuling's parents were like Bihua's parents who had been eager to benefit quite a lot from their daughter's marriage. Yuling's mother acted like Mrs. Hou and even matchmakers were unwilling to speak to her. Mr. Zhu, a craftsman who came from Kaiyang and made articles from bamboo strips was regarded as a gypsy. He had worked both in Guaizaoping and Yanerpo and got along with the villagers. He knew about our father's worry: his youngest son needed a wife, so he became the matchmaker, and later a wedding was held.

Yuling and Chunshang were about the same age. The most important thing was that he had a brother working in Chengdu and had a brother-in-law working in Lijiayan as a village party secretary.

"After you visit our dad's graveyard on the 100th day," Chunhong said to me, "you should have a talk with the woman who has an affair with Chunshang."

"There are millions of people in a city. How can I find her?"

"I'll get her phone number."

She asked Yuling to check Chunshang's phone, and the latter found a special name "Hey".

Chapter 26

I went to Baima the day before the 100th day after our father's funeral. I booked a room in a hotel located on the right bank of the Zhou River and in the north of Laifeng Road. I always chose a hotel in the Laifeng Road which was a national highway. I passed by the Laifeng Road when I took a train to go to university. I had never seen a city before I became an undergraduate. The hotel I stayed at was elegant, but it was close to the street and noisy. It should have been quiet. Now I was agitated and I was thinking about Fang Yun rather than Hey.

Fang Yun and Ziguo went to Wuhan. The machine was sold and the case was not accepted by the police station. Chen Shuliang's five siblings had had a grudge against the penny pincher so much so that they hid their mother in a cave in which food and water had been provided. After five days, they drove their mother to Wuhua Town and then she returned to the city by bus. The local people cursed Shen Shuliang: he was a zillionaire and he would not lose much money if he gave some to his siblings, but he would rather donate to the county government and the public security bureau.

Fang Yun frequently asked the police station when his case would be solved, but he always got a perfunctory answer. Meanwhile, I did not know what to say to him. I called him after he went to Wuhan, he soon hung up the phone. My relatives would not need to return to our hometown on the 100th day after our father's funeral, and I would not have to meet him. However, I was thinking about that when I was getting near my hometown.

The longer I worked in another city, the less I could do for my relatives. I could not return to my hometown in glory. When I was reading or writing at home in Chengdu, melodies far away reminded me of my hometown and my days there. But I could not do anything useful for it. I was not good enough to have nostalgia.

Chapter 27

I kept sitting in the hotel room until 4 p.m., and I wondered if I should meet that woman. I was fretful and hungry, so I walked on the street which looked like the new street in Huilong Town. The landform in Baima resembled that of in Chongqing full of crooked roads. I wanted to know why Chunshang had fallen in love with that woman.

I came across Baima Newspaper Office to which I had frequently been. I'd had friends there but gradually I lost contact with them. When a road which I had often passed by seemed strange to me, it was because that the people had become strangers rather than it had been changed. Everything would fade away.

A thin woman sat next to me and talked with me cheerfully in a low voice. After a moment I realized that she would let me join the church.

"I read the Bible," I said. "But I'm not a church goer."

"You should listen to God's words to understand the Bible better," she said. "And I'm telling you the details."

"You are not God."

She glared at me.

"Thank you, madam." I bowed to her and left.

I walked into a tea house and had a cup of tea. Some customers were playing cards, but that did not bother me. Later I could have a meal here.

Now I thought about a joke about "Hey" told by Chen Ya in Huilong Town. When Guangwen, Wan Ping, Chen Ya, and Zhang Dachao were still good friends, I had dinner with them one day. Chen Ya cracked a joke: "People usually go nuts when they catch adultery in the act. A woman named Flower did it in a different way. One day she went home and saw her husband having sex crazily with another woman in bed. She was surprised but soon she closed the door softly and went shopping. After she returned home again, she found everything clean and tidy. What she saw several hours ago was just an illusion. Hey! She was different from others."

When I thought of that joke, those two "Heys" still cut. I finished my meal at 6:30 p.m., and then I called the woman named Hey.

Chapter 28

I believed there were traditional, generous and merciful women such as Chunhong and Fengjuan. You could feel that they had forgiven you, accepted you and protected you, but you might not understand them. Hey was distinctive: she let you understand her but she did not care if you could feel it or not.

"Who is that speaking?" I asked on the phone.

"This is Ho Yi," she said cheerfully.

People nowadays usually wore various masks, but she was genuine.

"Are you having a relationship with Chunshang?" I asked.

"Oh, it's you, Chunming. Where are you?"

I was surprised and I could judge that they did have an affair.

"I'm in Baima," I replied.

"Let's have dinner together. It's my treat."

"I finished my dinner a moment ago with my friends. I'm in the Sandalwood Tea House nearby the newspaper office."

After twenty minutes she came and called my name. I used to get annoyed when Ruisong said that Chunshang and I looked alike. The genes mattered and we were siblings.

She was plump but did not look like a local woman.

"I had studied for 19 years from kindergarten to senior high school," she said lightly. "I had forgotten many classmates except the ones I had tried to please when I was in Huilong Town. I could not recollect Xu Chunshang until I saw the graduation photo of junior high school the other day. I felt that I had never seen him before, but one of my classmates told me that he had been sitting in the last row of the classroom and had been silent for three years. Hey!"

I had a cup of tea at once lest I should laugh. She frequently said "Hey", and that was why Chunshang had saved her name on his phone as "Hey".

She had been treated as an outcast, but Chunshang had been ignored by her, too. As a result, she felt so embarrassing that she got his phone number through all her connections. Chunshang was excited to receive her call, and she invited him to dinner because she had never given him any meat-filled steamed bun when they studied in the same classroom.

"Oh, it should be my treat," Chunshang said awkwardly.

"You should listen to me," she said.

In their conversation, she found that he would be at a loss if she treated him politely, and he would become submissive if she treated him aggressively.

"Your mother died when you were just a kid," she said. "A child who has lost his mom will always be hungry for milk just like a pup even after he grows up. The milk will control his mind in the way that the authority does. There are many people like you although their mothers are still alive. Parents don't teach their children to be independent and thoughtful, and most of the people are servile."

"Chunshang met me twice in Baima, she said to me. "We had dinner and had tea."

I asked a waiter to prepare boiled dumplings because she had not had supper. She looked charming when she laughed.

Did I need the so-called authority? It had nothing to do with beauty.

When she was eating the dumplings, I asked, "May I smoke?"

"Just do what you like," she said lightly.

I lit a cigarette.

Chapter 29

"The other day Chunshang called me to wait for him in a motel," she said. She was glad although she did not need to meet a man in a cheap motel.

"We spent three days and three nights in the motel," she added. "I got married many years ago, but now I'm a celibatarian."

"The first two nights he told me about his sad stories," she continued. "He was looked down upon by his wife and his siblings. They refused to go to his house to celebrate their father's birthday, and even his last one was held in his eldest sister's house."

And then she told the details about what happened on the day before our father's last birthday.

"He cried in my arms," she said, make gestures. "He nearly called me mother. I would say yes if he called me, but he did not."

"Did he say anything else?" I asked.

"He did not speak ill of you. From his words I could understand that he had been treated well by you. He is submissive, hey, and he needs to be treated by you in the old way. On the third night Chunshang wanted to have sex with me, but I refused. I just wanted him to hold me in his arms, and I told him not to do anything that he might repent later. And I hoped that he could call me mother."

She was lonely.

"Thank you," I said.

"Do you ask me to leave now?"

"No. But I do thank you."

"Don't worry. I won't meet him again. He is a man now. When your eldest sister called him, I heard her shouting. She was wrong."

"I apologize to you on behalf of her."

"She should not have wronged Chunshang. I think she is too stern."

"But she is kind-hearted. After our mother's death, our family might have collapsed if without her."

"I see what you mean. I have to go now."

She paid the bill and I let her be a protective host.

Chapter 30

I returned to the hotel after I sat in the tea house for 30 minutes. I received Chunhong's call as soon as I entered the elevator. She spoke in a low voice lest Hey should hear it.

"I could not meet her," I told a white lie. "She did not receive the phone call with an unknown number."

"Oh, it's futile," she said in disappointment. "Do you need Yang Jin to pick you up?"

"No. I'll stay in the hotel."

I kept thinking about Ho Yi for many hours and then Yaqiong came to my mind. After Yaqiong's son had been scalded to death for two years, I met her only once.

When Xiaolan and I were walking on the street, I came across Yaqiong. She tried to grasp Xiaolan's sleeve at the sight of her.

"I'll go shopping with my uncle," said Xiaolan. She pulled her sleeve back so hard that Yaqiong stumbled.

"Oh, you are a beautiful woman with high cheekbones," Xiaolan consoled her.

"A woman with high cheekbones brings ill luck into her family," an elderly woman nearby a store argued. "Yaqiong's son had died because of her, and her husband will never return home. The spirit without a graveyard in its hometown can't bring good life to its offspring."

"But pop stars love high cheekbones," Xiaolan retorted.

"Those women do not love their family!"

Yaqiong was smiling and grasped Xiaolan's sleeve again, the latter flung her hand off her sleeve immediately. Suddenly the elderly woman's grandson ran out of the room. Before Yaqiong hugged the boy, the elder woman yelled and she flinched. But soon she embraced the boy, kissed him on the forehead, and then she fled. The grandma cursed her and hurled her walking stick at her. Yaqiong heard the sound and turned around, looking happy.

I considered whether Ho Yi resembled Yaqiong in some way.

The connection between human beings would become a part of our life although it might be inexplicable. That reminded me of the nurse Ms. Cheng during our father's hospitalization. She had helped me quite a lot, which did not make me feel remorseful during our father's last hours. Chunhong often told others that I was a filial son, but I knew that it was Ms. Cheng who had enabled me to have the good reputation. Later I could not find the nurse. Did I repent? I should regard her as the Saviour. Was Ho Yi the Saviour of Chunshang? Did he really "grow up"?

Chapter 31

I had not got up when Yang Jin called me. It was 7 a.m., and he was waiting for me outside the hotel. Yang Jin carried my bag as soon as he saw me, and then Jiao Yan came out of the car. Chunhong had told me that Jiao Yan should not have been invited for our father's funeral because she was a home wrecker. When I looked at Jiao Yan, I realized that she must have spent the night with Yang Jin in the hotel in which I stayed, which made me uncomfortable.

Jiao Yan let me sit in the front passenger seat which was regarded as an important position by villagers either because of being ordered by a senior leader or of protecting the leader from bullets. But I would rather let Jiao Yan sit beside Yang Jin.

"She should sit in the back seat," said Yang Jin. He did not mention the interesting subjects such as Guangwen, Huigoer, or Ho Laosan's son, perhaps he was too tired last night. The trip to Huilong Town was silent.

Jiao Yan got off the car when we heard chains clang, but the shouts weakened. I got off halfway although Yang Jin wanted to drive me to the riverside road.

The deserted oil-pressing mill was still there but the chained old dog had been gone, which made me less worried. People did not need to care about how things disappeared. They should recognize and discard difficult problems in their life rather than solve them, and they would idle away their whole life when there was no difficult problem. However, the chained man could not even live like a dog.

Chunhong was waiting for me to have breakfast. Her husband and son had finished their meal. Li Zhi went to play snooker and his wife sent their child to school.

"Guangwen contacts another driver to take us to Yanerpo," said Chunhong. "Yang Jin's car can't provide sufficient space for so many people. By the way, what did you say to Hey?"

I fudged the answer.

"Was Jiao Yan in Yang Jin's car?"

I smiled. She knew that it was yes.

Last night Chunhong called me. She went to Huang Ermei's store and the latter sent goods to an elderly crippled woman.

"You'll pick up Chunming tomorrow morning," said Chunhong.

"I'll go at once," Yang Jin said excitedly, stripped to the waist. "You may tell this to my wife once she returns."

He took a shirt and got on the car. After ten minutes Huang Ermei returned and had a chat with Chunhong, and then the latter went home.

When Chunhong was watching TV, she received a call from Huang Ermei.

"Yang Jin has a quarrel with another driver because of scratches," said Huang Ermei. "He will pick up Chunming tomorrow."

"Is he all right?" asked Chunhong. "Tomorrow is the 100th day to visit my dad's graveyard."

"She must know that her husband was not telling the truth at that time," Chunhong said to me.

I was quiet because I did not know what to say.

Chapter 32

The sacrificial offerings were ready. At 10 a.m., Chunshan asked us on the phone to buy fish for our lunch. After we bought the fish, Chunhong said that she forgot to take a bag of pesticide which was asked by Zhanhui to give her husband. We should go at once, but Yuling insisted that our dad loved cooked fish. When they were talking loudly, I looked around.

The courtyard was forlorn. One of the dogs or cats perhaps had gone to the mountains for more food, and the sycamore tree had died because of excessive firecrackers during our father's funeral. On the day of his burial, the morning sunshine on its leaves became its last charm. Now only a dark tree stump was left. More things had disappeared in my hometown.

Yuling put two large pieces of fish into a bowl. Meat, incense, fish tallow, and joss paper were placed in front of the graveyard when Chunshu was chanting. The seller of hell bank notes said that the deceased man in the nether world would become a zillionaire if joss paper of large denominations could be burnt for him.

"Our dad will become much richer than Chen Shuliang after piles of paper are burnt," said Chunshan.

After Chen Shuliang's mother was kidnapped, one villager said to Chunshan and Chunshu, "Chen Shuliang is a miser! But your relatives Guangwen and Chunming are generous."

"I'm not a rich man," Guangwen retorted. It seemed that it would be a sin if he was a miser.

"The ghost money will be burnt for the deceased man," Chunshu chanted, holding three sticks of incense. "And he will become wealthy in another world."

Before the firecrackers were set off, Chunshu let us kowtow, but he would not kowtow. He had been engaged in funeral business for so many years, and he was asked by Chunhong to chant.

My female relatives kowtowed and then they laughed.

"Three or four kowtows?" Xiaolan asked her father.

"Don't be swayed by Xu Xing!" Chunhong snapped.

"In the past people dwelling near the Qingxi River made three kowtows for a dead man and four for a living one," Chunshu explained. "But now three kowtows for a living man and four for a dead one. That's wrong."

Xiaolan made three kowtows and Qingmei four.

"You should follow the rule!" cried Chunhong.

"You should protect Chunshang from bad things!" Yuling said loudly, kneeling.

We became quiet.

Chunshang was moving his lips.

"Anybody to kowtow?" Chunshu asked impatiently.

We kowtowed at once and then Chunshu set off firecrackers.

When smoke was flying in the bamboo forest, we went to Chunshan's house. The ceremony of the 100th day after our father's funeral was ended. We would not think about our father except on anniversaries.

Chapter 33

In early October Swallow called Chunhong.

"Did you join the ceremony of the 100th day after my grandpa's funeral?" asked Swallow.

"You should have called us much earlier," replied Chunhong.

Chunhong heard Swallow sobbing before she hung up the phone. The younger relatives neither called their parents nor returned for the ceremony, and they were busy.

"What has happened?" Chunhong asked anxiously.

"Dayou has been having an affair with Qiuyue," said Swallow.

One day she read a message sent by Qiuyue in Dayou's phone: "I'll always remember the day when I became a woman. That was on June 4."

That day was the 22nd day of the fourth lunar month, also the burial of her grandpa.

Chapter 34

We remembered that day, too. We had breakfast after we returned from the graveyard. Chunhua, Chunying, and my wife went to Chunhong's house with Qingmei. Guangwen and other brothers-in-law left to avoid more quarrels. After lunch Chunhong and I went to the town.

"Qingmei is not at home," Chunhong said. "Where is she?"

"She goes to her mother's house," replied Chunhua. "And she will pick up Dou."

When Guangwen came out of the bathroom, his wife asked, "Why are you still at home?"

He did not answer that question. Instead, he continued to talk about the funeral: Chunshu did a good job in chanting, Chunshan made good preparations, but Chunshang did not do anything useful.

After a moment Chunhong called Lily. After lunch Yang Jin drove Lily and Peiliang to the railway station.

"Did you get back the money you'd lent?" asked Guangwen.

"I did not know how to properly talk about it with my siblings," his wife answered.

"They won't repay us."

The tardy repayers had let Chunhong down.

"The more money they have, the more unwilling they are to repay," said her husband. "Even Chen Shuliang is a miser."

Swallow came.

"Where is Sixi?" asked Chunhong.

"He left by car-pooling," replied Swallow.

"He must have cadged money from your parents again, and they should have stopped giving him any money. Where is Dayou?"

"He and I visited Xiaolan and then he called his mom, but he said that he would go to the county and have his phone repaired because of a low sound."

Guangwen lit a cigarette and then gave me one. "There are phone repair shops in the town," he said.

"Dayou said that his phone speaker had broken down," Swallow explained, "and the shops in the town could not provide the accessories."

"Where is Qiuyue?" he asked, glaring at Chunying.

"She is shopping," replied Chunying.

"But her shopping is too long!" he shouted. "Even the tardy Uncle Chenggui can return early!"

After Huatian went to school in Qingping by boat, Qiuyue told her parents that she was so tired that she would take a rest and return the next day. She went to the market and did not have lunch. Her mother called her, and she told her that she was meeting one of her friends in a restaurant.

"I saw Qiuyue carpool," Guangwen argued. "But I know that she has a carsickness." At that time he gave cartons of cigarettes to senior leaders to express his gratitude to them who had given wreaths to his father-in-law. At 10 a.m. that day, he was in Yang Jin's store and asked Huang Ermei about the things bought by his brothers-in-law on account, and he came across Qiuyue.

"Qiuyue was neither in Huilong Town nor in Qingping Town!" Guangwen said loudly.

Swallow blushed. Dayou left at 10 a.m. and he declined her company and would let her have a good rest at home. A car-pooling driver was waiting for the last passenger and Dayou got in the car. Barber Sun's store was far away from Yang Jin's store.

Chunying called her daughter, but her phone had been turned off. Swallow went outside after her call to Dayou was not answered.

"Where are you, Xianhe?" Chunying asked on the phone, changing her shoes.

"What's he doing?" asked Chunhua.

"He is playing mahjong with Hongquan, Bihua, and Fang Yun in Hongquan's house."

Chunhua went outside at once because she got angry as soon as she heard that her husband was playing mahjong – he was always a loser.

"Dayou and Qiuyue must have spent the night in a hotel room in the county," said Guangwen, closing the door.

"Watch your tongue!" Chunhong snarled.

Guangwen lit a cigarette and gave me one. Chunhong shouted angrily and sadly while her husband looked like a poor man. He had been respected by the villagers but he did not know that his wife had told his affair with the other woman to me and my wife.

"Qingfang's husband would not have died if you had not appeared," Chunhong yelled. "After that she lived with a bad man and became a victim of domestic violence, and she hanged herself one day."

Now my wife and I knew who was Qingfang.

Chapter 35

"I'll call Qiuyue," I said, trying to avoid a quarrel between Chunhong and her husband.

"It'll be useless!" Chunhong snarled. "And you should not have pampered Qiuyue, Chunming!"

"How many times has Chunming met her?" Chunhong argued.

"She has let me down," Chunhong said sadly after a moment of silence. "I planned to introduce her to Li Chengzhong, one of my adopted sons. He told me that he would choose her as his girlfriend after she grew up. I thought that she would be a lucky girl if she could marry him. He is a handsome young man Who will secure a promising career upon graduating from the military academy. I've seen through her and it's a good thing that she did not have a relationship with Chengzhong. She slept with Dayou, the husband of her cousin, on the day of her grandpa's funeral. Shame on her!"

"I've found her out," said Guangwen.

"I've insinuated it to Chunying and her husband," said Chunhong.

"Did you persuade Qiuyue?" Guangwen asked me.

I did not believe that Qiuyue had slept with Dayou. I called her but her phone had been turned off. In the era of phones, it would be like falling into an abyss if you could not reach someone. I wanted to shirk the responsibility and I tried to keep myself far away from the bad thing which was going on. It would not have happened if I had allowed her to depart Dayou by various means this morning.

"You should not have acted like a coward, Chunming!" Guangwen said angrily.

That reminded me of what Chunshu had said: cowardice was worse than violence.

"Parents should educate their children well," Chunhong argued. "Xianhe said that he would rather let her daughter have a better-off life, but a girl would want more and more. Qiuyue should not have watched men seductively, and Swallow should not have been such a fool. Dayou is a dirty man! People from Cotton Infertility are indecent!"

That reminded her of Lianwazi's mother. The two women used to have bad quarrels, and Chunhong could not gain an advantage. As a result, she always remembered that.

Chapter 36

Guangwen changed his shoes.

"Where are you going?" his wife asked. "Chunming and Li Jing will leave tomorrow. And you should accompany them. When parents are alive, their children can have a home; after they leave the world, their children will find their way."

"You are and will always be with us," said Li Jing.

Guangwen hesitated when he was standing at the doorway.

"We'll go out, too," said Li Jing.

"And I'll return soon," said Guangwen.

Li Jing would let Chunhong join us, but she did not hear what she was talking about. I pulled my wife's sleeve and we went outside.

Chunhong had to be alone at home and was at a loss. Whom should she call? Her daughter and son-in-law were sitting in the train; her son was either fishing or playing tennis; and her siblings were busy with their own business. It was not noisy in the street because it was not the market day. Everything was going on as usual even though a man from Yanerpo had died. My wife and I were walking shoulder to shoulder silently. But the silence was unbearable, and everything would rot in it. It was hot outside. Li Jing would rather stay indoors, but she would not let Guangwen feel awkward if he was forced to stay by his wife.

We saw Guangwen sitting in Yang Jin's store. Yang Jin might be on the way home or would go somewhere else. Huang Ermei in a yellow dress appeared in the street and then returned to the room.

"We won't go there," said Li Jing.

My wife and I were unwilling to greet her. The world would become better or worse if people did not greet each other. We chose to go back. But soon Chen Ya in a hardware store greeted us. He would not have said hello to us if we had not turned around suddenly. He had small talk with me although he looked awkward. He did not attend my father's funeral, Guangwen's former buddies did not, either. Chen Ya pretended that he did not know about the funeral, so I talked with him perfunctorily and declined his invitation to dinner. And then my wife and I returned to the riverside road.

We sat along a bank. I did not want to face Chunhong's loneliness, just like my unwillingness to be with my father alone. Whenever I went to my brother's house, I did not want to be lonely, either. My wife would leave and have to look after her mother, and soon our son would take the college entrance examination. I thought that Chunhong was forlorn and needed solace. But how could I console her even though I might extend my stay in her house?

Chapter 37

Dayou returned to Swallow's house in the evening.

"Where is Qiuyue?" Chunhong asked on the phone.

"I did not see her," replied Dayou.

"They are not together!" Chunying snapped after a whole afternoon of silence.

Xianhe called Qiuyue but she did not answer it. It was much more serious than her being with Dayou.

"We should call the police," said Xianhe.

"Let Dayou answer the phone, Swallow," said Chunhong. "Did you meet Qiuyue, Dayou? She has not appeared and we'll call the police."

"I did not see her," he replied.

"Call the police now, Xianhe," Chunhong ordered. She was unwilling to do so because it would be known by everybody and Qiuyue would bring shame on the family and become a laughing stock.

Soon Qiuyue came.

Qiuyue silently changed her shoes and looked grim. Chunying and her husband did not speak, so Chunhong said to Qingmei, "You'd better persuade Qiuyue."

After a moment she came back. "I've told her about it," said Qingmei, "and she said that she knew what she should do."

What we had been worried about became true.

Chapter 38

"I'll divorce Dayou soon," said Swallow.

"You should not divorce soon after you remarry!" Chunhong yelled.

"But Qiuyue is waiting for Dayou in Anhui. He will elope with her."

Swallow sent Chunhong the messages between Dayou and Qiuyue. Chunhong was shocked when she read them.

"It's so good to have bodies." – sent by Qiuyue.

"Guess which part of your body I love most?" – sent by Dayou.

Chunhong considered that they did not have anything except bodies.

She sent all the messages to Chunying. Later I received a call from Chunying.

"How dare Dayou do such a dirty thing to my daughter?" she cried madly. "She is just 16!"

Xianhe cried, too. He would go to Anhui and kill Dayou.

After Xianhe found her daughter in Anhui, he asked her to quit her job and go to Guangdong with him.

"You did not care for me when I was a child," she argued. "And I don't need your care after I grow up!"

She did not give a glass of water to her father and even tried to drive him away. She could live without her parents, but she could not live if without Dayou. But now her calls to Dayou were not answered because his phone had been turned off.

Chapter 39

Meanwhile, Dayou and Swallow returned to Chunhong's house in Huilong Town. Dayou knelt as soon as he saw Chunhong.

"It's useless," she said to him coldly.

"Dayou is kneeling in the living room," she said to her husband on the phone. He hung up the phone impatiently.

At night she showed the messages to her husband, but he threw her phone on the sofa.

"I'm not interested in the family affairs of your sisters!" he said in an annoyed tone of voice.

She had only accepted Guangli's kowtows, but she was angry about Dayou's sin which was commonplace in men. Guangwen would solve the problem anyway just like he solved the problems in the village although he got irritated at first. He was angry with Swallow who should have taken his advice. Later Chunhong saw Swallow alone in the living room. Dayou went to Chunshu's house but the owner and his wife had gone to Yanerpo; Dayou went to Guaizaoping, but Chunshang and his wife had gone to another province for work.

Chunshang was unwilling to leave after the 100th day of our father's funeral.

"When will you go to work?" Yuling snapped. "You have been tardy with various excuses! Are you still waiting for that woman?"

Ho Yi had changed her phone number and Chunshang, holding a poker, yelled at Yuling although his mother-in-law was still there.

"Are you going to beat me for that woman?" Yuling shouted. "You must look after me if I become a disabled woman, and you can stay with her if I die!"

Chunshang threw the poker into the fireplace in a sulk.

"Oh, it stops," his mother-in-law said at the doorway. Yuling closed the door at once.

Later Chunhong told me that Chunshang and Yuling became a sweet couple and went to work in another province. Chunhua and Chunying refused to help Chunshang to find a job because they did not think that Chunshang and his wife were good enough for the job. Chunshang had to call Stone who was operating a construction project in Henan province. Stone let him join his work team reluctantly.

Dayou went to Yanerpo and entered Chunshu's house. Chunshu was shocked to see Dayou kneeling. The pigwash wetted his knees. Chunshu recognized Dayou and worried what had happened to Chunshan and his wife who were picking up pine nuts for selling.

"I was wrong," Dayou said sadly.

Chunshu and his wife did not know that Dayou was still having an affair with Qiuyue. The family members usually did not tell Chunshu and his wife about the bad things happened among the sisters because they could not get any sympathy from them.

"What's wrong?" Chunshu asked.

Dayou told him everything.

"Mrs. Hou will tell this to everybody," said Zhuqing. "I'll go to find your parents."

Chapter 40

Chunshan and Fengjuan came back after several hours. Dayou carried Fengjuan's basket, entered the room and then knelt down. Chunshan went to make fire and his wife tried to support Dayou to stand up.

"You are a man and you should not kneel," said Chunshan.

"It's my fault," Dayou said sadly.

"Your kowtows can't turn your wrong deed into a good one," said Chunshan.

"You should kowtow to Qiuyue's mother," said Fengjuan.

"She is far away now," Dayou replied.

"Does Qiuyue know this?"

"No. But I will say goodbye to her."

Fengjuan realized how Sixi had deceived so many girls.

"I'll invite more people over to my house, if you don't rise to your feet now." said Chunshan.

When he heard Mrs. Hou talking, he quickly supported Dayou to stand up.

"When did you come back?" Mrs. Hou asked Dayou. "Where is Swallow?"

"She is in the town," replied Dayou, trying to keep calm.

"Is she pregnant?"

"No. She is busy."

"My husband hasn't shat for a week. I'll dig sweet potatoes and cook food for him."

Dayou left after he had supper with Swallow's parents.

Chapter 41

Xiaolan danced nearby the lotus pond and then went to Chunhong's house. When Chunhong was speaking to me on the phone, she pointed at a glass of water and let Xiaolan pass it to her. Meanwhile, Swallow was washing the dishes.

"Swallow will divorce anyway," Chunhong said to me. "That's not a good thing for a woman."

I felt too sad to say anything. A poet might be inspired by sorrow, but what else could he do?

Chunhong could not get any suggestion from me and her husband did not allow her or Swallow to talk about it during supper. Li Zhi was not at home, Qingmei and her daughter had supper in her mother's house. Before Chunhong could say something, Guangwen went outside.

Chunhong received a call from Chunying while Swallow and Xiaolan were sitting on a sofa.

"Dayou implored me to forgive him," said Swallow. But she did not want to be heartbroken again and again.

She mentioned Chunshang's father-in-law. He had been diagnosed with alcoholic hepatitis before he got liver cancer. He heard that a kind of herbal medicine could cure it, so he bought the medicine and had it every day. He began to drink again after his pain was gone. His wife yelled at him but could not stop him from drinking. At last he got cancer and died, and his wife did not cry for him at all.

"I've given him a chance to repent," Swallow added. "But he has let me down again and again. I won't feel sad if he dies."

Swallow received a call from her father and he told her that Dayou had knelt before him. She hung up the phone.

"He had loved Qiuyue crazily before I found him out," she explained to Xiaolan. "But he knelt to my parents and relatives after it was discovered. He is a bastard. He told me that Qiuyue was not a virgin and she had lied to him. He should not have seduced my cousin!"

Those things were remembered by Xiaolan. Afterwards Qiuyue sent messages with rude words to Swallow, but she turned silent after Xiaolan sent her Dayou's words and video of his kowtows. Qiuyue's parents took her to Guangdong at last.

Chapter 42

Xiaolan recorded the video when Dayou was kneeling towards Guangwen. Dayou knew that Guangwen and I would be the key to solving the matter. But I was not in the town at that time. He kept waiting for Guangwen in his house until 11 p.m. He knelt down when Guangwen changed his shoes. Meanwhile, Xiaolan recorded the video curiously.

Guangwen ignored Dayou.

"Cook a bowl of ginger soup for me to avoid a cold," Guangwen said to his wife.

She took off his coat and found it wet. "What did you do?"

He did not reply.

He went to see Qian Wen. Before supper, he came across Qian Wen in the street and the latter shuddered at the sight of the former.

"Why are you shivering?" asked Guangwen.

"I'll repay next month," Qian Wen replied in a trembling voice.

"I can trust you this time," said Guangwen, smoking.

It was still hot but Qian Wen was wearing long trousers and walking with a limp.

"I'll meet you tonight," Guangwen added.

"I was wrong," said Dayou, moving closer to Guangwen with his knees.

"You are a rapist," said Guangwen. "Qiuyue is still a teenager although she asked you to spend one night with her in a hotel room. And you should be sent to prison in Dalugou."

The prisoners in Dalugou would have to dig coal and Dalugou was a notorious name in the areas around the Qingxi River.

"The messages between you and Qiuyue will be sent to the police station," said Guangwen, looking at the shuddering Dayou with scorn. "And Chunming will write an indictment."

Dayou cried.

We did not call the police and Dayou had helped us quite a lot during our father's funeral.

"Qiuyue was wrong, too," said Chunhong. She hated Dayou but she would rather protect Qiuyue from being criticized. What was more, she persuaded Swallow not to divorce. However, Swallow was determined to divorce Dayou, just like she used to be determined to marry him.

The house bought by Swallow and Dayou was owned by Swallow alone, but she needed to repay 20,000 yuan to his parents. She did not want the money which was earned by Dayou's mother during her stay in the house.

Dayou did not care about his parents nor his son after he divorced. After many months, people said that he went to Qingdao, Shandong. His younger female cousin went to work in Qingdao when she was a teenager and met a middle-aged labour contractor. The contractor divorced his wife and married her. When Dayou met her, she had a five-year-old daughter and operated two supermarkets. She took away all the money and went to Tibet with Dayou. After one month she came back like a loser and her husband vomited blood.

When those things were known in Huilong Town, Chunhong sighed, "Dayou can't change himself."

However, Dayou's mother had been living in Swallow's house. The woman acted madly when Swallow asked her to leave, and she cried in the street that her money had been stolen by Swallow. The latter had to sue the woman but the lawyer said that she must find Dayou who had conned his cousin of a lot of money, bought a car, and run over and killed a man and escaped. Both his license plate number and identity card were fake, and he had been at large.

Chapter 43

"Do not offend a base person," said Tan Ruisong.

Two years after Swallow's divorce, I met Single Braid and Ruisong in Chengdu, and we talked about Dongxuan.

Single Braid lived on the top floor and built one more floor for tenants, and he could earn 8,000 yuan each year. Bijia Mountain had become a part of the county and the submersible bridge would be dismantled. For better transportation and sightseeing, Mr. Zhang, the secretary of the County Committee, adopted the experience of the bamboo cable bridge across the Minjiang River, and invited engineers to design a similar bridge. The county was getting larger and larger and landlords were eager for more and more money. However, Mr. Zhang asked all the illegal buildings to be demolished.

Mr. Zhang had been working in Dongxuan for three years and he would rather stay here and build a well for the locals. When he took the college entrance examination, the title of the Chinese composition was *Dig A Well*.

His essay was included into *Excellent Selection of Writings for National College Entrance Examinations*. It said that a leopard would focus on its target until it could catch it. Through field researches and experts' argumentation, the natural gas discovered in Huilong Town and Mafu Ridge could be nationally owned rather than be locally owned by Dongxuan.

But Mr. Zhang often focused on environment protection and would create local tourism. The pit would not have existed if his predecessors had not set up upscale buildings. What was more, Mr. Zhang would put into practice and demolish illegal buildings. As a result, Single Braid would lose nearly 10,000 yuan each year.

Single Braid had spent a lot of money on exploration of cultural relics. He used ropes and entered a cave and found six sarcophaguses. He took pictures and wrote reports and submitted them, but his efforts became futile for the sixth time. All of us had trouble. I talked about Swallow's house.

"A base person will bring you endless trouble if you offend him," said Tan Ruisong. "But he can sharpen himself through the trouble, just like Chunshang. You will find the meaning of life when you have to deal with others who may be your enemies. My brother deals with leaders and he will make a fortune even though he may not become a billionaire."

He gave us the famous cigarettes he had received from his brother.

"Your brother has done a very good job," said Single Braid.

"There are few statesmen and entrepreneurs," said Ruisong, smoking, "and most of the people are calculating. And they can do everything when they have power and money, which is the highest standard of the society."

"You want to become foolish," said Single Braid. "But you are smarter than us."

"It is much more difficult to make a smart man become a fool than make a fool smarter," said Ruisong. "Wear a mask in the complicated world. Oh, let's change the subject. By the way, how is Guangwen, Chunming?"

"He remains the same," I replied.

After our father had passed away for one year, he called me five times within three minutes on July 22 and talked about the total solar eclipse. On the whole he called me less and less.

Three months ago, Chunhong told me that Mr. Li was promoted to secretary of the party committee in Wuhua Town, and Mr. Han was promoted to town mayor. Guangwen invited them to dinner. After he returned home, he slept on a sofa but fell to the floor at midnight. Qingmei and Dou stayed in his house. Dou heard it before she went to the bathroom. She rushed to support him to stand up but she was just a child. He yelled but his wife, his son, his daughter-in-law, his daughter and his son-in-law could not console him; he had sacrificed for his family, but only his granddaughter cared for him.

"That night windows were closed because it was windy," said Chunhong. "Guangwen would have become a laughing stock if his words had been heard by others!"

"What happened next?" I asked.

"He became shy and laughed when I mentioned this the next morning."

Alcohol made Guangwen speak the truth. He had done quite a lot but he could not be promoted; by contrast, others could. Guangwen was dependent upon me and considered that I could have helped him because I worked in Chengdu and I should have provided better connections and resources for him. Once dependency has taken root, it is not easily dispelled.

Chapter 44

"Too many leaders in Dongxuan have been removed from office," Ruisong explained. "And more will be sent to prison. My brother has better connections, so he is safe now. What's your brother-in-law's name?"

"Li Guangwen," I replied.

"I asked my brother about the village leaders who had been chosen, and Li Guangwen was not one of them. That's not a good thing."

I avoided the subject and Single Braid was not interested in it. When Ruisong was having tea, Single Braid asked, "Do you know about the progress of the local tourism?"

"Mr. Zhang says that the extraordinary Baili Canyon should be taken as the crucial scenic spot," said Ruisong. "Giant salamanders live in rivers with good water quality, which means ecological environment is very important. Drifting channels will be built but they'll be far away from the town. A special road with fast transportation can solve it."

Single Braid wanted to know about the cultural conception. Mr. Zhang, the secretary of the County Committee, said that a scenic area must have cultural significance, and he would create such an area for the people in Dongxuan. Therefore, Mr. Zhang divided culture into explicit culture and implicit culture. A temple was a part of the explicit culture while myths and legends belonged to the implicit culture.

He preferred the implicit culture. There were temples in Dongxuan but they were not as famous as the Shaolin Temple. There were two eminent men in local history: Wang Chuan and Luo Siju. Wang Chuan was assigned as a commissioner after the founding of the People's Republic of China, but he was sent to prison during the Cultural Revolution and died in it. Luo Siju, a man from Laojun Mountain, had been assigned as the provincial commander-in-chief and the prince's tutor, and he had been chosen to meet the Emperor and also had suppressed the uprising of White Lotus Society. On the whole, the culture in Dongxuan was not as good as that of in the county in which Mr. Zhang had served. But there was Banese culture on which buildings were created locally, such as the Banese Plaza and the bronze sword. Mr. Zhang knew a man named Zhou Xuan who had published papers on the Banese culture. Zhou Xuan was Single Braid.

After Single Braid was standing awkwardly in Mr. Zhang's office for a long moment, Mr. Zhang asked him to sit down. Mr. Zhang talked with his honoured guest on the Banese culture for two hours.

"You may study more on it," he said to Single Braid.

Single Braid called Ruisong excitedly.

"Success is like pregnancy," said Ruisong.

Ba Valley and Qianfeng Ridge were on the list, too. The Ba Valley was an inaccessible place but the Qianfeng Ridge had cultural relics and was one of the three extraordinary geographical locations; the other two were Shennongjia and Zhangjiajie. At last, however, Baili Canyon was chosen. Before that, more than ten experts from other cities or provinces were invited and their field researches lasted for more than 15 days, but Single Braid was not invited.

Chapter 45

"Mr. Zhang asked you to study more," said Ruisong. "His true meaning was that your researches were useless."

Single Braid tried to laugh to cover up his embarrassment.

"There is farm land in the Qianfeng Ridge," Ruisong explained. "The Ba Valley provides natural gas and there is an industrial park to be built in the Boar Ridge."

"The culture is for industrial and agricultural production," said Single Braid.

"The world is full of illusions and the fake may become the fact. Your researches should be used for the internal mechanism, otherwise they will become useless. Love and prostitution are alike: for survival."

"The world you mention is lifeless."

"You should be satisfied. The senior leaders invited you to take pictures in Baili Canyon for publicity."

Women and landscape, such pictures were the best. But the women should not be the pop stars because nobody could afford the appearance money. Ordinary women were the choice. Naked pictures should not be taken, and daughters of his friends should not be taken as the models, either. Single Braid had to visit women household after household, but he was laughed at as an impotent man. At last he had to choose two girls in a night club.

He developed the photos in Chongqing and framed them and sent one to Mr. Zhang.

"That's a wonderful picture," said Ruisong. "Good landscape with charming girls in sunset. Do you have one, Chunming?"

"No," I replied.

"It should have been published in the illustrated magazine. Single Braid paid 3,000 yuan to hire the two girls including meals and transportation, and he should have got more remuneration."

"That's an advertisement," said Single Braid.

"You are stubborn. What if Mr. Zhang knows that you'd hired two girls in a club? You tried to please him with two hookers although you dislike my cigarettes."

"They are beautiful women anyway," Single Braid argued, blushing.

"You are a quick learner. Hookers and women must serve the internal mechanism. I'd rather be a prostitute!"

The guests in another table looked at him and then laughed.

Chapter 46

I did not think too much of Ruisong's words at that time. But one day I realized their meaning when I was sitting in the meeting room of Grandeur Hotel, a five-star hotel located in Beijing Road, Chengdu. A live-action drama or a stage show would be held in the scenic area. Due to geological limitations in Baili Canyon, a theatre would be built and a drama on Banese culture would be shown. Famous directors were invited from Beijing and the team members visited Dongxuan for three days. Experts and professionals talked about the script in the Grandeur Hotel.

I was surprised to see that I was one of the experts. Five days ago I received an email of the script, and I felt uncomfortable as soon as I read the title *Dream Back to the State of Ba*. *Dream Back to Tang Dynasty* was very popular, but what would be the content of *Dream Back to the State of Ba*? Wars, migration, or destruction? Even the love story was just men and women running nearby a river. Awe in the Snake Banese and the Tiger Banese could not be shown. The bronze sword discovered in Huilong Town meant that the Banese used to live in the areas around the Qingxi River. The king in the play wearing a crown looked like cheap stage props. Actors standing on the bamboo stood for the battle fought in the river; and the king's marriage was held in a temple and his courtiers offered jade ware. In fact, the Banese worshipped mountains and forests and the best gifts were the prey. I wrote my suggestions to make contributions to my hometown.

Mr. Jiang, Director of Propaganda Department in Dongxuan, greeted me and he was one of the experts. We shook hands. Before I stepped into an elevator, he rushed to stop me.

"Mr. Zhang is satisfied with the script," he whispered. "And he will not need any suggestion."

My suggestions became useless. Mr. Jiang rushed to greet the President of the Historical Society of Sichuan Province who had deeply studied the

Banese culture and who had made a field research on the bronze sword discovered in Huilong Town. During the 2.5 hours of discussion, everybody approved of the script and the team concerning stage art, music, Banese culture, and high technology. Ruisong's words came to my mind.

Chapter 47

I was in a quagmire. We were like bloodsuckers and we would still need the rotten things in our life. I remembered when Ruisong came back from the south, he cursed and slapped himself and would atone for what he had done to his wife in the rest of his life. After he and his wife had made peace for one year, I saw him look pale. Later he told me what had happened.

The woman who had seduced him hoped that he could return to the south after she heard that he was getting better. She kept bothering him so much so that he avoided her crazy messages and calls. Gradually she stopped pestering him, but he felt empty – he had been a leech upon the negative side of life.

We were the same. We were unwilling to lose something in our life even though it might be bad.

"Craziness is loneliness," said Ruisong. "Human beings either love nobody or love someone madly. There is loneliness."

Chapter 48

After the discussion was over, I had a dream that night: I was sleeping under a straw shed with a leaky roof. I was soaked with the rainwater and it was pouring. I held a broom but I saw Chunying come out of the muddy ground.

"When did you come back?" I asked. "You should go to the room."

"You are in the muddy ground, too," she said.

I turned around and saw nothing. The next morning I received a call from her.

Chunhong and I asked Chunying to educate Qiuyue: stop her affair with Dayou and stop doing stupid things, but Chunying thought that we were wrong; what was more, she cursed and threatened Swallow. Since I could not help Fang Yun, Chunhua had seldom contacted me, and Chunying seldom called me. I did not want to meddle in my family affairs anymore. When our father was alive, our family was like a honeycomb; after he passed away, it produced no honey but brought dangers.

Chunying talked with me about Qiuyue on the phone. Xianhe thought that Qiuyue would get better, but she acted like a lifeless girl. Chunying considered that her daughter should have a boyfriend who came from a remote place because her reputation in her hometown had been ruined.

"A matchmaker introduced a man named Yi Kaimeng to my daughter," said Chunying. "He worked as a clerk in the factory operated by his father. A local man in Guangdong is unwilling to marry a girl from another province. But Yi Kaimeng was attracted by such an enticing girl as Qiuyue. They fell in love soon and she lived in his house. Now she is seven months pregnant."

I was sad when I heard that, but I was shocked by the following words.

"Yi Kaimeng refused to marry Qiuyue," she added. "My husband and I gave 60,000 yuan to Qiuyue to buy clothes and food for the baby. But her parents-in-law asked Qiuyue to give the money to them. We did not know the local custom in Guangdong, but we supported our daughter. To our disappointment, Yi Kaimeng was rude and irresponsible. Now Qiuyue is living with us. After the baby is born, we'll give it to Yi Kaimeng and keep ourselves far away from him and his parents."

"Did you tell this to Chunhong?" I asked.

"No. They are rich and they can't understand us."

"You'd better follow the local custom and you should care for the baby."

But that was not what Chunying wanted to hear. She soon hung up the phone and she might consider that I and Chunhong were the same: the rich who would not sympathize with the poor.

Chapter 49

I was writing a poem before I received the call from Chunying. I planned to console her with the verses, but I realized that would be useless. Did money outweigh kinship? The baby in Qiuyue's belly would become a motherless child, which would be the baby's fate. I lost my mother when I was a child, and the fear made me call Chunhong immediately.

"Let them decide," said Chunhong.

She had got tired of the trouble of her family members.

"Our grandma had asked me to speak less," she added. "The young people are different from us. We hold on regardless of difficulties but they give up."

Chunhong did not know Yi Kaimeng. She had talked with Swallow to persuade her restore the marriage with Sheng Jun, but Swallow refused.

"Now I'm worried about Qingmei," said Chunhong.

Chapter 50

Would Qingmei divorce, too?

"She wants to leave," said Chunhong. "Two weeks ago she let Dou spend the night in my house. She turned off the light, otherwise her daughter would not grow tall. Lily and Li Zhi are not tall because they had often slept with the light on when they were children. Later Qingmei carried a large bag and told us that she meant to leave. I thought that she would go to work in another province with her husband, but she would leave us. My husband said that he would treat her as his daughter, and we would take good care of Dou and educate her to have a bright future. Qingmei cried and took away some clothes, and nothing more. After my husband smoked too many cigarettes, he cursed Li Zhi on the phone. Li Zhi was still confused and worried if Qingmei had had a car accident. My son idles away his life and he does not care about Qingmei at all. After Li Zhi came home that night, he was punched by his father and his mouth was bleeding. When my son wielded a knife, my husband withdrew his hand. He was so sad that even his son let him down. Li Zhi threw away the knife and cried about his life. He said that we had treated Lily as a diamond but him as dirt. He wanted to operate a tea house or a foot bath parlour, but his father argued that either a gambler or a lecher would do such business."

I could see that Guangwen had changed although he kept doing his job. When he mentioned this after many years, he said that he felt like falling into a river with his body full of rocks. The three bodies from Lijiayan which had sleeping at the bottom of the river suddenly rushed at him. He would have screamed if his wife had not yelled at him.

"You should have become a competent man!" Chunhong roared, slapping Li Zhi.

He rushed into the bedroom and slammed the door. Chunhong stood outside the door and heard Qingmei crying.

"Now they make peace," said Chunhong. "My husband asks them to have a second child so that Qingmei will not leave. This is a woman's fate."

Chapter 51

Luo Siju, a historical personage in Yanerpo, wrote an autobiography in his declining years. It depicted his hometown and he started his military career in Laojun Mountain and Mount Lordhou. Villagers in the two places were connected: any subject would be spread in each other's place. A political commissar from Laojun Mountain was sent to prison and Zhu Zhanhui from Mount Lordhou got ill.

Zhu Zhanhui looked younger and her husband joked that he was beneath her. In fact, she had got scleroderma and had to stay in her house in Yanerpo. Her tongue was hardening and might fall into her belly. She had had several months of penicillamine, but later it became useless. She and her husband had to buy medicine online from a hospital in Shanghai, and it could stop her tongue from falling but could not stop her whole body from hardening.

The topic about the political commissar lasted just for a few days, but the gossip about Zhu Zhanhui's illness lasted on and on because it had never been heard of. Chunhong chatted with two female friends on the subject.

"How is Zhanhui?" asked Chunhong.

"I don't know," said Jin's wife. She was about the same age as Chunhong, but she had grey hair.

"People may get ill someday," said Chunhong. She talked about our youngest aunt who died two weeks ago. We did not tell our aunt's family members that our father had passed away, and her family members did not tell us about her funeral, either.

"Zhanhui's medicine is expensive," said Chunhong. "Each pill costs 8 yuan and can make her feel better for several hours."

"Last week I returned to Yanerpo," said Jin's wife. "My husband did not harvest the corn." Her husband had done a lot of jobs but could not earn much money. His wife asked him to do farm work, but he idled away his time in a tea house. Therefore, she had to do the farm work all by herself.

"I saw Zhanhui taking medicine," said Jin's wife. "Her throat bulged after she spoke a few words. I told her to look after herself. Her throat was growling."

"Her husband helps her to take medicine," said Chunhong.

"At that time I asked her husband to help her. He was scattering chemical fertilizer on eggplants."

"Zhanhui had a long talk with Huang Yan the other day," said Xiangsan's mother. "And she always wears a mask."

Jin's wife and Huang Yan were sisters-in-law but on bad terms. Huang Yan often boasted that her son had joined the navy and now he worked in a court in Qinghua District, Baima city. A car horn made her shout that the leaders in the court would pick her up, but neighbours gossiped that she had committed a crime because it was related to a court. Jin's wife did not laugh at her but sighed that her own two sons were bricklayers.

"Illness can make a patient's condition good or bad sometimes," said Chunhong. "Her husband cares for her."

"Her son has earned a lot of money by picking up customers on his motorbike," said Jin's wife. "But his money is used for buying medicine for his mother."

"He is a filial son but he can't look after her all the time. Zhanhui has a good husband."

"But she has had affairs with other men," said Xiangsan's mother.

They did not mention Chunshu. But Chunhong knew what they were hinting at.

"I'll go to the grocery store," said Chunhong.

Chapter 52

Chunhong called me. I thought that she would talk about Qiuyue, but she talked about Zhanhui.

"I feel pity for Zhanhui," said Chunhong. "Chunshu has not visited her yet but Zhuqing has. Zhanhui can't look after Tian now. Chunshan has to find other babysitters, but they are expensive and can't provide good food for Tian."

I knew Chunhong had funded the raising of Tian. Qinglian, the daughter of Chunshang, failed to be admitted to a senior high school because of low marks. Through the connections of Ruisong, I let her become a transferred student at the expense of a lot of money. Chunshang and his wife had been working in another province, but their money was either borrowed by their cousin or was saved. They would call me and Chunhong whenever they needed money.

Qiuyue had given birth to a child. I did not know what happened later. When we were young, thought outweighed cowardice; but as years went by, cowardice outweighed thought.

Chunhong was seven years older than me and she did not contact Chunying. Her contacts became less and less, and she did not know what to say when she held the phone. Money was not the only thing that separated the family members.

"What goes around comes around," said Xiangsan's mother. "The wrongdoer will be punished by God sooner or later."

Chunshu was a wrongdoer, too, but he might be ignored by God. He had promising children. Xiaolan and her husband could earn more money, their daughter Clever became a hardworking student and became No.2 in her school in the senior high school entrance examination, and was admitted to the senior high school in the county. Hongquan and his wife became richer and had a son named Ben.

"Call me dad," said Hongquan on the phone.

"Give more money to my grandpa," said Ben.

Hongquan provided living expenses for Ben and his grandparents each month and had to give more.

"Only Chunshu has a good life now," said Chunhong.

When a party was held for the one-month-old Ben, I let Chunhong send my gift money to Ben.

"Lily hasn't been pregnant yet," Chunhong complained on the phone. "I asked her to have a baby for the sake of her husband, but she refused."

My family members had their own problems.

"But we are much better than Zhanhui," she added.

A comparison made us realize that we were not in the worst situation.

Chapter 53

According to Luo Siju, if a villager in Laojun Mountain was sent to prison or got ill, a villager in Mount Lordhou had committed a crime or died. Was that true? Natural gas had been exploited in Mount Lordhou, but petroleum had not been discovered in Laojun Mountain.

Part Seven

Chapter 1

Our mother was born on the 18th day of the ninth lunar month, and it was Chunhong who had burned joss paper for her during these years. If she forgot, our father would remind her.

"Our dad has been gone," she said. "If I forget it, nobody will remember it." She was angry that her brothers did not visit our mother's graveyard.

She and her husband went to Yanerpo to visit our mother one day, and then they went to Zhu Zhanhui's house. As soon as Guangwen entered, he received a call and was asked to have a meeting at once.

Mr. Jia, the county head, arrived in Huilong town for the first time with his publicity team within the three months following his assumption of office. He would finish his task of "Red Lanterns". The team would go across the county and all the leaders must attend it.

Mr. Jia used to be a lecturer in a university before he became a leader in the government office. He had been studying *Sorrow after Departure* written by the famous Chinese poet Qu Yuan, and he considered that loyalty should result in inclusiveness and politics should be included into maths which could show the secret of politics. He also said that the "Red Lanterns" would become a political feat for Mr. Zhang and all the citizens and leaders should carry it out: loyalty and filial piety, sense of propriety, justice, honesty and honour. Each household should have these moral standards and hang a red lantern at the gate; if without it, the household would not be trusted by neighbours. To develop local tourism, moral standards were very important; without them, even good landscape could not attract tourists to stay longer. After they left, they would publish their travel recordings online; if they were bad, no tourist would go to Dongxuan. That's why Mr. Jia made the rule.

"No tourist will visit the household without the red lantern," Mr. Jia explained, "and he will not consume. Our people are kind-hearted and 5% the households will hang the red lanterns. If all of them do so, it will become meaningless. The communities will choose the 5%."

Mr. Jia stressed that the county government would fund the red lanterns. There were more than 1.3 million people in the county, or more than 300,000 households. Even if one person was living in the house, that would be taken as one household, and the 5% would be nearly 500,000 households. If one lantern was 10 yuan, the county government would have to pay a lot of money. But some households could not have the lantern anyway.

Chapter 2

Guangwen walked out of the town government building at noon. There were 3,484 villagers in Lijiayan, or 765 households; 5% would be nearly 40 households. He considered if these 40 households were worthwhile to hang the red lanterns. Some villagers' family members had been sentenced to prison because of larceny. Yan Min died during adultery but the wife of her lover Li Baoshun became a victim – should they hang a red lantern? Yan Min's husband Li Cai was a victim, too. After she died, Li Cai did not remarry; instead, he took good care of his child and his parents-in-law – should they hang a red lantern? Li Changxue's mother often cursed others but he and his wife and his father were kind-hearted. Mrs. Hou, Xu Limin's mother, was just like her, but Limin and his wife did not live with his mother. By comparison, Li Changxue still lived with his parents. There were so many difficulties that Guangwen would hold a meeting. The meetings were usually held on the street. But today Guangwen went to Lijiayan because it was so important. He knew the situation of each household, but he would need detailed suggestions on the spot.

Chapter 3

Guangwen told Mr. Jia's points to everybody and talked about Li Cai.

"Li Cai's household should hang a red lantern because he is a filial son-in-law and a good father," said Li Pu.

"But Yan Min's name is still in the registration booklet of Li Cai's household," Li Qiantao argued. He glanced at Guangwen, and only he could understand the latter.

If Li Cai's household could hang a red lantern, how could Guangwen treat the other villagers fairly? Even Huigoer's household should hang a red lantern because he needed respect; if without it, he would keep making trouble.

When Guangwen gave cigarettes to others, someone shouted, "Mr. Li! Something serious happens!"

The comer was Jin Erwa, a fool from Tongzishuyan.

"My wife is going to have a bottle of paraquat," Jin Erwa said, panting.

"Why?" asked Guangwen.

"She has been cursed by my mom." He ran backwards at once.

"His wife may die after he runs home," said Guangwen.

Jin Erwa's wife was Lin Xiuying, a beautiful woman who had poliomyelitis in childhood. She walked with a limp but she could do all the farm work. However, she was looked down upon by her mother-in-law and was often cursed by her. Guangwen used to persuade them to make peace, but that did not work. Later people said the mother-in-law doubted that Lin Xiuying had had an affair with her father-in-law. Lin Xiuying could be free if she died.

Guangwen would have to solve it although he could have called Shen Mingyi, the group leader in the village, to do it.

"Who will go there?" asked Guangwen.

"I'll," replied Li Qiantao. He drove to Tongzishuyan by motorbike, but he did not return.

Chapter 4

Guangwen called Li Qiantao, but it was not answered, so he called Shen Mingyi.

"I did not see anything serious happen," said Shen Mingyi. He went to Jin Erwa's house and saw him sleeping and his family members doing farm work.

It was at 3 p.m. Guangwen's calls to Li Qiantao were not answered. Meanwhile, Shen Mingyi and other men were looking for him. Guangwen had a presentiment of danger. He and other villagers searched for Li Qiantao on their motorbikes.

Guangwen had seldom sat in Yang Jin's car during these six months. Yang Jin had been in love with Jiao Yan, and he often cooked in her parents' house and was liked by them. Huang Ermei, the wife of Yang Jin, became a laughing stock although she was a good woman. People would either laugh at others or be laughed at by others. Chunhong asked her husband to stop sitting in Yang Jin's car so that she would not sadden Huang Ermei. Meanwhile, he would not choose another driver for the sake of long years of cooperation between him and Yang Jin. Guangwen planned to learn in a driving school and would buy a car. His wife persuaded him to keep a low profile among the village leaders. At last, Guangwen drove a motorbike.

When Guangwen stopped in front of a precipice, he worried if Li Qiantao had fallen off. At 6 p.m. Guangwen returned to the village and told this to Lu Xiaoyang, the wife of Li Qiantao. He asked villagers to search for him. They kept shouting for the whole night but could not find the man. Guangwen called the villagers in Lijiayan. Everybody except students and the disabled went to look for Li Qiantao. Only blood was found in the forest. A beast?

The historical personage Luo Siju was perhaps watching all this with scorn.

Chapter 5

Lu Xiaoyang took a white sheet out of the cabinet, tore it up and used one piece to wrap her head, and then she went to build the mourning hall. Guangwen was unwilling to watch all this. Chunhong joined the searching team and she would always be the first one to carry out the task assigned by her husband in the village. Her granddaughter went to the best elementary school in the county and Qingmei looked after her. Chunhong used to be worried about Li Zhi who did not want to live in the county, but he went to search for Li Qiantao with his friends, and his face was scratched in the forest. After Lu Xiaoyang put on the funeral kerchief, he went to a restaurant with his friends. Chunhong had to stay for the funeral.

This was the first funeral in Lijiayan without the body of the deceased man. When the three men died in Lijiayan many years ago, there was no mourning hall or funeral. Villagers said that they might be alive. Lu Xiaoyang insisted that the funeral must be held for her husband and she invited monks to chant for him. A dummy wearing blue clothes and stuffed with the clothes which had been worn by Li Qiantao was placed in a coffin. A piece of face-shaped wood was put on the head and the face was covered with a piece of paper, and shoes were put on the feet. The whole thing looked like Li Qiantao's body.

It was death in line of duty. Guangwen turned the funeral into a memorial meeting and eulogized Li Qiantao. The rural customs should be followed: funeral geomancers would be invited for the procedures. Guangwen acted like Limin who had done the same thing during our father's funeral.

Chapter 6

During our father's funeral, Li Qiantao invited performance teams and gave 3,000 yuan to us. Chunshan, Chunshu and Chunshang shared the money. Now it should be repaid, and they had a discussion.

"The teams were invited by Li Pu, Guangwen and his adopted children, and Yang Jin," said Chunshu. "Each household gives 1,000 yuan. Let Chunhong send it to Li Qiantao's wife."

Chunshan and Chunshang agreed with the suggestion. The latter was in Henan province and would not return for this.

On the eve of the funeral, Chunshan called Chunhong. It was not answered, so he called her husband.

"Li Qiantao's family members are not short of money," said Guangwen.

"The teams and the instruments can't be easily available," said Chunshan.

"But people must attend the funeral. No participants, no funeral."

"Li Qiantao worked for Guangwen," said Chunshu. "Everybody knows that he was not poor." He was angry that he was not invited by Guangwen as one of the funeral geomancers of the funeral. There were rules in Laojun Mountain and Mount Lordhou, but the host would decide.

Chunshu did not attend the funeral. After Chunshan got there, he realized that Chunshu was right. Chunshan was like the fifth wheel. He went to the kitchen and gave 3,000 yuan to Chunhong, and then he left without having a meal.

When Chunshan was walking along the river, he heard Guangwen's low, sad voice from a loudspeaker. He was eulogizing Li Qiantao, which was worthwhile for his life. A farmer's funeral would be provided with an oration, but Li Qiantao was a village leader and he was admired by Chunshan. The words in the loudspeaker were not clear enough.

Chapter 7

The Qingxi River originated from Baizhi Mountain in the northeast of Chongqing. Water resembled tears of the mountain and expressed its sadness to the world. Baizhi Mountain was only a few dozen kilometres away from Damian Mountain. The weathered black rocks could be seen at 2,700 meters high. Experts said that these rocks had existed for 500 million years. Sometimes sounds of wind and river running could be heard. There was a gap less than two meters high in the east of the level ground. Stone grooves covering long miles could be seen. The stones were like those of in the level ground, but the wind in the stone grooves had been roaring. The water flowing in the grooves was destined to go across the mountain and become a large river to nourish everything and create history of civilization.

The river had been known as Middle River before it flowed into Dongxuan. It joined Yexi River at Golden Town and formed Qingxi River. The Qingxi River went westwards and joined two rivers in Golden Town: the Ba River in the north and Behindba River. The ancient Banese found shelters in the Qingxi River through droughts, floods, beasts, weapons, and meteor showers. Perhaps the Qingxi River was born for the Banese.

The world used to move slowly, but one day it moved so quickly that human beings' hearts resembled sharp knives without blessings to the world. People treated the world and the rivers with sharpness; as a result, the Qingxi River had been dirty for decades. People could swim in the Qingxi river in the past. But now there was scum, pungent smells, and dwindling fish in the river. Nobody knew how many corpses had been buried at the bottom of the river. Accidents and plots had been on and on since rivers and human beings came into existence. The dirtiness of a river was far more than what the eyes could see.

Chapter 8

Mr. Zhang went by boat and inspected the county and Huilong Town on a sunny day. Local residents in the old street of Huilong Town usually dug holes in the back floor to pour excrement into the Qingxi River. As days went by, the River became dark and fetid. Before Mr. Zhang came, the government leaders in the town spent a lot of money on pollution treatment. Therefore, what he saw was a clear river.

Mr. Zhang exclaimed that anybody who dared to pollute the Qingxi River should not be allowed to hang a red lantern. That was told to me by Tan Ruisong, not by Guangwen.

Tan Ruisong was the reporter. After the news was shown on TV at night, he called me.

"Mr. Zhang came to Huilong Town," he said. "And his deeds were boasted. He commended my boss and the latter asked me to express his gratitude to Mr. Zhang."

"We were unaware that the Qingxi River ought to be considered our mother river until the central government imposed environmental protection measures," Ruisong added. "Su Causeway was built after Su Tungpo visited the West Lake, and Sea Weir was built after Fan Zhongyan visited Taizhou. They had their own opinions and would do good things for the people. But the leaders nowadays have no insight. Views are the best result of biological evolution."

I did not agree with him. Mr. Zhang had insight, so he initiated the "Red Lanterns".

Chapter 9

Red lanterns could be seen along the way. Guangwen entered a residential quarter which had been built by the local environmental protection agency to sell to the staff at a cheap price. He bought a house from a man who worked in the local food bureau and whose wife was the deputy director of environmental protection bureau. The couple sold the house covering 140 square meters priced at 600,000 to Guangwen, and they got the profits. The house was located on the fourth floor. Guangwen's house in Huilong Town was also on the fourth floor. The positions were auspicious. He found no red lantern in the third floor, but he felt proud when he saw the red lantern at Room 402. The lantern was made by Dongxuan County Committee.

"Look at the red lantern!" Qingmei called Chunhong yesterday.

Chunhong called her husband. He did not feel assured until he could see it.

"Red lanterns will hang in Huilong Town soon!" said Chunhong.

Guangwen told her that he would go to town for business and told others that he would go to see his granddaughter. But he wanted to take a good look at the red lantern.

Qingmei took videos and she had been selling cosmetics through WeChat. She put on a facial mask and took it off after twenty minutes; she took photos to show the comparison and the quality.

The plastering was bad. It had been made by Guibing who would not have made a fortune if without Guangwen's support. Only material fees were charged, but the work was not good enough.

"You may ask Guibing to repair the ceiling," said Qingmei.

Guangwen was in a sulk.

"Why does Room 301 have no red lantern?" he asked.

"The son of that family stole a phone," replied Qingmei. "He was so agitated that he went to the Sï-Shen-Tsï Methodist Church the next day to repent. The phone owner was in the church, too, and caught the thief. The son's family members had a quarrel with others."

"Why?"

"God will forgive the man who has repented. The son returned the phone to its owner and was released from the police station."

Guangwen thought if investigations had been made on the family before a red lantern could be shown.

"A red lantern should hang at the door of their house," he said after a moment of consideration.

"You look tired. Take a nap and I'll cook lunch."

He closed his eyes and soon snored. Qingmei continue to take videos.

Chapter 10

Guangwen was snoring but he was clear-minded. When he talked with me about it, the ceiling came to his mind. Guibing let him down. When someone told Guangwen about Guibing's ingratitude, Guangwen did not say more, but he realized there must be something more in it, and he had not been able to figure it out. The son of the neighbour living in Room 301 went to the church, which shocked Guangwen. He did not know penitence. Nobody had seen God. A man's wrongdoing should not be known by another one, which was his understanding. But why did the family members of Room 301 quarrel with others?

The selection of poverty-stricken households followed the Red Lanterns, and more subsidies would be provided. The households who had been doing business in other provinces let their parents live alone: these old men could not do any farm work and could not have sufficient food, so they would be taken as the poverty-stricken households. There used to be 765 households in Lijiayan, and now the figure became 834. 38 households were not allowed to hang red lanterns, and now the figure became 42. In Yanerpo, 91 households were the extra. As a result, Xu Bing, the village party secretary, had been fretful.

Guangwen called the family members who had separated from their parents temporarily.

"You are taking advantage of the policy," he said. "And your household is not moral enough to hang a red lantern."

"How many subsidies will be given to us by the country?" one of the family members asked.

"This is an honour, not money."

"Any punishment if without the lantern?"

"No punishment. But it'll be embarrassing."

"We are just ordinary people and we don't care about being embarrassing."

"Dongxuan will be built into a famous county for tourism. If you don't hang a red lantern, tourists won't trust you, or have meals in your house, or buy the things made by you."

"They won't go to a poor place."

"So you won't hang the lantern?"

"No."

Guangwen asked their parents, too, and they had discussed the subject with their children.

"It'll be useless," said one of the elderly men. "We'll need to cook every day and the smoke may make a red lantern become a dark one."

Guangwen submitted the list of the households which were not suitable for hanging red lanterns. His method was soon adopted by other counties, including Golden Town upstream and Qingping Town downstream, and the task could be finished within several days. But Liuye Village in Qingping Town was different: all the households hanged red lanterns for the sake of a good reputation. As a result, the village party secretary had to persuade rich families to remove the red lanterns.

Guangwen realized that he should have been praised by the secretary of the party committee. The occupants of Room 301 had quarrelled with others. Skeletons seemed to come out of the bottom of the river and rush at him. There was no way out. He stopped snoring. It did not last for ten minutes and the mask was still on Qingmei's face.

Chapter 11

Qingmei removed her facial mask at once and poured water for her father-in-law. Guangwen asked her about Dou and her schoolwork. He always gave money to Qingmei and gave more if Dou made progress in her studies. Qingmei deposited the money in her own bank cards. Guangwen realized that he should stop giving money to her to avoid her selfish calculations, but he could not control everything. In fact, Qingmei did not want much more. The house in the county was registered by Guangwen and his wife. Lily would not possess this house but Qingmei felt that she was idling away her life and getting old although she was just 25.

"You may have lunch at home after you have a walk," said Qingmei.

"I'll be busy and won't have a meal here," said Guangwen.

"Where is Li Zhi?" asked Guangwen, standing at the door.

"He went to the town and bought a pencil case for Dou," replied Qingmei.

Guangwen did not see Li Zhi and considered that his lifeless son acted like Ho Laosan's son. The latter screamed less and less; he was blind and the chains were removed from his body. He would die sooner or later and would not squander money.

Guangwen found that Qingmei was not pregnant. His daughter had not been pregnant, and Peiliang's parents might be worried about that. Guangwen wanted a grandson but his son and daughter-in-law seldom stayed together.

Chapter 12

Guangwen would visit Sï-Shen-Tsï Methodist Church. He had often passed by it but had never taken a good look at it. When he heard the church organ and the choir, he did not enter.

He saw pigeons in cages when he was walking on the crowded street. They were screaming and pouring shit on others' legs because they would be killed for food. After he walked past Fuzi Lane, The Third People's Hospital, and Ballad Plaza, he entered the Central Garden. The Sï-Shen-Tsï Methodist Church was located nearby the Central Garden. He did not choose the path. He stopped in front of Stone Pot Tofu Restaurant and recollected his dining in it. He put his hand on a stone lion. It was made by white marble but it became dirty after so many people had touched it. He would leave after he smoked a cigarette. Suddenly he heard "Welcome Home," it was Longxin Hotel, the most luxurious hotel in Dongxuan. The sweet voice came from eight tall, charming women in blue cheongsams. Middle-aged women were dancing in a parking lot when cars were driving something else. A large advertisement with words "Water is the Source of Life" could be seen, two sexy women in the spray. That was the publicity photo taken by Single Braid for Baili Canyon, which meant that the tourism was in full swing. Guangwen felt tired and sat down in a rock. He was preoccupied with so many things that he did not hear the loud music.

"I'm not religious," he thought. "An unreligious man goes to a church just for sightseeing. I'm not a tourist in Dongxuan."

He had been to Thailand with his friends. They must obey the rules when they were visiting a local temple: do not point at a Buddha figure, do not step on the threshold (the threshold stood for Buddha's shoulders), do not tread on a monk's shadow (the shadow was the monk himself). The rules made you feel the holiness rather than restrain yourself. But that was not the important thing.

His friends contacted him less and less. He had decreased his contact with Yang Jin since he stopped sitting in his car. The money deposited in Yang Jin's bank account was still there. Sand excavation had been forbidden since Qingxi River was controlled. Nobody would buy the sand excavation vessels from Ho Laosan and the vessels gradually became scrap iron. Diggers were sold to a labour contractor in Golden Town. The cooperation with Ho Laosan was ended, just like a couple stopped having meals together and sleeping together. But everything would become habitual. No hope, no motivation.

He did not go to the church. He might have the meal cooked by Qingmei, but that would be uninteresting. It was a boring trip in the town.

Chapter 13

Guangwen was nostalgic. When Yang Jin was with him, he felt that he was the lead role and Yang Jin was the supporting role. But now Guangwen felt that he was a fool without the supporting role.

He wanted to visit Peiliang's parents, but soon he felt that would be duller. He walked forwards and saw many shops with eye-catching foreign names. The shop owners preferred using the word "international" to make it impressive. A foot bath parlour with an international name located in Bijia Mountain in a remote town looked ridiculous.

When he came across a man, he recollected the reciter in Li Qiantao's funeral. Did he have anything to do with Li Qiantao? Guangwen wanted to see him clearly, but he walked into a building. Perhaps he was not the man in the funeral.

Guangwen went to the riverside road. It was much longer than that of in the town. The smells of food were mixed with urine. There was no public toilet along the road, so people had to pee around the railings at night. Men in fishing boats removed dirty things from the river. A woman screamed at the sight of a hungry rat, and her boyfriend trampled it to death. Guangwen became gloomy and walked into an alley.

Chapter 14

It was Water Chugging Alley nearby a market selling aquatic products. It was so smelly, thick, dark, and long that Guangwen felt like walking in intestines. The mothers in Huilong Town often cursed their children whenever they got angry: "You came out of my intestines!"

Guangwen lifting trouser legs walked carefully on the wet ground.

"Uncle!" someone yelled at him. He was surprised to see Swallow.

After she divorced, she could not get back her house and had to stay in her hometown for three months. Later she went to work in Zhejiang. After two years she returned but could not become the true owner of her house. When I talked about this with Ruisong and Single Braid, Swallow had to deal with Dayou's mother every day but she could not find a countermeasure against her. Guangwen had to entrust Huigoer with solving this issue. During those days, Huigoer slept in the hotel room at night booked by Guangwen, had tea in Suwan in daytime, and peed and shat nearby the entrance of Swallow's house. But those measures did not work after one week. He adopted new methods: he followed Dayou's mother when she went to buy vegetables, and he spat at the vendor who had sold vegetables to her; what's more, he lay down on the ground nearby the vendor, rolling his eyes silently. The vendor asked Dayou's mother to go away so that he could avoid Huigoer. As a result, she could not buy any food, and her grandson and other kids would have to be hungry. At last, she gave the key to Swallow. The latter gave 20,000 yuan and the interest to the former, changed the lock and went to Zhejiang. But when did Swallow return to Dongxuan?

Chapter 15

Swallow worked in a hair salon. Guangwen entered it and the disinfectant made him feel uncomfortable. Two women in their forties were sitting in front of mirrors. Guangwen thought about the joke told by Chen Ya: a middle-aged man dressed himself up because he had a lover, so his wife often changed hairstyles. But things might be much more complicated.

One of the two women was focusing on her phone anxiously and her head was covered with yellow hair dye looking like shit. A hairdresser, standing behind the other woman, was holding an iron tooth comb in his left hand and a hair dryer in his right hand. The hairdresser in his early thirties was bald. Swallow gesticulated towards him, and he smiled at Guangwen, and then he went to deal with the customer's hair. Swallow let Guangwen sit down, but he would rather keep standing because of the smell, the noise and the shit-like thing.

Before Guangwen left, the hairdresser gesticulated towards Swallow.

"He asks me to buy water for you and let's have lunch together," she said.

When Guangwen gave a cigarette to him, he was stopped by her.

"The smoke will make hair dye burn," she explained.

"You may go to Huilong Town someday," Guangwen said to the hairdresser.

Swallow invited Guangwen to have tea. She ordered Kunming-Puer tea for him and buckwheat tea for herself.

"When did you return to Dongxuan?" he asked. "Or did you stay here?"

"I've been back for months," she replied. "Stone mills have been demolished because of low standards. It's difficult to earn money in other provinces now."

"So you are a hairdresser now." He thought her hairstyle was like weeds. Many young hairdressers had strange hairstyles.

"You asked him to go to Huilong Town. Well, that's funny. Don't you see that he can't speak?"

"Can you gesticulate?"

"Yes."

"You should tell this to your parents. By the way, Barber Sun is different from you."

"We are much better than him. His service is 5 yuan each time, but our service is 500 yuan."

"Oh, your aunt would have squandered money if she had been served in your hair salon."

Swallow laughed. Later she rubbed her left thumb with a tattooed flower.

She told me and Chunhong that Dayou had got hurt at work; in fact, it was she who had got hurt and there was a scar in her left thumb, and that's the reason for the tattoo.

Guangwen felt that the light on her had been gone.

"I'm pregnant," she said. "He is Qin Xuan. His dad used to work in a chemical fertilizer plant. The factory is not as good as before, but he has retirement pay. His mom is an insurance canvasser. His younger sister is a nurse. He is two years older than me and has not married. I wanted to be single, but I can live with a mute man because he has no sweet talk. I've told my story to them and they did not say no. You may tell this to my parents, or you may say nothing about it."

Chapter 16

Guangwen was thinking about Qin Xuan on his way home without having lunch. Swallow and he had got the marriage certificate and their parents should meet each other. That reminded him of Qian Wen who had to walk with a limp. Now he saw him entering a building with a board written Department of Retirement Affairs. The Department was relocated ten years ago and the rooms were used to do dirty business. Guangwen thought that his trip in the town was so bad except the red lantern. Did he really want to see it? He was unclear. He got tired of staying in the town and he could not have suitable card players. In Huilong Town, only Blacksmith Zhang was prospering. Just like Swallow said, it was difficult to earn money in other provinces, so the workers could not send more money to their family members in their hometown.

The village was like a deserted place. Except some dogs and chickens, only old men could be seen. They silently sat down against the wall and thought about the past and they had no future. When Guangwen greeted them, they looked at him with cloudy eyes.

"Oh, Mr. Li!" they said after a long moment of silence.

He could see the marks of old days and he had changed, too.

Many villagers had died. Mrs. Hou and her tardy husband were still alive in Yanerpo. By contrast, many old men in Lijiayan had gone to another world one by one. The other day Guangli died but his wife did not know that. She had to carry him on her back and went home, and then she called the doctor.

Rural doctors and medical rooms had been provided since last year, but villagers would rather go to the township hospital if they got ill; what's more, some poor villagers could have free medical treatment. Nowadays they chose to go to a county hospital. A poor villager from Yaqueliang enjoyed free hospitalization in spite of huge medical costs.

People said that Li Zhengshe had taken away Guangli. Li Zhengshe, who died three months ago, used to frequently bully Guangli. After Guangli became one of the adopted sons of Guangwen, Li Zhengshe dared not to push around him.

The young people would rather live in a city although they might be jobless. They returned to the city after they took a rest in their hometown. In the city, they became idlers or trouble makers. Guangwen knew that some state-owned institutions would not hire new employees although the old ones had died. He was still the village party secretary of Lijiayan and was worried that someday the seal in his hand would be taken away by King of Hell. He would leave as soon as he gave some money to Li Qiantao's wife.

Chapter 17

But the village party secretary must solve problems. Some of the selected poverty-stricken households were really poor, but most of the them were unwilling to hang the red lanterns. Leaders gave food to the impoverished families, but the better-off families envied them and made trouble.

They complained this to Guangwen.

"After the county becomes famous for tourism," he said to those better-off families, "tourists will go to your houses and you will get more."

However, but poor families took advantage of the policy and made things hard for the leaders. When it was pouring, Guangwen was having a meeting in the town, he asked Li Pu and other men to help Li Chao. Li Chao had a poor family and an ill wife. They helped Li Chao to remove rainwater from their house, but Li Chao was just an onlooker. Li Chao said rude things to Li Pu, but the latter did not retort. The senior leaders would need satisfaction from villagers, so Li Pu had to endure.

"I'll quit," Li Pu told Guangwen on the phone.

After Li Qiantao died, Guangwen let Li Pu in his sixties solve many problems because the latter was familiar with the affairs in the village.

Chapter 18

The local government would build houses for the poor families, but the better-off ones became much more jealous. As a result, Guangwen had to make a speech again. Yang Jin, general managers of the natural gas company, local leaders, and I had wanted to know why Guangwen could be eloquent. Now I came to know that he had learned all this by himself and could put it into practice.

"We all know the good emperors in our history: Yao and Shun," Guangwen exclaimed. "When Emperor Yao saw two thieves get caught, he said that he should be sent to prison rather than them, and he said that he should have educated his people well. Look at us now. The government will build houses for us, and we should be grateful rather than become the thieves. Let me tell you the buckets effect: the capacity of a bucket depends on the shortest board. When the water is full, that'll be the best result. For us, our life will become better and better."

But the villagers were confused. Guangwen always received applause whenever he finished his speech in the past, but now his listeners were silent. He wanted to make peace and gain support, but now he found things had become unpredictable, and he could not make them definite.

Chapter 19

The local leaders in Dongxuan required the poverty incidence in each town should not be below 11% so that they could keep the title of national-level poverty-stricken county and get more subsidies. In the past, the subsidies could be used by the local leaders at will; but now the money must be given to the poor family. Many leaders including Guangwen regretted that they should not have rated Lijiayan as a poor village. He realized that his judgement had got worse, so he would stop Lijiayan from being rated as a poor village and would stop Huilong Town from being in the same situation. All in all, he would avoid trouble. Mr. Han was different from his predecessors who could become friends with Guangwen. The county leaders dispatched 800 appointees to work as the No.1 secretary in each village, a position higher than the village party secretary.

A director of teaching and discipline in a local middle school was sent to Lijiayan. He knew that Li Guangwen was an influential man in Lijiayan, so he went through the motions and returned to the school. A man named Hua Yunxiang was sent from Chengdu Archives Bureau to Yanerpo. He was so serious that he criticized Xu Bing, so the latter made things hard for him. In spite of that, Hua Yunxiang asked one of his comrades-in-arms to invest in Yanerpo and plant gastrodia elata and rhizoma bletillae. The investor provided road hardening and convenient transportation for the villagers in Yanerpo. The villagers complained that I was useless and could not do things for my fellow-villagers although I had been working in Chengdu. What was more, Xu Bing was also the topic.

Guangwen considered that his position would be negatively influenced by the No.1 secretary. Hua Yunxiang's friend could bring more benefits to the villagers in Yanerpo, but the villagers in Lijiayan could not get more money. In the past, the villagers supported Guangwen, but now they didn't.

A bad mood would result in gloom, like a shadow watching a man's life. Guangwen considered if the figure he had seen was Qian Wen. His elder brother had stopped trusting medicine since his wife's leprosy could not be cured; as a result, he started to believe in destiny. A fortune teller once told Guangwen that the back of the hand contained much more important information than the palm did. He used to see people and control them through eyes, but now he realized that the shadow was much more meaningful. Qian Wen's shadow might be premeditated.

Chapter 20

Guangwen did not want to stay in the town or in the village. When he realized that, he missed Li Qiantao who could understand and help him. Li

Qiantao had met different people, so Guangwen would not feel bored in the town. However, he did not have their phone numbers. After Li Qiantao died, Guangwen still kept his phone number, and sometimes he was eager to call him.

One night Guangwen played cards and drank a lot, and he walked home at 2 a.m. The breeze made him sober, so he began to smoke. Everything was dark and quiet, but Li Qiantao's number jumped into his mind suddenly. He could not find Li's phone when he died, but now if he called him, what if someone answered it?

He managed to retrain himself from calling Li, yet he could not contain his bad mood. At last he had to stay at home.

Chapter 21

Chunhong and her husband had been married for 30 years. He often worked and entertained outside but she did all the housework. After she made tea, she put the cup on the table. When her husband did not take it, she realized that she was alone at home. Now he had tea at home, but she felt emptier.

"You don't have to work?" she asked.

Her husband stayed at home for three days and looked unhappy, and she knew there was something in his heart that he was unwilling to say.

He was watching cartoons and she laughed.

After a few days, she called me.

"Zhanhui died half a month ago," she said. "Chunshu carried her coffin and chanted in her funeral."

Zhanhui's belly had become very large before she died. Few men could be contacted to carry the coffin. Weaksight started new business and could earn more money. Crap build a new house at the foot of a hill. The house was surrounded by reeds, but crops could still be planted.

Chapter 22

Chunhong talked with me about Chunshang and Yuling, and I should be a good listener.

"Chunshang's daughter Qinglian went to a third-rate college because of her low marks in the national college entrance examination," she said. "Even the lectures were perfunctory. Many of her classmates fell in love and lived together. Now she works in Fujian province. Her younger brother Zhaohui studies in a higher vocational college. He is single but he is addicted to his phone."

Chunshang and his wife were working in the construction site operated by Stone, but it was in a worse situation and they could not earn much money. After the No.1 secretary finished his task and returned to the city, the business in the village such as Guaizaoping or Yanerpo was gone.

The boss only hired Magpie to watch the site. The female dog had a son named Leopard, but its parents were dead now. Some other dogs were either killed or were hungry, and one of them was kept by Magpie.

"Leopard barks at people except Magpie," said Chunhong.

Villagers used to give some food to their dogs although they were impoverished; after they had money, they stopped doing so. However, city dwellers loved pets. The decline of agriculture civilization began with less care for animals.

"Something serious has happened to Bihua," Chunhong added. "The company in which she worked produced high-quality fake phones, and the case was prosecuted. Bihua was an accountant and became one of the principal criminals and was taken to the police station. Later everybody knew that. Zhuqing cursed that Sixi should be imprisoned. Sixi returns to Baima and lives with Kang Furong whose benign tumour has been removed from her head. A man from Poplar Terrace has met Sixi and said that Sixi has been financially supported by Kang Furong but he still sleeps with other women. Hongquan paid the fines and his wife was released. Other criminals were sent to the procuratorate. Zhuqing said that they had solved it by themselves, even Xiaolan said so."

Chunshu and his wife, and Hongquan did not tell me about it. They knew that I could not help them and they regarded me as a useless man although I had been working in the city.

"As for Swallow," she continued, "I wish she could get better and better."

Guangwen went to work after his wife called me. He had spent four days at home and many things had happened within these four days. He was not worried about Lijiayan because Li Pu did not call him, but he was worried about the provincial and national inspectors who disguised themselves as the locals. The things Guangwen thought about at home over the past four days have dispersed like a wisp of smoke. The repayment of debt came to his mind. Rural infrastructure had not been improved although national payments had been provided. The village could not make profitable business.

Zhao Daping in Cypress Ridge called Cao Xia, one of the poverty-alleviation leaders, whenever he saw a meeting on TV. "You are sitting in the platform for too long and you should have visited me much earlier."

Zhao Daping asked Cao Xia to send food to him at once. In fact, Cao Xia had visited five poor households including him according to the requirements of senior leaders. (One poverty-alleviation leader was asked to visit 16 poor households in Baima city.) Cao Xia's travelling expenses would not be reimbursed and most of her salary was used to buy gifts for the poor households.

When she complained this to her boss, she was questioned: "You said that you had visited them. Any proof?"

Two poverty-alleviation leaders were asked to visit one poor family. They would take photos and videos in the house, and they must repeat their names so that the villager could remember them. Cao Xia felt that she had to go through the motions, but she would rather record the fact. What's more, these leaders were asked to have meals in the poor households and give money to the villagers, but the latter did not say thanks.

"I'd rather die," cried Cao Xia. She implored Zhao Daping to ask for less.

Hua Yunxiang was not a rich man and his wife had to do street vending at night; their son was studying in a middle school. Whenever he heard the difficulties of a villager, he would give money to them. One day he visited a woman named Ma Cui (she talked to Chunhong in a pigpen on the day of our father's death), she cried that her daughter had killed herself by having pesticide because of a hard life. Hua Yunxiang gave 300 yuan to her. He had 700 yuan totally, but now he had only 400 yuan left. The other villagers wanted more money, but he could not give them. They battered him and took off his clothes. He ran to the village committee wearing underpants only.

Xu Bing laughed, but Mr. Han got annoyed.

Mr. Meng, the director of poverty relief bureau in the county, inspected Huilong Town. Mr. Han took him to Yanerpo in which gastrodia elata and rhizoma bletillae brought profits. Unluckily it rained before they went to the planting regions.

"The road is slippery and muddy," said Mr. Han.

"The television reporters are here," said Mr. Meng.

"Let's take photos outside the village committee," said Xu Bing. "It's just like in the planting area."

"Is it possible?" Mr. Meng asked, looking at the sky.

Xu Bing got an umbrella at once.

"I don't need the umbrella," said Mr. Meng. "Mr. Zhang does not use it even in heavy rain."

"I dislike formalism!" cried Hua Yunxiang. "You'll go there but I'll stay here to write the information sheets."

"OK," said Mr. Han. He gloated that Hua Yunxiang did not join them.

Later Xu Bing apologized to Mr. Meng and Mr. Han because of Hua Yunxiang.

"A leader should get familiar with the local customs when he works in a village," said Mr. Meng. "The village party secretaries should do their job well even before the No. 1 secretary came."

Xu Bing apologized again. But Mr. Han did not apologize because he should not offend Mr. Meng. Mr. Han told Mr. Meng that Hua Yunxiang used to run to the village committee wearing underpants only.

"Oh, he worked really hard," said Mr. Meng. He laughed.

Chapter 24

After Hua Yunxiang finished his task, he wrote *My 730 Days in the Village*. After his trousers were taken off by force, he returned and put on new trousers and went to the field. He considered that it was a difficult job for the local people to survive. Poverty brought them no civilization. In fact, a man with spiritual richness was usually poor, but poverty made the uneducated men become either humble or rude. He concluded that gastrodia elata and rhizoma bletillae could not bring more wealth; what's more, these plants were owned by bosses, not by villagers. Investors needed good manpower. The No.1 secretary in Maliu Village, Jichang Town, Qianfeng Ridge said that a boss would plant Mangnolia officinalis and Gardenia jasminoides, but he went home as soon as he reached the village: no young manpower. Yanerpo was in the same situation.

He contacted two bosses to plant rattan pepper, Chinese yam, ophiopogon japonicus, and edible wild herbs in Yanerpo. But the bosses returned to the city because of few young manpower. At that time Yanerpo was no longer a poor village, and he left as a loser. The accident happened in Happy Home in Zhongba Town could be seen in many places. When leaders visited such a place, the performance team would do a good job while unmanned aerial vehicles and stereoscopic shooting would be adopted. Nearly 30,000 yuan was wasted.

Chapter 25

Guangwen did what he should do. Yang Jin once said that Mr. Li was a loyal man, and you could not understand him if you were not as loyal as him. Yang Jin had seen much of the world.

Guangwen realized that he must know the latest information. He could not stop others from speaking even though he knew it. He missed the days when he could control others. He had been a victim of poverty and only three households helped him at that time, including Li Baoshun. When he was a child, Li Baoshun's grandpa gave him some pork lung for the Spring Festival. After he grew up, he often visited the elderly man's graveyard and burned a cigarette for him. However, the villagers he had served during these years had never helped him; what's more, they even treated poverty as a means of getting more money. He must serve the villagers whenever he was needed. Sometimes the people and the things which he had tried to forget agitated him again. But a chance came when things got complicated.

The local government had built houses for the poor villagers nearby the high-speed intersection. It was Longjingwan which used to be a canyon and which was filled with earth for a desulphurization plant. Now Longjingwan looked like crumpled sheets. Bosses had planted landscape trees and would sell them to city dwellers. The poor villagers had to walk hundreds of miles to farm. Later the government asked the poor villagers to plant honey plums which would be sold at 50 yuan per 500 grams. In addition, the plums would be sold to foreign countries through e-commerce platforms, and the villagers would become rich, proud Longjingwan dwellers. But when could it come true? Both the poor and the better-off villagers disliked that, and some poor ones were unwilling to relocate.

Chapter 26

The villagers in my hometown neither hung red lanterns nor relocated. Limin would rather let his parents stay in Yanerpo for the good funeral. Xu Bing said that cemeteries would be established in Longjingwan. Mrs. Hou cursed her husband because she dared not curse Xu Bing. She died two years earlier than her husband. The body would be cremated in Longjingwan and Mrs. Hou would not go to a strange place to avoid strange souls in the nether world.

Chunshan wanted to relocate because he had got 10,000 yuan given by the government. He was eager for a house so that he might sell it someday. Xu Bing said the governmentally-supported households for relocation must have their houses demolished, and the land would be used as plantation or forests, and he asked the villagers to pack up.

Chunshan would rather stay. The old house was still strong and the memories came to him.

After our mother died, our father often visited her graveyard and talked to her. The neighbours laughed at him and said that he could not raise his children. After six months he built new houses.

Our father did not hire men to cut down trees because he could not afford to provide meals for them. I considered the meals would be so delicious that they would surpass luxuries. He went to the mountains all by himself and had to cut saplings sadly. Later Chunshan helped him. Chunshu went to the mountains sometimes, but he was still an avid reader. Our father and Chunshan usually came home holding trees at midnight. Our father hired workers to build houses for Chunshan and Chunshu, and later they got married. But he did not build a house for me because he told others that I would work in a state-owned institution, and his youngest son would live in the old house. Our father was like a cornered animal and he spent the rest of his life in worries and could not realize his strengths and shortcomings.

Those days made Chunshan weep now and his wife asked him what had happened.

"I miss our dad," he said, sobbing.

That was the first time that he cried after our father's funeral.

The night when our father's body was moved from the freezing coffin to the wooden one, he cried too. But it was not just for our father, at least not entirely. "I want to stay here," he said.

His wife was preparing for relocation, and she got confused now. Just like Chunhong, she would stay with her husband wherever he went.

Chapter 27

Limin and Chunshan would rather live in Yanerpo. Chunshu and his wife enjoyed their life in the town, and Hongquan asked them to raise Ben in the town, too. Chunshu and his wife did not return to Yanerpo after gastrodia elata and rhizoma bletillae were planted, and they would rather get a new house.

If villagers were willing, they would relocate; some were rich but they would rather save their money. Huigoer was unwilling to relocate because he could enjoy the benefits of being a poor and a non-poor household at the same time through the advantages of the policy. But now he was short of money because Guangwen stopped letting him do various things. Huigoer felt that he was losing his value; he was getting old but he refused to live in the nursing home located in Golden Town.

"I won't stay with those drooling old people!" Huigoer retorted.

He often played cards and lost more money, but he refused to take Guangwen's advice. But Guangwen always invited him to dinner and gave him cigarettes whenever he came across Huigoer. The latter looked embarrassed if he was not asked to finish a task. In the past he would do his best after he received the money and he thought that he would be invited again. But now he felt that he became useless.

After Guangli died, Guangwen gave money to his wife and she gave local specialty to him in return. After Li Qiantao died, he gave money to his wife, too. He said the money was provided by the local government, in fact he used his own money.

Huigoer was a nuisance but he was needed by Guangwen to some extent.

Guangwen hoped that Huigoer could live in another place. The true name of Huigoer was Li Dengfu.

"You will get 10,000 yuan if you relocate," said Guangwen. "You are a household enjoying the five guarantees, but Magpie in Yanerpo is not. He can stay there because he is employed to guard the forests for more investments in Huilong Town. The other day Mr. Meng inspected Yanerpo led by Mr. Han. Mr. Meng shook hands with Magpie. You did not watch TV. Longjingwan is a good place and you can have a free life there."

Huigoer started to sweep the floor. He had not cleaned his house for decades.

Chapter 28

The houses in Longjingwan would soon be finished. The government leaders in the county required that all the villagers should relocate before the New Year's Day, and Mr. Zhang would cut the ribbon. Guangwen was in a difficult situation: the villagers in Lijiayan focused on Huigoer while other villages focused on Lijiayan. People gossiped that the No.1 secretary in Lijiayan had been driven away by the competent Li Guangwen. The other villagers said that they would relocate after the people in Lijiayan did; the villagers in Lijiayan said that they would go after Huigoer did. Huigoer had been a pawn used by Guangwen, and the latter had to go to the village and talk with him again.

Some villagers in Lijiayan whispered: "Mr. Li Guangwen does not deal with many problems now."

Guangwen used to ask Huigoer to clean dirty walls.

"We haven't seen Huigoer for a long time," a villager said.

Li Pu thought if Huigoer went to receive the subsidies. The latter came to Li Pu's courtyard after he lost his money in playing cards.

Li Pu went to Huigoer's house at once. Huigoer usually hung straw on the door before he went outside, which meant that he was still alive. Some dead villager was not discovered until his body was rotten. Li Pu opened the door but could not find Huigoer who had no family member, no friend, no phone. Li Pu called Guangwen immediately.

Guangwen was riding a motorbike and rushed to the village after he received the call. He searched for Huigoer just like he searched for Li Qiantao. Huigoer might be dead or be missing. When Guangwen reported this in the town government office, everybody felt relieved.

"It'll be a good thing if the troublemaker dies," said the director of civil affairs bureau. "His residence information will be cancelled if he is missing for many years."

After half a month, someone said that he had met Huigoer in Laifeng Road: he rummaged through a trash can and then ate a banana skin. He became a beggar in another place, which was a good thing for his hometown.

Chapter 29

Chunshan refused to move and he was followed by others.

"We'll move if Chunshan moves!" said the villagers.

Mr. Cui, a philosophy graduate, persuaded Chunshan and his wife sincerely: "You get stuck in agricultural society and you treat the land in which you have been living as your hometown. Now we are in the urban society. The developed countries have world cities which challenge the countryside and break conformism. Cosmopolitanism will replace hometown and the capital will replace the traditions. All in all, we should keep pace with the times."

Chunshan and his wife got worried about the bad result, so they just sat there silently.

"That's Spengler's point," Cui explained.

Chunshan had never seen Spengler on TV and thought that he might be a provincial leader.

"My third brother works in Chengdu," he said.

"In which department?" Cui asked.

Chunshan did not know, so he fudged an answer: "Nobody is allowed to enter the place if without a notice and a permit."

Before I went to have a meeting in the Provincial Party Committee Propaganda Department several years ago, I was questioned at the gate in details. Later I told this to my family members. As a result, Chunshan remembered that.

"You should support his work," Cui said humbly.

"My wife will cook poached eggs for you," said Chunshan. "I won't take your money. The poverty-alleviation leaders usually have meals with us, but I won't receive their money."

That was true. Limin and Chunshu took the money, but Chunshan and his wife, and even Mrs. Hou did not.

"I'm not hungry," said Cui. "It is required that we should not have a meal in the villager's house at will."

"It's my treat."

Chunshan had a nice chat with the young man and the latter had a delicious meal. However, Chunshan refused to relocate. Mr. Han could find it out because he knew me. I was just a poet, not an influential leader. I often had dinner with my friends, and one of them was Tan Ruisong who had had an affair with a young woman in the south and who had to return to Dongxuan as a loser. What's more, I did not build a road for my fellow-villagers. I was a useless man.

Gossip could travel fast. Later Guangwen told me that he was not valued by Mr. Han because I did not have important connections. Someone from Huanghua Town in Mafu Ridge worked in the government office in Shanghai. When he returned to his hometown, he was warmly received by Mr. Zhang and his hometown was built into a peach demonstration garden.

"You could have become influential if you had shown what you could do," Guangwen said to me. "The natural gas would not have been discovered if the land had not been excavated."

He sighed and then talked about Bihua. They did not contact me to solve such an important problem. He was disappointed. He had let his daughter have higher education so that she could have a secure job in a government office, and he had spent 90,000 yuan on finding a good job in a state-owned institution for her, but I had failed to make her become an official employee. Now she worked in a joint venture company and could earn much more.

Chapter 30

"Can I be rated a poverty-stricken household?" Chunshan asked anxiously.

His name, Xu Chunshan, would be inspected, otherwise Xu Bing and Mr. Han would have to take the blame. Even though he returned the 10,000 yuan, he would have to be sent to the new house located in Longjingwan. He realized that he must accept the reality although he loved his old house in his hometown. Therefore, he became desperate and would fight back if he was forced to move, and he might burn the man who dared to ask him to go. He asked his wife to leave but she was determined to stay with him.

Chapter 31

When Chunshan cursed his wife, Guangwen, who came here by motorbike a moment ago, gave a cigarette to him. Chunshan stopped yelling and his wife gave a basin of water to Guangwen to wash up. Soon Limin came, too.

"Barber Sun died when he was having supper last night," said Guangwen.

"Last night I saw a lot of hair in my dream," said Mrs. Hou. "And that was a harbinger of Barber Sun's death."

"His funeral is conspicuous," said Guangwen.

"His grandson teaches in a university," said Limin.

"He can meet a lot of senior leaders," Guangwen explained. "They would rather let him teach their children. Sun Jun was a visiting scholar. He spent the Spring Festival in Finland three years ago. Thousands of Chinese people sang our national anthem in a hall. He also had the Loong Boat Festival in Canada and saw the Chinese national flag and the Canadian. The Vietnamese and the Italians can't have their national flags raised when they have their traditional holidays in Canada."

"We don't know that our country is getting stronger," said Limin, receiving a cigarette from Guangwen.

"The government could not have built new houses for you in Longjingwan if our country had not become stronger," said Guangwen.

Limin laughed but Chunshan glared at him.

"Sixi is such a bad son!" cried Chunshan. "Tian hasn't been registered in the household booklet and my house covers 75 square meters. This year I can't register for him because I was told that some poverty-stricken household had provided fake information to get more areas of structure. Limin has six registered family members excluding his parents but he pays the same as I do."

"So you get angry about it?" asked Limin.

"Our country should not lose the greater for the less," Guangwen explained. "If you move, other villagers will move, too."

"Will I be thrown into a dark room?" asked Chunshan. "I heard that someone had been locked."

"That's gossip!"

Guangwen left in a sulk. He had wanted to communicate with Chunshan to avoid trouble and Mr. Han asked him to do so, too. However, Chunshan refused to take his advice.

Chapter 32

Chunshan wanted to live. His son had not repented, but his daughter and her mute husband had a lovely son. Qin Xuan was a good man and he would not have married Swallow if he had not been a disabled man. Chunshan worried that he would be locked and his old house would be demolished. He realized that he should ask for help and called me.

"The villagers in dangerous houses should be relocated," I explained.

"But my house is safe," he argued. "You may tell the man in the poverty alleviation office to cancel my name."

I did not know those men but I had to finish the task although his name should be on the list.

When the Red Lanterns were carried out in Qingping Town, 90% of the poverty-stricken households who had said that they would not hang the red lanterns changed their mind. The poverty alleviation leaders gave 30 ducks to each poor household and gave 20 to each better-off family.

Dream Back to the State of Ba was shown in Baili Canyon and it turned out to be a great success. The tourism in Baili Canyon would positively influence other counties and the red lanterns must be hung to attract more tourists. At last, all the households except prisoners' families should hang the red lanterns; in addition, each family, both better-off and poor, would be provided with 30 ducks.

Chapter 33

The Red Lanterns appeared in Huilong Town. The relocation was postponed and Mr. Zhang would cut the ribbon after the Spring Festival. Limin's household hung the red lantern, but Chunshan's and Chunshu's did not. Zhuqing got angrier and hated Chunshan and his wife, and me.

I took my wife and my son toChunhong's house during winter holiday. After we had lunch, we hired a car and returned to Yanerpo to visit our parents' graveyards. We had supper in Chunshan's house. Later we visited Chunshu. He treated us coldly and his wife was in the room. After we smoked two cigarettes, we left.

"Chunshu and his wife are unhappy," I said to my wife. "They don't hang a red lantern but others do."

"Your relatives are cruel!" she yelled.

I told her the details of the red lantern.

"I did not let them hang one?" she shouted.

Our son was talking with his girlfriend on the phone sweetly and did not notice us.

Chunshan and Chunshu cold-shouldered me because I was unserviceable. Chunshan had blamed me that I was not in the same group with him.

"Everybody has to follow the trend of the times," said my wife. "He will be forsaken when others move on, and he should take the consequences. You have done quite a lot for your relatives, but they don't care for you! You are a poet, but your righteousness becomes fake!"

My relatives had borrowed money from me and my wife, but they had not repaid. What's more, we had paid 17,000 yuan to build a cemetery hill for our parents. At last, I was treated as trash by my relatives and by my wife.

Chapter 34

Limin and Mrs. Hou hung red lanterns, but Chunshan and Chunshu did not. Few people would visit Chunshu and his wife. She seldom went outside unless she needed to go shopping and take her grandchildren to have a walk.

"You look pathetic, mom," said Xiaolan.

Yaqiong's household did not hang a red lantern either, so she would get one anyway.

One day Yaqiong's neighbour walked into the wrong house when she came back. The red lantern confused her: when did Yaqiong's house hang one? On the same day someone said that his red lantern had been stolen. It was said that the mad Yaqiong would steal one which was located far away.

Later 40 households had lost their red lanterns. Middle-aged women were asked to find out why. 36 households did not hang red lanterns, 35 of them had Spring Festival couplets on their doors, and only Yaqiong's household hung one red lantern. An elderly woman found that and knocked hard at the door of Yaqiong's house. Nobody opened the door and Yaqiong had not been seen for many days.

The neighbourhood committee pasted a note on Yaqiong's door. After two days, there were some words in good handwriting on the note: "I picked up the red lantern on the road. But who has taken it away?" The neighbourhood committee could not open the door and had to take away the lantern. However, more households had lost lanterns. Surveillance cameras had not been installed in Huilong Town except in the savings bank. The town was full of acquaintances and the cameras would record all the strange and embarrassing behaviours of the dwellers. However, the red lanterns were the symbol of morals, and cameras were installed within half a day. But more than ten lanterns were stolen at night, so the videos were viewed and a woman with dishevelled hair was recognized. Three policemen went to Yaqiong's house.

Chapter 35

Two of the policemen were familiar with Yaqiong's house. When the five-month-old boy was scalded to death, she shouted at home so madly that her neighbours had to call the police. Now the policemen burst the door open. And saw Yaqiong sitting on a sofa, holding a baby bath tub which had been seen by the two policemen, and talking gibberish. They asked her questions but she gave no answers.

The bedrooms were full of quilts, sheets, and spider webs. The whole house was like hell. The three policemen found 70 red lanterns in the balcony and then put them into bags.

"Why did you do that?" asked one of them.

She was silently holding the bath tub and looking happy. The policemen looked at each other, walked out of the house, and removed the red lantern. On that night she stole six lanterns again. The local government and the police station did not know how to deal with an insane woman.

The officers asked residents to bring the lantern into the room before they slept at night. If it was stolen, the government would provide a new one after a few days. However, the lantern was the symbol of honour and of wealth, especially those hanging on the stores to attract tourists. The countermeasure should be adopted to scare the thief. Afterwards, a woman's screams could often be heard at night.

Chapter 36

The screams woke Zhuqing up.

"Stop beating Yaqiong!" she shouted.

"Mind your own business," said her husband.

Huigoer appeared when Yaqiong was shrilling at night.

Guangwen could not find Huigoer, so he gave some money to Li Zhi and asked him to search for Huigoer in the county and city. Li Zhi and his buddies enjoyed themselves. During their fun, the searched a few streets, but could not find the man.

Huigoer returned to the town unexpectedly and quietly. He was sitting in a dark corner and watching a woman crawling in front of a store and wiping the blood with her sleeve. Animals often howled and fought at night for this area. The woman's yelling could be heard far away, and he kept sitting until morning came. He walked to the township government building and waited there. Nobody knew when he left.

He went to buy a packet of cigarettes. He had had a shower and worn new clothes, with a smell of lemon in his hair. Nobody could recognize him. Soon he was taken to a special room in which food, water and cigarettes could be provided. He was not set free until Li Qiantao, who was said to have been dead, appeared.

Chapter 37

Many people, including Lu Xiaoyang, believed that Li Qiantao was still alive. After the funeral, she considered that her husband could not have had an accident because he had been familiar with the route. She dialled his number and a woman answered the phone. She wanted to speak to her husband, but the woman got annoyed. She kept calling until she was blacklisted by that woman.

Only Guangwen believed that Li Qiantao had died. He had had a presentiment of disaster caused by money. Li Qiantao had taken charge of the finance in Lijiayan, and the accounts should be changed.

"You should hide yourself in an unknown place," Guangwen said to Li Qiantao. "I'll ask you to come back at the right moment and I'll look after your wife and children."

Someone had warned Guangwen to be cautious about the people around him. Did he test Li Qiantao? When Guangwen was thinking about a good plan, Jin Erwa reported that his wife had had paraquat – that would be the best chance because a search and witnesses would result in a plausible disappearance of Li Qiantao. Guangwen winked at him and the latter did it.

He pushed his motorbike into a valley – Guangwen, Li Pu and others found the marks of the motorbike along the escarpment. He took the SIM card out of his phone, scratched it, bound it on a stone with weeds, and threw it into a forest. He ran westwards and avoided sitting in a steamboat – he knew the driver who came from Huilong Town. Wearing a hat and holding a hoe he walked fast on the hillside field. At dusk he came to Qingping Town, hired a motorbike and went to the county. He had a bowl of noodles and then hired a car to go to the city.

Even Guangwen was unaware of his whereabouts. On the 27th day after Li Qiantao's "funeral", Guangwen walked towards home at 2 a.m. and called Li Qiantao.

"The number you dialled is currently disconnected."

Guangwen felt relieved but called again and again. He got home just before dawn.

The audit teams were sent to the towns by the county government on that day (on the previous day actually). The financial accounts of the villages within these five years should be submitted to the town government office. The accounts of Lijiayan would be those made after Li Qiantao's "death". After the "funeral", Guangwen and other leaders forced open the drawer in Li Qiantao's desk. There was only a mouldy cigarette and two coins with the denomination of 1 yuan. They searched Li Qiantao's house and found nothing useful. People said that he had committed suicide to escape punishment. No evidence had been left.

The local leaders, including Mr. Han, explained this to the audit team. They did not say much more, but Guangwen felt that their silence was too meaningful. He waited and endured until the wee hours. He could not reach Li Qiantao, but he felt relieved to some extent. As the sun rose, the darkness would be gone.

Chapter 38

"I'd been ensnared," Guangwen said to me.

At that time he was in the prison. One of the classmates of Tan Ruisong was the security section chief in the Dalugou Coal Mine Prison. Through his connection, I would be able to visit Guangwen.

Ruisong and I were led by his classmate, Mr. Xia. Yesterday Ruisong called him, and then he told it to Guangwen. We first went to Mr. Xia's dormitory. He went home in the county at the weekend. His dormitory was dirty and smelly.

I was eager to see Guangwen, but I had to obey Mr. Xia. He gave two glasses of water to us.

"The yellow stains on the interior of the glass are like urine," Ruisong joked.

Mr. Xia laughed. Ruisong gave cigarettes to us.

I had lunch with Ruisong, his younger brother, and Single Braid today. Ruisong said that he would meet a friend, and his brother had the abalone porridge spoon by spoon. He paid the bill and would visit Mr. Wu for approval for his new project. He gave two packets of cigarettes to Ruisong.

"I carried four packets of cigarettes and at noon my brother gave me two," said Ruisong. He put five on the table and Mr. Xia took away two. Ruisong gave me one, but I did not receive it.

"Take it," said Ruisong. He did not see my bad mood.

"Let's meet Mr. Li now," said Mr. Xia.

Chapter 39

The prison had been built in a tunnel in the deep mountains. We saw the cells after we walked past wooded land and flower stands. A prison guard was sitting in a watch room. Mr. Xia talked with the guard and then the latter opened the gate with clunks. We walked towards the abyss-like cells, bungalows built by cement. White-covered Bafine cigarettes and wafer biscuits were sold in a small, wooden store.

Bunk beds were installed in each cell. I saw "0019" on the beam and someone sleeping in the upper bed and covered himself with a purple blanket. I thought he was Guangwen.

"This way," said Mr. Xia.

Guangwen was sitting alone in the bed behind the door and stood up as soon as he saw Mr. Xia. He looked thin and his shaven head surprised me. The number on his uniform was 7295.

My father was Xu Chengxiang and his admission number in the hospital was 00033428. Li Guangwen, the husband of Chunhong, was numbered 7295 in prison.

"Your brother-in-law visits you, 7295," said Mr. Xia. "You should make yourself better and better."

"Thank you very much, sir," said Guangwen, giving a bow.

Mr. Xia looked at the neatly-folded quilts and went outside, followed by Ruisong. Guangwen smiled at Ruisong gratefully because the latter had visited our father in the hospital and kowtowed in front of our father's graveyard with his friends.

"You sleep here?" I asked, pointing at the lower bed.

"Yes," Guangwen replied.

Both of us sat down. I wanted to give him famous cigarettes, but that would irritate him, so I gave him ordinary ones. I lit up one for him. He was poker-faced when he was smoking. He had told me that relatives always wanted more and better things from the family member who was a leader or a boss. I thought about Ruisong's brother having abalone porridge and his arrogant manners.

"Are the meals good here?" I asked. "How many hours do you work in the coal mine each day?"

He fudged the answers. I saw the festering wounds in his hands caused by broken bleeding blisters as a result of holding a pickaxe for long hours.

He withdrew his hands. "Does your sister know you come here?"

"No," I replied.

"Do not tell her." He did not want his wife to see his hands.

She had visited him and could speak to him through a window. She called me but could not tell me the details and she sighed.

"I'd been ensnared," Guangwen whispered to me.

Mr. Xia and Ruisong were cracking jokes at a distance.

Chapter 40

Mr. Han was the plotter. Hatred could be much stronger than love, and Mr. Han's jealousy was growing more intense, that was because Guangwen was influential. To bring him down would be the solution.

Feng Quan made it happen. He had been promoted but one day he got detained and interrogated: his embezzlement and bribe-taking had reached more than 160 million yuan, and he had slept with 72 women. He refused to tell the details of the money, but he told the thing which had happened in Huilong Town: five people died after a boat capsized. Three deaths in an accident would make the leader jobless. Li Guangwen, the village party secretary of Lijiayan, helped him and made the three bodies stay at the bottom of the river.

Guangwen was just a small potato but Feng Quan's words could send him to prison. Guangwen did not know about Feng Quan's situation, but Mr. Han knew the details. The good connections between Guangwen and Feng Quan had been gone. In spite of the wild gossip, Mr. Han secretly found the families members of the three dead men and asked them about the accident.

Chapter 41

"It has been solved," the three families said.

"Very good?"

"Yes."

"You may go now."

They returned as soon as they walked out of the room. "The accident happened many years ago. But why do you ask about it now?"

"Your satisfaction is important," replied Mr. Han. "Now and the past."

He started to read the documents. After a moment, he saw they were still in the office. "You…"

"May we make a request?" they asked.

"Tell me."

"We want their bodies to be salvaged and will bury them in the soil."

"But their bodies may be in the ocean now."

"They are still in the site where the boat capsized."

"The river keeps flowing."

The family members looked at each other.

One of them was a man named Li Kui in his seventies who had lost his daughter in the accident. "The bodies had been bound with rocks."

"What?" Mr. Han asked in surprise.

Li Kui told the conversation of Li Guangwen to Mr. Han. "Mr. Li cared for us."

"The senior leaders can make a proper judgement," said Mr. Han, smoking.

"Anything more?" asked Mr. Han.

The family members were silent.

"If you want to protect Mr. Li," said Mr. Han, "you should let the bodies sleep in the river."

"He is a good man," said Li Kui. "But…"

"Tell me the details, and that's protection, too."

"Mr. Li did not negotiate with us before he made the decision although he gave sufficient money to us afterwards. He has nearly 20 adopted children, and they ride the high horse in the village. He often asks the troublemaking Huigoer to bully the villagers he dislikes. He has had an affair with a woman but he fell out with her and trampled on her breasts."

Li Kui stopped and fearfully looked at the other two families who were lowering their heads.

"Anything more?" asked Mr. Han.

They were silent.

"You may go home now."

They left in a hurry and forgot their request.

Chapter 42

Huigoer left after Mr. Han had a talk with him. After a few days, he returned amid a woman's screams. And within one week, Li Qiantao, who was thought to have been "dead", was brought back. In fact, Mr. Han asked Huigoer to find Li Qiantao and gave him some money. But soon Huigoer played cards and lost the money. Mr. Han had been suspicious of Li Qiantao's death during his "funeral". After Mr. Han became the secretary of the county committee, he could have more power and had Huigoer do the secret job. Qian Wen was also an important pawn because he had been crippled in an accident caused by Guangwen. Li Qiantao's had gangsters bring Qian Wen to a deserted place in Qianfeng Ridge. The naked Qian Wen knelt in the snow and kept kowtowing until blood could be seen in his forehead. Someone kicked him hard in the buttocks. He was nearly frozen and he was allowed to go home after those men finished having their wine. However, his legs were ruined.

Qian Wen went to the building with the board written Department of Retirement Affairs, and his figure was seen by Guangwen. Qian Wen met Mr. Jiang, a well-known man in the underworld of Dongxuan. Mr. Jiang had been engaged in usury and had his men batter or kill the tardy debtors. He was renowned for valuing friendship: if his friends wanted him to do it, he would do it; if not to do, he would not do. Qian Wen would give him a lot of money, but Mr. Jiang would not punish Li Guangwen.

Mr. Han had heard of Qian Wen, so he had a talk with the latter.

"I hope you can write a report in details," said Mr. Han. "And I'll tell you when you can submit it."

After Li Qiantao was found, the report was submitted.

Chapter 43

The financial accounts made by Li Qiantao were without problems. The money had been used for building roads, weirs, reservoirs, compensation for demolition, and supporting poor families. People said that Li Guangwen must be protected. He was sentenced because he had been connected with the organized criminal gangs to hurt an innocent man. The source of his property was suspicious, but he had operated excavators and sand excavation vessels. Before he bought a house for his daughter, he wrote an IOU (I owe you) to me. It was a fake one, but his property could be secured, and that was the only thing that I could do for him.

Chapter 44

I returned to Huilong Town. Chunhong and Chunshu went to Yanerpo to help Xu Xing to relocate Zhu Zhanhui's graveyard. Chunhong cooked meals and Chunshu dug a graveyard, carried the coffin, and buried the deceased woman. The poor families in the village had moved to Longjingwan. Chunshan realized that he should keep pace with the times, but his house in the village was still there. Leaders would inspect Longjingwan, and one occupant must stay in each household. Fengjuan and Zheng Saner stayed in Longjingwan, Mrs. Hou and her husband were in the old house. Elderly men stayed in Yanerpo, and Chunshan, Limin, Chunshu and Magpie could help Xu Xing.

On the twelfth day of May in the lunar calendar, Xu Xing visited his mother's graveyard and burned joss paper for his father and his wife. He could hear someone crying and thought it was an illusion. At night his wife came into his dream.

"We hang a red lantern," said Xu Xing. He had spent a lot of money treating his wife's disease but he refused to be rated a poverty-stricken household. He wanted a red lantern which stood for good morals to protect his wife from being the gossip.

"I'm not interested in the lantern," she said. "I've got the same illness in the nether world, but I'll recover if my graveyard can be moved to a new place."

"Where?"

He could not get an answer. He fell off the bed and woke up. However, he did not see her in his dream again although he slept early at night. He asked Liu Xianwen about it.

Chapter 45

"Xu Xing wants the power of the witch?" asked Liu Xianwen. "That's ridiculous! The ancestral grave should not be moved at will! A witch used to be powerful but now is powerless. The funeral geomancers will have a meeting in the nether world each year. That's to say, I'll lie in bed and wake up a few hours later. The so-called meeting is to let my mind wander in Hades full of stenches. One day King of Hell sat in an impressive sedan chair and led us to a place. His Majesty would reward his workers. But someone shouted, followed by the stink. Some bearers died and some would become a disabled man in the human world although he could survive. As soon as His Majesty stepped out of the sedan chair, the ground was fully covered with coins and banknotes. 'This is the smell of money,' said His Majesty. He waved his hand and the coins and banknotes became the destroyed human beings."

Liu Xianwen was making his speech outside a postal savings bank and was surrounded by listeners. They did not know the human beings, either sinners in history or greedy officials nowadays, mentioned in his speech; but they were worried about their future, especially those who withdrew money a moment ago.

"People must pay for your service," said a woman, carrying two piglets in a basket.

"That's the beneficence which will make the deceased man's soul suffer less in the nether world," Liu Xianwen explained.

"The more we pay, the less the deceased man will suffer?"

"Zhu Zhanhui might have been alive if she had asked me for help. The souls have three grades: the top one is goodness, the middle one is toil, and the last one is cleaning." He made his right hand into the shape of an eagle claw and waved his arms. "The first flourish is the symbol of becoming a lake," he chanted, "the second one is the symbol of becoming a river, the third one is longevity, and the fourth one is free from ghosts. Zhanhui had been controlled by the ghost. If the soul is graded as the top one, it will hear the wails and the ghost will run away. If the soul is graded as the middle one, the person will need food and rest. If the soul is graded as the last one, the spirit will be laughed at by the ghost because the funeral geomancer is not powerful enough."

"Your service is expensive," said the woman.

"We'll need to survive, too. The money will be received by gods. I can invite gods and have them do things for us. If a funeral geomancer is not powerful enough, he can only invite gods but can't let them work, and that'll cost much more."

"Will the money be given to immortals and King of Hell?"

"Yes. They are our bosses."

"They should be sent to the smelly valley."

She was being watched angrily by the other listeners and even the growling piglets on her back seemed to criticize her, so she left. They said that she would be punished by God because of her rude remarks, but Liu Xianwen did not retort because he had seen the world through and through.

A witch in the past was reasonable and responsible: she could tell the reasons for relocating the grave and went to the grave, and she stuck her neck out after the grave was dug; an executioner would withdraw his machete if he saw white ants, and he would thrust the machete into her neck if he did not see the white ants. The witches nowadays were talkative but were irresponsible. No awe, no good world of gods or of humans. If verbal tricks worked, it would be a very good result; if not, a bad result.

Chapter 46

Xu Xing went to Liuye Village in which there was a woman named Sun Feng. She was an ordinary girl before she was 10 years old. After her tenth birthday, she fell off an escarpment but she survived; it was said that an immortal with wings took her to heaven through 49 days and met celestials. Since then she had worked as a sorceress for 40 years.

When Xu Xing came, Sun Feng walked out of the latrine pit.

"I thought you would not come here," she said.

Xu Xing got surprised because she knew who he was although she had never been to Yanerpo.

"I had planned to visit you," he said. "But I could not find the way."

"Your mind will lead the way."

She reached out her hand to him, and he gave him 600 yuan. She touched his forehead and chest, asked him to close his eyes, and then she chanted incantations and drew strange patterns on a piece of paper. When he held the picture with rocks and flowers, he asked her about it but could not get an answer.

"I'd like to know if I can relocate my wife's graveyard," he said.

Silence. He found himself in darkness and he had to leave. According to the picture, he found a place full of rocks and flowers in Zhenxun's ancestral grave. Zhenxun and his family members had left and would not return. His ancestral grave was full of weeds, and the area with rocks and flowers was next to Zhenxun's mother's grave. It might be a miracle. Zhanhui had had an affair with Zhenxun, and he had done a lot of farm work for her. But she was so greedy that her spirit would get a piece of land in his ancestral grave. It might be her destiny.

"When did Zhanhui get ill?" Liu Xianwen asked.

"She could not pick up her chopsticks at breakfast and she could not speak clearly," replied Xu Xing.

"It might be at 9 a.m. A hungry spirit met a patient's spirit. Her grave will be dug at 5 a.m. and be buried again at 9 a.m."

Chapter 47

When I returned to Yanerpo, Zhanhui's graveyard had been relocated and Chunhong was cooking. Xu Xing was still busy in the cemetery hill but other men went back. Magpie went to the forest and would come when the meal was ready. Chunshan, Chunshu and Limin held the red envelopes given by Xu Xing who could not pay more. Limin told Xu Xing to give some money to the workers so as to avoid bad things, Xu Xing felt embarrassed and rushed home. The money was put in red envelopes which looked like the paper torn from the Spring Festival couplets. Two banknotes with the denomination of 10 yuan were put in each envelope, and the three men laughed. The money was not enough for the fare by motorbike.

"I worked for Xu Xing and provided a piece of cured meat for him," said Chunshan.

"Chunshu should have done this for Zhanhui," said Limin. "But you are his elder brother."

Limin's mother came.

"I'll inspect the cemetery," said Mrs. Hou. "I don't know if my husband will live there this year."

In fact Mrs. Hou wanted to get more information about Zhanhui's new graveyard. Xu Xing cleaned Zhenxun's ancestral grave and kowtowed, weeping.

"Burning and cleaning are necessary," said Limin.

"I don't think the relocation is a good thing," Mrs. Hou argued. "Her coffin had no dirt and Liu Xianwen had chosen a good place for her."

Mrs. Hou walked home and got some fun in her curses. Her husband was in Longjingwan and she would go there to cook for him because her daughter-in-law would not do so.

Chapter 48

Chunhong and I stayed in Chunshan's house for one night. I wanted to have a talk with her about her husband. She would burn joss paper in front of our parents' graveyards. She and Chunshan were busy in front of the graveyards, but I just used a shovel to make fashion.

We talked about the old days when our parents were still alive.

"We could not have gone through the difficulties if without our dad," said Chunhong. "A lifetime hard work is amazing."

We thought that our parents could hear our talk. We had parents and grandparents although our grandpa's graveyard was not here. They had always been with us.

I would have to mention Guangwen if I was alone with his wife. I would not tell her about the details when I visited him in the prison. When he saw me, Mr. Xia, and Ruisong out, I was shocked by the eagerness for freedom and hostility towards free individuals that filled his eyes: the higher the free men went, the deeper he was in the abyss.

"It was said that I had forced Sun Qingfang to commit suicide and said that I'd had an affair with Huang Ermei," Guangwen told me.

The written judgement showed that Guangwen had been corrupted by indecency. In fact, he had no affair with Huang Ermei. Yang Jin seldom went home after he had a relationship with Jiao Yan, but Guangwen often went to Huang Ermei's store. When Yang Jin went home during Jiao Yan's performance, he came across Guangwen and gave him cigarettes.

"I'll sit in your car," Guangwen said to Yang Jin. "It's not convenient to ride a motorbike in the village."

Yang Jin wanted to return to his normal life because he could not endure the vagrancy and uncertainty in Jiao Yan. However, he was treated as an outsider by Huang Ermei after he returned home.

Guangwen persuaded Yang Jin to cherish his wife, but at last people said that he had an affair with Yang Jin's wife. Guangwen had done quite a lot for the villagers in Lijiayan, but on the day when Guangwen was arrested, they set off firecrackers to ward off him. He was saddened and he thought that he had been supported by them.

"Li Kui had pesticides and died," he added. "I would not have a grudge against him if he criticized me overtly."

I would not tell those things to his wife.

Chapter 49

When I knocked at the door of Chunhong's house, I did not see the red lantern.

"It was taken away in the afternoon two days ago," said Chunhong. "It would have been removed much earlier if someone had not supported my husband."

The house was clean and forlorn.

"Where is Li Zhi?" I asked.

"He has changed himself since his dad was sent to prison. The price is too high. He is working in Jiang Hua's restaurant in Fujian and can earn 9,000 yuan each month. Jiang says he is smart and offers good suggestions. Jiang is a trustworthy friend through thick and thin and will give dividends to him."

I wanted to boil water.

"Let me do it," she said.

After a moment she poured me a cup of tea. The cup had been often used by her husband. I got nervous at once because she found that I had visited him in the prison.

"He was a prisoner more than 30 years ago," she said.

She told me their life in Xinjiang.

Chapter 50

Guangwen stole 300 yuan from his uncle Huang Zhong. He calculated the fees of learning materials, postage and others; the total cost was below 300 yuan, but prices of commodities had been increased. He furtively pried open the drawer at midnight and found 900 yuan, but he only took away 300 yuan according to the calculation. The next morning the aunt yelled and her husband called the police at once. Guangwen and his wife soon were arrested in the railway station. They had not bought train tickets and had only paid 0.4 yuan to take a bus. Guangwen did not argue and he would spend three years in Beiye Prison.

The uncle visited Guangwen.

"I hope you can change yourself," he said to the young man. "My wife asked me to write a letter to your village. I did it but I did not send it. She is an illiterate."

"He should be imprisoned for the rest of his life!" the aunt yelled at Chunhong. "And he should be executed by shooting!"

Chunhong looked at her silently and did not argue. She did not take part in the theft, so she was not sentenced. She became a laundry worker nearby the Beiye Prison. However, she was pregnant and should go home for the survival of her child. She returned 10.4 yuan to the uncle, bought some clothes for her husband and gave him some money. She returned home alone.

"The uncle was kind-hearted," said Chunhong. "And the villagers did not know about it."

Guangwen was released after three years. Those memories seemed to have been buried when he was sitting in the train to go home. But the prison had become a sinful scar. I remembered that he got angry when Zhang Dachao was mentioned. "He's a prisoner!" That reminded him of his years in Xinjiang.

"I should not have put away his good wine," Chunhong sighed.

"His two imprisonment is related to poverty," she explained. "The first time was caused by his own poverty, and the second time by other's poverty. He should have retired much earlier."

And then she talked about the strengths of her relatives. Even when she mentioned Sixi, she said the reason why he lied was not because he was a bad person, but because he had no truth to tell. She forgave others.

Chapter 51

When I was sitting in the high-speed railway to Beijing, I received a call from Chunshan.

"Chunhong hanged herself," he said. "She had gone through so many difficulties, but she could not endure anymore after the red lantern was removed from her house."

"When did it happen?"

There was no service in my phone when the train rushed into a tunnel.

475

Afterword

I went to Lushan County in the western Sichuan province on a cold autumn day in 2016. It was a task assigned by the institution in which I had been working. An earthquake hit this place three years ago, since then the local people had been working around the clock to restore economy. The Federation of Literary and Art circles in which I would take a temporary post was not helpful. It acted like a publicity department and only had a vice chairman, but there was no specific work in the literary federation. My suggestions, such as the establishment of writers' association, seemed to be unnecessary because writing should be independent and personal.

When I worked in the Federation of Literary and Art circles of Xuanhan County in the northeast Sichuan one year ago, the County was developing tourism. That was my hometown and I had congenial friends there. They drove me through the Bashan Grand Canyon, and we visited rural households, chatted with them and spent the nights in their houses. We had to walk six hours in the steep mountain road, and we could enjoy delicious meals provided by the villagers. It was summer but fire was needed at night. The next day we felt exhausted and our legs hurt. We saw the sources of rivers and felt their nourishing of everything, and we also saw ancient paths which had been used to transport lychees from the south to the Shaanxi province in the north for the Imperial Concubine Yang in the Tang Dynasty.

I wrote articles about Xuanhan and published them in *Guangming Daily* and *People's Literature*. I wanted to write books about Lushan, so I should understand the local writers and their creation. They were busy and I could not join their talks. I should consider whether they needed my job or not, otherwise it might cause disturbance.

I revisited Baihuo Village. No mark of an earthquake had been left except the word epicentre painted on a rock. There was no occupant in the new houses in Baihuo Village. The elderly men and children stayed in the village and the young went to work in different cities. I walked through streets and remembered the names of places and stores. I ate in restaurants when I was hungry, one meal or five meals a day. Lushan is next to Wenchuan in the north and is connected with Tianquan County in the south; Aba prefecture and Garze are nearby. Xuanhan has a population of 1.3 million; Lushan has a population of 100,000 and has nearly 20 ethnic minorities. The county is open and bleak.

Few people could be seen in the well-known root carving street. Lushan is famous for root carving because of the good texture of Phoebe zhennan S. Lee. There are many root carving artists and dealers in Lushan. I stepped into Mr. Wu's store. The wall was full of certificates of merit and most of his works had been focusing on withered lotuses for 20 years. I asked him why, he said that the withered lotuses would have rebirth. The orders for his works increased after the earthquake. Mr. Yu, a dealer, led me to visit his exhibition hall. His wife was making tea for me although I would not buy any. He said that he had three halls which had collections and products to be sold. He would have to give one collection to a leader for free if he liked it. If the leader did not know how to appreciate it and gave it to another man in your presence, that would sadden you. He hired no man in his halls; if he got raw materials, he would had professionals do it; but the employee would do anything he liked on the materials. What's more, he did not trust the person who claimed that he could do everything. He, patting me on the shoulder, said, "Don't believe the man who says that he is an all-round doer because he is a liar."

After I returned to my room on that day, I wrote the beginning of the novel: "My emotions and thoughts are rushing when someone is knocking at the door. The knocking sounds the same as the one who talks in his sleep."

I did not know why I wrote like this and I had not thought about the content. I returned to Chengdu from Lushan. When I was having lunch one day, I cried when I saw men and woman wearing folk costume walking in the farm land, singing and dancing on TV. My son asked me what had happened, my wife said that I was pining for my hometown. Their voice was their ancestors' – they had been toiling in the farm land, their hair with the token of love. Human beings had gone through endless days, and they were strong and lonely. On the day when I left Lushan, I could feel the quietness of the scenery.

The song I was hearing had the solitude. My wife was right.

The loneliness came from my hometown. It is located in Laojun Mountain. There are many mountains with the same name across China. In the novel, Laojun Mountain is inconspicuous in the Daba Mountains. Starting from Motian Ridge and going southeast, the Laojun Mountain is forlorn in the northeast corner of the county. In Ming Dynasty people from Hunan province came to Sichuan province. They would have reached Chengdu Plain if they had held on, and they might have reached Kaijiang County, Chengdu in miniature; but they lived there and built Qianhe Village. In addition, they gave their children names with the meaning of water. In fact, there was only one river, and that was the Qingxi River in the novel. My ancestors would rather live in the mountains for the sake of safety: walk in the steep mountains. By contrast, the rivers were imaginary. The first generation died in the mountains. My parents' graveyards were surrounded by weeds and the land was their hometown.

This place had often been trapped by scarce harvests and famine. Historical records showed that the local people in the poverty-stricken Puguang Town, Xuanhan County had to eat grass, trees and soil. Hunger had always been there. Nowadays the people in Qianhe Village still use large bowls for meals; when they are invited to dinner, they will worry if they can have full stomachs when they see small bowls. I wrote *One Hundred Years of Hunger* more than ten years ago, and you will find the connection between the two novels. *One Hundred Years of Hunger* is about a story happening in the mountains while *Who Is Knocking at the Door* a story happening around a river. Mountains and rivers show the relations between traditional culture and modern culture.

The French historian Braudel said: "Great history, both its advantages and disadvantages, is not welcomed in the mountains." That's true, but civilization has to be accepted and it is handed down through acceptance. Mountains, human beings and civilization resemble flowing rivers. A river should keep running. One droplet of water and another one form a large drop of water, just like the relation between water and river, like between yourself and others, and like between an individual and the times. All the eras are connected and ancient melodies still resound through human beings' hearts.

Our ancestors' sacrifice and loneliness exist in our life. We should move on. Our happiness and sadness show that we are living our lives. I'm deeply touched at the thought of this.

After that lunch, I started to write this novel. Qingxi River and Lushan River would turn into one – rebirth and growth. The names I'd heard in Lushan might appear in my novel. I don't like writing an outline and I need to protect the secret feelings in writing from being foreknown. But I have to pause and think about the names of the characters, and I meet them every day during my writing. I know some writers will list an outline of nearly 50,000 words if his novel may reach 100,000 words, and they will have few revisions. But I enjoy revising my novel.

The original name of the novel was *Trilogy of the Rapids*, but that was presumptuous – I should not compare myself with the famous Chinese writer Bakin (Li Yaotang). I used a new name: *Who Is Knocking at the Door*. The river in my hometown is surging. I touch my heart and feel my ordinariness, struggling, tears and laughter.

I express my gratitude to Guangxi Normal University Press and the editor Ms. Liang Wenchun.

April 2020
Chengdu